D1066226

# THE CLOSE-UP

——

## SARAH SMITH

carina
press

**carina press®**

Recycling programs
for this product may
not exist in your area.

ISBN-13: 978-1-335-01482-5

The Close-Up

Copyright © 2022 by Sarah Smith

For questions and comments about the quality of this book, please contact us at CustomerService@Harlequin.com.

Carina Press
22 Adelaide St. West, 41st Floor
Toronto, Ontario M5H 4E3, Canada
www.CarinaPress.com

**Printed in U.S.A.**

To everyone who's been hurt or broken
and built themselves back up.
This book is for you.

# THE CLOSE-UP

# Chapter One

Nothing good comes from a dick pic. I know that now.

It's not that I ever thought highly of them. Like so many other women, I've been sent more than my fair share of unsolicited penis photos. They're never, ever fun. It's just that tonight I discovered the kind of irreversible damage they can inflict.

Tonight I watched my year-and-a-half relationship go down the drain, all because of one ill-timed junk shot.

"Think of it this way," my cousin Harper says, pointing her martini glass at me. "At least you found out now what a gross crap-weasel Brody is. At least you weren't married. And at least you didn't have kids together."

I squint at her over the rim of my second Amaretto sour in the last half-hour. Harper is many things: my cousin, birthday twin, best friend, and a workaholic architect who earns an impressive mid-six figures in the Bay Area. One thing she's not? An emotional shoulder to cry on. She's always pragmatic and logical, even when I want to trash my cheating ex over drinks.

My cheating ex as of three hours ago.

I drain the last of my drink, then slam it on the table. "Yeah. Finding out my boyfriend cheated because he mistakenly texted a picture of his penis to me with the words, 'Miss you, Laura. General Monster Dong is aching to be inside you, baby,' is so much better."

Just speaking that heinous nickname Brody came up with for his penis makes me want to crush my empty glass in my bare hand.

"It *is* better, Naomi. Imagine how much worse it would have been if you had been home with kids and you got that text."

She's right. "Of course it's better. But it still absolutely sucks to know that I wasted the last year and a half with him. I thought he was…"

"What exactly did you think Brody would be?" Harper narrows her hickory-hued eyes.

But I can't. No matter how long I wait for the words to come, they can't hide the truth: my relationship with Brody wasn't going to last anyway. And I knew it the whole time I was with him.

I glance around this dive bar that somehow exists in the upscale Nob Hill neighborhood of San Francisco, desperate for a distraction. I try staring at the scratched-to-hell hardwood floors, the impressive layer of grime that coats every single one of the ancient light fixtures in this basement bar. When that fails, I try gazing at the handful of other bar patrons, all of whom are either enraptured by the basketball game playing on the flat-screen or staring into their drinks. Nothing works. And that's when I face the truth.

Brody was a bad habit, a go-nowhere relationship that I had gotten used to being in. We were never going to get married, buy a place together, have kids, or do any of that long-term life stuff you typically want to do with your significant other. And I knew that.

When I turn back to Harper, I expect to see her lips

pursed and one eyebrow raised, her signature "I told you so" face. She's had it ever since we were kids.

Instead a soft expression radiates from behind her thick bangs. It's pure empathy.

"Don't get me wrong," she says. "If I see Brody's smug face again, I'm going to punch it. Cheating is never, ever okay. If he was unhappy with you, he should have broken up with you. That bastard hurt you in the worst way, but you weren't right for each other in the first place."

I picture five-foot-two Harper wailing on six-foot Brody and almost laugh. She's got the no-bullshit personality of a prison guard when she's pissed off, and Brody wouldn't stand a chance.

The lump in my throat dissipates as I swallow. I was so enraged when I received the accidental dick pic this evening that I immediately marched into the bedroom where Brody was and yelled, "My name isn't Laura, you asshole." I recommended he give "General Monster Dong" a more realistic nickname, like "Private Average Sized At Best." Then I stormed out of the apartment while dialing Harper. I didn't have the time to throw on makeup before leaving like I would have on a normal night, but now I'm silently grateful. At least this way I won't have mascara streaks running down my cheeks if I end up crying.

I wait out the urge for two long seconds, thankful it doesn't take hold. "Why do you always have to be so insightful?" I let slip a joyless chuckle.

She reaches over to smooth the ends of my shoulder-blade-length hair. "Because as best friends *and* cousins, we know each other better than anyone else. You call me out on my shit, and I call you out on yours. We've been doing that since we were in diapers."

I let a small smile break free, the pain in my chest easing. "Right."

Harper looks up to thank the bartender, who drops off another gin martini for her and a bourbon for me.

"If you knew Brody wasn't right for me all along, why didn't you say something?"

As loving and protective as she is of me, she's not one to hold back her opinion. She's never mean about it, unlike some people who use honesty as a flimsy excuse to be assholes; she's just blunt. And she always, always acts with care and concern.

"Meddling's not my style. Bringing you here to Spud's Bar to drink away your post-breakup frustration is more my speed."

"Here's to that." I raise my glass in a mock toast. "And here's to no more relationships for me. Ever."

Harper frowns. "Come on, Naomi."

"Hey." I point my glass at her. "No meddling, remember?"

Her mouth twists as she sighs.

"I'm serious. I'm done with relationships. The few long-term ones I've had have brought me nothing but heartache and frustration since I started dating as a teenager. And they all ended in disaster. Brody cheated. The guy before him, Tyler, ghosted me after nearly a year together. The guy before that—Aaron—never, not once referred to me as his girlfriend for the two years we were together, only as 'the girl I'm seeing.' And what's-his-name before that broke up with me on my twenty-first birthday. While we were out having drinks with my friends. Then went home with the bartender. Remember?"

Harper winces.

"Clearly, happily ever afters are not in the cards for me. So from now on, it'll just be me."

This is what a lifetime of idealizing your parents' perfect marriage does to a person. When you grow up with parents like mine who never fight, who can't keep their hands off each other even after nearly forty years together, who still go out on weekly romantic date nights, it warps your expectations. It makes you think that you too will someday meet that perfect someone and have an equally perfect relationship.

But sixteen years of failed relationships have taught me one thing: it's never gonna happen.

Harper shakes her head, clearly disapproving of my relationship ban. "Fine. Keeping within my *style*, I won't say a word about your ridiculous ban. You know what else is my style? Cheering you up when you're feeling down. And you know the best way to do that?"

"No clue." I finish off the bourbon in two more gulps. I don't even stop to taste; I just guzzle and let it burn down my throat. I'm instantly light-headed. I hardly ever indulge in alcohol, so three drinks in less than forty-five minutes means I'm well on my way to drunk.

Harper signals the bartender to refill my glass. Scratch that. *Four* drinks.

"The absolute best way to cheer yourself up is to find a new hottie to cleanse your palate." Harper fixes her gaze on a guy sitting at the bar, his back to our booth.

My brow flees to my hairline. "What?! No way am I hooking up with some rando!"

She takes my shrieked response in stride, shaking her head. "For god's sake, Naomi. I'm not suggesting that. I just think you should flirt with someone a little."

"Oh." I inhale, relieved. "I'm not really in the mood."

"Come on, Miss No-More-Relationships. There's no better way to kick off a relationship ban than flirting with a hottie, zero expectations attached. You can cross it off your fuck-it list."

My fuck-it list. I haven't thought of it in years. When we were teenagers, Harper and I came up with a list of silly and crazy things we'd like to someday do, like bungee jumping and making out with a hot stranger at midnight on New Year's Eve. We joke about it whenever we feel the urge to make fun of our naïve teenage selves.

"The sooner you move on—the more you look at other guys, even if it's just for a fun conversation that won't go anywhere—the easier it will be to get over Brody."

Harper's words take hold in my brain, like an anchor digging into the ocean floor. That actually makes sense.

I grip the table to steady myself. "I think I might be a tad too drunk for this."

"Flirting is always more fun when you're a bit drunk."

She says it in such a matter-of-fact way, I believe her. I stand up and smooth down the front of my flowy white blouse, which I'm wearing with a slate gray pencil skirt and black heels. I push up the sleeves, annoyed that I didn't think to change out of my work clothes before I stormed out of the apartment in a rage.

"You look amazing as always," Harper says, as if reading my mind.

I run my fingers through my hair. "I don't feel very amazing at the moment."

She pins me with you've-got-to-be-kidding-me eyes. "Naomi, you're tall with long arms and legs, perky tits, and a bubble butt. You're probably the best-looking woman that's ever walked into this dive."

"Next to you." Even though I appreciate Harper building me up, she's a stunner. She's got an adorable girl-next-door face, and the petite and busty figure I've envied since we hit puberty together. We both share the same background—Filipino and Caucasian—as well as the same dark hair, dark eyes, and tan skin.

She winks at me. "Now go get your flirt on with Mr. Broad Muscly Back over there. He's been eyeing you since we sat down."

I turn on my heels and pause for a beat, taking extra care to make sure I don't fall.

"Wow," I mutter to myself.

Just the sight of this dude from behind is impressive. His crisp dove gray dress shirt is an inadequate cover for the toned muscle underneath. Sculpted shoulders and thick arms highlight his broad frame perfectly. The back of his head is covered in cropped light brown hair. Judging by the slicked-back style he sports on top, he's got one of those trendy skin-fade haircuts that European soccer players and male models favor.

I lick my lips. I don't even need to see his face. There's no doubt it is just as attractive as the rest of him. No way would I ever approach a guy this hot if I were sober. He is unquestionably out of my league.

I take a breath, and the moment of insecurity passes. This is just for fun—a simple distraction.

"Fuck it. Let's do this."

Liquid courage takes hold, and I stomp up to him, leaning my hand on the bar top. "Hey!"

Judging by the way his shoulders jump to his ears, I'm way too loud. I bite my lip to stifle a laugh. Uh-oh. I've hit the giggly marker of drunk.

He turns to face me. "Hey, yourself," he chuckles.

I dry swallow the air in my throat. Just as I suspected: when this guy smiles, he is off-the-charts hot.

Gold-brown eyes, thick pouty lips, and a jawline so sharp you could cut diamonds on it. I pause at his nose. The crooked bump along the ridge tells me he must have broken it at some point. But instead of making his face look imperfect, he looks rugged. And yummy. Like a sexy caveman who broke his nose fighting off a saber-toothed tiger.

"You're hot." I immediately clamp my hand over my mouth. Not only does the alcohol have me operating at a deafening volume, it also seems to have misplaced my filter.

He bursts out laughing once more. "Oh. Uh, thanks."

He rubs the scruff on his now flushed cheek. The facial hair he sports is thick but trim. Not a beard, but more than a five o'clock shadow.

"Sorry." I hiccup. "I've had a bit too much to drink."

"You don't say?" He flashes that winning smile once more. My knees are actually weak.

"But you must hear that all the time, looking the way you do."

He doesn't answer right away. In the moment of silence that follows, I study him. Something about this guy is familiar, but I can't put my finger on it.

"I don't actually." His eyes fall to the bar top, like he's embarrassed about something.

"Well, I'm telling you. You're mega, crazy, super-hot."

His expression slides to amusement. Inside I feel a ping of pride at getting this guy to laugh and smile.

A fresh bout of dizziness hits me. This time it's more intense, though. I swallow.

The handsome stranger's eyebrows knit. "Are you okay?"

I nod, even though I'm not. I grip the bar top for stability.

Gently, he steadies me with a hand on my arm. "You sure?"

The look of concern in his eyes has me feeling something familiar again. Just then a tiny bell goes off in my head. I've seen him before, but without facial hair. I just can't remember where or when…

I start to wobble, but this guy's got me upright with just his hand. He's still on the barstool, but he's leaning on it now instead of sitting. The almost-standing position he's assumed makes it look like he's keeping guard for me. If I weren't fighting to stay up, I'd swoon.

"I'm sorry," I mumble. "It's been…kind of a rough night."

"Sorry to hear that." Sincerity radiates in his eyes and his gentle tone. Even though he's probably just being polite, it sounds like he means it.

"Do you wanna talk about it?" he asks. "Maybe over a glass of water?"

"Water? How smooth."

The corner of his mouth quirks up. "On any other night I'd offer to buy you a proper drink, but it seems like you've already had a few."

"And on any other night I'd admire you from across the bar instead of marching right up to you and calling you hot. I have two Amaretto sours and two bourbons to thank for that. Because I'm in fuck-it mode. And you are number one on my fuck-it list."

The things my liquor-laden brain comes up with. Christ.

"What's fuck-it mode? And a fuck-it list?"

"'Fuck-it mode' is me downing more alcohol in forty-five minutes than I have in the past four months combined because I found out my boyfriend cheated on me tonight. I broke up with him, of course. And now I'm chatting you up. Because fuck it. See? Fuck-it list."

"I'm still not sure I understand what a fuck-it list is, but I'm sorry you went through that. Your ex is a prick for sure. I'm kind of glad to hear that happened, though."

"Sorry, what?" I hiccup.

"I'm glad because if he hadn't screwed things up with you, I wouldn't be chatting with the most beautiful, hilarious woman I've met in a long time."

There's the slightest gleam in his eye when he speaks.

"Whoa," I say through a hot exhale. "You are smooth…"

"Simon," he says with a boyish half-smile.

"Naomi."

He gives the spot on my arm where he's holding me a gentle squeeze. I pat him just above his knee and promptly salivate. My oh my, that is one firm quad.

"It's nice to meet you, Simon." I let my hand rest on his thigh, fully expecting him to politely mention that I could take my hands off him at any point.

But he doesn't. Instead his smile softens; he keeps his eyes locked on mine. That gleam in his stare sharpens, and my stomach takes a tumble. In my head, I run through everything that tells me this impromptu flirt session has gone from playful to something more.

We're openly touching.

Our faces are mere inches apart.

He's looking at me like he's starving and I'm the snack he's hungry for.

It all gives me confidence to see if I can take this exchange to the next level.

"Sorry for disrupting your quiet night," I say. "Judging by the way you're holding me and letting me touch you though, you're into this."

"You're the kind of disruption I'm happy to have. But you're drunk."

I'm certain my cheeks and neck are as red as the letters on the exit sign above the back door. "Oh…yeah. I—I'm sorry, I…"

He pins me with those soothing gold-brown eyes. They haven't lost one ounce of intensity, despite him putting the brakes on our exchange.

"I'm definitely into this—into you. But you need to be sober for this to go anywhere. How about we exchange numbers and tomorrow you can text me where you'd like me to take you for a drink?"

His sweet offer delivered with that killer grin takes the edge off my momentary embarrassment. He whips out his phone, I give him my number, and he calls me. I make a mental note to save his number when I fetch my purse.

My eyes fall to the floor. "Sorry for my, uh…drunkenness."

He lets out the sexiest growl of a chuckle. "Don't fret about it. We've all been there."

*Don't fret about it.*

Those four words hit like a Mack truck to my brain. It's a phrase I remember from many, many years ago.

In a split second, I'm transported to my college dorm room. I'm alone in bed on a night when my roommate is out, my laptop propped on my pillow, my hand down the front of my pajama shorts. On my screen plays a naughty video of a gorgeous college-aged man on his knees in front of his girlfriend's bed.

The lucky lady is lying on her back, her legs hanging over the edge of the bed, her naked body open to him. The webcam recording their every move is positioned in such a way that you can't see her face.

But you sure as hell can see his. He scoots closer to her legs, rests his hands gently on the tops of her thighs, then twists his head to the camera. His mouth stretches into a smirk that somehow looks more kind than smug. He winks. Then he turns back to her open legs, lowers his face, and goes to town. Her moaning, panting, and screaming are all that can be heard for the next few minutes.

Only this isn't just some random college couple filming their bedroom escapades for thrills.

This is the most popular cam guy online at the time, someone who millions of college girls like me watched, fantasized about, and pleasured themselves to because most of the videos he streamed were of him orally pleasing whatever lady he was seeing at the time—always with her enthusiastic consent.

He was the guy we all wished our college boyfriends were more like. He was the guy our boyfriends crudely dubbed as the "pussy whisperer" because of how easily and often he could bring his partner to climax.

Those four words became his trademark. He'd make a woman screech to high heaven in record time, and she'd always giggle an apology for being loud or making a mess on his face. Every single time he'd say, "Don't fret about it," like an unofficial catchphrase.

That popular cam guy? Simon Rutler—the same Simon standing in front of me, holding my arm, tensing under my palm, about to flirt my skirt off.

My heart thunders, transporting me back to the present. I blink through the dim lighting of the bar. This is the cam guy I pleasured myself to countless times during college. And I just made an absolute fool of myself in front of him.

"Oh my...shit."

I just drunkenly threw myself at the pussy whisperer.

I stare at him, my jaw hanging in the air, as if I just watched the Loch Ness monster trot through the bar.

"Are you okay?" he asks.

My lips purse as I almost call him the nickname, but I catch myself. I remember reading on some blog way back in the day that he hates that nickname. Saying it right now would undoubtedly piss him off, which would make this mortifying moment even worse.

Just then my stomach seizes. Of embarrassment? No, wait. That's the bourbon.

I grip the metal bar just below the bar top as my stomach lurches once more.

"Sorry, I'm...gonna be..."

I don't get to the word "sick" because hot bile shoots up my throat and out of my mouth, landing on his shoes. There's no time for apologies, though. I need to make it to the nearest toilet before I turn this entire bar into a biohazard by upchucking the contents of my stomach. I press a hand to my chest, as if that's going to somehow keep me from vomiting everywhere.

I burst through the door, ignoring Simon calling behind me as I dart to the nearest toilet and spew into the grimy bowl. My eyes burn with tears as I gag and purge. Seconds later, the putrid smell of hard alcohol mixed with the gyro I had for dinner hits my nostrils. I jolt back, crashing into a pair of legs.

"Naomi?" I register Harper's voice from above. "Holy crap…are you…are you okay?"

There's not a word that exists in the English language that fully captures this feeling of next-level humiliation. Of unknowingly hitting on my college fantasy while intoxicated, then vomiting on him.

Wiping my mouth on my sleeve, I heave a breath. "Nope. I'm definitely not okay."

## Chapter Two

The sound of my phone buzzing with a text is the worst sound in the world. Probably because I'm hungover.

Perched at my desk in my office in the Tenderloin district, I glance at the screen.

Harper: How are you holding up?

I rub my temples with my fingertips, willing my throbbing headache to ease. I take a long moment to close my eyes, breathe deeply, and will myself not to vomit all over my desk. Once my stomach is settled, I open my eyes and quickly type a response.

Me: How do you think I'm holding up? You fed me drinks the whole night, then I chatted up the cam guy I crushed on in college, then I vomited on him. I'm feeling pretty freaking embarrassed. I also feel like death warmed over.

For the briefest moment, I contemplate texting Simon an apology for how I acted last night. But what in the world could I say to him that would make things better? I'm sure as hell never going to see him again after the horrific display I put on last night. Best to forget about it and move on.

Harper texts back a string of laughing emojis. From anyone else, I'd be raging, but since they're from Harper, all I do is sigh. She's the queen of giving people a hard time when they're whining, and it would feel weird if she weren't.

Harper: At least you're not thinking of Brody, right?

She's right. Not once has Brody popped into my mind, even though on paper he should be the only thing I'm thinking about, given it's been less than twenty-four hours since we broke up.

No comment is all I text back to her.

She sends a winky emoji before reminding me to drink loads of water and eat something greasy.

I'm chugging water just as my boss, Fiona, stops at my open door.

"Morning, Naomi," she says without looking up from her phone.

I tell her good morning in response, then wait quietly as she gazes at her screen. This has been our morning routine ever since I started working here three years ago. Perfectly polished Fiona in her power skirt suit stops at my office to check in on whatever project I'm working on, always while reading something on her phone. It's a bit micromanage-y for my liking, but nabbing a digital editor position at Dash, one of the most popular websites in the country, has been a dream of mine ever since I graduated college. This high-end lifestyle website is the epitome of its name. Everyone who works here is expected to look stylish and professional while producing creative content centered on the chic and cultured lifestyle theme. If I have to follow a bunch of nonsensical rules to jibe with the office culture, I'll do it.

I smooth a hand over my hair, hoping I don't look as haggard as I feel. I put on extra concealer this morning to minimize the hangover-induced dark circles that have set up camp under my eyes.

I update her on the interview I have lined up later this week with a former pickpocket-turned-popular YouTube home chef. Fiona looks up from her phone, a wide smile on her face. I blink twice, stunned. I've never, ever seen her smile that big. She's usually so calm and composed, her emotional range drifting from mildly content to focused.

When she falls into the chair across from my desk, her expression doesn't budge. "There's been a change in plans."

I steel myself. Whenever a boss has spoken those words to me in the past, it's always been code for bad news. Either a deadline has moved up to an impossible time frame or I lost out on an assignment I'd been vying for.

"Care if I get a bit personal?" she asks. "Promise it'll all make sense in a minute."

"Of course." I try not to sound too shocked. In the time I've worked with her, she's always been tight-lipped about her personal life.

"I'm being whisked away to the Seychelles with my husband." She waves a hand in the air. "For our anniversary."

"Oh, um…"

Her announcement throws me for a loop. All I know about Fiona's home life is that she's married to Jeremy, an investment banker, and they have one college-aged daughter named Cece. Whenever I've asked about weekend family plans, she always gives me a bare-bones explanation. A couple sentences about whatever trip they're planning or home project they're undertaking. She's never randomly offered up any cute story or fun moment with her husband. I just figured she was intensely private about their life together. Or there wasn't much to say about it. Until now.

"I know what you must be thinking," she says, pulling me out of my confusion. "I've never been all that chatty about my personal happenings. That's because I've always thought you should keep home at home and work at work. But something happened over these past few months to turn my whole world upside down."

Now that I think about it, Fiona has actually seemed a bit more smiley and cheery lately.

"People always say that you should never stop dating your spouse. Well, we definitely didn't follow that advice. When Jeremy and I had Cece, our whole lives became her. And then when she left for college, it was like we had nothing in common. We argued constantly. I thought we were near the end. But these past few months, there was this change in him. He started being more attentive. He'd clean up the house without me asking him to and order dinner for me from my favorite sushi place when he knew that I'd be working late. He'd take me for walks on days when it was nice weather. And he'd make sure the fridge was stocked with my favorite pressed organic juices."

I almost say "huh" out loud but stop myself. Getting surprise pressed juice deliveries must be the rich people equivalent of receiving an impromptu bouquet of grocery store flowers.

"Would you believe I thought he was cheating at first?" When she laughs, I let out an awkward chuckle.

"I checked his phone. And emails. He wasn't cheating. But I was so thrown by his sudden change in behavior. It had been years since he had done so many thoughtful, romantic things for me unprompted. I should have been making an effort too. Yet for so long it was me doing it all—reminding him of birthdays and anniversaries, taking care of the house, doing all the gift shopping and putting both of our names on the card. It was nice to be the one being attended to for once," she says. "I was afraid that if I asked him about it, it would jinx everything, and things would go back to where they were. Complacent. Unhappy. Meh."

I nod along, wondering what compelled a man on the brink of divorce to recommit himself to his marriage.

"Last night at dinner, he explained that he was doing all this to be a better husband after years of falling short. He said he was committed to being a more attentive and loving partner to me. Then he pulled out his phone and showed me two plane tickets to a resort in the Seychelles. We're staying over the holidays this year to celebrate our twenty-fifth anniversary."

"Holy crap."

She grins so wide I wonder if her face hurts. "That was my exact reaction."

"That's wonderful, Fiona. Truly."

"After the shock wore off, I said yes, of course. And that's when it all clicked. This is what Jeremy had been working toward these past few months. He was dating me again—he was asking me to fall in love with him again. And I absolutely did."

"Wow. If only more men took the initiative he did," I say.

Fiona raises her brow at me. "It wasn't all him."

She pulls out her phone, swipes her finger across the

screen, and hands it to me. When I look at it, I nearly choke. It's a smiling headshot of Simon Rutler in a suit.

"This man is the reason we're headed to a tropical getaway instead of calling divorce attorneys. And he's your new interview assignment."

"Um…what?" My head snaps up.

I take a minute to process the craziness of this moment. Just last night I was hitting on Simon—my college crush—and now he's my new work assignment? What the hell are the odds?

I shove the thought aside and skim over his "About Me" section. Simon is a licensed individual and couples' therapist. He conducts one-on-one and couples sessions out of his home office but also holds seminars for men who want to be better husbands and boyfriends. Dozens of testimonials on his site speak of how he helped people strengthen their relationships.

"Don't worry, Simon's not one of those loathsome pickup-artist types." Fiona wrinkles her slender nose.

I read on and see that Simon addresses this exact issue in the latter half of his "About Me."

*Warning: This is not pickup-artist garbage. Men who teach other men how to degrade and disrespect women are not welcome in any of my classes. I focus on improving relationships through self-examination, becoming more emotionally aware, and learning to be more vulnerable with yourself and your partner. If I catch any of you PUAs in my classes, I'll throw you out myself.*

I hand Fiona back her phone.

"You're going to convince him to do his first-ever exclusive interview," she says.

For a second I don't say anything as I try to process all that Fiona has thrown at me.

"I know you normally pitch your own ideas, and I appreciate the initiative you take," she says after a moment, seeming to notice my hesitation. "But I don't want to sleep on this. My instinct tells me that this is going to be a huge hit. And you're the only editor at Dash who I trust to do this interview justice."

I soak up the compliment. Fiona isn't one to throw around praise willy-nilly.

"Next week is August. I want three ten-minute interview segments we can run with ads at the beginning of the month." She studies her phone screen once more. "See when is the soonest you can talk to him. I want him on Dash before anyone else has a chance to snag him."

Her confidence in me unleashes a quiet motivation inside. I probably have close to a zero percent chance at sitting down with Simon after what happened last night. But I have to at least try.

"I won't let you down," I say to Fiona before she walks to her office.

My phone buzzes with another text from Harper.

Harper: Did you eat yet? You need to eat.

Me: Screw eating. CALL ME! You won't believe what just happened.

One unanswered email and one voicemail later, still no word from Simon.

With any other assignment, I'd call this typical.

Loads of the people I contact for interviews take at least a couple days to get back to me. But I haven't vomited on any interview prospects before. Or shamelessly flirted with them. That's likely why I haven't heard from Simon.

As I sit on Harper's plush couch, I mindlessly scroll through my email. It's another late night at work for her, so that means I get her one-bedroom apartment in Nob Hill all to myself. I glance at the pile of boxes in the corner of her apartment by the door. I'm staying with her until I can find a place of my own.

Sighing, I set my glass down on the coffee table and pull up Simon's website and read through all the info. A section in his bio catches my eye:

*Yes, I was a cam guy. No, you can't call me the p\*ssy whisperer. No, I'm not ashamed of it, but I'm a therapist now and I want that to be my focus. Please respect that. But what I will say is this: it was fun as hell to cam. You'd be a lot less angry and judgmental—and a hell of a lot happier—if you spent more time focusing on yourself and less time policing the sex other consenting adults have.*

I burst out laughing. His sense of humor and no-nonsense tone makes me think he'd be a lot of fun to interview.

I play a two-minute-long clip from one of his seminars at a crowded conference room. A thirty-something man in the middle of the rows of chairs stands up and describes his relationship problem: his girlfriend complains about how he's not as thoughtful as she wants him to be.

The guy shrugs. "I mean, I do a lot, you know? I go to work every day. I take out the trash. I remember her birthday. I remember our anniversary. It just rubs me the wrong way that she thinks it's not enough. And then when I ask her what more I should be doing she gets mad. I'm just trying to communicate."

I roll my eyes.

Simon stands at the front of the room, his knit eyebrows indicating that he's listening intently. "Let me ask you something…"

"Miles," the guy says.

"Miles, what do you do for work?"

"I manage a sales team for a medical software company."

"How would you feel if one of the people on your team came to work and did the bare minimum every day?" Simon asks. "They never exceeded goals, they put in just enough not to get fired. And when they did, they sat around the rest of the day. Then, every once in a while they asked if you needed anything. How would that make you feel?"

"I guess I'd feel kind of annoyed."

"I bet that's exactly how your girlfriend feels. She has a job too, right?"

Miles nods.

"Having a job is baseline—you and everyone else who is able *should* have a job. To use that as a reason to be patted on the back is kind of ridiculous."

Murmurs of agreement rumble in the background.

"I don't say that to call you out, Miles. I say that to be as straightforward as possible. Because I get the feeling you're a guy who doesn't like to beat around the bush. You want to get straight to the point, right?"

Again, Miles nods. Simon asks him to recount what his girlfriend does for him. She cooks dinner every night, keeps a schedule of all their social activities and appointments during the week, plans vacations, remembers important family events for both of them, and takes care of most of the household cleaning and bill paying. She even planned a surprise birthday party for him earlier in the year.

"Here's the point: you're doing the bare minimum and expecting your girlfriend to be wowed by it. But she's not. And she shouldn't be." Simon pauses, presumably to let his words sink in. "Every single one of you is here because you acknowledge that you're falling short in some area of your relationship. I'm not saying your partners are perfect. I know they're not because no one is. And I'm sure some of your partners are falling short in some way too. But women in relationships tend to take on the majority of housework, social scheduling, childcare, looking after elderly parents, all that. Statistically speaking, your partners are doing so much already that you don't even acknowledge."

He pauses once more, presumably to let that point sink in too.

"So yeah, maybe in this one area of your life, *you* should take the initiative. Own your mistakes and show your partner that you're committed to being better. And to do that, first you need to realize what it is that you're doing wrong. So where are you falling short, Miles?"

Miles shakes his head, then looks like a light bulb has gone off in his mind. "I… I think my issue is that I'm not taking initiative like she is."

"Your girlfriend makes it a point to do all this unprompted," Simon says. "Every time she has to spell out what exactly she needs from you, it's frustrating and hurtful to her. You should already know to do those things. You're not a kid. You're a grown man, and grown men should pay attention. Grown men shouldn't have to be told ten times to do something, especially by their partner."

There's a faint chorus of hums and yesses from the audience.

Simon goes on to explain the emotional labor Miles's girlfriend is likely doing, managing her emotional responses to his lack of initiative. When he mentions how women are stuck doing the emotional labor in most heterosexual relationships, I find myself nodding along. That's the story of every adult relationship I've ever had. When the camera pans back to Miles, he looks awestruck. Simon finally gave this guy the ass-kicking revelation he needed.

Miles's head droops. "Man, I… I suck."

"It doesn't have to stay that way," Simon says. "Now you know your problem. And you know how to fix it, don't you?"

Applause follows Simon's encouragement. And then I realize I'm clapping too. I stop once I register just how silly it is for me to be applauding a prerecorded video. I can't help it, though. Simon is a genius, but it's not because he's delivering groundbreaking information. All of what he said is stuff that women have been telling their partners for years. The groundbreaking part is the fact that Simon, a guy, is calling other guys out instead of commiserating along with them. It's one thing for your partner to call you out, but it's something else entirely when a fellow dude takes you to task and says you need to do better.

Just then my phone rings. It's Simon. I take a second to breathe before answering.

"Hello, is this Naomi Ellorza-Hays?"

"Yes! Simon. Um, hey there—hi."

He chuckles, and I register that he actually said my full last name, hyphenate and all. Most people go with one or the other, which never fails to annoy me. My parents gave me both of their names, and I've proudly worn that hyphen my whole life. The fact that Simon didn't just brush my name off like everyone else makes me like him even more.

"This doesn't happen to be the Naomi I had the pleasure of meeting last night, does it?"

I cover my face with my free hand. "That's me. The shoe-vom girl. Very sorry for how things went down."

"Don't apologize. I thought it was cute," he says, his tone easy.

*Cute.*

That single word has my chest fluttering.

"But, the vomiting…" I drift off, too embarrassed to say more.

"I worked as a nurse's aide in grad school. Do you know how many times someone's vomited on me? You barely got my shoes. It's really not a big deal."

Not only is he dynamite in bed and rehabs mediocre males, but he was also a caregiver. A professional nurturer. Cue all the swooning.

"Thanks. I appreciate how gracious you're being."

"Don't fret about it." Thank goodness he doesn't know just how triggering that phrase is for me. I get another visual flashback of him leaning away from his thoroughly satisfied partner and wiping his lips with the back of his hand before saying those same words.

When he clears his throat, I'm back to the present.

"Look, I know you called about an interview, but—"

I interrupt him before he can say more. I know the tone, the implication of "look" said in this way. It's been thrown at me a million times before whenever I've asked for an interview from someone who is hell-bent on saying no. But if I can interview him and introduce him to the masses, he could reach even more people.

I swallow back all my residual embarrassment and put on my fearless interviewer hat. "You still get people calling you the pussy whisperer, don't you?"

For a long second all I hear is silence. My heart thuds, wondering if he'll hang up on me. But then he clears his throat. "Unfortunately, yes."

"Doing an interview with me could change that for you. Right now, so many people think of you as the cam-guy-turned-relationship-guru. And there's nothing wrong with that. You should be proud of your cam work. You were incredible."

I bite my tongue. I sound like a pervy fangirl. Must stay on message.

"But people should know you as a therapist first. This interview could help solidify that. We have an impressive reach."

I run through a few stats about the average daily views on our site and how often we're mentioned in other media outlets. The way he hums makes me think he's almost convinced.

"When I got your messages, I watched some of your interviews," he says. "I love how you work. You let the subject say their piece and ask open-ended questions. You never try to trip people up, like some interviewers."

"I would never. I promise to let you tell your own

story the way you want to, in a way that's comfortable for you."

"I don't know you very well, Naomi, but I trust you a hundred percent on that."

I hold my breath, hopeful that this might actually work out.

"Okay," he finally says.

I swallow back the victory squeal I want to let out. Instead I fist-pump the air.

"Free tomorrow?" he asks. "You can drop by my home office in the morning and we can get rolling on this."

"I'll be there."

# Chapter Three

By some coincidence, Simon's apartment is right next to Nob Hill, just a handful of minutes away from Harper's place.

Standing outside his building, I slowly inhale to calm my crackling nerves. I'll have to look at him for the next couple of hours. I'll have to gaze into his eyes, inhale the scent of his cologne, and pretend that I didn't used to fantasize about him. I haven't the slightest clue how I'll be anything other than flustered to the max. I hit the buzzer to his building intercom anyway.

"Hey there." Simon's voice sounds tin-like through the speaker.

"Hey, Simon. It's Naomi."

"Naomi." He practically chants my name. It makes the ball of nerves at the center of my chest loosen a tad.

"Sorry, I'm here a little earlier than we said."

"Don't fret about it."

That phrase again. It unleashes another naughty memory of Simon lying on a bed, his partner riding his face. One more blink and I get a killer view of his backside as he slowly, smoothly takes her from behind.

"Come right up," he says.

I reach for the door to his building, my face hot from

the images tainting my brain. No more blinking allowed. Just a deep, centering breath.

When Simon lets me into his place, he's the picture of ease, with an effortless half-smile on his face. As he helps me with my bags, we exchange pleasantries. Now that he's standing up straight and not slouched on a stool, I notice he's tall as well as broad. Maybe a couple inches past six feet. Just standing next to him makes my five-foot-seven-inch self feel dainty.

He gestures to two armchairs near the bay window in his living room. "I figured this would be the best place to shoot, because of the lighting and the space."

"It's perfect."

He settles into the chair across from me while I set up the tripod and camera next to my seat. Unlike at other media companies, most Dash producers and editors are a one-person show, often doing all of the research, storyboarding, interview questions, camera work, and hours of editing themselves. But I'm suited for it. Even in college as a film and TV production major, I loathed group projects, always preferring to work on my own and commandeering the bulk of the editing and post-production to ensure the assignment was as close to perfect as possible. As nice as it would be to have my own staff someday, I relish having this much control.

I do a slow scan of the cozy mid-century space and quietly freak out that I'm in Simon Rutler's home. But then I promptly tell myself to get it together. I'm in and out of people's homes and offices on an almost daily basis when I'm shooting interviews. I've filmed in much weirder places—everywhere from abandoned warehouses to crowded street festivals. This isn't a big deal at all.

We sit down, and I give Simon an overview of the

points I plan to cover. When he says he's ready, I hit Record on the camera and take a silent deep breath.

"Tell me how you got started as the Bay Area's most sought-after therapist for men trying to be better boyfriends and husbands."

Simon's eyes drop to the floor as he chuckles through a smile. "I'm hardly that."

"Based on the number of people singing your praises and your full practice, you most definitely are."

His cheeks and neck flush pink. He must be one of those people who doesn't take compliments well, and it's utterly endearing.

"Honestly, I just give them a new perspective and a new set of tools to approach the issues in their relationships. The hard work? They do that themselves."

"Spoken like a true expert."

My comment earns a soft laugh.

"So when you were a kid, did you always want to grow up and be a relationship therapist?" After doing interviews professionally for the past ten-plus years, I've learned how to ask different versions of the same question to get a better response.

"Well, when I realized that I couldn't grow up and be Spider-Man, I had to find something else to do."

"We all have to give up those childhood fantasies," I say.

"The short answer for why I got into the field is this: I grew up watching my parents fight constantly. As a kid, I wished that I could make them get along. But of course, at that age, I didn't have a way to help them, so I just watched as they fell into this unhealthy cycle of arguments and resentment until they got divorced."

"I'm sorry to hear that."

Even though he's discussing an indisputably personal topic, he doesn't seem to be bothered. He keeps steady eye contact and a relaxed posture as he speaks.

"Lots of kids go through the experience of watching their parents split up, but it really affected me," he says. "I ended up seeing a counselor during my teen years to help process a lot of that anger and pain I held. That inspired me to think about psychology and specifically therapy as a career path when I was older."

It's refreshing how candid Simon is about his own experience with therapy. There's still a stigma around mental health services and seeking professional help, and hopefully hearing Simon speak openly about it will help normalize it.

"I wanted to help people the way my therapist helped me. So I studied psychology during undergrad and earned a bachelor's, then I got a master's in counseling psychology."

He explains that after he earned his supervised clinical hours and started practicing as a therapist for couples and individuals, he noticed how emotionally guarded a lot of his male clients were in their sessions and in their relationships.

"So many were hesitant to open up both to me and to their partners," Simon says. "And after spending so many years studying psychology and working in therapy, I learned it's because men are socialized not to be vulnerable or emotional. It's seen as a weakness."

"That's so true. I mean, it's messed up, but that's exactly what I've observed too."

"It's upsetting because there's nothing weak about expressing how you feel. It actually shows how strong you are as a person, that you're comfortable enough to let your guard down and tell your partner what you're feeling. You're brave enough to open about what you're going through instead of hiding it, like so many people have been taught to do."

I nod along in agreement.

"I related to that mentality," he says. "I grew up with a dad who hardly ever expressed his emotions. He bottled things up and refused to talk about his feelings. I don't think I ever saw him cry. I was like that too until I started seeing a therapist as a teenager and realized how much better it felt to express my feelings instead of repress them or joke about them.

"I started to drive home the importance of that with male clients. A lot of them fought me pretty hard, they said it felt weird and awkward to talk about their feelings. But just like with anything else, the more you do something, the more comfortable you get doing it. Every time they did a session with me, either alone or with their partner, I tried my best to create a supportive, non-judgmental environment. And that helped them see the benefit of being open and talking about their feelings in the context of a relationship. Yeah, you'll still disagree and argue with your partner. But if you can get to the point where you're talking to each other in a respectful and sensitive way about how you're feeling—both the good stuff and the stuff that's bothering you—it feels amazing. Like you've unlocked this whole new level where you're having a healthy back-and-forth and not just fighting all the time because one person's upset that the other isn't being open and honest."

The smile he flashes has a tinge of shyness to it. "I feel like I'm babbling."

"You're not. At all. So that's when the light bulb went off for you?"

"That's when I started marketing myself to men who were having issues in their relationships. I filmed YouTube videos explaining these concepts while I built my practice and shared them on social media. After a couple of months, the videos got to be so popular and widely viewed that I started doing seminars in addition to individual therapy and couples therapy. It's been great because doing both seminars and therapy engages me in different ways. I love the one-on-one dynamic of therapy sessions, and I also enjoy public speaking and engaging with large groups. Both formats fill my tank in different ways."

"Love the way you put that," I say. "Things took off quickly for you, then."

"Not gonna lie, my camming background helped me gain a bit of a following at first."

"How so?" I'm shocked Simon mentions it. I figured based on the disclaimer he posted on his website, that topic would be off-limits.

"I honestly think a lot of people started attending my lectures initially out of morbid curiosity. I think they assumed the guy who used to have sex on a webcam couldn't possibly be a competent therapist."

I shake my head. "I don't get that. We're not all one-dimensional people who are only interested in one thing. Most of us are multifaceted, complicated human beings who crave different experiences. And that extends to our careers."

When Simon pauses to stare at me for a second, I suddenly feel self-conscious. God, that must sound like such an amateur analysis of the human condition to a guy who spent ten years studying psychology and counseling.

But then he smiles. "I couldn't have said it better myself."

I feel my cheeks warm at his compliment. "I figured you wouldn't want to talk about camming in this interview."

He shrugs, easy smile on his face. "I don't mind talking about it when it's relevant to the conversation. I fully admit that I wouldn't have the successful practice I have today at thirty-four if I hadn't cammed in my twenties. In a way it's kind of made me a unique provider in this space. Like, here I am, this guy who comes from an unconventional background with my camming work, using unconventional methods to reach out to people— by holding seminars aimed at men to help them become more comfortable with their emotions and openly admit where they're falling short in their relationships."

"Do you think the other side of that is a benefit to you, though? Like, maybe because of your background and your methods, you're able to reach a demographic of people who wouldn't normally consider therapy or relationship counseling?"

I mention his use of YouTube and social media to promote himself early on in his career.

He smiles shyly. "Maybe. I never really thought of it in that way."

"I think it's clear you have. When I was researching for this interview, I noticed that your audience and clientele skews relatively young—a good chunk of your clients and couples are in their late twenties to thirties. I think that's worth noting that your work resonates with younger people who maybe wouldn't think to reach out

to a therapist when they're having personal issues or relationship issues. And it ends up being a good thing that
they do know you through camming because they probably see you as sex-positive and nonjudgmental, and
feel more comfortable opening up to you because of it."

He takes a second, his expression turning thoughtful. "That's incredibly insightful."

I realize that this sounds more like a conversation
between friends than an interview. I ask him about what
his long-term career goals are.

His face takes on a thoughtful edge. "I love what I
do. I can't imagine doing anything else."

"There's nothing else you want to try?"

"I'm down to try almost anything."

I could swear he gently wags one of his eyebrows,
but I can't be one hundred percent sure. I bite my lip,
feeling strangely intrigued.

I ask him the rest of my questions about upcoming
seminars and if there's anything else he wants to add.

"There's no shame in seeking out therapy or counseling. We all need it from time to time. I see a therapist too, periodically. It can help your relationship and
marriage immensely. That and foreplay. Lots and lots
of foreplay."

I burst out laughing.

"That's the last time I throw back to my camming
days, I swear," he says.

"Oh, anytime you want to revisit them, I know a few
million people in the Bay Area who would be thrilled
about it."

"There are enough of my old videos floating around
online still. No need to add more." He chuckles.

"Your old site is still active?"

"No, but some old videos still circulate online on random sites. Even though I'm focused on different things now, I'm not ashamed of what I used to do."

"You shouldn't be."

His shy smile is back. This feels a hell of a lot like flirting.

I shove the thought aside as we finish, then I pack up my gear, confident this interview is going to be a hit. Simon was a dreamboat with his openness and honesty, and that confidence-without-cockiness he wears like a well-tailored suit.

"So," Simon says as he stands. "How did I do?"

"Brilliantly. My boss is gonna love this. Viewers will go gaga over you."

He flashes a flustered smile before his expression turns tender. "How are you holding up?"

It takes me a second to realize he's referencing my breakup.

"Honestly, fine overall. It sucks to be cheated on, of course, but now that I've had some time to process things, it's a good thing we're through. We weren't right for each other."

"If you ever want to chat about it more in depth—"

"Are you offering to be my therapist?" I almost chuckle.

"Actually, I was going to refer you to a colleague."

"I don't think I'm ready to now, honestly. But eventually I think it would be good for me to talk to someone."

He says he'll text me his colleague's contact info.

"Gotta say, I don't know if I'd feel comfortable with you as my therapist given how we…met," I joke.

Simon laughs. "That would be pretty unethical for me to be your therapist."

"Really? I guess I'd think it would be more weird than unethical."

He raises an eyebrow. "It would be unethical because I'm attracted to you and I'd never take on a client who I felt that way about."

"Oh."

Simon is into me. Cue a million fluttering butterflies in my stomach. But a disappointing crash follows. There's no way this can go further. There's no official policy at Dash preventing employees from dating interview subjects, but a lot of higher-ups aren't fans of mixing business with pleasure, including Fiona. I've heard her make disparaging comments about other staffers who fraternize with their interviewees. I personally don't hold the same standards she does, but she is my boss. If I want to wow her, it's best that I stay as straight and narrow as possible. She would undoubtedly disapprove if she found out that I was doing anything romantic with Simon.

"Look, I won't lie. I'm attracted to you too," I say. "But it's important for me to be professional. We have a work relationship now. I don't want the lines to blur, so we shouldn't pursue anything."

Simon's cool, calm smile doesn't waver. "I respect that." He walks me to the door. "It's probably for the best since you're in the middle of a relationship ban."

I turn to look at him. "How did you…"

"You were talking kind of loudly at Spud's the other night."

"Well. That's embarrassing."

I brush aside a loose chunk of hair that's fallen from my ponytail.

"It was funny hearing you go off a bit." His tone is

as soft and comforting as his smile. "I'm still not sure what a fuck-it list is, though."

I cover my face with my hand. "It's just a silly thing my cousin and I came up with years ago. A list of ridiculous things we'd never be brave enough to do. One of mine was hitting on a hot stranger. She figured it would help me get over my breakup."

I notice his cheeks redden as he looks at me. "That's pretty cute."

"Cuteness aside, I'm a disaster when it comes to relationships. This ban is long overdue."

His head falls back as he chuckles. The space by his front door is narrow so we stand barely a foot apart, our eye contact alternating between each other and the floor.

"So!" I say through a breath while shuffling my feet. "I'll send you a link to the interview when it airs."

"Sounds great."

I stick out my hand for him to shake. He glances down, amused.

"I figured a handshake would be a little more professional than vomiting on your shoes."

He chuckles. As we stand in front of each other, palm pressed against palm, I can't help but notice the way my heart thuds, the way my breath quickens. I'm holding the hand of my twentysomething fantasy. It's warm and soft and firm all at once—and it feels so damn good. Too bad it's the most physical contact we'll ever have.

"Right. Professionalism." His voice is a soft growl that makes my mouth water.

When we finally let go of each other, I'm hot all over.

I reach for the doorknob and give Simon a quick smile as I turn back and tell him good-bye. Then I'm out the door, every inch of my skin engulfed in invisible flames.

If that's what a handshake with Simon Rutler does to me, would I be able to survive anything more?

As I make my way down the street, that flame inside me slowly dies down until it's a tiny ember. I can't ever find out the answer to that question—not if I want to play it safe for my job.

"Ten thousand. Can you believe it?" Fiona says as she sticks her head into my office, beaming.

It's midmorning the day that Simon's first interview segment has gone live on the Dash website, and it's gotten ten thousand-plus views in the first two hours. This is the best viewership any interview of mine has ever gotten.

She darts back to her office as stratosphere-levels of excitement rocket through me. Ever since we left each other in a cloud of palpable sexual tension the day I interviewed him, I haven't had the nerve to contact Simon. Because if I were to reach out, I know it would turn into a flirty exchange, just like every other conversation we've had so far. And I can't have any more of that. Must stay professional.

But I *did* promise to send him the link to his interview. He *is* the reason Dash's website is overloaded with views.

I text Simon a link to the video.

Me: Hey! You're a hit! 10,000 views in less than two hours.

Simon: Holy sh*t that's a lot of views.

Me: You're a hot commodity. And do you always self-censor your texts? LOL

Simon: New Year's resolution. I'm trying to swear less this year. And I don't know about hot commodity.

Me: You are most definitely a hot commodity. Accept it.

I scold myself right after sending that message. That's a bit on the flirty side.

Fiona walks back into my office, and I set my phone down so it hopefully looks like I'm giving her my full attention.

"Put all your current projects on hold. You're doing a full-blown series on Simon."

"Wh—I am?"

"Absolutely. With numbers like this, we'd be foolish not to turn this into a series. Obviously viewers love him and want more."

"Oh, um…"

I internally scold myself. If this were any other work assignment, I'd be ecstatic. This is what every Dash editor and producer wants, and it normally takes five-plus years of an impeccable work history before you're trusted with a series. And here I am with the opportunity dropped in my lap. No way should I let my crush on Simon affect that.

I straighten up in my chair, feeling enlivened.

"Okay, how about this: I embed with Simon. Follow him at work, during his seminars, and a few one-on-one sessions with a couple of clients. I could give an inside, close-up look into his home life too. People are dying for a taste of something real."

For a second she's quiet, and I panic that my idea is too far off the rails and borderline inappropriate. But then she clasps her hands, clearly thrilled. "Yes! It'll be this unprecedented deep dive."

Fiona goes on about how we can market it almost like a TV series for the site. I smile at her enthusiasm and propose eight additional episodes.

"I love it," she says. "We'll air the next two segments from your original interview with Simon later this week as planned. And we can plan for the premiere episode of the series to follow soon after." She tilts her head at me. "That was a damn good off-the-cuff pitch. Creative. Raw. Viewer-driven. Well done, Naomi."

Fiona trots back to her office while I take a moment to process what happened.

I just got my biggest assignment of my career...documenting my dream guy...who I'm struggling not to flirt with in the name of professionalism.

I make a noise that sounds like a cross between a groan and a laugh. Then I swipe my phone from my desk and text Simon.

Free for a chat? I've got a proposition for you.

He calls me ten minutes later.

"A proposition, huh?"

The obvious smile in his voice makes me giddy, but I take a moment to swallow it back. Get it together, Naomi.

I briefly explain what I just pitched to Fiona. He's quiet the whole time, which causes the slightest hint of doubt to gnaw at me.

"I know that sounds a little—"

"Okay. I'm in."

"Really?"

"Yeah. It sounds like a cool idea."

"Wow. I thought it would be a harder sell given how hesitant you were when I asked you to do the first interview."

"You let me tell my story on my terms. I imagine you'll take the same direction in this series?"

"Absolutely."

"Then I'm all for it. Also, because of your interview, I'm on track to fill every seminar and counseling session for the next three months. I'd like to keep that momentum going and I think an extended series would do that."

I have to bite back a squeal. I've been wanting a big project like this ever since I started working at Dash and it's finally happening. "Would it be totally unprofessional to tell you how psyched out of my mind I am? Like, I seriously wanna scream."

"Then scream." There's a playful edge to his voice that makes my mouth go the tiniest bit dry.

"No way. I'm in the office."

"When you get home, then."

I chuckle. "If it's okay with you I want to get started filming right away. Like, later this week, if possible."

"Shoot, I can't. I have a two-week couples' retreat in Lake Tahoe that kicks off this weekend."

I'm about to tell him that's all fine, that we can work something out when he gets back. But then the ambitious part of my brain pipes up once more.

"Can I come with you and film part of it for the series?"

Again he pauses before letting out a laugh.

"What?"

"You're tenacious as hell, you know that?"

I chuckle. "I'll take that as a compliment."

"Good. I meant it as one."

The growl in his voice sends heat across my body. Damn it. I'm gonna need to get that under control.

"I'll run it by the couples and see if any are on board to be filmed. We're all staying in the same Airbnb, so if they're cool with it, then you're in. And hey, if this ends up working out, you're cool with sharing a bedroom at the Airbnb we'll be at, right?"

"What? Are you serious—"

Simon bursts out laughing. "I'm kidding, Naomi."

I let out a breath of relief. "Thank god."

"If only I could have seen your face."

"You're insufferable." My tease earns me a throaty chuckle.

Two weeks in a house rental with Simon Rutler would have been a fantasy come true for early twenties me. If this works out, sharing living quarters with Simon could get a bit...intimate. We'll see each other at all hours of the day and night. Keeping to my self-imposed professionalism code is going to get real difficult real fast if I happened to see him shirtless or run into him in a towel right after he's hopped out of the shower.

I shake my head. This is ridiculous. As long as we abide by the boundaries that we've set for ourselves, attraction aside, we'll be just fine. We've managed so far. And I know better than to just think with my lady parts.

At least I think I do.

"You'd better get used to my insufferable-ness if you're gonna spend two weeks with me in Lake Tahoe." The tease in Simon's tone is crystal clear. And it does nothing but spur me on.

"Oh, I'm ready."

## Chapter Four

One week into this couples' retreat and I'm buzzing with excitement. Almost all of the seven couples here agreed to have a session filmed for the extended series. I've sent some raw footage and a few edited teaser clips to Fiona and I've never seen that many exclamation points in any of her past emails to me combined. She even typed a smiley face—she's never, ever typed a smiley face in anything she's sent me before. It's clear she's ecstatic about the series. She even bumped up the airdate for the first episode by one week. That means she has full confidence in what a hit this series will be.

As I open my eyes and stretch in bed, my smile doesn't budge. If I knock this out of the park, Fiona mentioned a promotion to senior editor and producer, which means I'll be able to spearhead more long-running projects. I'd get a staff of people to work with instead of doing all the storyboarding, researching, filming, and editing on my own. As much as I love having all that control, being able to share the massive workload would be a welcome change.

I climb out of bed and head into the bathroom to get ready for the day. The soft hum of the coffee grinder from the kitchen echoes from the kitchen down the hall.

That's probably Simon. In the time that I've spent sharing living quarters with him, I've learned he's an early
riser who fires up kitchen appliances first thing in the
morning. A perpetual late sleeper on my days off, I let
out a small groan of annoyance. But then I remember
that I get fresh coffee as a trade-off and my grumpy
mood slowly melts away.

While I brush my teeth, I frown at the state of the
bathroom counter I'm sharing with him. Almost all of
the contents of his toiletry bag are scattered over the
marble surface. As minorly annoying as it's been to navigate his mess each morning, it's also weirdly endearing. For years I saw Simon as this perfect, untouchable
fantasy that I watched and gushed over. But every day
since we've been on this retreat, I've see him perform
ordinary, unglamorous tasks like sweeping the floor and
taking out the trash, and it's humanizing him. He's no
longer the mysterious cam guy I used to lust after. Right
now he's my work assignment. A regular guy. Kind of
like finding out the celebrity you've idolized for years
and years uses the same discount fabric softener as you.

After I wash my face, I skip doing my hair and
makeup in favor of downing some coffee. I walk into
the kitchen, giving Simon a silent wave as I make my
way over to the cupboard for a mug. He responds with
a nod as he looks at his phone and takes a long gulp
from his cup. He's learned that I'm not a morning person and don't care to talk much before I've had my first
few sips of coffee.

I turn around and see him standing there, pot of coffee in his hand. When he pours it into my cup, I offer
him a sleepy smile of thanks before blowing on it and
taking a sip. He leans against one end of the counter

while I lean against the sink and drink quietly for a few minutes.

"Sleep well?" he asks.

I nod, taking in the gray sweatpants and tattered white shirt he's sporting. He's the only person I know who can wear morning grogginess attractively. His eyes are puffy, his face is covered in scruff, and his hair is tangled and mussed, but he looks just as dashing as he does clean-shaven and decked out in a suit.

I take another long sip of coffee and hum at the rich, full flavor. "You're a coffee god. How do you make plain black coffee taste so good?"

"The secret is the roast. And the beans. I found this little place in the Mission District that sells these incredible Ethiopian beans. Best I've ever had. And then you have to grind them yourself, right before you brew. That's it."

"Well, if your current job hits a snag, you can always be a barista. I'd pay you whatever you want for a cup like this. I'm hooked on this godlike coffee."

"Godlike, huh?" He inches closer to me. The cheeky way he raises his eyebrow has me giggling.

"Wish I could say the same about your cleaning skills." He laughs.

"You are a human tornado, Simon. You leave dirty dishes in the sink and wet towels on the bathroom floor like it's your job." I lightly knock my shoulder into his.

He winces at the floor and for a second I think I've taken the joking too far. As well as we've been getting along, we're still at the beginning stage of being friends and colleagues. Maybe I should hold back a bit.

But then when he looks up, he's grinning. He shrugs. "One of my few flaws, I suppose."

I chuckle, relieved that he's not offended.

"So. What's on the docket for today?" he asks as I down the rest of the coffee in my mug.

"Going to go through the stats on your interview videos while I try to wake up. You're still riding the wave of your first segment and getting record views on the Dash site."

I don't miss the way his cheeks flare red before I turn around to refill my mug. Very, very adorable. I grab my laptop from the kitchen counter and set up on the stool at the bar.

"Mind if I join you?" Simon asks. "I have a million emails to get through before breakfast."

I tell him of course and for the next ten minutes we work in companionable silence. I glance at my phone and notice a text from Harper.

Finally had a chance to catch up on your videos, nice work! And ooohhh boy Simon is yummy on camera. But you knew that already, didn't you? ;)

I roll my eyes and try not to let my smile grow too comically big, so Simon doesn't notice.

"Wow," Simon mutters as he stares at the screen on his laptop. "Some of the comments on these videos are…interesting."

I look over and see that he's reading the comment section of his interview.

I aim a pointed stare at him. "Simon. Don't you know? Never, ever read the comments."

He rubs his neck and shrugs. "I know, I know. Curiosity got the best of me."

I scroll down to the comment section of one of his

videos to check it out myself. The first few I skim are
compliments about how open and honest the interview
was. Then a handful from people saying they're going
to sign up for his sessions ASAP. And, a bunch about
how sexy Simon is and how they wish their husbands
and boyfriends would enroll in his seminars.

That's it! I'm signing my husband up for his seminar. He could
definitely use this guy's help. And also whatever diet and workout
routine he's into. What a stud!

A hot therapist schooling men on how to be better? Yes, please!

BRB, sending this to my boyfriend

"I think your fan club is growing," I say.
"Wow, five pussy whisperer comments," he says,
frowning at his laptop screen.
I whip my head at him. Momentary panic sends my
heart racing. The last thing I want is for Simon to regret working with me. I do a mad skim of the comments
and spot one mention amid the hundreds of comments.
Simon could be looking at an entirely different section.
"Crap, I'm sorry, Simon. I still think, though, that
this was the best way to establish yourself in your
current career. Some people just refuse to move on,
I guess."
He flashes an easy smile at me. "It's okay, Naomi.
I'm not naïve. I don't think people will magically forget
about what I did before. I just don't want to be defined
by it. And from the response to this interview, it's clear
that people are viewing me in a new light. And that's
thanks to you."

My chest swells as I stare at my phone screen, his compliment making me glow from the inside out.

"Oh. Good. Phew." I mime like I'm wiping sweat from my brow, then immediately regret it. God, he must think I'm such a weirdo.

But he just laughs and turns back to his computer. We continue to work silently before his phone alarm goes off. He shuts it off and hops off his stool.

"I'm gonna head out for a run. Wanna join me?"

I cackle, then immediately go quiet when I take in the confusion in his expression.

"Sorry, I, uh, don't really run. Unless something or someone is chasing me."

"Noted." The corner of his mouth quirks up. "I'm learning a lot about you. You're a coffee fiend who refuses to speak in the early mornings until you've had caffeine, and you don't ever run."

"I'm a fascinating being, no question." I grin so wide, my cheeks ache. "The only run I'm planning on going on today is a bakery run for some breakfast pastries, if you care to ditch your morning jog and join me?"

"I'll pass today, but tomorrow?"

"As long as you don't expect us to run there."

"I would never."

He leaves me with a wink and a grin that I can't seem to stop thinking about the rest of the day.

The next morning I'm driving the two of us in my rental car to a bakery in downtown Lake Tahoe.

"Are you ready for the best egg tarts you've ever had in your entire life?"

Out of the corner of my eye, I catch Simon shaking his head and grinning. "I guess."

"Wow. Your lack of enthusiasm for food is astounding."

"I just don't get that excited about food. Running, on the other hand…"

I roll my eyes and he laughs.

"I'm addicted to the endorphin rush," he says. "Sue me."

I throw my head back in a groan, then lightly shove at him. I immediately wish I could undo it. Damn it, I need to stop touching him. One, it's way too touchy-feely for how little time we've known each other. And two, it's probably not the most professional thing in the world to shove the guy I'm documenting for work, even if it is a joke.

*And even if his body is deliciously hard and firm to the touch.*

I ignore that last part. "Sorry about the touching," I mutter. I immediately purse my lips and sigh. That sounded a million times creepier out loud than in my head.

The sound of Simon laughing saves me from dying of embarrassment. When I glance over at him, he's grinning to himself. "It's fine. Really. I kind of figured given how handsy you were the night we met that you're a pretty tactile person."

"Oh. Um, yeah. I guess I am." I let out a strangled sound as I ease to a four-way stop. "But I should probably stop now that we're working together."

"It's okay. I like it."

I take an extra second to soak in his reaction before I press the gas pedal. It's not his tone that gives me pause. That was perfectly pleasant. Friendly, even. But the way he wagged his eyebrow as he spoke? I definitely paused at that. *That* was the right amount of suggestive and intriguing to leave me wondering if this is just us navigating our newly formed friendship and colleague status…or something else.

Just then Simon's phone rings. He pulls it out of his pocket and frowns slightly. "Ah, damn. It's my mom. I forgot she wanted to FaceTime this morning."

I gesture for him to answer it.

"Sorry, just a sec." He answers the phone, flashing a bashful smile at the screen. "Hey, Mom. Good morning."

"Hi, honey!" a cheery voice says. "I was just wondering what you were planning on giving your sister for her birthday next month. I was about to head to that spa she likes in Palo Alto to buy her a gift card, but if you were going to get her something similar, I'll get her a new purse or shoes."

"Feel free to go to the spa. I honestly haven't thought of anything yet."

"Oh, Simon. You always save this stuff to the last minute." The way his brow wrinkles when his mom tsks at him makes me laugh. He looks up at me and I grimace before mouthing, "Sorry."

"I've still got a few weeks left," he says. "How's your car running?"

"Oh it's good, honey. Thank you again for changing the oil. You know I can take it into the shop no problem. You didn't have to drive all the way out here to do it."

"Mountain View isn't that far from San Francisco when the traffic's not bad. No sense spending money on something you can make your son do."

"You're so sweet. Always making sure I'm okay."

The way Simon's cheeks flush pink immediately after his mom's compliment is all kinds of adorable.

There's just something about a big gruff guy going all puttylike around his mom that is insanely endearing.

Simon asks her how her shifts at the hospital are going while I pull into the downtown area of Lake Tahoe.

"Is that Simon?" a sweet elderly voice chimes in.

"Hi, Grandma," Simon says, upping the volume of his voice. She must be hard of hearing.

"Peanut!" she sings. I mouth "aww" at him when he shakes his head at me, that bashful smile still on his face.

"How are you, Grandma?"

"Oh, you know. Every day above ground is a blessing."

I grin at her phrasing as I search for parking.

"Can you help me with my phone, Peanut?" she asks. "I forgot the passcode."

"Of course. Mom, can you grab a pen and write this down, then tack it on the refrigerator for Grandma to look at in case she forgets again?"

"You got it, honey."

"Okay, Grandma. It's one-one-one-nine-five-seven. That's the month and year you and Grandpa got married, remember?"

I inwardly squeal at how attentive and patient Simon is with his family.

"Got it. Thanks, Peanut! Love you."

"Love you too," he says. "Okay, Mom. I'd better get going here. Promise I'll call you later this week."

"Wait, how is everything going on the retreat?"

"So far, so good."

"How's filming for that show you told us about? Are you nervous being on camera all the time?"

"It's going great. The editor, Naomi, is doing a wonderful job," he answers patiently.

I notice his expression turns tight for a second, but it eases when he glances over at me. I wonder if he's weirded out that I'm listening in on his family conversation. I'd probably be a bit self-conscious too if I were chatting with my parents in front of Simon. Not because I'm embarrassed of them, but because my parents tend to fuss over me like I'm a little kid despite the fact that I'm well into my thirties. I smile slightly to myself. Kind of like how Simon's mom is with him.

"And actually, I'm in the car with her now, so—"

"You should have said something! Can we say hi?"

Simon knocks his head to the side, his cheeks flushed. "Really, Mom?"

I pull into an open parking space and turn off the car. "It's okay. I don't mind."

Simon exhales in that low-key annoyed way you do when your parents are driving you the tiniest bit crazy, but you endure it because you love them.

He makes a slight grimace at me and for second I wonder if he's irritated that I offered.

"You sure you don't mind?" he asks.

"Positive." I smile, despite the tinge of awkwardness I feel too at the prospect of having an impromptu chat with Simon's mom. At least Simon and I are sharing in the feeling.

I unbuckle my seat belt and pivot so I'm closer to him. He scoots closer and turns the phone to me. "Hi there. I'm Naomi. It's nice to meet you."

His mom's eyes go wide as she beams at me. Instantly I recognize that warm hue and kind sentiment. Simon's eyes are just like hers. So is his light brown hair color. But every other feature of her face is too delicate to resemble Simon's. The rest of him must come from his dad.

"Naomi! What a pleasure. I'm Barbara." She pivots her gaze to Simon. "Shame on you, Simon. You didn't mention how lovely she is."

"God, Mom," he groans, scrubbing a hand over the side of his face.

Now I'm the one blushing. "Oh wow, thank you, Barbara. That's so nice of you to say."

"Mom!" she calls over her shoulder. "Come here and meet the person who's filming that show about our Simon! Look at how cute she is."

"Sorry," he mutters. "They get like this whenever I mention there's a woman in my vicinity."

"I get it. My family is the same way."

Just then Simon's grandma pops into view. Behind her thick-rimmed glasses are those same golden brown eyes that radiate softness. She grips the frame of her glasses between her left index finger and thumb, squints at me, then grins.

"Well, have a look at you. So pretty! I'm Miriam."

"Thank you, Miriam. You're lovely, by the way. You and Barbara both. I can see where Simon gets his eyes and hair."

"Oh, stop!" they say in unison.

Miriam runs her hand over her shoulder-length gray-brown waves. "You should come by the house some time. Simon, bring her by for dinner one of these nights. I make the best homemade ravioli you'll ever have. You can even film it for the show!"

I pivot my gaze to Simon. "Ravioli's my favorite." He shakes his head, laughing.

Barbara cuts back into frame. "I just have to say, Naomi. I love the series you're doing about our Simon. It's so fun to see him in those videos." She darts her eyes to Simon. "If only your dad could have taken a class like yours back in the day."

"Okay, Mom, Grandma, we'd better get going. Nice to talk to you both."

They exchange I-love-yous and we tell them good-bye.

Simon hangs up and shoves the phone in the pocket of his gym shorts.

"Sorry about that." There's the slightest gleam of self-consciousness in his eyes when he speaks. "I love them, but they can be a little over the top."

"Don't even worry about it, Peanut."

His expression turns full-on playful. "Ha. That's the first and last time you call me that. That embarrassing nickname is for my grandma's use only."

"Why does she call you that?"

"Apparently when I was a baby, I was bald for a while and looked like a giant chunky peanut."

I press my hand to my heart. "Oh my god. That might be the cutest thing I've ever heard. But seriously, your mom and grandma are so sweet. And relatively low-key compared to how my family gets every time I've brought someone new around."

"How so?"

"Well, for starters, everyone expects a hug. They'd probably fawn over you because you're tall and hand-some. They'd ask you a million questions about your work and family. One of my cousins would make you do a karaoke duet with them. They'd force-feed you food until you burst. And that's just my mom's side."

A dazed look flashes across his face. "Wow. I don't know if I'd survive."

"Oh you would. They'd want you to come back for every family gathering ever, so they need you alive."

As we both laugh, a sense of comfort settles over me. Despite the few awkward moments Simon and I have shared at Lake Tahoe, being around him feels so natural. And easy. He's a blast to chat with, whether we're working together or just hanging out—the kind of person I can imagine being fast friends with.

I climb out of the car and head toward the bakery, which is at the end of the block.

Simon squints at the sign bearing the name Lorelai's above a tiny brick storefront. "Let's see if these egg tarts live up to the hype."

"Oh, they will."

"So confident."

"Just wait until you taste them."

# *Chapter Five*

Simon pulls into a parking spot downtown in front of the bakery we've hit up almost every morning since I took him here a handful of days ago.

"When are you going to just finally admit it?" I tease as we climb out of the car.

Simon rolls his eyes as a smile tugs at his lips. "When you stop pestering me."

"Not gonna happen."

He folds his arms across his chest and sighs, his expression playful. "Fine. Egg tarts are better than running. There. Happy now?"

I flash what I hope is a smile that's equal parts smug and sweet. "See? Was that so hard?"

He shakes his head and his smile turns wolfish. He gently pats my arm, nodding toward the entrance of the bakery. "Come on. The sooner we get in there and order, the quicker you'll be stuffing your face and I won't have to listen to you gloat."

Together we jump into the ten-customer-deep line. I was right about the fast-friends feelings I had the other day. Even though we haven't known each other long, Simon definitely feels like a friend at this point. Each day the awkward moments are fewer and farther between. And playful teasing is another hallmark of getting to know Simon better. As important as it is to me to maintain professional boundaries with him, it's been fun joking around and getting to know him better on this retreat.

As we wait our turn in line, I notice the attention Simon gets right away and smile to myself. It's been like this every other morning we've come here. I don't blame the half-dozen people in the vicinity who all slowly turn their gazes on him. Tall and broad Simon looks dashing even in worn jeans and a rumpled hoodie, his hair mussed to high heaven.

At least his admirers are discreet about it. They do quick, seconds-long glances before turning back to the menu board or their phones. Except for the teenage boy behind the counter who stops mid-crouch at the display container to gawk at him with wide, unblinking eyes before the older lady at the register snaps at him to hurry up. He's stared at Simon with heart eyes every day we've seen him at the bakery.

I've always been a woman who had more female friends than male friends, so being out and about with my hot male work colleague and witnessing all the attention he receives is entertaining.

Simon leans down to me. "Can you imagine if this place existed in San Francisco?" He nods his head to the glass-front displays near the counter, which hold dozens of delectable baked goods. "The hype train would hit it instantly and we'd never be able to get in. The line would be miles long."

"All the more reason to come here as often as possible," I say. "I'm gonna miss it when we head back to the city."

The line moves forward and we take a step up, but then the woman standing in front of us tumbles back, crashing into Simon.

He steadies her with both hands on her arms and casts a watchful glance over her. "You okay?"

She nods, a slow smile crawling across her face. She looks like a taller, leggier version of Margot Robbie. She also looks positively smitten to be in Simon's arms right about now.

"Yes, thank you. Sorry about that. It's these wedges. Still trying to break them in."

She glances down at her towering sandals, then tugs at the hem of her navy blue romper. "No worries." Simon gives her a light tap on the arm before letting her go.

Instead of turning back to the front of the line and ordering like I expect her to do, she stays standing and staring at Simon.

"I'm so clumsy." She chuckles, twisting a lock of hair between her fingers.

I have to bite my lip to keep from chuckling at her very obvious flirting. But Simon doesn't seem to be fazed. Judging by his non-reaction at all the attention he received when we first walked into Lorelai's, he's clearly aware of his effect on people and doesn't seem to care.

"It's really fine," Simon says, his cheeks growing pinker the longer she looks at him.

But before she can go any further, the customer ahead of her pays and leaves.

"Next!" the lady at the register shouts.

Margot's sexy smile takes on a sheepish edge. "I guess that's me. Thanks for breaking my fall."

"Sure thing," Simon says.

She turns away, orders, picks up her pastry, then strolls to the entrance of the store, giving Simon one last dose of googly eyes before brushing past him and disappearing.

"Well, then," I say.

He chuckles and we order. With our bag of egg tarts, we snag the empty bench right in front of the store front window. I open the bag, inhale, and groan.

"Should I leave you and the bag alone for a minute? I feel like a third wheel here."

I pull out a tart, hand it to him, and dig one out for myself. I take a giant bite and close my eyes the moment the rich custard coats my tongue.

"Oh my god," I say around a mouthful.

When I look up at Simon, he's chewing and frowning. "So you don't just do that when you eat at home?"

"Do what?"

"Sound like you're having an orgasm when you take your first bite of food."

I cover my mouth as I laugh. Once I'm sure I won't choke on my food, I finish chewing and swallow.

"Oh come on," I say. "You're telling me you've never made a sound like that enjoying incredible food?"

He tugs on the string of his hoodie, then grins before looking away.

"I'll take your silence as a yes," I say.

We share the rest of the egg tarts while people-watching.

"Did you decide on a name for the series yet?" he asks.

I nod while I finish chewing. "I was thinking *Simply Simon*."

The second I say it, a grin dances on his lips. "I love it."

"Yeah?"

"It's perfect. Direct. Self-explanatory. Easy to remember. A lot of people think my life is weird. Or pornographic. But it's really not. When you get past all the preconceived notions, I'm pretty basic. It's cool that you get that."

"Thanks. That means a lot," I say.

When he sticks his hand in the front pocket of his hoodie, he frowns. "What the…"

He pulls out a scrap of paper and shows it to me.

*I live in San Francisco too. You're hot. Call me sometime.*

A phone number is scrawled underneath.

That must have been the whole reason for the Margot Robbie look-alike falling into him minutes ago. I let out a cackle that has everyone walking nearby gawking at me.

"What?" Simon stares at me.

When I catch my breath, I explain it to him.

The look in his eyes is a mix of disbelief and amusement. "I've never had a woman slip me her number like that before. They usually just type it into my phone. Or they outright ask for mine."

"Oh dear god. That is such a humble brag," I groan. "Actually, that's not even that humble. You're basically saying that you're so irresistible, women come up to you regularly and try to pick you up."

He tilts his head at me. "That's how we met. Remember?"

I push his arm, but he doesn't budge. He's too sturdy.

"What can I say? I'm clearly irresistible."

He wiggles an eyebrow at me and I laugh at the mock-arrogance in his comment. But really, it's not arrogance. More like confidence. Maybe if I hadn't witnessed him patiently walk his grandma through using her smart phone the other day, I'd write Simon off as just another cocky guy who's all too aware of his attractiveness. But he's so much more than that.

"Will you bust out that modest charm when you call her?"

He studies the brown bag. "I'm not sure if I'll call."

"Why not?"

"You don't think that would be weird?"

"What do you mean?"

"Well…because of how…you know. You and I met."

His gold-brown eyes search my gaze and that's when I realize he's waiting for my response. He's waiting for me to tell him it's okay to date another woman…even though if I hadn't been sloshed the night we met, it's almost guaranteed that we would have ended up together.

Just the thought sends goose bumps across my skin. I take another gigantic bite of egg tart to divert my focus. None of that matters now. Yeah, I still find him insanely attractive, but we're solidly in the friends camp. And it needs to stay that way, given we're working together and I don't want anything coming in the way of this series and my promotion.

I finish chewing, swallow, and smile at him, hoping he can't decipher the flurry of hot-and-bothered feelings that rest underneath.

"Look, I know I technically tried to pick you up the night we met, but it didn't end up working out. And honestly, I think we're working out pretty well as friends and work colleagues right now. So you're free to date whoever you want."

He blinks before nodding, smiling slightly. "Yeah,

definitely. Maybe I'll call her when we get back to San Francisco, then."

He tosses his crumpled napkin in the nearby trash can before standing up, then sticks his hand out to help me up from the bench. We hop into the car and head back to the Airbnb.

"Coming to you changed everything for us, Simon. Truly." Cole, one of Simon's clients, gushes while holding the hand of his wife, Tamara. They're one of the married couples who have agreed to let Dash document their counseling session with Simon for the series.

They sit in dual armchairs just a few feet from Simon in the living room of the Airbnb. It's currently a make-shift therapy session space since the floor-to-ceiling windows overlooking the crystal-blue expanse of Lake Tahoe offer the perfect light for filming.

I stand quietly in the corner behind the camera, taking notes to reference when I edit the footage later on.

Simon returns a smile. "How have you two been doing since I saw you last?"

Cole and Tamara explain how they both have been working on their argument style—trying to remain measured in their tone and avoiding hurtful language when they're upset.

"We've come a long way since all that door slamming and storming out. Oh, and my personal favorite: the cold shoulder," Tamara says.

Cole gently squeezes her hand, then leans over to kiss her forehead. I recall the info they jotted down on the waiver I emailed them to fill out before the retreat. Married fifteen years with three kids, living just outside the Bay Area. Cole was a workaholic, and over time Tamara grew tired of him working impossible hours and weekends in his hospital executive job and not helping at home with their three kids. They had argued over the issue for years, Cole still kept working while Tamara struggled to keep things afloat at home. When she threatened to leave him, that's when Cole knew he had to make a change. He had heard about Simon through a friend, and he and Tamara started seeing him for counseling.

"I was just so fixated on money for the longest time," Cole says. He's mid-forties but possesses the energy of someone half his age. Everything from the animated way he gestures to the twinkle in his eyes reads young.

"I wanted to earn enough so that we didn't have to worry. I mean, the Bay Area's expensive. I know this sounds ridiculous, but I didn't realize that I was neglecting my marriage and my family so much in the process." He turns to Tamara, a regretful expression on his face. "When I started cutting back at the hospital and working more reasonable hours, remember what you said? How you told me how much happier you and the kids were to have me home more often and that you didn't care if we had less money or if we had to move to a smaller house? It was like a light bulb went off in my head at that moment. All those times when you asked me to help more and I chose work instead, I was outright dismissing your feelings. I was dismissing our marriage and our family. It didn't seem like it to me at the time, but I get it now."

"I didn't handle it the best way either," Tamara says. "I would bite my tongue for weeks on end and just let my frustration bottle up until I was so stressed and so angry that I would snap at you and we'd yell at each other. That wasn't the right way to deal with it."

"But I get why you handled it that way, sweetie. I wouldn't listen when you'd try to bring it up in a calm way. I probably would have done the same. It would all culminate until we were both so frustrated that we'd explode on each other." Cole scoops Tamara's hand in his.

Simon compliments them on the physical affection they're expressing. "It's huge when couples can go through a tough time and continue to express affection for each other. I want to commend you two for that."

They practically beam. I quietly note how supportive Simon is with every couple he counsels. He affirms with compliments often, and if someone is being closed-off, he asks questions gently to coax them to open up. His demeanor is so inviting and nonjudgmental.

"When you two have a disagreement now, how do you handle it?" Simon asks. "Are you bringing up the issue as soon as it starts to feel like it could be a problem?"

Tamara nods. "It was so hard to do that at first. My instinct is to avoid rocking the boat. I'm so used to just quietly letting things slide—that's how I grew up so it was ingrained in me. But I learned that bottling things up just results in those feelings festering until you can't take it anymore and have an outburst."

"That's such an insightful observation, that you're able to identify the root cause of that behavior. Well done," Simon says.

"I've gotten better about not saying 'you always do this' or 'you never do that' because now I realize how hurtful that is to hear," Tamara says. "So instead, I say how I'm feeling, I take ownership of that feeling, and make it clear to Cole that I need his help. I tell him I can feel myself heading toward anger and resentment, but I also make it clear that I'm not there yet. And I won't get there as long as I feel like he's supporting me, listening to me, and doing what he can to help out."

Simon compliments them on the progress they've made in their relationship. At the end of the session, I thank them again for letting me document the session for the series.

"We're happy to," Cole says.

Tamara nods along, her jet-black bob as polished as the impeccable red lip she sports. "Hopefully it helps more people get on board with the idea of going to couple's therapy. Goodness knows if we had seen something like this, we might have gone to see a therapist much sooner."

She excuses herself to return a call to her mom, who's watching their kids.

When she heads down the hall to their bedroom, Cole turns to Simon and starts excitedly talking to him about a surprise he has planned for Tamara. I leave the two of them to talk while I put away my camera equipment. I'm in my bedroom going over footage for the series when Harper texts me.

Hey! Haven't heard from you in days and I'm dying to know…what's it like shacking up with your college fantasy?? Tell me you've at least made out!

I roll my eyes.

Me: You need to grow up.

Harper: Come on! Honestly, I'm surprised you haven't texted me sooner to gush about what it's like being around your dream guy 24/7.

Me: Okay, you wanna know the truth? It's pretty normal. Not at all as exciting as you think. But in a totally good way.

A minute later she calls me.

"You're gonna need to explain that because it makes no sense to me. How in the world can you be so relaxed about sharing an Airbnb with Simon? I saw your face that night at Spud's Bar. I remember distinctly how you had zero chill around him. And that mischievous gleam in your eye when you told me that it was your idea to stay with him for two weeks in Lake Tahoe."

"Mischievous gleam? What the hell even is that?"

Harper scoffs at my shoddy excuse.

"Okay, look," I finally say. "Yeah, Simon's hot and I used to be a fangirl of his back in the day when he cammed, but I see him in a whole new light now. I've gotten to know him as a work colleague and a friend. He's just a regular guy who's a therapist committed to helping people, specifically men, be more open and comfortable with their emotions so they can be better partners in their relationships."

"And that's *not* super hot to you?"

*Yeah, it's crazy hot. And maybe if we weren't working together...maybe if that night at Spud's Bar I had said "no" to one or two drinks, I would have been a bit more sober and we would have hooked up and—*

I shake my head, halting the thought as soon as it formulates in my filthy mind.

I swallow. "Okay, fine, yes, it's an attractive quality." I wince at how pitchy my tone is and how weirdly diplomatic I sound. "But I'm not a cavewoman, Harper. I can acknowledge when a guy is attractive, but that doesn't mean I'm automatically going to pounce on him."

"Well, damn. That's pretty boring. I was hoping for some super-juicy details. My life is so boring, dealing with zoning laws and blueprints and building permits."

"Sorry to disappoint."

"I guess you won't need that surprise I packed in your suitcase."

"What surprise? What are you talking about?"

"Check the very bottom of the zipper compartment."

With my phone pinned between my cheek and shoulder, I unzip the compartment, dig to the bottom, and promptly freeze.

"You didn't," I mutter.

"Oh, I did."

I almost growl at the giddy tone of her voice. And then I growl for real when I pull out a three-pack of condoms.

"Harper! Are you serious right now?"

"Hey, I just want you to be safe and prepared in case you and Simon get it on."

"I can't believe you."

"Come on, Naomi." I can practically hear her roll her eyes over the phone. "I remember the way Simon looked at you at Spud's Bar the night you chatted him up. He's totally down to bone you."

I chuck the box of condoms back in my suitcase. "You know, when you talk like that, you sound like an annoying high schooler, not a thirty-three-year-old corporate architect."

"It's true."

"It doesn't matter. Simon and I aren't going to sleep together. I don't even think of him in that way anymore."

The lie dances like fire on my tongue.

"You're a god-awful liar, you know that?"

I sigh. "Okay fine, yes, I still think he's super hot and I'm attracted to him, but like I said, I'm not going to do anything about it. You know how straightlaced Fiona is. If she thought I was screwing around with Simon, she'd lose all respect for me. I've got a promotion on the line with this series. I'm not going to let a little bit of flirting and attraction get in the way of that."

"Aha! So you two *have* been flirting! I knew it!"

I groan as Harper giggles.

"Good thing I packed those condoms," she says. "You'll thank me later."

I shake my head at her smug tone. "Good-bye, Harper. I've got a ton of work to do."

"Oh, and I packed a little something else for you right next to the condoms—to help you blow off steam while you work up the nerve to pounce on your dream guy."

She says a quick good-bye before hanging up, and I immediately dig into my suitcase once more. As soon as I feel the long, thick rectangular box, my lips purse in irritation. Of course she would pack this. I should have seen it coming.

But as I pull the brand-new pink vibrator tied with a red ribbon out of my suitcase, I have to bite my tongue to keep from screaming. My annoying meddling cousin. Once I'm back in San Francisco, I'm going to kill her.

## Chapter Six

From the massive mahogany desk in my bedroom of the vacation rental, I clean up an audio clip for episode one of *Simply Simon*. I probably could have gone with the one I saved two versions ago, but I'm a perfectionist—I always have been. And I want everything about the premiere episode to be just right. I save it, then I check the views on Simon's videos that are posted on Dash. It's the last day of the retreat with everyone taking off tomorrow morning. All the couples are out for a hike near the lake and Simon took off for a jog, leaving me some quiet time alone to work. All three segments from the very first interview I did with him at his apartment are live and every single video has garnered thousands of views in the first few hours of being up on the site. Everyone adores getting to know the Bay Area's most sought-after relationship expert, it seems.

I check my calendar on my laptop and see that I have a week until *Simply Simon* airs. I pause and take a deep breath, equally excited and nervous. I'm thrilled with how Dash viewers have fallen in love with Simon—and I want the series to be a huge hit that meets all of their expectations.

I silently tell myself to stop worrying. I've gotten loads of great footage on the couples' retreat. It's going to make a killer premiere once I'm done editing it. Viewers will love seeing Simon in his element as a therapist. In every email Fiona has sent me, she's been so supportive and positive about my work. I'm going to knock this out of the park.

*I'm going to knock this out of the park.*

"I'm going to knock this out of the park," I whisper to myself.

When that does nothing to calm the nerves whirring inside of me, I gaze out the window right in front of my desk. Since I'm on the back side of the house, I can't see the lake, but I've got a killer view of the lush green yard and the trees lining the edge of the property.

A few seconds of gazing has me a bit calmer. I turn to my laptop and check the comments section on Simon's videos. I don't normally care to check comments, but the one time I did it with Simon, I saw just how overwhelmingly positive the feedback was and want to see if it still holds true. I let out a soft squeal when I see that the majority are raving about Simon and expressing their interest in the upcoming *Simply Simon* series, which Dash just started promoting on the site. Of course, there's a smattering of comments about how hot Simon is. He's a good-looking, charismatic, and intelligent guy who's just been delivered to the online masses. There's guaranteed to be some fawning.

But then one comment catches my eye.

Hot damn the pussy whisperer grew up nicely. Though I do miss his old work.

I don't have to click on the link to know what it is.

One of Simon's many fans has linked to one of his old camming videos. I roll my eyes, annoyed that someone thought it was appropriate to bring up Simon's past in his present career.

I click on the comment to delete it, but my fingers slip on the keyboard of my laptop. I accidentally click the link instead and am taken to a page where a video screen pops up.

"Shit!"

I absolutely did not mean to click. To watch an old video of him right now, even by accident, crosses every single professional boundary I've set for myself. Yeah, I used to watch him years ago, but that was before I knew him personally, before we started working together.

As fast as I can move my fingers, I go to close the tab, but a low, breathy moan hits my ears. It's deep, throaty, guttural…male.

My hand stills as my eyes drop to the image on the screen. It's a naked, younger Simon sitting on the edge of a bed, his partner kneeling in front of him, her head between his legs. You can't see her clearly. But Simon is on full, unobscured display. And judging from the caveman-like sounds he's making, he is having a hell of a good time.

My lips part as I inhale sharply. Somehow I missed this camming video all those years ago because I don't remember watching it. My jaw plummets to the floor as I take in the visual. His bare, muscled chest that heaves with every desperate breath he takes. The sunlight from a nearby window that paints him in a light glow. How his long, sculpted arms tense with each second that passes. That delicious way he white-knuckles the edge of the bed, a clear sign that he can barely take the pleasure he's receiving.

Seconds pass. My brain scolds me that I shouldn't be doing this—I shouldn't be gawking at this incredibly hot video of twenty-something Simon getting it on with his lady at the time. But I'm hypnotized. I couldn't peel my eyes off the screen if someone waltzed in and offered me a million dollars to move my eyes six inches to the left.

Because there's something addictive about the presence Simon has when he's on screen. It's the same presence he possesses in everything I've seen him do. Whether he's receiving pleasure, delivering it, or conducting a therapy session or seminar, his energy is always the same. Confident, but gracious. In control, but not a control freak. Selfless, yet self-assured.

A slow wave of heat washes all the way up my chest, my neck, my face. I could swear I'm breathing as fast as he is. Observing Simon get so worked up is having a similar effect on me. Inside I'm tingling; between my legs, I'm aching.

I really, really shouldn't be. I know I shouldn't.

Because this is wrong. So, so wrong. I drew a line—I'm supposed to have a friendly and professional relationship with Simon. But that line is long gone now. I set fire to it the minute I decide to watch this video. And if I'm being honest, I'm not the least bit interested in stopping.

With wide eyes that refuse to blink, I continue to gawk. Simon's head falls back and a hard swallow moves down his throat. His face is flushed, along with his neck and torso. His chest is pumping faster and harder, a surefire sign that he's about to lose it.

Jaw muscles bulging and abs tensing, he lets out a grunt that echoes loudly in the room.

Having been Simon's fangirl all throughout my twenties, I'm familiar with his O face. And I can spot his tells from a mile away. But every single time I see it, it gets me. It's like this cocktail of giddiness and nerves. There's something so intrusive about watching someone lose themselves to pleasure, even when they open themselves up to it—even when they want you to watch.

Now I'm holding my breath. I know what's coming. My blood is hot as it pumps through me; my breath is fire every time I inhale. No matter how wrong it is, no matter how many rules I've broken in the past ninety seconds, I need to do something to relieve this full-body throb. Otherwise I'll disintegrate.

Just as Simon starts to fall off the cliff, I hear the sharp sound of metal clanking on concrete. It's so loud and sudden, my shoulders jerk and my gaze darts from the computer screen to the window. Like a reflex, I smack the laptop shut and stare wide-eyed at the yard.

Oh no. Oh no, no, no. Not this. I absolutely, most definitely don't need to be seeing this right now.

But I am. I'm staring wide-eyed and open-mouthed at shirtless Simon, clad in just a flimsy pair of gym shorts, back from his run, standing right in front of me in the backyard.

And my god, what a sight it is. From where he's standing he can't see me—he's faced away and looking toward the trees, hands on his hips as his chest heaves with each breath he takes. There's a dumbbell at his feet on the concrete patio next to the grass—probably where the harsh sound seconds ago came from.

"Fuck," I mutter as a hot breath shoots from my lips.

This is a hell of a scenario. Seconds ago I saw Simon all sweaty and breathless while in the middle of a sexy act and now I'm seeing him all sweaty and breathless from his workout. It's a distinction my brain doesn't care to make. All it cares about is that I'm seeing Simon in real time, in the flesh, just feet away from where I'm sitting, making a lot of the same movements and sounds he made in that sexy camming video.

He's just as sweaty. His skin is flushed the same shade of pink. His muscles are bulging just like they were in that video. His chest is heaving just as hard. His jaw is just as tight as it was. And my body. My poor body can't take it.

When he bends down to pick up the dumbbell, he makes a grunting noise that lands deep in the cave-woman recesses of my brain. It's the same sound I heard him make on camera seconds ago. And it's the last straw for me.

I jolt up from the chair, nearly knocking it over, and scramble over to my suitcase. I dig out the vibrator Harper packed as a joke, rip off the packaging, and instead of the bed, head straight for the bathroom. I need the water to muffle the ungodly noise I'm guaranteed to make. Plugging the drain of the tub, I undress and climb in. I set the vibrator on the ledge of the tub, then slip my hand between my legs and let my fingers take over as the water level rises around me. It's not long before I'm shaking and shuddering, gasping and yelping. I'm careful to cover my mouth with my free hand so I don't make too much noise. I'm gone before the water level makes it to my ankles.

But I can't stop there. That first orgasm was a quick one, something to take the edge off. Masturbating has always been a regular activity for me, but since ending things with Brody, I haven't been in much of a feisty mood. Apparently all it takes to turn that around is a two-minute video of Simon being turned on followed by forty seconds of watching him work out shirtless in front of me.

This time when I touch myself, it's slower, more measured—more civil. I'm not a crazed animal satisfying a carnal urge anymore. I'm slightly more human and have the mental fortitude to remind myself that I like the buildup just as much as I like the payoff. I've always been someone who preferred long, drawn-out sex and masturbation, so I give myself exactly that. After a few minutes and when the water starts to cover my belly as I'm lying down in the tub, I hit climax number two. This time, I let out a breathy yell. It's quieter than the one before, and I'm glad. That means I have the energy for one more.

I go for the vibrator this time, building myself up just like I did before with gentle, teasing pressure from my hand. Minutes pass until the water makes it all the way up to my chest. Holding my breath, I kick the faucet off with my foot. My chest heaving, my eyes pressed shut, my breath ragged, I press the pink silicone against my most sensitive spot. My mouth falls open and I let out a moan to end all other moans. I quickly cover my mouth with my free hand. Thank god Simon is outside and everyone else is out of the house because even against my palm this sound is unholy. The heat builds to that unbearable point, where pleasure and frenzy combine. Inside I burn hotter and hotter until I just can't take it—

There's a knock at the bathroom door, and my eyes fly open.

Shit.

I think—is that Simon?

"Naomi? Are you in there?"

Yup. That's Simon.

I try to lower the volume of my voice, but it's too late. My body is too far gone. It doesn't matter that my brain is sending messages to the rest of me to get myself under control and be quiet.

Because right now climax has taken hold of me. It is in control. It's calling the shots, and it doesn't give a flying fuck that Simon is on the other side of the door, about to hear the orgasm that's about to claim me.

I try to loosen my grip on the vibrator, but it's no use. It's like my hands are acting of their own volition. My uncontrollable shout bounces off the walls of the bathroom. It's so loud my ears ring. There's no question that Simon can hear it too.

"Are you okay?" His voice is urgent.

All I'm able to do is yell-gasp the word "yes" as the orgasm rips through my body.

Finally my hand releases the vibrator. It lands in the cradle of my belly, but this orgasm is strong as hell. My arms and legs thrash against the tub, water splashes onto the white tile floor. The opaque shower curtain tangles against my arm so tight, the shower rings rattle against the rod up above. I don't even have time to feel embarrassed about it. I'm caught up in the sensations, my hands gripping the tub to weather the ecstasy convulsing through me.

"You don't sound okay. Crap, did you fall?" Simon hollers.

Panic and pleasure shoot through me while I thrash. I open my mouth to tell him "No," but I can't form any words. The most I can manage is dialing back my scream to a moan.

"Hang on, I'm coming in!"

When Simon bursts in, I'm at the tail end of climax. But these are monster aftershocks after an orgasm like that. My limbs are trembling, my breathing is ragged and loud, my chest is still heaving—and it's clear as crystal what I've been up to.

The whole thing only lasts seconds, but it's long enough for me to feel the burn of utter mortification. Because as Simon stands above me processing the image of me splayed out in the tub, it doesn't take long for him to figure it all out.

That twist of concern in his face soon morphs into confusion. A beat later there's surprise. Then recognition. I watch it all play out from his eyes to his mouth, to the red flush on his skin.

His eyebrows dart all the way up to the top of his forehead. "Oh," he finally says.

There's nowhere for me to hide, so I don't even bother. But I do manage to slip one hand over my crotch and slide my arm over my breasts.

"Yeah, um. I didn't, uh, fall."

His complexion is now beet red as he does a slow scan of my body. It takes a moment before his eyes shoot back up to my face. His stare turns shy and embarrassed, as if he's just now realizing that he probably shouldn't have checked out my naked body.

"I see that."

My eyes drop to the front of his pants, which showcase a generous bulge.

"Oh." It's the same word Simon just said, but when I say it, there's a hitch to it. A glimmer of intrigue I didn't feel until this instant. Because that bulge is broadcasting that Simon is totally into this—he's into *me* in this moment.

Something inside of me turns bold. It's like the embarrassment from moments before has evaporated, leaving behind arousal and amusement. And I'm so very on board.

Mustering all the arousal-fueled courage in my body, I hold Simon's gaze. And then I raise my eyebrow. The corner of my mouth soon follows.

It's a silent question I'm asking him—and I think I already know the answer.

I wouldn't normally be so brazen, but this isn't a normal situation. It's a comedy of errors that's just turned into the hottest moment of my life. I'm asking if Simon is game to join me. And judging by the slow rise of his bare chest, that hint of a grin playing on his lips, the way he keeps looking at me with hunger in his eyes, he's up for it.

Screw professionalism. Screw every other excuse I've come up with over the past couple of weeks as to why I can't give in to my attraction to Simon. None of it matters right now when we're seconds from pouncing on each other.

"Come here." The words fall in a raspy whisper.

My heart thuds as I watch the slight upward curve of his mouth turn into a full-fledged grin. He steps toward me and moves to shut the door.

But then the front door slams.

"We're back!" A gaggle of excited voices follow.

Someone announces that they're going to fire up the grill. The sound of glasses clanking echoes.

"Hey, Simon! We got that Scotch you like!"

I sit up, head twisted in the direction of the noise, mouth open in disbelief.

You have got to be fucking kidding me.

I fall back into the tub, water splashing all around me. I groan, then laugh, then groan again.

When I look up at Simon, his face is twisted in a pained expression, like he can't believe this is happening either.

With my eyes on his, I sigh and shrug. He shrugs too before letting out a flustered laugh. He heads out of the bathroom, shutting the door behind him.

As soon as he's gone, I slide under the surface of the bath and let out a scream that I'm grateful is muffled by the water.

As I hold my breath, I tug at my sopping-wet hair, my brain a flurry of disbelief and panic. How the hell do we move on from that?

## Chapter Seven

It turns out that avoidance is my preferred method of moving on.

I avoided Simon's gaze that entire night when we all had dinner together at the Airbnb. I avoided talking one-on-one with him when I woke up at the crack of dawn yesterday, said good-bye to everyone, and drove my rental car back to San Francisco.

And today as I attack my to-do list at work, I'm trying my damnedest to avoid thinking about him and how, had everyone come back just an hour later from their hike, Simon and I would have totally had sex.

I go dizzy at the thought as I try to focus on my computer screen. What the hell was I thinking? Okay sure, even as I look back on it now, it was insanely hot to have Simon walk in on me masturbating, see how turned on he was, and then to witness him make it very clear that he was down to take it further.

But…

That would have been a mistake. A very foolish mistake. Because as amazing as I'm sure it is to hook up with Simon, it would have derailed me. It would have shattered my self-imposed professional code for this series. It would have most definitely thrown me off my game—I'm already thrown off my game after *almost* hooking up with him. I'm fairly certain that had we actually gone through with it, I wouldn't be able to concentrate on anything other than just how dynamite he is in bed and how...

I shake my head, annoyed that once again I'm losing focus. This is why getting cockblocked by the couples at the retreat was a good thing. Now, I still have my professional code. I can at least look Fiona in the eye when she asks me how the series is going. I can tell her that I'm working hard on loads of compelling segments instead of fumbling and stammering and hoping she won't be able to tell something's off whenever I talk about Simon, which could then lead her to question my capability to spearhead *Simply Simon*.

*Simon.*

At some point we're going to have to talk again. We're going to have to meet up, I'm going to have to interview him and film more segments of him...

I slump over in my desk chair and groan softly into my hands, cringing at how I'm going to approach the subject with him.

I haven't even told Harper about it—and I tell her everything. But I can't stomach anyone, not even my best friend and cousin, ever finding out about my most mortifying life moment. Simon knows, and that's already one person too many.

"Excellent work on the first cut of the *Simply Simon* premiere, Naomi. Everything—the scene transitions, the shots, the editing—is so clean and streamlined," Fiona says as she walks into my office, snapping me out of my mental reflection. I jerk my hands from my face and straighten up in my chair.

She walks to my desk while reading something on her phone. "We're still going strong on the views for his first three segments. People are dying to watch the series premiere. And we've gotten two more advertisers on board because of his strong showing. A men's razor company and this custom boxer brief clothing line."

"That's great," I croak out.

"The way you've cut episode one is brilliant. Everyone adores this insight into his work life. It's both slick and compelling."

I mutter a thank-you, then take a sip from my coffee mug, hoping the caffeine will jolt me out of my humiliation stupor.

"God, this guy," she says while checking something on her phone. "Good-looking. Sex positive. Smart. Cultured. Sensitive to women's issues in relationships. Willing to hold other men accountable for their shortcomings."

I nod along with Fiona's assessment, chugging from my mug, unsure of just how long I can endure her going on and on about Simon's appeal. It's all true, of course, but every mention of him makes it harder and harder for me to distance myself from the memory of him bursting into the bathroom, his eyes bulging at me as I sprawled out all wet and naked just a few feet in front of him, my eyes falling to his crotch because I was so turned on that of course I would gawk at his junk.

"He's the whole package, wouldn't you say?"

Fiona speaking the word "package" unfortunately coincides with my recollection of Simon's package, and I can't help but gasp as my immediate, involuntary response. Too bad I'm also drinking at that exact moment.

I choke on the sip. When I look up, Fiona is staring

at me, something between a frown and surprise clouding her expression.

"Are you all right?" she asks.

I nod before coughing for another several seconds, then swallow.

"Down the wrong pipe," I say, my voice raw.

"Hate it when that happens." She waves a hand. "I was thinking, really go for it in episode two of the series. I think it would be compelling to see Simon doing something outside of his work. Something raw. Up close and personal."

My throat goes dry. If only she knew how up close and personal we've already been.

I clear my throat. "What do you mean?"

"Something non-work related. Take him out on the town. Show what he likes to do for fun. Or, I don't know, working out?"

Coffee won't do anymore. I need to cool off, so I drain the water bottle on my desk. And then I process Fiona's micromanage-y suggestion. As confident as I am that I can come up with my own ideas, I can't just blow off Fiona's suggestion—she's my boss. And I'm going to have an aneurysm if I have to film Simon all sweat-soaked, his muscles bulging while he's panting during a workout after what happened the last time I saw him working out. All that grunting and gasping and groaning and sweating and writhing and...

I shake my head to rid the visual from my mind, then wipe away beads of sweat that have suddenly formed along the back of my neck, close to my hairline. The last thing I need after our last semi-sexual encounter is to be around Simon when he's doing the second sexiest thing a man could ever do.

But there's no way around it. Fiona's hell-bent on this more personal angle for upcoming episodes.

"Okay, yeah, I'll um, text him about it right now."

"Oh, no need. He's on his way here so you two can talk about it when he arrives."

"What?"

Fiona frowns at my sudden sharp tone. I clear my throat and mumble something about my throat being sore from all that coughing. She explains that the art department needs to take photos of him for the series promo content, so he's stopping by to do that right now.

She looks out the glass floor-to-ceiling wall of my office, which faces the elevators. Then she grins and waves. "Simon!" she sings.

Whipping my head around at lightning speed nearly dislocates my neck. In walks Simon, from the elevators right into my office. A dozen heads pop up from the nearby cubicles. It seems like everyone at Dash is eager to see Simon in the flesh.

He stops in my doorway, his posture easy and the smile on his face natural. I swallow all the saliva in my mouth.

No…just…no. This cannot happen. The first time Simon and I see each other post-almost-hookup fiasco cannot be at my workplace, where I have to exude professionalism and competence. Not when I'm a tangle of nerves and indiscernible syllables at just the thought of him.

Now that he's here in front of me, I'm supposed to just pretend that we didn't almost have sex two days ago?

Before I can stammer out an unintelligible greeting, he shakes hands with Fiona.

"It's a pleasure to finally meet the man who helped save my marriage," she says.

He thanks her for the kind words, and they chat briefly about the series. Fiona talks about how she feels so newly loved-up by her romantically reformed husband that she's been doing more thoughtful things for him too, like making him breakfast in bed and surprising him with box seats to all the Giants' home games this season.

The entire time, I gaze up at them, still seated in my office chair, in awe of how easy and calm Simon seems. Is he totally over what happened between us?

She mentions their anniversary trip to the Seychelles and asks if he travels much.

"Not as much as I'd like. I'm headed to Napa with my mom, grandma, and sister next month for a long weekend, though."

Fiona's face lights up. "Oh, that would be great to chronicle for an episode. We could get an inside look at you spending quality time with your family. What do you think about accompanying Simon to Napa, Naomi?"

As I stammer out a response, Simon interrupts. "Actually, I'll have to run that by my family first."

Fiona smiles warmly. "Of course. Look at me, throwing out all these ideas. I should really leave it up to Naomi. She's doing a brilliant job of things so far."

Fiona raves about the just-edited first episode of *Simply Simon* at the couples' retreat.

"You're our most-watched online series to date," she says.

Simon blushes. "Wow, really? Thank you for even

wanting to produce a series about me. It's been a joy working with Naomi."

Fiona looks at me. "I meant to ask earlier, you two have a nice time in Tahoe together?"

My throat goes dry once more, but this time it's because I can't think of a single thing other than Simon seeing me touch myself in the tub. It's like when someone points out a tiny stain in an otherwise beautifully pressed and laundered shirt. Every time you look at it, your eyes can't help but zero in on the flaw.

"It was, um…"

Simon's brow wrinkles as I stammer my way to something resembling a complete sentence. I have zero doubt that he knows what I'm thinking at this exact moment and why it's messing up my ability to speak.

"It was great," I finally say.

"Yeah, we really got to know each other," Simon says.

"Good to hear." Fiona taps on my desk before turning her attention back to Simon. "Naomi and I were just discussing ideas for your upcoming episodes. Viewers seem to want more personal footage of you."

"Personal?" Simon asks. There's a twitch in his brow line when he says it. I wonder if that word is conjuring up the same sort of inappropriate images as it did for me.

Fiona nods. "In addition to the qualified and intelligent therapist that you are, people want to see you let loose too. So show them. Don't be afraid to get real. Show us what you're like in the mornings before you've had your coffee. Show us what you like to do for fun. Show us what you're like when you get a little flustered."

Even though I'm sitting down and Simon is standing a few feet away, I can see his eyes dilate the moment Fiona says the word "flustered."

"Feel free to take off early if you two want to head out and brainstorm ideas," she says to me. Then she walks to the open doorway and looks between us. "Don't be afraid to be real. To get dirty. Viewers love that."

When Fiona's out the door, a soft strangled noise escapes from Simon's throat. Her phrasing has made me want to melt into the floor—but that's not a realistic option. So instead, I do the next best thing I know how to do: I joke.

I muster the last bit of nerve I have and look him square in the eye. "If only she knew just how dirty it's been already." I try for a smile.

Simon's expression goes from flustered to a full-on grin. "Exactly."

The laugh we share helps melt the tension in the room.

"After I finish up in the art department, should we meet and talk about ideas for what's next in the series?"

"Sounds like a plan," I say. "Where should we go?"

"How about Spud's Bar?"

There's a gleam in his eye I can't help but chuckle at.

"You think we should meet at the bar where I hit on you, then vomited on you, to brainstorm 'dirty' ideas for the series?"

"I can't think of a better place, given our history."

"We're really going for it, aren't we? Just putting it all out there."

He shrugs, sly smile on his face. "I've been putting it all out there my whole life. I don't know how else to be."

Simon's ability to confront the tension between us head-on with humor has me feeling a million times lighter.

"Spud's Bar it is."

The dim lighting at Spud's Bar illuminates Simon perfectly as he sits across from me in this corner booth.

"Just water for you?" he asks before sipping from his Scotch.

"Remember what happened the last time we were here and I drank something other than water?"

My gaze flits to the bar, then the bathroom. Simon brings the glass to his mouth, hiding his smile.

"I think it's best I stick with water," I say.

"Suit yourself."

I eye my glass of ice water as I work up the nerve to say what I've been planning to say ever since he left my office earlier today. Yeah, we're here to brainstorm ideas for the series, but I also need to address the elephant in the room: how we almost had sex.

Because even though we had a relatively pleasant interaction just hours ago, we still need to actually talk about the event in question. It's what mature adults would do.

"We should talk. About what happened. In Tahoe." I internally roll my eyes at my stilted tone.

My nerves go haywire, even though they shouldn't. Simon's a cool guy. I probably couldn't have picked a better person to accidentally have an orgasm in front of, then proposition for a hookup. He's progressive about sex and is open to talking about anything. But that's just one part of it. How in the world do I begin to talk about an event that makes me want to melt into the floorboards?

His expression goes soft. "You're right. We should."

I trace the rim of my water glass as I work up my nerve once more before looking at him. "I'll be honest. I'm pretty embarrassed."

Simon frowns like he's confused. "Why?"

I force my gaze to stay on him instead of darting all over the room. "Because what I did was incredibly unprofessional. First of all, masturbating so loudly that you heard me and thought I was hurt."

The corner of Simon's lips twitch, as if he's trying not to laugh. My face bursts into flames.

"Very sorry about that," I mumble before taking a long gulp of ice water. "And just as a sidebar, thanks for rushing in to help me when you thought I was hurt. I did sound like a possessed she-demon."

He grins, then coughs. "It was no problem."

"But after the…confusion of that moment was cleared up, things should have ended. I shouldn't have… demonstrated…that I wanted something more to happen with you…on a work trip where I was assigned to film you for my job."

Simon squints at me like he can't quite understand what I mean.

"Naomi, I…you don't need to apologize. I mean, yeah, I was caught off guard a bit, but after I realized you weren't hurt, I was into it. I thought that was clear."

"No, I mean, yes. I mean, I could tell you were into it. I just…" I close my eyes and shake my head. "To be honest, if everyone hadn't come back at that exact moment and interrupted us, I would have been down to… you know."

His mouth twitches again.

"But in the end, I'm glad we didn't end up doing… that…together."

"You are?" His voice is stilted.

I nod. "It's probably not the smartest thing in the world to hook up with someone I'm working with. It's probably hard to believe, given how you've seen me behave so far, but I've always been a stickler about professionalism and boundaries. Fiona, my boss, is even more so. She turns her nose up at employees at Dash who fraternize with their interview subjects."

"I see."

"And if she found out that we almost…you know…it would most definitely tarnish her opinion of me. I want to avoid that at all costs. I already feel like I started out in an awkward, semi-unprofessional place given how I threw myself at you when we met. Fiona's been really impressed with my work on your interviews so far and that means a lot to me—this series means a lot to me too. And if it goes well, I'd be in line for a promotion. I don't want to lose that opportunity."

"That makes total sense. I get it."

Simon takes a long sip while I down the rest of my water. He signals the bartender to refill my glass, and I say a quiet thanks.

"So could we maybe just move on and forget it ever happened?"

"Absolutely. Consider it forgotten."

"I'd love it if we could just be work colleagues. And friends."

"I'd love that too."

Even though Simon sounds sure, there's a glimmer of something extra in his gold-brown eyes.

I ignore it in favor of moving on. "Okay! Now that's squared away, how about we come up with some ideas for episode two of *Simply Simon*."

"I'm all ears."

"Good, because the idea that I have is a little out there, but I think it could be great."

I pull out a small notepad from my purse, rip out a page, then hand it to Simon along with a pen.

"I want you to make a fuck-it list."

He raises an eyebrow.

"Fiona wants something gritty and fun and real for episode two—a close-up of something that shows a side to you that's different from your work as a therapist. So I thought you could make a list of random and wild things you've always wanted to do. Then we can film one for the series."

Simon stays quiet for a moment before a smile pulls at his lips. "I'm down. But you have to make your own fuck-it list too and do something from it as well. Fair's fair."

I roll my eyes. "Fine. But I'm not doing it on camera. This series is supposed to just be about you. I'm making a list because fair's fair, and you shouldn't be the only one doing something."

"Okay, deal."

For the next minute we quietly scribble. When I finish, I slide my list to Simon; he slides his to me.

When I read the first item on his list, my eyes go wide. "Are you serious?"

His expression remains confident. He doesn't even blink. "Dead serious. I've always wanted to."

I stammer as I grin, positively giddy at the prospect of Simon doing this on camera for the series. When he winks at me, I could squeal. This dude is unflappable and so self-assured. I love it so, so much.

"Yours is a lot tamer than mine," he says while squinting at my list. "And you only wrote one thing down."

"I guess I'm just super boring."

"Not boring. Just different. I like it."

There's the hint of warmth in my chest. I focus back on his list and circle number one. "I'm psyched to see you do this. You sure you want to?"

"Positive. I can't wait, actually. We can do both of ours the same day. Or night. Night might be better."

"Okay. Sure," I say, despite the grimace on my face.

Simon's smile turns gentle. "If you're not comfortable, Naomi, you don't have to do it."

I shake my head. "No. I want to. I've always wanted to. I just may need your help."

"At your service."

I ignore the butterflies that statement sends to my stomach.

"When should we do it?" Simon asks.

"How about Saturday? In the Castro district."

That glimmer in Simon's eyes shines brighter than I've seen. "Can't wait."

## Chapter Eight

I stand outside the entrance of Bangerz, a popular male strip club at the edge of the Castro District, my stomach in knots. I shouldn't be. I'm not the one entering their amateur night. Simon is.

But as I fumble with my phone to double-check that it has enough battery for this evening, I know we have to be strategic about this. It's challenging enough that I'll be filming this on my phone—there's no way any strip club would let me bring in my clunky bag of camera gear and openly film someone performing at their establishment. I'm also gonna have to play it off like Simon and I are together and I'm just filming him for shits and giggles. If they knew it was for an online series, it would result in loads of release forms, getting permission from the owner, and a million other pain-in-the-ass things. I need to make this look like an authentic spontaneous moment.

And then I have to hope that the footage will be good enough to use in episode two.

I take a deep breath and straighten my cross-body bag, then zip up my jacket against the damp chill of evening that's a trademark of San Francisco nights, even in the summer.

I remind myself that it'll all work out. The premiere of *Simply Simon* happened days ago and was a mega-hit. It garnered more views in its first few hours on the Dash website than any of the interview videos posted. People are going to love episode two just as much. I just have to have faith.

I scan the street for Simon and spot him crossing the street down the block. He's wearing a dark gray bomber jacket, dark shirt, jeans, and sneakers. For a moment I wonder if he chose such a simple outfit because it'll be easier to strip off. My cheeks are fire at the thought.

I watch him stroll along the pavement, his posture and his expression easy, not looking the slightest bit nervous.

He grins as he walks up to me. "Hey. You weren't waiting long for me, were you?"

"Nope. Just a couple of minutes. Are you ready?"

"Always." His tone is as steady as his eye contact. Does anything faze this guy?

We line up at the door and wait for a few minutes before the bouncer starts to let people in. Right below the glittery Bangerz sign that sits above the entrance is a marquee with interchangeable letters. "Amateur Night! Saturday at 9 p.m.!"

Once we're inside, a wave of pulsing EDM music hits my ears. I look over at Simon and make an exaggerated whiny face as I cup my ears with my hands. He rolls his eyes and laughs.

Over the deafening music, we somehow communicate via shouts and hand gestures that I'll get drinks while Simon signs himself up at the DJ booth. I order club sodas for both of us. Even though I know Simon would prefer hard alcohol, San Francisco law prevents any club that serves alcohol from being fully nude. Since Bangerz allows nudity among its performers, we're stuck with nonalcoholic beverages. While I wait for the bartender, I notice that the stage is empty. They must be setting everything up for amateur night. Drinks in hand, I weave through the dense crowd and scan for an open table. By some miracle there's a two-person table free halfway to the stage. I hustle over and nab it, set our drinks down, then wave Simon over when I see him looking around.

He sits next to me and I slide him the club soda.

"Liquid courage to fuel you through your performance tonight," I joke.

He winks at me before taking a long sip, then gazes around the all-onyx space, which is bathed in dim mood lighting.

"Now this is the best way to spend a Saturday night. Crossing off item one on my fuck-it list."

I wrinkle my nose. "It's weird hearing you swear."

"You know what else is weird? The fact that you only had one item on your list."

I shrug. "It's the only thing I could think of."

"Come on. There's gotta be some other exciting thing you've always wanted to do," he teases.

"I'll think about it and add it to my list. I'll even show it to you when I do. Promise."

I chuckle as I sip my drink, taking in the décor. Every surface is painted black or red. Strobe lights illuminate the raised stage, which looks like it was shellacked with liquid glitter. The high-tempo dance music sets a frenetic tone. But it's a few notches below the deafening volume that hit us when we walked in, so I'm thankful. Now we can actually talk to each other.

"You know, this would be a great moment to check off item number two on your fuck-it list," I say to Simon. "This is the perfect place to give a huge, impromptu toast that makes the crowd go nuts."

Simon laughs. "Not a chance."

I set down my drink. "Okay, so here's our game plan. As soon as it's your turn to go up there, I'll grab my phone and film you. I'll probably do a lot of ridiculous shouting and hollering to make it look like we're together, that way no employees suspect that we're doing this for a show. If anyone asks, we're a couple having a wild date night. Sound good?"

Simon bites his bottom lip, clearly trying not to laugh. "This isn't some covert military operation, Naomi. We can just go with the flow."

I eye a server who stops by the table next to us, careful to keep my voice as low as the overhead music allows. "I just don't want it getting out that we're filming this for a show. A lot of businesses wouldn't allow us to film if they knew that—they'd want to draw up a contract or paperwork that entitles them to rights and profits, all that. And we don't have the time or the budget."

Simon nods his understanding, even though that smile still dances on his lips. "Makes sense."

The server turns around to take our order. "You two doing okay?"

Simon slips his arm around my shoulders. "Would you be able to get a cranberry juice with ice for my girlfriend? If you're not too busy."

I scrunch my face in an attempt to hide the incredulous smile I'm aching to let loose. As soon as the server leaves, Simon drops his arm from my shoulders. I playfully shove his arm.

"Hey, I was just getting into character."

The lights dim and the DJ's voice echoes around us.

"Ladies, ladies, ladies! And gentlemen too! Who's ready to kick off amateur night at Bangerz?"

A wave of screams and cheers follows.

"Please put your hands together for the first fresh meat of the night, Freddy the firefighter!"

The entire audience erupts as a tall, muscled guy from one of the tables in the middle of the club walks to the stage. He's all smiles as he jogs up the steps and places a red plastic fire hat on his head. As the shouts and whistles persist, he takes his place in the middle of the stage and stands with his back to the crowd. Then the music starts. The beat for Ginuwine's "Pony" drops and I squeal.

"Oh that's brilliant." I clap.

Simon brings his fingers to his lips as he whistles and cheers him on. Then he leans to me, his mouth a whisper away from the shell of my ear. "Firemen get you all hot and bothered?"

His warm breath sends a surprise tingle down my neck. I close my eyes for a second, reminding myself that this sensation means nothing. He's only talking this closely to me because the music is so loud.

"Haha," I manage.

The crowd goes wild as Freddy drops to his knees and pulls an impressive spin move. I wonder if he's a dancer.

The server returns with my drink and I thank him as Simon hands over cash. Freddy finishes to enthusiastic cheers and the DJ announces the next contestant, who chooses an R&B slow jam. The crowd clearly loves it, judging by the shouts and hollers.

"Gotta say, I'm surprised you'd want to do this," I say to Simon, appreciating that I can talk at almost a normal volume since the song is slower.

Simon raises an eyebrow. "Why? Because therapists can't be into wild stuff like stripping?"

I stammer, my face suddenly hot. "No, I…sorry, I didn't mean it like that."

"I'm kidding. I get what you mean. It seems more in line with when I cammed, right?"

"Yeah, I suppose. But I didn't mean it in that way, I swear. I just meant that the stereotype is that the younger you are, the more willing you are to do wilder things."

"I see that. I consider myself a pretty uninhibited person most of my life, but the thought of performing at a strip club when I was younger freaked me out. I think I had to gain some confidence before I could be secure enough to want to try something like this. Now that I'm in my thirties, I feel a lot more sure of myself."

"Really?"

He nods.

"Actually, wait a sec." I pull out my phone. "This is really great stuff you're saying. Can I film it so I can include it in episode two of the series?"

Simon says of course.

"So how would you reconcile these things that you do? What would you say to people who would criticize you for being a therapist who also wants to participate in amateur night at a strip club?"

"I'm a sex-positive person. I always have been and I always will be. And I don't think there's anything wrong with pursuing things that you enjoy, as long as they're safe and you're not hurting anyone. No matter how off-the-wall they seem—no matter what other people think.

"And I'd tell anyone who would criticize that to stop and examine why they feel the need to shame anyone for doing something that's perfectly safe and legal. Fine if you don't want to do something, but why do you feel the need to judge others who do? I think there are a lot of people who are quick to shame others who do things that they find unusual. But they criticize because there's something in their background that makes them feel insecure or uncomfortable or ashamed. And if that's the case, I encourage those people to dig deep and explore that feeling. Figure out why you started assigning shame and disgust to certain activities. Once you understand why you do something, you can figure out how to stop doing it. And you can start learning how to be more open about things instead of judging them for their perceived value or stigma."

I nod along enthusiastically at everything Simon is saying. I also take a moment to admire just how much his belief system aligns with his public work persona. Loads of people act one way publicly and are totally different behind closed doors. Not Simon, though. There's a genuineness he possesses that's so evident whether he's in a therapy session, presenting a seminar, or on a night out with a friend—like he's living the words he preaches to his clients about always striving to be uninhibited and vulnerable.

"And I also want to show that you can be a multi-faceted person who excels in a field while having lots of different interests," he says. "It's a good thing to be open to new experiences."

"Like a therapist who kicks ass at amateur night at a strip club."

He grins. "Exactly. I admit, it took me a while to get to this point. We all have to confront those insecurities and biases that we internalize. I mean, when I was in my twenties, I was totally comfortable having sex on a webcam, but I couldn't take my clothes off onstage in front of a few dozen strangers."

His expression turns the slightest bit sheepish. I rest my hand over his arm. "I don't think that's weird at all. Those are two totally different scenarios. I mean, when you were camming, you were able to control so much about it. It was just you and your partner in a room. Yeah, people were watching, but I'm sure that felt a bit removed in a way. Like, because you couldn't see the viewers, it maybe took a bit of the pressure off. But it was still exciting because you were sharing the act with an audience, but on your own terms. A venue like this is totally different. You're right there in front of all these people. They're watching you as you perform just a few feet away—and you can see them, feel them watching you."

Simon stares at me, his mouth open slightly.

"Oh crap, sorry! I hope I didn't just freak you out about performing just now."

It's a second before that dazed look in his eyes disappears. He shakes his head. "No, not at all. I just… you described how it feels perfectly. It's like you read my mind."

"Oh."

I play with the straw in my drink, feeling weirdly giddy that I'm so good at articulating Simon's feelings when we've only known each other a few weeks.

Just then the DJ announces performer number three, who looks like a preppy country club boy. He jumps onstage and starts grooving to some rap song I don't recognize as he unbuttons his shirt.

Simon points at him. "That guy is definitely your type."

"God, no way."

"Oh, come on. Look at how wholesome he is. That clean-cut blond hair and boyish smile. I bet he even rows crew for whatever college he goes to. Or plays water polo. That's the kind of guy you bring home to Mom and Dad, and then jet off to the nearest strip club and cheer him on as he drives the place wild. Win-win."

"First of all, I'm not into dating guys who are ten years younger than me. That guy looks barely old enough to get in here."

Simon's brow starts to lift, but I shake my head. "I'm so over college guys. I was over them was I was in college."

"Fair enough."

"Besides, I won't be bringing anyone home anytime soon—or ever. I'm in the middle of a relationship ban, remember?"

He nods yes as he downs the last of his club soda. I slide him my drink to finish, which he happily accepts. Just then the song ends and frat boy takes a bow to raucous applause.

"Up next is… Simply Simon!"

My jaw drops.

"I thought it would be good promo for the series." He stands.

I hold up my phone. "I'm ready. Break a leg."

He leaves me with a grin then jogs up the steps to the opening bars of "No Diggity." I nearly drop my phone as I laugh. And then I hold my breath as Simon completely dominates onstage. He moves to the beat of the song, teasing each piece of clothing like a pro. First he tosses aside his jacket, then he lifts the hem of his shirt, moving his hips gently. The crowd loses it. People jump from their seats, hollering and whistling, clearly loving the show Simon is putting on for them.

It soon gets so rowdy I have to stand up and move closer to the stage to get a clear view of him as I film. The second verse hits and Simon is bare chested, a giddy smile plastered on his face.

I wonder just how far he's going to go. The guys before him all stripped down to their underwear and opted to leave them on. Will he do the same?

He goes to pull his belt loose, and tosses it into the audience. My jaw drops. Holy crap. He's really going for it.

"Yes, baby, yes!" a woman at the table next to me screams. A guy behind me howls.

I realize that my mouth has been open the past several seconds as I take it all in. I quickly close it, swallow, and contribute my own pitchy "Woo-hoo!" To the tidal wave of screams as Simon's jeans fall to the floor. He's left in a snug pair of dark gray boxer briefs that showcase just how well-endowed he is.

If the crowd was wild before, they're unhinged now. I hold my breath as the final bars of the song play, wondering if this is it…or if he'll go full monty. He looks off to the side and finds me gawking at him. We make eye contact and the corner of his mouth tugs up into the surest, smuggest smirk I've ever seen. As the song fades out, he winks at me, spins around so his back is to the audience, and pulls his boxer briefs down, treating everyone to a full-on view of his flawless, muscled ass.

"Holy god," I mutter to myself.

But I can't even hear my own voice. The audience has just lost its collective shit and the volume in the room is decibel-shattering. My ears will be ringing for days after this, if not weeks.

But I'm all smiles. I'm giggling like I've just had a hit of laughing gas. That was the single most entertaining thing I've ever seen. It was equal parts hot, adorable, and endearing—just like Simon.

I stop recording on my phone, slide it back into my pocket, and run over to him as he exits the stage.

He's pulling his shirt back on as he scales down the steps, blushing as hordes of people shout how hot he is and how much they love him. A few blow kisses at him.

Weaving through the crowd to get to him is a monumental task as everyone is on their feet cheering and hollering. I bump into a million people along the way. I'm nearly to Simon when an overenthusiastic fan jumps up from her chair, running into me, and I fall into him. He catches me in his arms and I let out a giggle, in awe that this embrace isn't awkward at all. Maybe it's because in the few weeks we've known each other, we've gotten as personal as you could possibly get—I hit on him, he's seen me naked, and we almost slept together. But we worked past it all and now a unique comfort exists—the kind of comfort you feel with a friend you've been through the wringer with.

That feeling lingers as Simon pulls me into a hug. The rumble of his laughter vibrates against my chest. I can't help but laugh too, feeling a whole new kind of giddy.

"Holy hot damn, am I right, everyone?" the DJ hollers over the speaker system. "Let's hear it for Simply Simon!"

The crowd whistles and cheers around us.

When Simon and I pull apart, the first thing I see is his smile. It's as wide as mine.

"How did I do?" he asks.

"Like you don't already know." I give him a light shove on his shoulder. "You smashed it."

"You ready?" Simon asks as we stand on a random street corner in the Castro district, just a few blocks from Bangerz.

"I think so." I let out a breath and look around. The streets are crowded tonight, but no one seems to be paying attention to us. Typical San Francisco mentality. People are on the go and rarely care about what's going on around them.

I wonder if they'll pay attention to me when I start singing.

Just as the nerves creep up my stomach, I breathe, then focus on that giddy feeling that flooded me less than an hour ago. The high from witnessing Simon's killer amateur strip club performance is what's going to power me through this.

"Are you ready?" I ask him.

He holds up the harmonica that I'm surprised stayed in his jacket pocket even as he whipped it off during his striptease.

"Ready and raring to go. Are we still doing 'How Will I Know'?"

"Yes. Let's do it."

I glance around as a crowd of people moves past us

in every direction on this busy weekend night. Simon plays a few bars on the harmonica to get the right key for the song. I take a long, deep breath and hum softly to make sure I have the pitch right. And then I open my mouth and sing.

I don't miss the way Simon's eyes go wide as I nail the beginning of the first verse. Inside I'm soaring at his stunned reaction, then he catches up to me as he plays on the harmonica.

It's a weird combo for sure—I don't know if many street performers choose to play Whitney Houston's most popular hits on the harmonica. But there's a first time for everything. Just like this is the first time I've ever sang in public.

I've always loved singing karaoke at family gatherings. I've done it since I was a little kid. It's a tradition in my family, to have karaoke going on in the background while we visit, eat, and play games. And everyone, no matter their vocal ability, is encouraged to sing. It's about having fun rather than showcasing talent.

But my family has always complimented my voice. I can carry a tune well—I just never had the nerve to sing in front of a crowd. It's one thing to sing for fun in front of supportive family at home. It's a totally different ball game doing it in public, in front of strangers who aren't afraid to heckle or berate you if they don't like the way you sound.

Heckling isn't what I hear, though. I hear whistles and a few soft cheers. A handful of people stop to watch. One person even pulls out their phone to record us.

I smile as I look at Simon, who is impressive on the harmonica. He winks at me as he glides it along his mouth. More and more people stop and as I hit the bridge of the song, there are "woos" and people clapping along.

At my final run of the chorus, I do my best to belt it out. When I finish, there's a roar of applause.

I cup my cheeks with my hands at the response. I can hardly believe it. I sang in public, in front of strangers—and they actually liked it.

My heart races, but this time, not because of nerves. Because of the adrenaline. I did something I never thought I would. And I kicked ass.

I turn to face Simon and squeal. He pulls me into another hug, this time lifting me off the ground and spinning me around. When he sets me down, I can't stop smiling.

"Holy shit," we say in unison.

"That was amazing, Naomi. You have an incredible voice. Damn."

"Thanks." I scrunch my face, overwhelmed at his compliment and at the enthusiastic response from passersby.

"We need to celebrate," he says, pocketing his harmonica. "We both conquered items on our fuck-it lists."

My stomach growls, a reminder of how I skipped dinner because my nerves were so out of control in anticipation of how this night would go.

"Yes. Food. Now."

He laughs. "You got it."

## Chapter Nine

Forty-five minutes later we're sitting on a bench in front of a burrito joint on Eureka Street. I'm chowing down on a surf and turf burrito while Simon rips into a giant chicken quesadilla, both of us still riding the high from conquering our respective fuck-it lists.

"I haven't had that much fun in…honestly, I can't remember," I say between bites.

"Really?"

"Really. Most of my Saturday nights were spent lounging at home with my ex bickering over what show we should watch on Netflix."

Just saying that out loud colors my good mood with a tinge of sadness.

"I guess that should have been a sign. We argued about so much, even little things like what to watch together. And even when we weren't fighting, being together wasn't really that fun. Just, 'meh.'" I tuck the wrapper around the last third of my burrito and shove it into my purse.

Simon finishes the last bite of his quesadilla, then pivots to face me. "The end of relationships are rough. That moment when you know it's not going to work out anymore—even though you know it's for the best—it can be really painful. You're separating from a person you've bonded with, who you've built memories with."

"I guess we both just got complacent. Well, Brody got a bit restless too, given he started screwing someone else behind my back."

Simon's expression turns sad as he gazes at me, then pats my hand. It's the perfect comfort.

"It's okay. I'm happier now. Doing this—random fun things with a friend—is a million times better than being in a dead-end relationship."

Simon murmurs a "yes" as he downs the last of his horchata.

"So. I feel like I've given you a thorough workup of my relationship history. What's yours?"

He looks down at the ground and rubs the back of his neck. Before he can say anything, a tall guy in a suit and a woman in a cobalt blue party dress walk by us.

"Hey! Simply Simon!" The guy flashes a thumbs-up at him, which makes Simon chuckle.

"We love your show, man," the guy says.

Simon flashes a shy smile. "Oh. Thanks."

"And the show you just put on at Bangerz." The woman wags her eyebrow at Simon. Suit guy rolls his eyes as he smiles.

Simon full-on beams and thanks her. Suit guy introduces himself as Paul and tells Simon that because of the series, he and his girlfriend, Anna, the woman he's with, started to see a therapist.

"Gotta admit, I wasn't crazy about the idea of counseling," he says. "But I figure if the camming legend himself is a therapist now, I should give it a try."

Simon blushes before reeling in his expression.

"Well, I'm glad that you reconsidered. How are things going for you two?"

They explain their arguments are improving. Specifically they're not yelling and name-calling as much anymore.

Paul shuffles back a step. "Didn't mean to interrupt your night. Just wanted to say a quick 'hey.' We're big fans."

As Simon thanks him, Anna leans toward me. "You're a lucky lady."

It takes a second before I realize what she's implied. "Oh! No, we're not... I'm actually the creator of the *Simply Simon* series. We're just colleagues. And friends."

"Oh! Sorry!" She chuckles.

Paul looks between us before his gaze lands on Simon. "So you're single?"

"Yup," Simon says, his expression the slightest bit strained.

"A single relationship therapist? Really?"

The way Paul says it sounds like he's joking, but I don't miss the way Simon flinches at the comment.

Anna frowns at Paul, clearly annoyed. And really, it's a pretty ignorant remark. I can't let it slide.

"Actually, the relationship status of a therapist is pretty irrelevant. Simon has more than ten years of education and training in therapy, psychology, and counseling. There are thousands of people and couples who can attest to what a brilliant therapist he is and how he helped save their relationships and marriages. Do you have to have children to be a good pediatrician?"

Paul stares at me wide-eyed. "Um, I guess not..."

"Exactly. So why would you hold up such an arbitrary standard for a relationship therapist? His work speaks for itself."

Anna aims a satisfied look at Paul, who lets out a flustered chuckle.

"Y-you're right." He turns to Simon. "Sorry, man. Didn't mean any disrespect."

"No worries," Simon says.

When they leave, Simon turns to me. "That was…"

"Sorry. I'm just now realizing how rabid I sounded." I stand up to throw away my wrappers and napkins in a nearby trash can. "I can get really worked up about stuff like that. To question you, a qualified therapist, is pretty obnoxious. Like anyone has the right to comment on your relationship status and how it informs your work as a therapist when you've already proven just how competent you are."

I turn back around to face Simon, whose expression is a mix of shocked and bewildered. Then his face splits into the biggest smile.

"Nope. Don't you dare apologize. That was…" He shakes his head, like he's searching for the right words. "Thanks for defending me. It means a lot."

We walk toward Harper's apartment in Nob Hill. I take a breath, relishing the feel of the air as it coats my lungs. It's both cold and wet—a weird combo, but I've always loved the way the air feels at night in San Francisco.

"So that's you rabid, huh?"

"Ha. Not really. I'm way worse when I lose my cool."

"What exactly are you like when you lose your cool?"

I pause, wondering if there's a way to word this to not sound completely unhinged.

When I look over at Simon, amusement takes over his expression as he zips up his jacket. "Tell me."

"Promise you won't hold it against me? Or think I'm a maniac?"

There's a gleam in his eyes. "When you put it that way…"

I elbow him gently and he laughs.

"Okay, okay. Promise."

I explain the disaster ending with Brody.

"Oh and the best part? I told him to rename his dick from 'General Monster Dong' to 'Private Average Sized At Best.' I shouted it. I'm sure the neighbors on the other side of wall heard my very vulgar suggestion."

Simon bursts out laughing and starts to tear up. Soon we're both cackling so hard, we have to stop walking and brace ourselves against a nearby brick building. A few people walking by glance at us like we've lost our minds.

"Christ, that's hilarious," he says after catching his breath.

We start walking again.

"I swear, I'm like a douchebag magnet. Every guy I've dated has been a piece of work. I wonder what that says about me."

I bite my tongue, wondering if Simon's therapist brain is quietly analyzing the insecurity that emanates from me in that single statement.

"Is that why we get along so well?" The corner of his mouth tugs up.

"Of course not. You're one of the most emotionally aware people I've met. I don't get any of the douche vibes I got from my exes."

He shakes his head, smiling slightly. "Yeah, but I'm

no angel. Maybe I wasn't Brody level, but I've definitely been dismissive and hurtful to an ex before."

"Really?" My mind is blown. I probably shouldn't be this shocked. Simon is human. He wasn't always the emotionally aware, nonjudgmental therapist he is now.

"I was a young and arrogant jerk who thought I knew everything," he says, glancing at the ground. "Thankfully going to therapy and studying it in school helped me realize how wrong it was to act that way—and working with my therapist helped me put a stop to that behavior. But I still feel bad about how I hurt my ex Tessa when we were together."

"What did you do? If you don't mind my asking."

He gazes ahead at the busy street ahead of us. It's almost midnight but San Francisco is still very much alive on this Saturday night. We stop at the edge of the street and wait as a cable car glides by. Half the passengers holler nonsensical noises at us and wave as they pass. Simon and I wave back.

"I used to be one of those insensitive a-holes who thought Valentine's Day was pointless. The epitome of a commercial holiday," Simon says as we cross the street. "It felt like greeting card companies and jewelry stores manufactured it to guilt guys into spending way too much money on pointless crap. Tessa disagreed. She said she didn't care what the holiday meant; it was an excuse to be romantic. She always wanted to us to go out to dinner, exchange gifts, flowers, all that. But I was more interested in proving a point than recognizing what really mattered: that my partner wanted me to meet her needs in this completely reasonable way. That day was important to her, and for that reason alone, it should have mattered to me. But I was selfish. I didn't get it at all."

"We've all done hurtful and insensitive stuff. Every single one of us."

He takes a long breath in, his posture straightening. "Honestly, we weren't right for each other anyway. I can see that now."

"How so?"

"She wanted to spend her life traveling the world. I wanted to settle down in San Francisco, go to grad school, be close to my family. It was never going to work. It was sad ending things, but I knew it was the right thing to do. We're still on good terms. She's making her way across Asia with her fiancé currently. I'm happy for her, truly. But still. I recognize that even though we weren't meant to be, our relationship would have been better had I been a more empathetic partner."

"I think the fact that you recognize this about yourself shows how much you've grown."

We walk up a steep hill, stopping as another cable car crosses, but this one is only half-full with much quieter passengers.

"That was a bit of a weird confession," Simon says through a laugh when we start walking again.

I turn to him. "Look, I know that we're thrown together because of work circumstances, but I'd like to think that we're getting to be pretty good friends now. Any time you want to talk, I'm here."

I'm holding his arm, gazing into his eyes as I say it, hoping he understands just how much I mean it.

His soft smile indicates my words hit home. "Well, now you know one of the many things that make me a good candidate for a relationship ban of my own," he jokes. "Or at the very least difficult for someone to want to date."

"You hate Valentine's Day? That's child's play compared to what makes me undateable."

"Really?"

"Hell yes, really. Wanna hear my list of impressively undateable qualities?"

He nods, the look in his eyes something between doubtful and expectant.

"I can't deal with loud snorers, so if a guy I'm dating snores, I give him two options: start wearing one of those breathing strips on his nose, or sleep on the couch."

Simon cackles so loud, a guy riding a bike in the street next to us jerks his head in our direction.

"I'm nice enough to buy the first box," I say. "But after that he's on his own."

"That's not terrible. Sleeping with a loud snorer is the worst. What else you got?"

"I call dibs on all restaurant leftovers. It doesn't matter if you want them for lunch the next day. If I see them in the refrigerator and I'm hungry, they're mine."

"What if they're labeled?"

"Nope. Food is a nonnegotiable for me. I'm extremely selfish in that respect."

"What else?"

"Work comes before relationships, always. I've canceled so many dates, I'm probably on some sort of dating app blacklist right now."

He lets out a sympathetic wince. "Damn, so we're both workaholics, then?"

When I high-five him in affirmation, he laughs yet again.

"I hate it when the guy I'm dating chats while I'm watching TV or a movie. So if I'm watching something, it needs to be as quiet as a church. Oh, and the most embarrassing one."

I take a breath before I gear up to admit my biggest offense. This is something I have no problem admitting to my friends. And if Simon and I are now friends, I should be honest with him too—especially since he was just honest with me about his ex.

"I have an extensive array of sex toys. Sadly, a lot of the men I've been with have found that threatening."

Simon's jaw goes slack, as if I just told him I'm a member of the Illuminati. "You're joking...right?"

"I'm dead serious. Not all guys are as sexually enlightened as you. I mean, a lot say that they are, but when it comes to sex toys, that couldn't be further from the truth. In my experience, at least."

One of the reasons I and so many other women drooled over Simon as a cam guy was because of how open-minded he was in the bedroom with the women he was with. They often used sex toys in their play together. Their openness and willingness inspired me to purchase my very first vibrator as a sexually shy nineteen-year-old. I contemplate revealing that tidbit of personal information but decide against it. I'm already on an oversharing kick as it is.

I clear my throat. "A lot of guys thought it was a personal attack on their sexual prowess that I wanted to use sex toys on my own and even more so when I wanted to use them on myself while I was with them. I think they took it like being with only them wasn't enough. But that wasn't the case at all."

Simon nods along, a mix of seriousness and sincerity

in his stare. "Exactly. Different things get people off. There's absolutely nothing wrong with using sex toys in any situation. I'm sorry that guys made you feel that way, but I need you to understand: it does not make you undateable. It just makes them insecure pricks."

His reassurance sends a wave of warm and fuzzies through me. "Thanks. That's nice of you."

"Seriously. It's off-the-charts hot when a woman is confident in herself sexually."

His words cause my mouth to go dry. Hearing him admit that he finds this quality of mine attractive is so sexy.

If I didn't already know what a supportive and engaging person Simon is in his real life to those he cares about, I'd think he's flirting with me. But he's not. He's just being a good friend—like I was being to him. Nothing more. Nothing less.

The sportsmanlike pat on the shoulder he gives me is another reminder of how platonic our acquaintance is in this moment.

"Thanks. That's…good to know," I manage to mutter after a few seconds.

I direct him to take a right at the upcoming street. Harper's apartment is a few blocks down.

"And just for the record, you disliking Valentine's Day is low on the list of things that could ever make a guy undateable. Especially a guy like you who is good-looking, sensitive, emotionally mature, and gainfully employed."

"Oh, you haven't heard the worst of it, Naomi."

I wait for him to elaborate, but he doesn't. Instead he continues to stare at the ground as we walk.

"Why don't you tell me, then?"

He looks straight ahead, like he's considering. I gently tug at his arm to get him to look at me. We stop walking.

"Hey." I point at myself. "Friend. Remember?"

A small smile cracks out of him, but a second later it's gone.

"The real reason things ended with my most recent ex is the same reason why every relationship I've had after Tessa has failed." The heavy sigh he lets out matches the weightiness of his demeanor. "It's because I used to cam. My ex wasn't a fan."

My chest tightens. Something a lot like protectiveness rockets through me.

"Are you serious?"

"Yup. Surprising, isn't it? You'd think San Francisco would be the easiest place in the world to find a like-minded partner. But I've realized that no matter where in the world you live, a lot of people seem to have the same hang-ups about sex, specifically anything related to camming."

He tugs a hand through his hair. "The worst thing about it is, they all started out the same. They initially said they were okay with my past. But eventually the truth comes out. You can't hide it forever."

"I'm sorry, Simon."

"It's all right."

"It's not, though. What you did as a cam guy was amazing. Do you know how many female friends of mine had unsatisfying sexual experiences because the dude they were sleeping with had no idea what he was doing? Or because he educated himself by watching degrading, unrealistic porn?"

A guy unlocking the door to his apartment in front

of us whips his head to look in our direction when I say the word "porn." I mutter "sorry" then offer a cheery, "Have a nice night!" as we walk by.

I turn back to Simon. "When my friends and I found you online, it changed everything. Thanks to you, we had somewhere to send our boyfriends so they could learn exactly what we wanted. You helped a lot of people, more than I think you know."

As I speak, I notice the slow turn of Simon's features. His mouth isn't in a hard line anymore and his eyes shine a tad brighter.

"Anyone who would ever use that as a reason not to be with you is a small-minded jerk."

"It's just hard, realizing that's the common denominator in most of my breakups. It's such a mind-fuck." He winces at his curse. "Like, my camming stuff is actually a turn-on for them at first. But after a while, reality sets in. They want me to meet their families, friends, co-workers, all that. Eventually they realize they don't want to have to introduce a former cam guy to their friends and family as their boyfriend. They don't like the stigma that comes with it, I guess. For a while, I felt ashamed. Like my real self wasn't good enough for them. But then I realized that was ridiculous. Because…"

"Because you have nothing to be ashamed of, Simon."

"Right," he says quietly. "With my most recent ex, I thought we were solid. We even lived together in my apartment. And she was open to her friends about me, which I thought was a good sign. Her family lived across the country, so I never met them. She said she told them about me. But then…" He pauses. "But then, a year into living together, we got an invitation to her cousin's wedding. I'd be meeting her entire family." A heavy sigh rockets out of him. "And that's when she sat me down and said that if anyone asks what I did before I became a therapist to just say that I was a nurse's aide and never mention my camming. Which wasn't totally a lie since I was a nurse's aide for the first year of grad school."

"But that's so messed up," I mutter.

"Yeah." He says it like a long, drawn-out groan. "I mean, I'm not naïve. I understand that it wouldn't be appropriate to bring up my camming at a family wedding. Obviously I would have been discreet about my work. But what hurt was that she was ashamed of me— of what I did. We broke up that night when I refused to go along with her lie. And I haven't been interested in a serious relationship since then."

We walk in silence for a minute.

"Even if I were okay lying about it, there's no use," Simon says. "These days everyone googles you before your first date. I mean, I get it. You want to make sure the guy you're going out with isn't a serial killer. But that means it's only a matter of time before people find me online. Which is fine. Like I said before, I'm not the slightest bit ashamed of who I am or what I've done. It's made me the person I am today. But it's sort of become this bizarre litmus test for relationships. I'm not interested in being with someone who's ashamed of me. I just didn't realize so many people would fall into that category."

"Simon, I'm…" I stop myself before I can say "sorry." I've said it enough times.

I contemplate going a different route, telling him how wrong he is to give up after a few narrow-minded jerks broke his heart. How I could call up every single one of my college friends right now and hook him up with a woman who is more than okay with his camming experience. How there are loads of single women who would happily line up for just a chance with him.

But I don't. Because that's not what he needs. He doesn't need me to fix this for him. He just needs me to be his friend, to empathize—to let him know that there's not a single thing wrong with him. To tell him he's a stellar person worthy of love, no matter how his exes treated him.

"Hey." We stop walking and I rest my hand on his arm. "It's your ex's loss. You're a hell of a catch."

His face brightens, his eyes sharpen, and his mouth curves into a genuine smile. "You think so?"

"I *know* so. Your past does not make you undateable. It just makes your exes insecure pricks."

He chuckles when I quote the exact words he used on me earlier.

"Thanks for that," he says. "It's been a nice break honestly, focusing on myself and my work. Maybe someday the right person will come along and it'll work out. Now if only people would stop bringing up my single status whenever I mention I'm a couples' therapist."

"I'm here to set them straight whenever you need me to."

We walk the last block to Harper's building.

"This is me. I mean, this is my cousin's apartment. I'm just crashing here until I have the time to hunt for a place of my own."

"Damn. It's really nice."

He stares at the white multistory beaux-arts-style building. Even in the dark, the sweeping arches and thick columns of the classical Greek and Roman-inspired architecture stand out.

"It's freaking expensive too. I could never afford to live here on my own," I say as I dig for my key in my purse.

"Maybe someday. Like after this series goes viral and you get a million-dollar raise."

"Ha! That will never happen. Honestly, I'd settle for a decent building in a good neighborhood with a house-mate who's not a serial killer."

Simon chuckles. "Good luck with that."

"Thanks for walking me home," I say.

"It's no problem."

I ask if we're still on for filming a one-on-one session with one of his clients at his home office on Monday, and he says yes.

"You were a good sport tonight," I say.

"It was a hell of a night."

"You're going to crash the Dash website when episode two goes live next week."

He shoves his hands in his jacket pockets and smiles down at the ground. "I guess we'll see." When he glances up at me, there's a warmth in his eyes I haven't yet seen.

He insists that I'm in the apartment building before he leaves. As I open the door, I turn around to wave good-bye. He walks backwards in the direction of his apartment and grins at me before turning around and taking off.

I quietly walk into the apartment and get ready for bed, careful not to wake Harper. And as I tuck myself into bed on her couch, I realize I'm still smiling.

A hell of a night indeed.

# Chapter Ten

I set up my camera in Simon's apartment, in the same spot where I interviewed him the first time. But today, we're interviewing a client of his who agreed to be in the series.

Simon stands in his kitchen just a few feet away, gawking at his laptop screen.

"Wow. Just...wow."

I grin as I adjust the height of the camera. "Still can't believe it, huh?"

"I honestly didn't think this many people would be into watching me at a strip club."

I scoff. "Oh, come on. You had to know it was going to drive viewers wild. Especially that move you pulled at the end."

My memory flashes back to the way he smiled at me before he spun around onstage and dropped his boxer briefs, treating the entire crowd to a view of his killer backside.

"Don't you remember how everyone absolutely lost it? It was a preview of how viewers were going to go nuts for it when it aired on the series."

Episode two of *Simply Simon* earned the most views the first hour it was up than any other video has ever gotten on Dash. Advertisers are flocking to the site and viewers are loving it too. Endless comments about how incredible Simon is—both for his work as a therapist and his sex-positive mentality that makes him engaging as hell to watch.

He raises an eyebrow at me as he tugs at the sleeves of his dress shirt. "I guess I'm just pleasantly surprised at the response."

My phone rings and I stop to see that my mom is calling. I ignore it, planning to call her back after I finish recording the interview, but then she texts me.

Anak! I need your help with something very important!

A minor wave of panic surfaces. I call her back.

"Hey, Mom. Is everything okay?"

"Oh yes, yes. I'm fine. I just need your help with this gift for your dad's birthday."

The tension inside of me melts as I bite back a groan of annoyance.

"Mom. Seriously? You made it sound like you had fallen off a ladder or something."

"Oh, Naomi. You know how seriously I take gift-giving."

It's true. She plans months in advance to buy gifts for my older brother, our dad, and me for birthdays and holidays.

I sigh. "What do you need?"

"Do you know if I can use superglue on ceramic? I want to try and put together that vase I accidentally broke. That really beautiful one he sculpted me for our first wedding anniversary, remember? I want to fill it with flowers from my garden and display it on the table when he comes home from work that day."

I instantly soften. That's such a thoughtful thing for her to plan to do for him. Dad sculpts as a hobby and will sometimes make Mom sculptures for gifts, which she loves. She adored that anniversary gift vase, but a few years ago she accidentally dropped it while unpacking after a move to a smaller house. When it shattered into a half-dozen pieces, she burst into tears, she was so heartbroken.

"Superglue on ceramic? Um, I'm not sure, Mom. I can look it up though after I get done with work."

Out of the corner of my eye, I see Simon's head pop up. "You trying to glue ceramic?"

"Hang on, Mom." I turn to him. "Yeah, a ceramic hand-sculpted vase."

He walks over and offers to explain to Mom how to put the vase back together.

I hesitate for a second. "You sure? I don't mean to ask you to walk my mom through an impromptu vase repair."

"It's no problem at all."

I put the phone on speaker. "Okay, Mom. My friend Simon is going to explain what kind of glue to use and how to put it together."

"Oh! How nice of you, Simon! Thank you! *Anak*, who's Simon?"

"He's the guy I'm filming for work, remember?"

"Oh! Simon from the videos, with the nice tush? Yes, I remember!"

I shake my head, quietly groaning. I turn to Simon. "She watches every video I ever put out," I explain.

"Of course I do! You're my baby and I'm proud of you," she announces.

Simon flashes an adorable grin. "Well, thanks for your viewership, Mrs. Ellorza."

"You had some excellent moves onstage. I need you to show them to my husband."

"Oh my god, Mom. Seriously. Can you not talk about that right now?"

Simon covers his mouth as he chuckles.

"Fine, fine," she says, the smile in her tone clear. "Simon, what kind of glue should I use for this?"

Simon recommends Gorilla Glue and for the next couple of minutes explains the best way to glue ceramic. When he finishes, Mom is practically giddy.

"Oh, I feel so much better about this. Thank you, Simon!"

"It's my pleasure."

"You should come over to the house sometime so I can make you dinner as a thank-you," Mom says. "Naomi, bring him over one of these days!"

"Okay, Mom. We've gotta go, though."

"Oh sure, sure. Thank you again, Simon. Love you, *anak*!"

Simon says bye the same time that I say "I love you too," and I hang up.

"Thanks for that," I say as I put my phone away.

"It wasn't a problem at all. Your mom seems sweet. And I'm holding you to that dinner." He shuts his laptop. "That's a really thoughtful thing for her to do for your dad."

"They are the epitome of couple goals. Married for almost forty years and act like they're teenagers in love. I don't know if I've ever seen them argue."

I tell Simon that Dad surprises Mom with her favorite white roses every week when he comes home from his Friday morning squash sessions. They make a big deal out of their anniversary every year, and always hold hands, even if they're just on a neighborhood walk or wandering around the grocery store. And they say "I love you" a million times a day.

"Seriously, the love between them is sickening—in the best way. They're a tough act to follow."

He looks at me thoughtfully, as if he's analyzing what I've just said.

"I don't mean to get all 'relationship therapist' on you, but do you think that you idealize your parents' marriage a bit?"

I frown at him. "How do you mean?"

"I just mean that you make it sound like their relationship is perfect when it's probably not. I'm sure they've gone through struggles just like any other couple."

I shrug. "Maybe. Probably."

"Do you think that factors into your relationship ban at all? Like, is there a part of you that thinks if a relationship can't be perfect, then it's not worth pursuing at all?"

I stand there and process his words for a few seconds, suddenly feeling exposed in a way I never have before.

"That got a bit heavy," I joke, but Simon doesn't laugh. Instead he looks at me expectantly. "Okay yeah, you're probably right."

"You shouldn't give up on relationships just because they're not perfect like your parents' marriage," he says gently.

"I'm fine navigating my dating and relationship life

in the way that I currently am. Thanks for the assessment, though."

I flinch at how my words come off sharper than I intended. Out of the corner of my eye, I notice Simon still looking at me.

I head to the kitchen for a glass of water, willing the slight tension in the air between us to dissipate. A second later, there's a knock at his door.

"What's this guy's name again?" I ask, glad that we can focus on the session instead of talking more about my personal life.

"Landon. He's been to a couple of all-day seminars," Simon says. "Do you mind grabbing the door?" He runs to the bathroom.

When I open it, I immediately bite my lip.

*Oh my.*

If I had walked past Landon on the street, I'd do a double take. He could be a stand-in for Tom Hiddleston.

I step aside so he can come in. When I close the door behind him, he turns to me, his hand outstretched, ready for me to shake. "You must be Naomi from Dash."

"That's me," I say, shaking his hand. "It's great to meet you in person, Landon."

There's the slightest wag of his eyebrow. "Likewise."

I take an extra second to peruse his tall, lean physique in that impeccably cut dark blue suit as he walks to the chair. And then I quietly tell myself off. This guy is here to improve whatever relationship he's in. I absolutely should not be checking him out.

As Landon settles in the chair, Simon comes out of the restroom. They exchange pleasantries, then dive in.

"How are things with Alana?" Simon asks.

Landon hunches over, his eyes falling to the floor. "We broke up, unfortunately."

"Sorry to hear that."

"It's all right. It's my fault, really."

"Tell me what happened."

Landon sighs, his chest heaving with the single labored breath he takes. "She wanted to move in together. I wasn't ready. And she wasn't willing to wait until I was."

He runs a hand through his thick mass of blond hair. "It was probably for the best. If I didn't feel ready to commit, we certainly shouldn't have moved in together. But…"

Sympathy flashes through Simon's eyes. "It's all right. Take your time."

"I just wish I knew why it was so hard for me. She was right for me in so many ways. We had the same interests, our values and beliefs were in line. I just… I couldn't take the plunge."

"Why do you think that is?"

"I don't know."

"Have you noticed feeling a similar hesitation in past relationships?"

Silence follows as Landon leans back in his chair and stares out the window. "I'm afraid to say it."

"It's important to be honest about your feelings. It's the only way to make progress."

"I just worry how that honesty will make me look."

"I'm not going to judge you, Landon. That's not why I'm here."

He pivots his gaze back to Simon. "The spark I felt for Alana at the beginning faded after a while. And I think there was a part of me that was scared to settle down because I was afraid of missing out on someone else who could give me that excitement."

A familiar, faint punch to my gut hit. That's exactly how I felt when I was with Brody.

Just then Landon turns to look at me. "That sounds horrible, doesn't it?"

"You're not actually supposed to talk to her," Simon says. "It stipulates in the waiver you signed that Naomi's here to observe, not interact with you during the one-on-one sessions."

This time when Landon wags his eyebrow at me, there's a cheekiness to it. I have to bite back a smile.

"Right," Landon says. "Sorry about that."

"Spark is what you make of it," Simon says. "I know it's fun to feel that initial excitement when you meet someone, but it takes effort to maintain. If you want a lasting, long-term relationship, you need to put in the work to make it happen. You wouldn't expect a lush garden to sprout up in the middle of some dry swath of dirt, would you?"

"I guess not."

"I know it's a simplistic analogy, but you can't expect passion and excitement with someone to magically happen when you don't put in the effort to create it."

"Well. I definitely dropped the ball on that one." Landon chuckles, almost like he's embarrassed. He rubs his face. "I guess when that spark started to fade, I didn't think about how to get it back. Jesus, you'd think I'd know better as a thirty-five-year-old man."

"We all make mistakes. It's just important that you acknowledge that about yourself—and figure out why you make those mistakes. If you know why you do something, then it's easier to pinpoint that behavior and modify it the best you can. If that's what you want."

He asks Landon about his past relationships, and Landon mentions his first serious relationship in college.

"It felt like I was the one planning most of our dates, giving gifts, remembering birthdays and important events, all that stuff. And she kind of just went along and never really seemed all that invested. All I really wanted was some reassurance from her that what I was doing meant something to her, and I never really got that from her. I always felt like I was bothering her—almost like she tolerated my existence rather than being happy that I was with her. I never brought it up though, I was too scared to rock the boat," he says. "It didn't work out obviously, and I think that hurt me—that I had put so much effort into something, into someone who didn't feel the same way. And I don't want to go through that again."

"That sounds like a really hurtful experience. I'm sorry that happened to you," Simon says. "It sounds like you're still processing the pain of that attachment injury you experienced with her."

He explains that an attachment injury occurs when one partner in a relationship fails to offer the comfort and care that the other partner expects during times of distress. Landon says that's exactly how he feels.

"I guess I've just been really guarded since then," he says.

I can't blame him. That's happened to me before and has definitely left me feeling skittish—and in a self-imposed relationship ban. As much as I want to believe that someday I'll be in a fulfilling relationship with a person who puts in as much effort and affection as I do, I can sympathize with Landon's reluctance. Sometimes it's hard to believe in something, even when you see it happening around you, when you've never experienced it yourself.

"I understand your hesitance," Simon says to Landon. "But it's important to say to whoever you're dating that you're feeling hesitant because of what you've been through. When you're feeling unsure or like you can't move forward, talk to her about that. Tell her that it's because you've gone all in in a relationship before and got your heart broken, and that's what's causing the hesitation. And reiterate that you want to find a way to work through it because you want to be with her now, you want to take your relationship to that next level, whether that's moving in together or getting engaged. Or maybe all you need is verbal affirmation from your partner that they love and care about you so you don't feel neglected. Or maybe you want them to hug you more often. It's okay to ask for those things."

Landon frowns slightly, but nods along with what Simon says.

"When you take ownership of your feelings and show that it's not the fault of the person you're with now, it goes a long way in helping your partner understand where you're coming from. And it helps make them feel like you're prioritizing their feelings and your relationship together."

I notice Landon's eyes glaze over the slightest bit before he blinks.

"I'll have to take your word for it," he says. "But I hope you're right."

"It's worked for my other clients," Simon says. He

purses his lips slightly. "It can work for you too in your next relationship."

They talk for a few more minutes until the session ends.

"Thanks again for seeing me when I'm such a mess," Landon says as he stands up to leave.

"We're all a mess in some way," Simon says, almost automatically.

For a brief moment, Landon's eyes dart to mine. "I definitely want to be better for my next relationship, though."

When Simon shuts the door after Landon leaves, I'm still processing that look—and those words.

"Do you feel like ordering lunch?" I ask while folding the tripod.

But instead of answering, he walks up to me. "Steer clear of that guy."

"Sorry?"

"He was totally checking you out."

Simon's got a hyper-focused look in his eye that borders on condescending. I feel like I'm a kid being told off by my teacher.

"You can't be serious."

"I am. And I think you should be cautious of him."

I frown, annoyed that he thinks just because a good-looking guy made eyes at me, I need a talking-to.

"Why, exactly?"

"That guy's broadcasting his player vibe like it's an air-raid siren."

"Why didn't you kick him out of here if you had a problem with him?"

"It's one thing for me to help someone work through their issues as their therapist. But that doesn't mean I have to like them as a person outside of therapy. This guy isn't someone I'd spend time with if he wasn't a client of mine."

"Look, I appreciate the protective sentiment or whatever it is you're doing, but I don't need you to watch over me. I'm perfectly capable of taking care of myself."

Simon's jaw tenses, and I fully expect him to say something back. But then he takes a breath, his expression easing from annoyed concern to mild disdain.

"Just trying to be a good friend."

He walks to his bedroom and closes the door before I can say anything more.

"You gotta admit," Harper says while lounging on her couch, her tiny feet propped against my leg. "It's kind of hot how Simon responded."

It's the evening after I recorded Simon's session with Landon and I'm with Harper at her apartment while we watch garbage on Netflix.

"It wasn't. At all," I mutter, gently dabbing the sheet mask on my face with my fingertips. "I mean, 'steer clear of that guy'? What the hell, does he think he's my dad or older brother?"

"You know your dad and your older brother wouldn't like it either if they had seen Landon trying to flirt with you," Harper says.

I roll my eyes even though I know it's true. Since I'm the only daughter and baby of my family, my older brother and dad have always made it an annoying habit to warn me off guys, even the ones I deemed worthy enough to date long term and brought home to meet my family. The absolute last thing I need is another overprotective male in my life.

I lightly smack Harper's socked foot. "That's exactly the point. Simon is my friend. I don't need him to be an alpha jackass or look out for me. I get enough of that already."

She squints from behind the eye openings of her own sheet mask. "Maybe he's one of those guys who looks out for his female friends when it comes to Bay Area dudes."

Fair point. Like every major metropolitan area in the world, there seems to be a plethora of jerkfaces to endure.

"Out of curiosity, what did this guy look like?" she asks.

"Like a carbon copy of Tom Hiddleston's character in *The Night Manager*."

"Damn. And he was super smooth too?"

I nod. "He just had this vibe. Like, super charming without saying a whole lot. It was all in his mannerisms, the way he smiled and made eye contact."

Harper lets out a low whistle. I smack her leg.

"Cut Simon a break," Harper says. "He sees this debonair guy walk into his apartment for a meeting fresh off a breakup, then try out a few flirty lines on you, his friend. He probably just wants to warn you because he cares."

Inside, I soften the tiniest bit. Even if Simon is jumping the gun, he's doing it because he cares about me.

"Maybe you're right."

I take in everything she's said while I remove the sheet mask and set it on a napkin on the coffee table. She hands me the giant bowl of buttered popcorn we popped earlier, and I munch on a handful.

"Thanks for hanging out with me tonight, by the way," I say. "I know you've been crazy busy with work."

I notice she hasn't checked her texts or her email once since coming home from the office this evening. Unusual for a workaholic like her.

"You're my cousin and best friend. Of course I'll do that for you."

"How's work going?"

Harper leans her head against the armrest of the couch. "Fine. I'm just freaking exhausted."

"Fifteen-hour days will do that to you, Harper."

"It's not just that."

Even with the sheet mask covering her expression, I can tell by her strained tone that she's stressed about something. It's a strange change of pace. She's always been someone who thrives off work stress. The more deadlines she has to keep up with, the more impressive her pace and stamina.

"What is it, then?" I ask.

She shrugs, then sighs. "I think I'm getting burned out."

"You've been working these impossibly long hours for the past what? Seven, eight years? You're well within your right to scale back."

"Yeah, but... I don't even know if I want to be an architect anymore."

I sit up to look at her. Her normally focused eyes now read weary. I can't remember the last time my unflappable cousin looked so unsure of herself.

"Seriously? That's all you ever wanted to do. Even when we were kids, you spent playtime drawing houses and buildings. You'd talk about how you couldn't wait to grow up and actually design them someday."

"Right. And that's exactly what I did. I think I'm just bored with it now."

I quietly muse over Harper's words. She's always been so certain of her career goals. But now that she's second-guessing her lifelong dream, I don't know even know what to say to begin to comfort her. So instead, I reach for her hand, hoping that it helps a little bit. The wet white material of the sheet mask crinkles as she smiles at me.

"Whatever you want to do, do it. You've spent years working so damn hard, you deserve to do something that makes you happy."

"What if I want to do some crazy, irresponsible thing?"

"Harper, I know you. You've got your retirement fund maxed out, a two-year emergency fund, and three years' worth of living expenses saved. You don't do irresponsible, at least not the way the rest of the world does."

"But what if one day I just said screw it. I quit my job and became a beach bum?"

"Then I'll pack extra sunscreen and spend every weekend visiting you."

I squeeze her hand in mine. Even with the barrier of the sheet mask, I can read the hesitation in her expression.

"Seriously. No matter what you decide, as long as it's what you want, it's the right thing to do," I say. "And I'll be there for you through it all."

"Thanks, Naomi."

My phone buzzes from the coffee table.

"Let me guess. A text from Simon?" Harper winks.

Simon: I owe you an apology.

Me: And egg tarts.

Simon: Of course. That goes without saying.

Despite my frustration at him, I can't help but grin. We've gone on two egg tart runs since coming back from Tahoe. It's become an unofficial tradition of ours and one of my favorite things we do together while working. He doesn't make fun of me when I make sex noises while eating. And he always knows that six is the perfect number to order. Enough for me to eat my fill at the bakery and for him to have some, with one leftover for me to enjoy later on in the day.

Simon: But seriously. I want to tell you how sorry I am.

Simon: It wasn't cool how I talked to you after Landon left.

And just like that, the last little bit of my irritation at Simon evaporates. He clearly knows how to apologize when he messes up, a quality I appreciate in a person.

Me: Apology accepted. Thank you. Although it took you long enough LOL

Simon: Ha yeah, sorry about that. I was busy.

Me: Work stuff?

Simon: Yeah. And a date last night.

Me: !!!!

Me: Ooohhh was it the Margot Robbie look-alike who was all over you at that bakery in Lake Tahoe??

Simon: Yeah actually.

Me: I want to hear all about it!

Simon: What are you up to tonight?

Me: Sheet masks and Netflix with Harper at her place. We had Thai takeout. Waaayyy too many leftovers. Very exciting night.

Simon: Sounds like a blast.

Me: Doing anything tonight?

Simon: Headed to Bangerz. My set's in 20.

> I let out a laugh.
> "You two made up. Yay."
> Harper gets up and walks over to the kitchen.

Me: Nooo! You can't perform without me there cheering you on!

> "Do you care if Simon comes over?" I ask Harper. With her head in the fridge, she sticks out her arm and flashes a thumbs-up.

Me: If you feel like trekking all the way to Harper's

apartment, come hang with us. We have plenty of left-overs. You can help us finish them off.

Simon: Whoa, hold on...you're offering to share left-overs with me??

I send an eye roll emoji.

Me: It's A LOT.

Simon: You convinced me. I'll leave my place in a lit-tle bit.

Me: You're really giving up headlining at Bangerz for me? I'm flattered :P

Simon: It's got nothing on you.

My stomach dips at his phrasing.

Me: Warning: We're doing a spa night and you have to join in. I'm talking hair mask, sheet mask, teeth whiten-ing, the works. Promise you'll look so, so pretty.

Simon: Can't wait ;)

## Chapter Eleven

Have you seen the stats for your latest video??

It takes a minute for Simon to reply to my text as I wait in line at the coffee shop down the street from the Dash office building.

Simon: No…is it good or bad?

Me: Good! Like very, very good.

I take a screenshot of the homepage, where the latest video I've posted for the series is the featured content. Then I text it to him.

I move up in line and order a double shot of espresso, hoping it'll power me through my walk to work this morning. I've been pulling loads of late nights editing Simon's series and brainstorming episode ideas and bonus content to include on the site, but I've been loving every minute of it.

No other project I've worked on has been this enjoyable to film and edit. Probably because I've become such good friends with my subject, and Simon is a blast to collaborate with. Every time we talk or hang out, time flies. It's less like I'm working on a high-stakes project and more like I'm spending time with a good friend. And even though it makes for groggy mornings, it's worth it because of how happy I feel and how well it's helping me do at work.

I check my phone as I wait at the far end of the counter for my drink order.

Simon: Holy crap 500k views??

Me: Yup! Viewers love you!

Simon: Well, they only love me because of you. You're the one filming and editing the series.

Me: I'm happy to take some of the credit.

Me: But seriously, it's all you. You're a hit.

"Naomi!"

I whip my head up at the sound of the barista calling my name. I walk over, grab my coffee, say thank you, then walk out the door. I head down the block, staring at my phone, turn the corner, and smack chest-first into a stranger.

I stumble back, quickly catching myself.

Espresso pools around the lid of my coffee cup, but I exhale in relief. Thankfully I didn't spill scalding hot liquid all over myself or the person I bumped into. And thankfully most of the coffee stayed inside the cup so I have enough caffeine to power me through the morning.

"Crap, I'm sorry," a male voice says in front of me.

"It's fine—" I look up and lose all my words. Because there stands Landon, Simon's superhot client.

"Hey," he says, brow raised.

I let out a flustered sound. "Sorry, that was my fault." I raise my hand that still holds my phone. "I was doing that super-obnoxious move of staring at my phone and not paying attention to anything around me."

Landon flashes a smile at me and my insides promptly melt. "Don't even worry about it." He tugs at the lapel of his suit jacket. "You could have thrown your coffee in my face and I still would have been happy to see you."

I laugh. "That's a bold thing to say."

He shrugs, then moves off to the side, closer to the building, to make room for the people walking past us.

I shove my phone in my purse. "Do you work around here?"

"Yeah, my office is just a couple blocks away."

I can't think of anything else to say as Landon smiles down at me looking impossibly handsome, so I just stare at the sidewalk and shuffle my feet.

"Hey," he finally says. "Sorry if I broke the rules when you were filming my counseling session with Simon. I didn't think talking to you during the session was a no-no."

"Oh, it's fine."

"It was just a little distracting having you there."

I let out a confused chuckle. "You knew I would be there. You signed a waiver, remember?"

"Oh, I remember." There's a lift to his voice, like he knows something I don't. "I just didn't know you'd be so gorgeous."

Way too smooth for his own good. I'm amused, though. "What a line."

"Okay yeah, it's a line. But it's also true."

My phone buzzes with a reminder that I've got a meeting in half an hour.

"I'd better get going," I say. "Nice to see you again, Landon."

He nods at me and I continue walking down the block.

"Hey wait," he calls behind me after a minute. I spin around. "Will you be at Simon's seminar tomorrow?"

"Yeah, actually."

"Maybe afterwards we can go for a drink? You don't even have to throw it at me."

I laugh. "Maybe."

Landon walks backwards in the direction of his office building. "See you then, Naomi."

I wave, turn around, and practically skip all the way to work.


"Any questions?" Simon asks at the front of the Le Méridien conference room.

A dozen hands fly up in the air. Simon answers each question from the seminar-goers patiently. From the back where I sit, I spot Landon in the back row. He twists his head around and grins at me. Then he turns back around to face the front of the room.

When the questions wrap up, everyone stands up and mills around or starts to file out of the room. Landon makes his way over to me as I pack up my camera equipment.

"I was thinking," he says, holding the bag open for

me. "It might be nice to grab something to eat. It's almost dinnertime."

I squint at him. "Are you always so suave?"

"What do you mean?"

"I mean that you originally asked me yesterday for a drink, but now you're smoothly turning that into dinner. Is that your usual technique?"

I wouldn't normally be so forward when talking to a guy. But now that I've sworn off relationships and dating, I have no time for second-guessing or wondering. From now on, if I'm going to spend time with someone, I'm going to be as direct as possible. That way there's no room for confusion or mixed-up feelings.

He holds up a hand, still grinning. "Okay, you busted me. Yeah, I was trying to rope you into dinner too because I want to spend more time with you than just one drink's worth."

Another too-smooth line. But honestly, I don't even care. Landon isn't someone I'd ever consider dating. His player vibe is off the charts with how he's got a smooth answer and quip for almost everything.

But I'm not interested in dating. I'm interested in having a good time. And as long as I'm enjoying Landon's company, I'm game for just about anything.

I take my time zipping up my gear bag before looking up at Landon. I make sure to give him pointed eye contact and a sly half-smile that says I can be coy too. "Dinner it is. Let's go."

Dinner with Landon wasn't what I expected. At all.

I expected a quick meal in maybe nearby Chinatown or one of the food trucks dotting this neighborhood.

But Landon insisted on Wayfare Tavern just down

the street from Le Méridien. The moment we walked into the upscale European-inspired bistro, I felt underdressed. I should have been wearing one of my cocktail dresses, not a casual button-up shirtdress and flats. But Landon didn't blink an eye as he led me to our table with his hand on the small of my back. He was perfectly dressed in his charcoal gray suit since he's a stockbroker who always has to look slick for work.

The moment we sat down, he set me at ease with his nonstop compliments about how nice I looked and questions about my work. And as we shared a burrata starter and fried chicken entrée, I felt myself start to ease up. This wasn't a date, and I shouldn't feel the need to impress. This was just dinner with a hot guy who I enjoy talking to.

And as we walk to a crowded English-style pub nearby, that's the thought at the forefront of my mind.

*No pressure. Just relax and enjoy.*

It seems like every local got word of this new place because there's zero seating available. But then I see a sign that points toward the back of the pub, claiming that there's seating upstairs.

I tug on Landon's jacket sleeve and point to the sign. "Try up there?"

We head in that direction at a slow pace due to the crowd. But then Landon takes my hand, steps ahead of me, and walks forward. People part around us, letting us through. We make it to a staircase and walk all the way to the top. It's considerably less plush than the sitting area downstairs. All that's available up here are simple wooden tables and chairs.

Landon stops to peer around the room. "Damn. All full."

Out of the corner of my eye, I see Simon waving at us from a tiny corner table.

"Oh, hey!" I wave back then lead Landon by the hand over to him.

The closer we get, the more it looks like he's frowning. His gaze drops to mine and Landon's linked hands. Like a reflex, I let go. I'm not even sure why. I can hold hands with someone if I want to.

I push the thought away and instead flash a smile at Simon just as he stands to greet us. "I didn't know you'd be here tonight," I say.

"I was having drinks with a friend when he got a work call and had to take off." He pivots his attention to Landon. "Good to see you, Landon."

They exchange a brief and cordial handshake.

"You guys wanna join me?" Simon asks. "It really picked up in here the last fifteen minutes. I don't know if they'll have a free table anytime soon."

Landon starts to hesitate, but I plop down across from Simon in the tiny corner table. "Sure."

The bench I'm sitting on is clearly meant for one person, but seeing as there are zero free chairs nearby, I scoot over to make room for Landon. When I look over at Simon, he sports a tight expression on his face. A beat later it's gone and he's back to looking at ease again.

"Sorry. I just didn't want to go searching for another bar," I say to Landon. I wiggle an eyebrow at him. "I'm pretty thirsty."

"Totally fine." He stands up. "What would you like to drink?"

"Something hard. Surprise me."

A cheeky smile dances across his lips. He dials it

back to polite before addressing Simon. "You want another?"

"Nah, I'm good."

Landon heads to the upstairs bar and I turn back to Simon. "Thanks for sharing your table with us."

"Yeah, no problem. I thought you didn't drink much."

"I don't, really. I just kind of felt like it tonight."

He raises his glass to his lips. "Why the change?"

"Because I'm thirty-three and if I feel like accepting a drink when someone offers, I'm well within my right to."

My attempt at a lighthearted tone falls flat judging by the way Simon jolts slightly at what I've said.

"Sorry...that came off a bit weird."

"It's fine." His tone is light, but his smile is tight once more.

For several seconds, we don't say anything. Simon stares off to the side. I swallow and dart my eyes. It's weird having this uncomfortable moment between us. Yeah, we're not always chatty, but we've been at ease around each other until now.

"So Landon gets you in the mood to drink?"

"What?"

Instead of repeating himself, Simon peers around the busy space. I pull his attention back to me with a firm, "Hey."

He turns his head to me.

"Is everything okay? You're acting weird."

His chest rises as he takes a breath. "Honestly?"

I nod.

"I think it's tacky that Landon asked you out at the seminar. And I'm kind of surprised that you said yes."

"What do you mean by that?" I have to bite the inside

of my cheek to keep from snapping at him. It sounds like he's questioning my integrity, which he has no right to.

"I'd just be wary of a guy who thinks it's cool to pick up a woman at a relationship seminar." Simon rolls his shoulders as he speaks. It's such a casual move—almost like he's trying to make it seem like he doesn't care what I'm doing when it's clear that he does.

"It's not like that," I say. "We're just hanging out. We can get together for a meal and a drink without any expectations for something more."

"You're an attractive woman, Naomi," he says. "Even if a guy like Landon says he's not interested in anything more with you, he's secretly always up for it. Always."

I let out a disgusted scoff. What he said comes off as so very condescending.

"Really, Simon?" I lean in closer to him. "Even if that's the case, does it mean that's what automatically happens?"

His jaw tenses. Something wild shines in his eyes. It makes my pulse beat faster, but not in a bad way—in an invigorating way. This is a strange brand of frustration he's eliciting from me.

"Just because a guy might want to do something doesn't mean that I'd just do it. Jesus Christ. Give me some credit."

He leans toward me. "That's not what I—"

Just then, Landon returns with two old-fashioneds. Simon immediately settles against the back of his chair.

"Hope this is okay," Landon says, scooting closer to me on the bench and gesturing to my glass.

"It's fine. Thank you." My tone comes off as harder than I mean it to. I quickly take a sip, letting the burn of the alcohol distract me from the charged exchange with Simon.

"So. What'd I miss?" Landon asks.

"How are you liking the seminars so far, Landon?" Simon asks, ignoring his question. He taps his fingers on the wooden tabletop, as if he's impatiently waiting for an answer.

Landon's face scrunches into a thoughtful frown. "I'm learning a lot. I can see now what I did wrong in past relationships, the mistakes I made."

"How so?"

Even though the expression on Simon's face seems friendly enough, I can tell by the hard look in his eyes it's all a farce. He clearly has it out for Landon. I open my mouth to say something to him, but Landon answers him first.

"It's just that now I can see how badly I screwed up in the past. I thought ghosting was a perfectly acceptable form of ending something. Terrible, I know."

"Yeah, wow. That's horrific," I say, giving him a playful nudge with my elbow. "We've all done crappy things. What matters is that you stop doing it and improve from your old ways."

Simon tilts his head at me. "Really? Have you ever ghosted anyone, Naomi? You don't seem like the type."

Pursing my lips, I let out a sharp sigh. "No. I haven't. Have you?"

Simon shakes his head, his gaze never leaving mine. Then he turns back to Landon. "Glad to hear you're not ghosting your dates anymore, Landon. I'm overcome with joy that my seminar could help teach you that."

"Jesus," I mutter against my glass just before taking another sip.

When I peer over at Landon, I notice the annoyed wrinkle in his brow.

"Look, man, I was definitely a douche back in the day. I won't deny that," he says. "That's why I'm seeing you. I want to be better for the next person I'm with."

Simon's jaw clenches. "So it's not at all douchey to pick up the closest woman in the vicinity during one of my seminars?"

"Simon. Stop. How many times do I have to tell you? Landon didn't pick me up. We decided to have dinner and a drink as friends. That's it."

Simon levels a glare at Landon. "Playing the friends card? Original."

Landon says nothing as he tugs at the collar of his shirt. Simon rolls his eyes and shakes his head.

"That's it." I slam my palm on the microscopic table-top before jolting up to my feet and bolting to Simon's side. I tug his arm. "Up. Now."

He stands up and follows me as I drag him to the corridor by the bathroom. With both hands, I press him against the wall in the farthest, dimmest corner of the area so hopefully no one can see.

Despite how badly I want to take him to task for his childish behavior, I'm expecting him to push me gently back with one arm, then walk away. But he allows himself to be pinned against the wall.

"What the hell is up with you?" I snap.

He says nothing, just staring at me with those warm golden eyes that always radiate kindness when they look at me, even when he's upset and frustrated.

A long moment passes without him saying a word.

"This alpha crap you're pulling with Landon is getting old."

It's a few seconds of him clenching his jaw and his eyes darting away before he says anything. "I don't like the guy, okay?"

"Are you kidding me? Are we in middle school? Are you one of the mean girls who expects me to stop spending time with someone just because you don't like them?"

Simon closes his eyes for a long second before speaking again. "I know I sound like an asshole right now, but it's just a vibe I get from him."

Hearing Simon curse is like an electric shock. It sounds so foreign from a guy who censors his own curse words when he texts.

"What kind of vibe?" I ask, the impatience clear in my stern tone.

"He comes off as too suave. Like he's playing everyone around him."

"Then why don't you kick him out of your class?" I retort, giving him a slight push with my hands still on his arms. "You make no qualms about that on your website, how you'd kick anyone out if you suspect they're there for the wrong reasons."

"It's not—look, that's not exactly it. I make a living reforming guys like him. They're welcome as long as they're actively working to better themselves."

When Simon speaks this time, his tone is softer, but the hardness, the conviction is still there.

"Then maybe Landon is in it for the right reasons," I say.

"Maybe. But I have a feeling spending time with him could get you hurt, Naomi."

Inside I'm two warring factions of feelings. One side of me is happy to have Simon's concern and care, but the other is annoyed that he thinks he has any right to meddle in my personal life.

"Look, I appreciate how you're trying to be a good friend and look out for me. You obviously can read people in a way that I can't. But I'm fully aware that Landon isn't an angel. And honestly? That's fine with me. I told you before I'm done with relationships and dating. I've spent enough years trying to be the good girlfriend only to see every relationship I've ever had fall apart. I don't need Landon to be a knight in shining armor or Mr. Commitment. I just want someone who's okay with having a good time for now and who respects my boundaries. That's exactly what he's done so far, and that's fine with me."

"It's just…" Simon's gaze turns impatient. He bends both arms up, cradling my forearms in his hands. It's the softest touch. My breath catches for the briefest second.

"I hate the thought of you getting hurt."

That touch and those words flip this moment on its head. Suddenly this interaction feels a lot more intimate than an argument between friends. There's passion and heat…and it has to stop.

Holding in my breath, I take a single step away so we're no longer touching. As soon as I'm out of his hold, it's like a spell is broken. Only the lingering heat of frustration is left.

"Listen. I get that you care about me, but it's insulting the way you infantilize me when it comes to Landon. I'm a big girl. If I want to hang out with a guy because he's fun to chat with and makes me laugh, I have a right to do that. And you have no right to say anything about it."

I spin around and dart away, ignoring Simon's calls

for me to wait. I stop at the table where Landon is sitting, dig cash from my purse and drop it on the table.

"Is that enough to cover the tip?" I ask.

He adds a five-dollar bill. "Now it is."

"Good. Let's get out of here."

He follows me back down the stairs, through the crowd, and out the door. We're half a block away before I register Landon saying my name. When I feel his hand on mine, I finally stop walking.

"What happened back there?" he asks.

"I don't want to get into it."

"Why not?"

I bite my lip. "Because Simon said some not nice things about you and I don't want to hurt your feelings."

"Promise you won't. What did he say?"

"He said he gets douchebag vibes from you. Sorry."

He shrugs, clearly unfazed. "He's not wrong. I'm kind of a douche. That's why I'm taking his seminar."

"It's not just that. He's my friend and he gets weirdly protective around me. Not sure why."

"You're kidding, right?"

I shake my head.

"Simon's into you. It probably pisses him off to see you hanging out with another guy."

I wave a hand in the air, dismissing his comment. "You should hear how he talks to his little sister on the phone. Super overprotective. And he fusses over his mom and grandma too. I think it's just that he gets protective of the women he's close to."

Judging by the tilt of Landon's head and the incredulous look on his face, he doesn't buy my explanation.

"Okay, full disclosure: we met at a bar one night when I tried to hit on him. I was drunk and there was an attraction there for sure, but we're just friends and coworkers now."

I silently scold myself for the lie I feed Landon. If that moment when Simon touched me as I backed him against the wall was anything to go by, that attraction is still alive and well. But that's all it is: a fleeting moment. There's no reason to give it more than a few seconds of thought.

Landon rests his hands in his pockets and takes a step toward me. "If you suddenly changed your mind one day and wanted something more with Simon, I'd bet my left nut he'd say yes."

"Come on, Landon."

He shrugs, his expression teasing.

"You know, for two guys who don't get along, you have pretty similar views."

"How's that?"

"Well, when I told Simon that you and I were just hanging out, he said the same thing basically. That you'd be up for it if I suddenly wanted to get physical with you."

A moment passes with Landon saying nothing. His expression softens while the look in his eyes goes dark. "He's not wrong."

My heartbeat skids. "Oh."

I shouldn't be surprised. The whole reason I'm spending time with Landon is because he's a charming and good-looking guy who's fun to flirt with. Still though, to hear him outright admit that he's up for getting physical with me catches me off guard. So few people have ever said that to me.

I take a step toward him. "So that means…"

Landon's hands fall to my waist. "That means I'd really, really like to kiss you, Naomi."

His voice is a soft growl I can't resist. Leaning my face up, I press a kiss to his mouth. I hum at the firm pressure combined with the soft feel of his lips.

For a few seconds, I let myself enjoy the sensation of my lips on his. But then he parts my lips open with his tongue. I'm nibbling at his bottom lip and teasing him back with the tip of my tongue. I run my hands through his thick blond hair, tugging at it to hold him steady as I go to town on his mouth.

The sharp sound of a whistle from down the block jolts us apart.

"Damn! Get a room already!"

Landon and I fall back at the stranger's comment, wiping our mouths and chuckling at the same time.

I drop my hands to my side. "Well. That was…"

"Hot?" Landon wags an eyebrow at me.

"Definitely that."

Crossing my arms, I shuffle my feet along the cracked pavement. Part of me is overjoyed that my first kiss in months was so natural and passionate. But the other part of me knows I need to make my intentions very clear to Landon—I don't want to lead him on.

"Look. I—that kiss was great, but I don't want to start anything right now, especially since—"

A soft smile spreads across Landon's face as he reaches for my hand. "It's okay, Naomi. It's not a big deal. Let's just have fun."

"So you'd be fine if all I wanted to do is meet up with you for drinks or dinner sometimes and make out?"

His smile doesn't budge. "More than fine."

I let out a small puff of air in relief at his response,

then kiss him. I check the time on my phone and see that it's almost eleven. "I'd better get home. Long day of editing tomorrow."

I order a rideshare on my phone. He stands with me until the car comes and gives me a quick kiss on the lips before opening the car door for me and waving good-bye.

It seems like Landon's going to be an interesting new buddy to have. I try not to think about just how pissed off Simon's going to be.

## Chapter Twelve

I'm on hour three of ignoring Simon's texts and calls at Harper's apartment.

He probably wants to apologize for going off on Landon last night, but I don't have the patience to deal with him right now.

I hit Save on the video footage I've been cleaning up for the next episode of *Simply Simon*, then hop up from the sofa and head to the kitchen for my third cup of herbal tea when there's a knock at the door.

Mug in hand, I check the peephole and let out a frustrated sigh. There's another knock, but I don't answer. Instead I plop on the couch, hell-bent on letting him have it out with the door until he tires himself out, gives up, and leaves.

"Naomi," Simon says from behind the door. "I could hear you sighing a second ago. Will you please just let me in so I can apologize to you already?"

I contemplate ignoring him. But then I won't be able to concentrate. So I stand up and answer the door.

"What do you want?" I say, crossing my arms.

Simon's face is twisted in worried wrinkles. "I want to say sorry for how I acted last night."

"You know that means close to nothing, right?"

His jaw tense, he nods. I take a second to size him up. His uniform of a crisp dress shirt and pressed trousers appears off today. The fabric is rumpled, like he didn't have time to iron his clothes—or he was so upset at how we left things last night, he didn't even bother.

It's the look in his eyes that gives it all away, though. His normally kind stare is tinged with sorrow. It's doing odd things to my chest—and my heartbeat.

But no matter how sorry he looks, I don't hold back. I need to make it clear to him how I feel.

"This can't keep happening, where you routinely pull that unwanted, overly protective bodyguard act."

"I understand. I'm sorry." He sighs, pulling his lips into his mouth for a moment before speaking again. "This isn't an excuse, I just want to explain why I acted the way I did. I had a bit too much to drink and acted like a jerk. And no matter how I personally feel about someone, I still need to be polite to them, especially if they're important to you."

The seconds of silence and intermittent eye contact that follow are tinged with tension. We're technically good again—I've made my expectations clear, he's apologized, and I've accepted. But inhabiting this unfamiliar territory of tension with Simon like this is beyond odd. I'm used to joking and chatting with him, not stewing in awkward silence. I don't know how to breech it.

I don't have to, though. A beat later, Simon pulls me into a hug. Instantly, I melt into him. I sink into his broad chest, burrowing my face in that lovely spot all guys seem to have, that thick, meaty mass where their shoulder meets the base of their neck.

And then I close my eyes and breathe in the musky, clean scent of his skin. The way he wraps his arms around me, it's like I'm being cradled. So soothing and comforting. Simon is a top-notch hugger.

"I'm sorry for being such a dick." His voice is so low and so soft, it could pass for a whisper.

I smile against his shoulder. "It's weird to hear you say the word 'dick.'"

He chuckles softly. I squeeze him tighter.

"I didn't know you were so into hugging," he says.

"Blame my family. We bombard people with hugs. At every family gathering you hug everyone at least twice, when you arrive and again before you leave. It's the greatest."

He pulls away, then bends down to grab a paper bag that's to the side of the doorway, out of view.

"What's that?" I ask.

"Egg tarts. Proper apology food."

I squeal and bounce on my tiptoes before snatching the bag out of his hands. "You turn apologies into an art form."

"Tell that to my mom. She said these would sweeten the apology."

"You told her about our fight?"

He winces, rubbing his hand behind his neck. "She called earlier to pester me about bringing you over for dinner one of these nights. And when I mentioned that I wasn't sure you'd even want to come, she got suspicious. Then she wore me down with questions."

"Ah yes. The mom interrogation, where they pepper you with questions until you can't take it anymore and tell them everything."

"Pretty much that." He sighs. "I'm not going around sharing our arguments with everyone, I promise."

"Don't even worry about it," I say after taking a

bite. "My mom does the same thing. It's why I don't pick up the phone when she calls if I happen to have had an argument with someone. I don't want to spill my guts to her."

He flashes a sympathetic smile.

I hum through another bite. "I'd love to go to dinner at your mom and grandma's house if the offer still stands."

"Really?"

I nod.

"Sunday, then?"

"Perfect."

"I gotta head back to work, but…" He takes a step back into the hallway. "We're good, right?"

I attempt to smile with my mouth full of scrumptious egg tart, relieved that Simon and I have navigated through this rift and we're firmly back to friends. But as he looks at me, I notice a hint of something in his gaze.

Something about it hits differently, like from this moment on, our friendship has shifted. I shove the thought away and tell myself not to think too hard about it. We've resolved this rift and we're back to being friends again.

"We're good." I smile at him.

He flashes a soft smile of his own, then darts down the staircase.

"You ready for this?" Simon asks from the driver's seat of his car.

"Absolutely. I'm starving."

As we head to his family's place, I gaze out the passenger window at the traffic whizzing past us on the 101, then glance in the other direction at the deep blue water of San Francisco Bay. The late afternoon sunlight casts a glowing orange beam across the water, which shines like glass.

"So will it just be your mom and grandma tonight, then?"

Simon nods, his eyes on the road ahead. "Yup. My sister can't make it. She's out of town for work."

"Should I know anything in particular about your mom and grandma? Any topics to avoid?"

"Nah, they're pretty open and kind people who love chatting about almost anything. Although if you compliment my grandma about her cooking, she'll love you forever."

"Good to know."

"The fact that you're bringing them flowers is enough to guarantee they'll love you." He glances at the bouquet of multicolored gerbera daisies sitting on my lap. "That's a nice touch, by the way."

"Promise I'm not trying to score points. I just thought it would be a nice thing to do since they're kind enough to feed me."

Twenty minutes later Simon pulls into the driveway in front of a tall and narrow two-story stucco house with a beige exterior and dark tile roof.

When he opens the front door, a chocolate Lab darts straight over to him. "Hey, Kiki!"

The dog spins around in excited circles, bumping into our legs. Her wagging tail hits my knee, and I lean down to pat her head. She responds immediately by licking my face. I fall back, laughing.

"Kiki likes you," Simon says as he gives her several pats.

"You're here!"

Looking up, I see Simon's mom, Barbara, walking toward us, a red apron tied around her waist. She claps her hands. "Kiki, come! Now!"

The dog obeys her command, instantly running over to Barbara. She pets her head, then points for her to sit on a nearby leather sofa. Then she tightens the ponytail holding back her light brown hair and turns back to us.

"It's so nice to finally meet you in person, Naomi." She pulls me into a hug.

I thank her for having me, then turn around and pick up the bouquet of flowers I placed on the floor when Kiki ran over to us.

"These are for you."

Barbara's mouth turns into a perfect O shape, indicating her surprise. "Oh my goodness, you didn't have to do that. How gorgeous! Thank you!"

She turns to Simon and hugs him with her free arm. When they break apart, she cups her hand over his cheek. "So good to see you, sweetie."

I can't help but smile at the sweetness and love in their exchange.

"Smells yummy," he says.

Barbara gestures in the direction of the kitchen. "You two go say hi to Grandma. I'm going to get a vase for these lovely flowers."

She heads down the hall and I follow Simon through the cozily decorated living room. In addition to the leather sofa is a plush recliner and what looks like an antique mahogany coffee table. There's a flat-screen TV sitting over a brick fireplace on the far side of the living room. The hardwood floors creak softly as we walk.

Framed photos dot the walls. Simon stares at me from each stage of his life so far: chunky baby, adorable toddler, sporty kiddo with missing front teeth, tall and broody teenager, then college hunk. My eyes fixate on the photo of him on a nearby shelf, where he's sitting on a beach with his shirt off, his light brown hair shaggy and soaked, beaming at the camera. Judging by the youthful look on his face, that was taken during his prime camming days.

I swallow back all the memories my brain aches to conjure up as we enter the kitchen. It's a long and narrow design, with one end where the sink and appliances are and the other end the dining area. Simon's grandma Miriam stands at the stove, her back to us. She's a tiny thing, nearly a foot shorter than Simon, with a slight frame. Her brownish-gray hair is in wavy curls today, and she's wearing a blue apron over dark leggings and a sweater. She's stirring what looks like marinara sauce at the stove while shuffling her feet in place, like she's dancing to music only she can hear. It makes me smile.

"Hey, Grandma," Simon says, his voice loud.

Miriam spins around, her eyes wide when she looks at us. "Peanut!"

She pulls him down into a hug.

"I got new batteries for my hearing aid so you can talk to me at your regular volume," she says.

"That's great," Simon says before introducing me to her.

I stick out my hand for a handshake, but she waves it away. "Only hugs in this house."

I chuckle as she wraps her arms around me. When she releases me, she keeps hold of my hands.

"Well, that's a lovely dress," she says, scanning the casual sundress I'm wearing. "Would you believe I had a dress a lot like that when I was your age?"

"I bet you looked lovely in it," I say with a smile.

"Oh I did. I was a looker back in my day."

Both Simon and I chuckle.

"Mom, look at the flowers Naomi brought us!" Barbara says from behind us.

She sets them on top of the dining room table, which is right next to a sliding glass door.

Miriam spins around. "Oh how beautiful!" She pats my arm. "Naomi, honey, you really shouldn't have."

"I wanted to. I can't wait to try your ravioli."

She beams, then directs us to sit down at the table.

"It's a good thing that dinner's almost done." He points his thumb at me. "This one hasn't eaten much all day and she gets hangry if she has to wait long for food."

I give his arm a light shove. "That's not true at all. I can be patient."

Both Miriam and Barbara chuckle.

"Oh honey, don't you worry," Miriam hollers from the stove. "I'm a beast when I haven't eaten. Or when I miss my afternoon nap."

"She's a beast too."

I roll my eyes as I laugh at Simon. Barbara walks over and musses his hair with a hand.

"You stop giving her a hard time already," she says good-naturedly.

"Are you sure I can't help with anything?" I ask.

"Positive," Barbara and Miriam say in unison.

As I settle in, I take in the scene, how Simon's mom and grandma work busily at the stove while he sets the table.

"You kids want some wine?" Barbara asks.

"Oh, no thank you," I say.

"Naomi's a bit of a lightweight," Simon says.

I roll my eyes at him when he nudges me with his elbow.

"Good for you, honey. Alcohol's no good for you anyway," Barbara says. "It completely dries out your skin. I still can't say no to my Friday night glass of wine, though."

"That's understandable," I say.

Barbara joins us at the table. Miriam follows with a ceramic tub of ravioli covered in red sauce, then sets it on the table with a heavy thud.

She beams at us. "Hope you're hungry!"

A half-hour later, I'm patting my aching stomach. Miriam starts to scoop ravioli out of the pan. "More?"

Holding up a hand, I shake my head. "I wish I could, but two helpings were more than enough. It was absolutely delicious. Best ravioli I've ever had, no question."

She beams. "I'll pack you leftovers to take with you. And dessert too. I made tiramisu."

Simon and I thank her.

"So!" Simon's mom claps her hands. "Can we talk about how exciting it is that our Simon is a TV star because of Naomi?"

"I'm not on TV, Mom. It's an online web series."

She waves a hand, as if that's some insignificant detail. "Same thing, sweetie." She turns to me. "I've been enjoying the show so much, Naomi. It's so exciting seeing him in action, what he does in his seminars and in those counseling sessions. And the way you edit the footage, it's so slick! It's like I'm watching a movie."

"That's kind of you to say, thank you. But really, Simon is the reason why it's so good. All the slick editing and filming in the world wouldn't make a difference if I didn't have such an engaging and charismatic star."

I look at Simon when I say the word "star." He rolls his eyes, flustered smile on his face.

"I just wish you could include some more real-life stuff," Barbara says. "Like, baby pictures or something like that."

Miriam claps her hands. "Oh that's a lovely idea! Simon was the cutest baby you've ever seen."

"No way you're airing baby photos of me."

"We're just so proud of you, honey. My baby boy!"

Simon sighs, though he's smiling. "Thanks, everyone."

Barbara and Miriam chat about how excited they are for me to film their family weekend trip to Napa for the series. After a few minutes, Simon stands up from the table to clear the dishes, then disappears to the other end of the kitchen.

Barbara turns to me, beaming. "So! How are you and Simon getting along?"

I clear my throat, suddenly nervous now that I'm the focus of Miriam's and Barbara's unblinking stares.

"Pretty good. He's been so fun to work with. And he's become a really great friend too."

"Just friends?" Barbara says with a hopeful smile.

The way Miriam and Barbara stare at me, their eyes unblinking and their grins wide, I know where this is headed.

Sweat beads at the back of my neck. This isn't the first time I've visited a male friend's family and had them allude to there being something more between us. It's always a delicate balance. I can't go off on them like I would if my own family were giving me a hard time—that would be rude. But I also don't want to evade the topic completely—that ambiguity could make them think that we're together when we're not.

Simon's back is to us as he washes the dishes and loads them into the dishwasher. With the water running and dishes clanking, I'm sure he can't hear a word of what his mom is saying. It would be nice if he could hear the conversation, then swoop in and change the subject. But it looks like I'll have to fend for myself.

I offer a polite smile. "We're friends and colleagues. And that's it."

"Well, I for one think you two would make a really cute couple," Miriam says, folding her napkin. Barbara nods her head in agreement.

I try to play it off with a chuckle. But the longer they stare hopefully at me, the clearer it becomes. I'm going to have to be a bit more blunt.

"Simon is an amazing person," I say. "But we're just friends. He's told me how he's focusing on his career right now. And I have a pretty terrible track record when it comes to relationships, so I've been concentrating on work too."

I brace myself for more teasing from Miriam and Barbara. But instead they exchange a knowing glance. Miriam excuses herself to go take her blood pressure medication. Then Barbara pats her hand over mine, the expression on her face warm. "Oh honey, dating and relationships are absolutely awful, just the worst when you're with the wrong person. But with the right person? Then it's easy. A lot like a friendship, in fact. Except there's the added bonus that you can't keep your hands off each other."

She winks, then stands up and walks over to Simon

to help him with the dishes. And I'm left sitting at the table, mulling over her words.

"Hopefully my mom and grandma didn't scare you off," Simon says on the drive back to his apartment.

"Not at all. They were so sweet and welcoming." I pat the cloth bag of Tupperware containers sitting on my lap. "And now we have a week's worth of lunches and dessert."

I almost mention his mom's comment about us as a couple, but bite my tongue. It's probably not worth mentioning for as much awkwardness as it might cause.

"So they didn't give you a hard time about us?"

"How did you know that?"

"I grew up with them. I know what they're like."

"They asked about us, specifically if we were together. I said no, we're just friends and added a bit about how I'm a walking relationship disaster to paint a more vivid picture. And then your mom said that when you're with the right person, relationships are a lot easier. It was actually kind of…poetic the way she put it."

"Poetic," he repeats.

"If only it were that simple."

I gaze out the window at the dark blue sky and the city lights glittering along the horizon. When I look at him, I notice his stare has gone intense. He's studying the freeway like he's trying to memorize every line in the road.

"Maybe it *is* that simple," he finally says.

"What?"

He clears his throat. "Maybe for some people relationships are that simple. Like your parents."

"Yeah. I mean, they hardly ever fight. When they

do, they resolve things right away. I've never seen them take longer than a few hours to make up. I don't think they've ever gone to bed mad at each other. They share a lot of the same interests. And they make each other laugh all the time."

Ever since I could remember, my parents seemed happy together. No, it wasn't rainbows and sunshine all the time. They get on each other's nerves like anyone else. But there's a baseline with them. They never insult each other. They're always kind to one another. And they always look at each other with adoration in their eyes. Always.

"They don't just love each other; they like each other too. I think that makes a difference," I say.

I recall the phrase they've said out loud a million times when others who have noticed their marital bliss ask them the same question.

"They say it's because at the core, they're best friends. That probably counts for a lot."

We hit a construction zone blocking traffic. Simon eases to a stop and turns to look at me.

He's not quite frowning, and there's a rawness behind his eyes that I can't ever remember seeing before.

"Naomi." His voice is gruff when he says my name. It makes my heart beat all the way up my throat. "I—"

The sound of my phone blaring makes me jump.

"Sorry," I mutter. "Let me get rid of this."

But then I see it's Landon calling. I feel bad about just ignoring him, so I answer the phone.

"Hey." His voice is breathy.

"Hey, how's it going?"

"Not great, actually."

"What's wrong?"

"It's just been...well, kind of the day from hell."

"What happened?"

"Just some annoying personal stuff. And work stuff. I don't want to talk about it."

Landon's clipped tone jolts me. I glance up and catch Simon rubbing a hand over his face.

"I just, um. Would it be weird if I asked you to meet up for a bit? Just for a drink somewhere?" Landon asks, his tone softer. "I can come to your neighborhood to make it easier. I just...you're the only face I want to see right now."

Inside I soften. Sure, it could be yet another one of his ultra-smooth lines, but I believe Landon when he says it. Because he sounds exhausted and pained and even though we're not anything serious, it means something that he chose to call me over anyone else.

"Of course," I say. "There's a martini bar on Polk Street. It's called Amelie. Wanna meet me there?"

"You're perfect, you know that?"

Hearing the smile in his voice makes me grin even wider. He says he's on his way, I tell him bye, hang up, and look back at Simon.

"Sorry about that. Landon apparently had a really bad day and wants to meet up at Amelie."

I can feel all the muscles in my shoulders clench at just having to mention Landon to Simon. The last time they were around each other, it led to an argument between us. Sure, he apologized, but I haven't mentioned Landon since.

For a second, Simon's expression goes tight. "Of course. You need a ride?"

"No, that's okay. It's just a few streets away, I can walk from here."

Traffic clears up and we start moving again.

"It's not a problem," Simon says while staring straight ahead.

The few minutes' drive to Amelie is silent. It's such a shift, the slight tension in the air between us now. Simon pulls over at the corner of the block where Amelie is, puts his car in Park, pulls out two Tupperware containers from the bag, then hands it to me. "Have fun with Landon."

His forced smile makes me flinch.

I nod and mumble a thanks, but as I go to climb out of the car, I turn back to him. I don't want to leave this cloud of tension between us yet again.

"Look, I know you're not Landon's biggest fan, and that's fine. It's just… You don't have to be friends, but can you just maybe try to exist in the same giant city together? And maybe be civil to him if you see him in another seminar? It would mean a lot to me."

He closes his eyes for a long second while he takes a breath. "Sure."

"Thank you. And thanks for the ride."

"Of course."

I start to reach for the handle, but stop to turn to him again. "Wait, what were you going to say a bit ago? Before my phone rang?"

His brow lifts slightly. When he doesn't answer right away, I wonder if he forgot. But the longer I gaze into his eyes, the less I think that's the case. Because he gives me that same raw look.

"I was just going to say that I'm glad your parents like each other. And love each other."

"Oh." It's all I can manage.

For a few seconds we say nothing.

I force myself to break the awkward moment. "Thanks again for letting me tag along to your family dinner tonight."

"You're always welcome," he says quickly. "I'll see you later."

I hop out of the car, shut the door, and he speeds off. And I stand there, watching until his car fades out of sight, wondering the whole time what Simon was really going to say to me.

# Chapter Thirteen

Landon waves to me from his seat in the middle row of the Le Méridien Hotel conference room. I smile slightly and wave back, then return to setting up my camera to film Simon's seminar today.

Ever since we met up for impromptu martinis last Sunday night, we got together at Spud's Bar the following night, which led to a tipsy makeout in the alley behind the bar.

But since then I haven't heard from him. I try my hardest not to read too much into the fact that I texted him the day after our hot makeout and he never answered me. This setup is supposed to be casual and not at all serious. The rational part of my brain knows there shouldn't be any obligations or expectation—like regular calls and texts.

Still, though. It stings to feel like Landon might be ignoring me.

From my spot at the back of the room, I see Simon finish chatting with a client and then approach Landon. His expression is serious, but lacks that annoyance he displayed when Landon and I ran into him at the pub a week and a half ago. I watch as Landon looks up at him, nods, and follows him to the corner of the room.

I can't hear what Simon says, but judging by his alert posture and the knit of his brow, he's apologizing to Landon. It's a few seconds before I realize I'm holding my breath. I shouldn't be nervous. We're good—and Simon promised me he'd be civil to Landon. But it's like a reflex to inwardly cringe when I see two guys who have a hostile history walk off together.

A second later, Landon's jaw tightens. He nods his head, then shakes his hand. I'm not an expert lip reader, but it looks like he says something like, "It's okay, man. Thanks," to Simon before he heads back to his seat. Simon walks back to the front of the room.

Landon turns his head and catches my eye, then offers a sly smile. The air I've been holding in my lungs comes out in a slow, quiet stream. They're good now. Simon's apologized and now we can all move on.

A minute later my phone buzzes.

Landon: Thanks for the apology.

Me: ???

Landon: Come on. I know you put him up to that.

Landon: I appreciate you doing that. I know the guy doesn't care for me, but I'm glad that he's willing to be civil.

Landon: And it's nice to know I don't have to endure more death stares from him.

Me: LOL

Me: But seriously, I'm glad to hear that.

Me: Sorry if I overstepped…but I just didn't want things to be tense anymore.

Landon: I get it.

I shove my phone back in my bag, glad the two buried the hatchet, but still annoyed that Landon hasn't referenced my flirty text from the other day. Simon begins the session, kicking off with his usual brief greeting and pleasantries, then dives right in.

"I thought we'd start today with a bit of a progress report. Anyone want to give an update on how things are going for you in your relationships?"

A handful of men raise their hands and talk about how things have been improving with their partners. One guy mentions how he feels closer to his fiancée after they started going to couples' counseling a few months ago. An elderly man talks about how implementing weekly date nights with his wife has given him an excitement he hasn't felt since he was a newlywed.

A tall man in his late thirties dressed in jeans and a sweater raises his hand.

"How are things going with you, Derek?"

Derek stands up from a chair in the middle of the second row and shoves his hands in his pockets. "Not great."

"Why's that? Last seminar you were in, you said you and Holly were hitting a major milestone in your relationship by moving in together."

"We were, but…" Derek winces before continuing to speak. "It's just gotten a bit awkward because she recently admitted to me that she hates one of my good friends."

My ears perk up and I adjust the camera to focus on Derek. This should be interesting.

"What's the story there?" Simon asks.

"I don't understand what her issue is. Gretchen and I have been friends since college. She's like one of the guys to me. And nothing's ever happened between us, so I don't see why she has a problem." Derek shakes his head and rolls his eyes. "Such a typical thing for a woman to complain about."

Simon's eyebrow quirks up as he stares at Derek.

"That's a pretty disrespectful comment to make," Simon says. "That type of insulting language isn't welcome here, Derek. You know it's not. If you have a concern about your relationship, fine. We can talk about it. But you will not make sweeping, disrespectful generalizations about women in this space. Understand?"

Derek flinches, then swallows. "Right. Sorry."

The room, though quiet since the seminar started, is now so deafeningly silent you could hear a pin drop from the fifth floor of the building. I've observed that during his seminars and therapy sessions, Simon doesn't hesitate to call out difficult behavior, always in a firm yet respectful way.

"This is just an observation, but I noticed something," Simon says. "You made it a point to mention that nothing's happened between you and Gretchen unprompted. And you said Gretchen's name and not your fiancée's when I asked you to explain the situation."

That's exactly what I was thinking too.

"Maybe that comes off a bit harsh," Simon says. "But

why is it that you jump to defend your friendship and not try to see your fiancée's point of view?"

Derek shrugs. "I don't know. Probably because I don't find jealousy attractive."

"What makes you think that Holly is jealous of Gretchen?" Simon asks.

"Well, for starters, Holly hates it whenever I go to dinner with Gretchen. But we work in the same industry. It's only natural that I'd want to meet up with a friend who knows what I'm talking about when I want to vent about my day. She hates how often I text her too, but she has no problem when I text my male friends. She thinks we're too flirty with each other for some reason. But that's just how Gretchen is around me. And sometimes when we meet up, I've given her my jacket if she gets cold. I guess that drives Holly nuts because sometimes I'll forget to ask for my jacket back and Gretchen will wear it until we meet up again. I still don't get that one at all."

The scoff I let out is a reflex to Derek's outright cluelessness. He's being so callous and insensitive.

Almost everyone in the room turns to face me, including Simon. My face ignites.

"Yes?" Simon asks. His tone is that stern, professional one he employs during his seminars. But his mouth is curved upward, like a smile is begging to take hold of his lips. The look in his eyes reads amused.

"Sorry. I'll be quiet."

"Aren't you supposed to film in the corner and not say anything?" Derek says.

If his tone were less indignant, I'd let his comment go. But that combined with his jealousy remark makes me not the least bit interested in acquiescing to him in any way.

"I only speak up when someone is being exceptionally clueless," I say, standing up. "Or a jerk."

Derek's brow flies up, as does Simon's.

It takes a few seconds for Derek to rein in his shock at my words. "Well, good thing you're not the one who's running this seminar, then."

He starts to turn back to Simon, but no way in hell am I letting go. Even though I'm not the one running this seminar, I'm a woman—and right now, Derek could use a verbal smackdown from a woman.

"Actually." I practically bark out the word as I step away from the camera and walk toward Simon. "I think I might have some helpful insight into this situation." I direct my gaze to Simon. "I'm not a relationship guru, but I've had a similar experience in the past. May I?"

Biting back a smile, Simon nods his head for me to continue.

I turn back to Derek. "Does your fiancée have any close male friends?"

He huffs out a frustrated sigh. "Yeah."

"Does she do the same kinds of things with them like you do with Gretchen? Does she go out to dinner with them regularly and text them at all hours of the day and night? Does she wear their clothes?"

Derek swallows. "I don't know."

"You don't know if your fiancée wears another man's clothes?"

He glares at me. "I don't think so."

"Would you like that? If she started hanging out with, oh. I don't know. Let's say Simon." I point to him. "If you knew that Simon was sending your fiancée flirty texts in the middle of the night, if you knew that Simon was taking her out to dinner—if you knew that she was going about her day, going to work, walking around in your house, spending time with you while wearing Simon's clothes. If you had to witness day after day as Simon employed all these low-key plays for your fiancée, how would that make you feel?"

"Um well, I guess I would..." Derek's face twists, like he's just swallowed something rancid. "That's different."

"Is it?" The rapid-fire rhythm of my questions and comments seems to catch him off guard. "Why is that different? Is it because *you're* the one having your feelings hurt in that scenario?"

When he says nothing, I keep going. "Or is it because it's okay for you to disregard and disrespect your fiancée's feelings, but it's not okay for her to do the same to you? Because if that's the case, Derek, I have to tell you, that is all sorts of screwed up."

Again he gives me nothing in response.

"Here's the thing. In addition to this crappy double standard you're employing in your relationship, your best friend is part of it too. Yeah, Gretchen may be your buddy and workmate and whatever else, but if she's being as flirty as Holly says she is, she's undermining your relationship with your fiancée. And she knows it."

Murmurs echo around me.

"Now, you say that nothing has ever happened between you two. I'm going to assume you're not lying, so I'll take your word for it. But if nothing has truly happened between you two, then Gretchen has been carrying a torch for you for years, it sounds like. She likes you, Derek. She likes hanging out with you, flirting with you, getting any bit of time you care to toss her way. Because she has a crush on you and is hoping that someday, you'll come to your senses and finally ask her out. And it sounds like you're either utterly clueless to it—and if that's the case, start forcing yourself to pay attention to the world around you because, my god, there is nothing more annoying than a grown man who has no awareness for himself or the world around him."

I raise my hand, pointing a finger to the air. "Or— and this is what my money's on—it sounds like you're the kind of guy who likes keeping a flirty female friend around for the ego boost. Every time Gretchen texts you or compliments you or goes out of her way to hang out with you, it's a pathetic little bump to your ego. It's so obvious. And I can guarantee your fiancée sees it too. And I can also guarantee that it kills her to see the man she loves disrespect her in this way."

When I finish speaking, I realize just how fast my heart is beating. I have to remind myself to breathe so I don't start panting.

There's a low whistle in the back. Someone in the front few rows says, "She's good."

Derek's expression is dazed mixed with embarrassment. Either he truly didn't realize any of this or he didn't think I would call him out in such a public way. Little did he know.

"And you know what? If your fiancée were here right now, I'd tell her to break up with you. Yeah, that's probably not what Simon would advise because he's a therapist and would likely recommend that you two at least consider counseling. And you should probably go to individual counseling too to figure out the root cause of why you keep engaging in behavior that hurts your fiancée's feelings even though she's asked you multiple times not to. But I honestly think she's put up with enough. She deserves better."

Nothing but silence meets my final words. With the adrenaline still pumping through me, I spin back around to my position in the corner, avoiding eye contact with everyone around me. I probably took it too far. But screw it. I've reached my limit when it comes to dealing with obnoxious behavior from men, no matter how oblivious or well-meaning. I've had to deal with Simon's overprotective alpha bodyguard act from the other week. I've had to deal with Landon's days-long radio silence. And I've had to listen to Derek act like it's no big deal that he openly and knowingly hurts his fiancée's feelings. I'm officially done.

Just then there's applause. I jerk my head up and see everyone clapping around me. I'm in shock as I take it all in. I catch Derek lowering back into his seat, a contrite look on his face.

The applause dies down, and Simon speaks. "Did you catch all that, Derek?"

His only response is silent nodding.

Simon turns back to me. "Thank you for that insight, Naomi. It was eye-opening to say the least."

I offer a flustered smile as a guy in construction gear sitting in the row in front of me twists around to offer me a thumbs-up.

"That was badass," construction guy says.

"Thanks," I say softly, still thoroughly flustered at the positive reaction I just received from everyone in the room.

"You two should do a seminar together. You'd make a killing."

I let out a soft chuckle. "Maybe someday."

\* \* \*

"Gotta say. That footage of you ripping Derek a new asshole? That was otherworldly." Harper points her sandwich at me in approval before taking a bite as we sit at a deli in the Presidio neighborhood of the city.

I chuckle, almost choking on the fries I just shoved in my mouth. It's the day after the seminar. Harper and I just finished a hike along the Batteries to Bluffs trail and are treating ourselves to greasy sandwiches at her favorite dive deli. While waiting in line, she asked how work went yesterday, so I showed her a clip of the raw footage that I saved on my phone.

"I'm serious." Harper squirts a hefty amount of ketchup onto her own basket of fries. "The way you laid the smackdown on that guy was a whole new level of epic."

"That guy either isn't aware of or doesn't care how much he's hurting his fiancée's feelings. He's too busy enjoying the ego boost from his friend. And there's a slew of men out there just like him. No wonder Simon has made this a career. Crappy men are everywhere."

"You should put it in the next episode," Harper says. "People will go crazy for you."

I shake my head, then gulp from my water glass. "No way. This series is about Simon, not me."

"You were in his interview episodes. And the strip club episode."

"Those are totally different. Of course I'd be in the interview episodes—I was the one asking him questions. And I was in the strip club scene for just a bit to help with the setup and when I asked him interview questions. I'm meant to observe and document the subject. I'm never supposed to make it about me. And that clip I sent you of me going off on Derek was definitely all me, not Simon. There's no reason it should be in the show. I just showed it to you because I know you love it when a jerk gets told off."

Harper shakes her head, clearly tired of listening to me. "Speaking of Simon, I still can't believe you've been working together for over two months and you haven't once fooled around with him."

I take a gigantic bite of my sandwich, hoping that Harper doesn't notice how red I'm turning at the thought of what almost went down between Simon and me during the couples' retreat in Tahoe.

I wait the several seconds it takes for me to clear that huge bite of food before I look up at Harper. When I do, she's frowning at me, clearly suspicious.

"Spill," she says.

"There's nothing to spill."

"Bullshit. You're as red as a beet. Did something happen between you two?"

Throwing my head back, I let out a groan. "Of course not." I sigh, realizing that I can't lie to Harper to save my life. "At least not in the way you think," I finally admit.

Her eyes go wide just as a giddy smile spreads across her full face. "Tell me!"

I give her a quickened version of how Simon walked in on me mid-orgasm in the bathtub and how I invited him to join me right before everyone barged into the house. Her eyes are bulging when I finish.

"Shit," she whispers, a dazed look on her face. "That's just…whoa."

I shake my head and wave my hand, like I'm brushing away that memory. "It's fine. We've moved past it."

I ignore the way she narrows an eye at me.

"Did you tell Landon?" she asks.

"Of course not. It happened before we even met. And it's not like we're official. We don't owe each other that kind of honesty," I say. "Plus, could you imagine how awkward that would make things between him and Simon? They're already not fans of each other."

"So you're liking Landon still?"

"It's going well so far."

He's amped things up and is sending flirty texts more often, much to my pleasant surprise.

"Landon aside, you must have given Simon some excellent spank bank material." She slurps the rest of her Diet Coke, then consolidates the trash from her empty basket with mine.

"God, Harper."

She raises an eyebrow. It's a look that silently conveys the phrase "you can't be serious."

We dump our trash in a wastebasket by the door, snake around the crazy-long line at the register, then make our way back outside and walk in the direction of Nob Hill.

"Naomi, Simon walked in on you. In the bathtub. Naked. And wet. I can promise you that image has been burned into his brain and he's fantasized about you. Multiple times."

We walk along the busy sidewalks in silence as I let what she's said soak into my brain. When we stop at a stoplight, I turn to her.

"That's ridiculous. He's dating someone right now. That incident we had is probably the last thing on his mind."

"If he's seeing someone now, okay fine. But before then, no doubt he thought of you. I remember the way he looked at you that night you two first met."

The crosswalk signal flashes and we cross the street

along with a horde of other pedestrians and make our way through the Marina District.

"I'll admit. There was a spark between us. It was definitely on fire when he walked in on me and we almost…you know. And I still think of him as an attractive and sweet guy. If we weren't working together maybe something would have happened between us."

My heart skids as I say it, catching me off guard. It sounded perfectly logical and harmless in my head. But to say it out loud conjures up something inside of me. The start of a shiver slides through my body…

When I realize just how long I've been quietly thinking about this, I look up at Harper. She wags an eyebrow at me. Clearly she noticed. I shove her lightly.

"But we talked about all of this," I say with renewed focus. "Simon agreed that in the end, it was good that we were interrupted because we're work colleagues now and it's not the smartest thing in the world to sleep with the person you're working with on a day-to-day basis. Things could get messy. And my job—this series—means more to me than a hookup."

When we stop at another stoplight, I notice Harper is suspiciously quiet. Normally she has a lot to say when it comes to my personal life.

"How's work going for you?" I ask, eager to change the subject.

"Crappy. I have to stop by the office later today, actually."

"It's Saturday."

She shrugs. "Duty calls."

Harper's eyes glaze over as we cross another city block. My mind flashes back to that night we shared sheet masks and prosecco at her place and she opened up about her doubts concerning her job.

"Is everything okay?" I ask.

Keeping her gaze ahead, she opens her mouth, but then quickly closes it. She shakes her head. "I don't really want to talk about it honestly."

We continue walking in the direction of her apartment. After a minute of silence, she finally speaks.

"You know when we stopped to take in the view during our hike this morning?"

I tell her yes as I recall the sweeping view of the Pacific Ocean as the chilly bay breeze whips around us. The sight of the deep blue water and endless bluffs jutting from the bay always makes me pause in awe. Even as crowded as the Batteries to Bluffs trail always gets—even as congested as San Francisco feels every single day—that killer view reminds me of what's out there. Vastness and beauty unbounding.

Harper's gaze falls to the ground. "Sometimes I wish I could say screw it and move to a place where I could have a view like that all the time instead of the inside of my office."

"You can do that, Harper."

"Right. Like, I just snap my fingers and it happens."

"Well, yeah. It's not like you have to answer to anyone but yourself. You can do whatever you want."

"Wrong. I have to answer to my job. And my boss."

"You've spent enough time, enough years working your ass off for them. You can take some time off or travel or try something completely different if what you're doing now isn't what you want anymore."

I stop her with a hand on her arm and move to the side so we don't block the sidewalk. "Look, I know

I've been really self-involved lately about work and I haven't done the best job of checking up on you and asking how you're really doing. I'm sorry for that. It seems like you're going through something right now. It's fine that you don't want to talk about it, I get it. But it seems like you want to make a change. And I think you should if that's what you want."

When she twists her head to look at me, I expect a cynical quip or complete dismissal of my idea. Harper has been a straightlaced hard worker her whole life. She's never once done anything that she hasn't spent days or weeks or months meticulously planning. But judging by the look in her deep brown eyes, I think my words are hitting home.

"You deserve to be happy," I say.

A small smile tugs at her lips. "Thanks, Naomi."

I stop and grab her hand. "Blow off work. Come with me tonight."

I tell her Simon's friends are hosting a party at a bar for him in Russian Hill to celebrate the success of *Simply Simon*. He invited me and told me to bring whoever I wanted.

Harper frowns slightly, but then purses her lips as she looks off to the side. Normally there's no convincing her otherwise when she's busy at work. But by the look on her face, she's actually considering ditching work and coming with me tonight. That's huge.

"You deserve a break, Harper. Come on."

She sighs, then smiles. There's a sparkle behind her eyes that heartens me immediately.

"Okay," Harper says. "I'll come. But only for a little while. One drink, then I'm headed home."

I beam at her and squeeze her hand. "Yay! We're gonna have the best time, promise."

## Chapter Fourteen

Harper and I take a rideshare to Simon's party at Robberbaron on Polk Street. Landon texts me that he's running late but will meet me there. When we enter the long and narrow space, I do a scan of the crowd to see if I can spot Simon and his crew. The dark paint on the walls combined with the mahogany wood fixtures, black décor, and mood lighting make it difficult to see at first. But then I spot him waving to me from the back of the bar. I smile back at him, then point him out to Harper.

He jumps up from the long table where he's seated along with a dozen other people.

"You made it." He beams at us as he pulls Harper into a hug, then me.

"I hope it's okay that Landon is coming too."

Simon's smile remains easy and relaxed. "Yeah, of course. Oh hey, my mom wanted me to ask you what colors look best on camera for when you film us in Napa. She's obsessing over what to wear."

"Your mom is the cutest. I can send you outfit ideas to show her if you want."

"She'd love that."

He introduces us to his friends. Most are other therapists and grad school classmates. A couple start to stand and offer us their barstools, but both Harper and I politely decline. Harper heads to the bar for a drink just as a familiar-looking tall and leggy blonde in a form-fitting dress, jacket, and heels slinks up to Simon.

He greets her with an arm around her waist and a kiss on the check. When she beams back at him, I realize it's the Margot Robbie look-alike from Lake Tahoe.

"Oh. Hey!" I nearly call her Margot, but I bite my tongue. That's not her actual name.

She flashes a dazzling smile at me and shakes my hand. "I'm Desiree."

I introduce myself and then Harper when she returns with a bourbon for herself and a glass of club soda with ice for me.

"So! You're the one who's responsible for making Simon the most famous therapist in the Bay Area," Desiree says as she wags an eyebrow at him. He shakes his head, smiling.

"He's a huge hit," I say. "The most successful online series Dash has ever had."

A few of Simon's friends whistle and cheer, which promptly causes Simon to roll his eyes.

Someone at the table calls for Simon and he steps away. Desiree leans toward me, her voice low. "I hope there aren't any hard feelings."

"Oh, um. About what?"

Her blue eyes sparkle as she looks at me. "When I slipped him my number in Tahoe, I mean. When Simon called me, he mentioned you two were friends and worked together, but I just wanted to make sure. A guy like Simon probably has women all over him. I'm sure some of his female friends have heart eyes for him and he doesn't even realize it."

"Oh. I mean, I don't really know. We've only been friends for a couple of months—ever since we started working together on the series."

"Right." She says it pointedly with unflinching eye contact. "So there's nothing between you two?"

I'm taken aback at how direct she's being. But maybe that's her personality. And part of me admires her communication style. Some people wouldn't be bold enough to address an issue like this head-on and instead quietly keep it to themselves as it festers within them.

I smile at Desiree, hoping that it looks genuine. "Simon and I are just friends. Truly. I'm actually seeing someone right now."

Relief paints Desiree's smile. I feel a warm hand around my waist. I twist my head and see Landon standing off to the side.

"Hey." He leans down to kiss my cheek.

"Hey." I introduce him to Desiree and everyone at the table. Simon's at the far end near the wall, chatting to one of his friends. He gives Landon a wave and goes right back to his conversation.

I look to the side for Harper, but she's gone. I turn and notice her chatting with a cute blond guy at a nearby table. He elbows his friend sitting next to him, who then stands up so Harper can take his chair. Her shoulders shake as she laughs at something the guy says. I smile, happy that she seems to be enjoying herself.

Landon heads to the bar for a drink. A second later a few people stand up from Simon's table and grab their jackets.

"Let's sit. My feet are killing me," Desiree says.

I follow her to the far end of the table. When I catch eyes with Landon as he makes his way back over from the bar, I gesture for him to take the empty chair next to me. Desiree sits down and Simon scoots a chair between the two of us.

"Having fun?" he asks me.

"A blast. It's very cool to see all your friends out and supporting you."

A guy sitting next to Desiree holds up his beer glass. "A toast to Simon. We're thrilled for your success, man. Now I can tell everyone I'm friends with a celebrity."

"Dude, how many times do I have to tell you?" Simon groan-laughs. "I'm not even close to famous."

The entire table ignores him, breaking into cheers. We all raise our glasses and clink them together. I glance over at Landon and see that he's frowning at his phone, still holding his glass of whiskey up long after everyone has taken a sip. I nudge him and he looks up.

"Huh? Oh," he says, the look on his face dazed.

He glances back down at his phone and takes a sip. I swallow back the annoyed sigh I want to let loose. I shouldn't be so bothered. He and Simon are sitting at the same table and being civil to each other—even if they're not acknowledging each other much. At least they're not staring daggers and exchanging passive-aggressive comments.

Desiree squeezes Simon's knee, gazing at him as he looks down at the ground, still blushing from all the attention.

"So. What do you two have planned for tomorrow?" I ask.

Desiree says they're headed to brunch at a restaurant in Jackson Square. "It's my mom and my dad's favorite place."

Simon looks at me. "Speaking of moms, guess who called me this morning?"

"Wait, my mom called you? How did she get your number?"

"I think she watched one of the *Simply Simon* episodes and saw my office info that Dash listed at the end."

"Wow. She's smooth."

"She wanted to thank me for helping her figure out how to glue your dad's vase back together. She said he loved it. He even teared up a bit when he saw it."

"That's my dad. One big mush."

"Like father, like daughter."

I lightly shove Simon's shoulder. "Oh my gosh, I haven't cried in front of you."

"Except when you eat ravioli."

I laugh at the smug look on his face.

"Okay, first of all, I did not tear up while eating your grandma's ravioli. I did stop mid-bite, close my eyes, and say, 'oh my lord.' I was overcome with emotion—it was the most incredible homemade ravioli ever. But I absolutely did not cry."

He pivots his smug expression to me once more. "Sure, sure. Keep telling yourself that."

I jokingly place my hand at the base of Simon's neck and squeeze gently like I'm going to strangle him, even though there's zero threat of danger. There's no way I could inflict any sort of lasting damage to Simon's thick neck with my hand.

"You're asking for it," I tease.

He leans toward me. "I'm asking for what exactly?"

The gleam in his eyes catches me off guard. So does the heat under my palm. His skin suddenly feels like fire.

It takes me a second, but I eventually recognize that look in his eyes. It's the same exact look he gave me while standing over me as I lay naked in that tub in Lake Tahoe, right after he nodded yes when I suggested he join me.

The sound of Landon sharply clearing his throat yanks me back to the present. I jerk my hand away from Simon's neck and to my lap, then guzzle the rest of my club soda.

"What the hell was that?" Landon mutters in my ear.

I don't answer him. I'm too focused on the expression on Desiree's face. Her perfectly sculpted eyebrows are right under her hairline as her gaze darts between Simon and me.

Clearly she's bothered by the way Simon and I were interacting with each other just now.

"Just friends, huh? That's pretty handsy for just friends." She scoffs and turns to Simon. "How do you know Naomi's mom? And when did you introduce her to your grandma? You haven't even introduced me to your grandma. Or your mom."

Simon looks at her, a tinge of guilt in his otherwise neutral expression. His face is red again, but I suspect for a totally different reason this time.

"My mom called me when we were working together one day, Naomi happened to be there, and she insisted she come over for dinner. That's all it was. She's like that with all my friends."

Desiree stabs her straw into her glass, which is mostly ice now. "Uh-huh. Sure."

"I'm sorry, Desiree," Simon says gently. "We've only been out on a handful of dates so far, and I honestly didn't think you'd be interested in meeting my family this soon."

"Oh, but you'll introduce your new female friend to them without a second thought." She slams her glass down, which causes the people at our end of the table to look over. "If you're bringing your female friend over to your mom and grandma's, it's a no-brainer that you should do the same with the woman you're dating. I can't believe you."

I contemplate getting up and walking away to give them privacy to talk. But before I can even move, Desiree darts to the back of the restaurant. Simon follows her.

"Are you gonna answer my question now?"

I whip my head to Landon. "What?"

"What is going on with you two?"

I press my hand to my forehead, tension building in my skull. "What are you talking about?"

"Desiree was right. You were getting pretty handsy with Simon."

"Landon, you know there's nothing between Simon and me." I dig through my purse for an aspirin.

"Do I?"

His indignant tone sets me off. "Yes. You *do* know, Landon. Because I've told you before, Simon and I are just friends. We just work together. Why are you acting like this?"

I try to keep my voice down so that Simon's friends at the table with us can't hear. Luckily the dull roar of conversation from earlier is now louder and judging by how everyone is turned away from us, engaged in their own conversations, they're not paying attention to Landon and me bickering.

"Maybe because you thought it was totally appropriate to grab his neck like you were trying to come on to him."

Landon's accusatory tone is the last straw. "Are you serious right now? I wasn't coming on to Simon. Okay yeah, we were joking around and I grabbed his neck because I thought it would be funny, but I didn't mean anything by it. I'm sorry that it bothered you. You're right, it probably wasn't the most appropriate thing to do, but I sure as hell wasn't coming on to him. Do you really think I would do that? In front of you? In front of Desiree? In front of everyone at this bar?"

When he says nothing, I walk from the table to the bar, but his hand on my arm halts me.

I start to jerk away until I see his regretful expression. "Hey, wait, okay? Please."

We stand facing each other, off to the side of the bar to avoid getting in anyone's way.

"You're right, I shouldn't have accused you of coming on to Simon," Landon says. "I just…it was weird to see you touch him."

I swallow. "I get it. I'm sorry. But I really didn't mean anything by it. We were just joking around. I won't do it again."

My stomach starts to churn. I'm genuinely sorry for hurting Landon's feelings, but I hate how placating I sound. This thing with him is supposed to be carefree and fun.

He sighs and tugs a hand through his hair. "Look, I have to run. Work emergency."

"On a weekend?"

"Yeah. I'll text you later, okay?"

He leans down and gives my cheek a quick kiss. I watch as he weaves his way through the crowd to the entrance.

I sigh, my head suddenly feeling as heavy as an anvil. Then I look for Harper. She's still at the same table, chatting with the handsome blond guy.

I don't want to interrupt her, so I head to the bathroom. A splash of cold water to my face is what I need right now after two train wreck conversations in a row.

I turn the corner for the women's restroom and stop when I see Simon leaning against the wall next to the door, shoulders hunched, his hands in his pockets.

"Hey," I say quietly.

He straightens to his full height when he sees me. "Oh. Hi."

"Everything okay?"

"Um, not really." His gaze falls to the floor.

"I'm sorry for upsetting Desiree."

"It's not your fault." He sounds so detached, it's unnerving.

"I shouldn't have grabbed your neck."

His brow immediately furrows as soon as I say it. "Probably wasn't the smartest thing in the world to do."

Even though it's true, his words still sting.

I swallow. "I can apologize to her if you think that would help."

He hesitates, then looks at the door. "I honestly don't think it would, Naomi. It would probably make things worse. She's really upset right now."

For a few seconds I just stand there. I can't think of anything else to say. "I'm sorry I ruined your night."

He clenches his jaw, then glances at the door to the

women's bathroom again. "Look, I know how awful this is gonna sound, but…she's in there cooling off. And if she sees you here when she comes out…"

I catch his drift instantly. My eyes burn and my throat tightens. Yes, I crossed a line when I put my hand on Simon while we were joking with each other. Yes, I deserve to be called out, and I deserve to leave. It still hurts, though.

"Got it. I'll take off."

I turn around, thankful that I was able to keep my voice steady when I spoke. Simon calls after me as I walk away, but I ignore it.

It's slow-going moving through the crowd once more, but it gives me time to collect myself, to take several calming breaths so I don't burst into tears.

"Naomi."

I turn and see Harper walking back from the bar, a drink in each hand.

"Everything okay?"

I force a smile. I don't want to put a damper on the fun time she's having by telling her how badly I just screwed up, how I ruined the night for Simon and Desiree and Landon.

"Yeah, all good. I'm gonna head home. Are you staying longer?"

"I was planning to." She looks over at the handsome blond guy a few tables away. He grins at her. "But I can come back with you if you want."

Her gaze is searching as she looks at me. She knows something's up, even when I don't say anything—she always does.

But there's no way I'm ruining her night too.

I reach over and give her arm a squeeze and put on

my best game face. "No way you're leaving, not when you've got a hottie like that to chat up. Have fun."

And then I dart as fast I can out of the bar. Once I'm walking along the sidewalk, my phone goes off. It's a text from Simon.

I'm sorry.

I ignore it as I pull up the rideshare app on my phone and wait for my car to come, trying my hardest not to cry.

## Chapter Fifteen

I'm posted at my regular spot near the wall with my camera set up for Simon's seminar today. He walks up to me, his eyes glued to his phone.

"About ready?" he asks.

"Yup."

He turns around, heads to the front, then greets the crowd. That short exchange is similar to all of our conversations this past week ever since that night at Robberbaron when things went south between us.

The fact that things are tense between us makes me a weird sort of sad. Yes, I've had arguments with friends in the past. They've often taken days or even weeks to sort out.

But this new rift with Simon feels different. So much of our lives have been intertwined with each other for the past two months. Simon has become one of my favorite people to talk to, spend time with, to joke with, to eat with.

But it's clear he's not interested in going back to what we used to be.

I close my eyes and sigh. My head spins as I think about working together these next handful of weeks. All the seminars and one-on-one interviews I still have to film with him, the shoot in Napa with his family. It's all sure to be awkward as hell.

My overwhelmed brain jumps to Landon. It's clear that he's done with me too. He never texted or called the next day like he said he would. It's an especially lonely feeling, losing a friend and the guy I was seeing at the same time.

I shift my focus back to filming today's session. Simon leads the seminar with his trademark confidence and ease, speaking with authority but without arrogance.

Someone raises his hand to ask a question. I can't see him from where I'm sitting, but when he asks about how to get his girlfriend to trust him more and stop accusing him of lying and cheating, my ears perk up. His voice sounds familiar.

"Why do you think she accuses you of lying and cheating so much?" Simon asks.

"Dude, I don't know." This guy's curt tone sounds vaguely familiar.

"You have to have some sort of inkling," Simon presses.

"Probably because of the way we started."

"And how did you two start?"

A sigh rockets from the guy, who I still can't see. "There was some…overlap… I guess you could say, between my last relationship and her."

"So you cheated with your current partner?"

"Jeez, way to sound judgmental."

"I'm not trying to sound judgmental," Simon says, a slight strain in his tone. "I'm trying to get the truth of the situation. It's the only way I can help, if you're open and honest with me."

"Fine. Technically I was still with my ex when we started up. It took some months before I was able to end things with my ex and fully commit to the relationship with my current girlfriend. But I don't see how that's relevant to our argument problem. I love her. I'm loyal to her. I don't see why you want to bring all that up."

Inside I'm starting to stew. This guy sounds unreasonably defensive given his history of lying and cheating.

"Look, you don't have to be here. No one's forcing you," Simon says. "But you need to come at this from a different angle if you want things to improve between you and your girlfriend. You can't approach a situation like this feeling defensive. You cheated on your previous girlfriend. And as a result, you now have this undercurrent of distrust in your current relationship. You need to truly understand that and take responsibility for it. There's no way to improve things in your current relationship if you refuse to do that."

My heart pounds. Jesus, this guy. To do something so hurtful and refuse to even see it.

I straighten up to get a better look at the guy Simon's addressing, but I can barely see the top of his head.

"It's just… I know we didn't have the cleanest start," the guy says, his tone dialed down. "But we just found out she's pregnant. And I don't want to fight like this in front of our child. I want to be in a good place for our baby."

"Okay, that makes sense. That's a wonderful reason to be here today—to create a healthier environment for your child," Simon says. "Part of that is trying to understand where your girlfriend is coming from. She was the one you were seeing in secret while you were in a relationship with someone else. Can you at least acknowledge her feelings of concern regarding that?"

"Yeah, I guess so," the guy mutters.

"It doesn't mean you're an evil person. It just means you have an issue to work through."

"Okay, yeah, fine. I get that."

"Have you two considered seeing a therapist to-gether?"

I straighten up as far as I can reach and finally get a look at the guy and instantly freeze.

It's Brody. My ex.

I fall back in my chair, coughing through a breath. My hearing goes fuzzy and I can't process anything else that happens for the rest of the seminar other than this: my cheating ex is going to be a dad.

The seminar ends and I shut off the camera. I quickly pack up my gear while everyone mills around.

I do my best to stay out of sight—I don't want to risk Brody spotting me.

I wait a couple of minutes, then sling my camera bag over my shoulder, grab my purse, and scurry along the back wall of the room. I pull out my phone and dial Harper, hoping that if I'm in the middle of a phone conversation, Brody won't bother me even if he does spot me. But when she doesn't answer, I swallow back a groan. Instead I text her, hoping that staring at my phone will deter him from coming up to me.

OMFG CALL ME AS SOON AS YOU CAN YOU WON'T BELIEVE WHO I JUST SAW

I'm nearly to the door when I hear my name.

Spinning around, I see Brody, his eyes wide and his mouth half-open.

"I thought that was you," he says, clearly in disbelief. He tugs a hand through his shaggy dark hair. "What are you doing here?"

Gripping onto the strap of my camera bag, I take a breath and contemplate offering him a polite smile, but my mouth twitches with the effort. And then my nerve catches up with me. I don't have to explain myself to Brody, not with the way things ended between us.

"I could ask you the same question," I say, my tone teetering on the edge of hard.

He frowns and tugs on the bottom of his shirt, the fair skin on his face flushing pink.

"Yeah, well. Trying to be a better man, I suppose," he mumbles.

For a second we stand and stare at each other. Harper's words echo in my mind the longer I look at Brody.

*You weren't right for each other in the first place.*

I let out a sigh. There's no use in being bitter anymore. The least I could do is try to make this interaction between us courteous.

"I'm filming a series about Simon for work," I finally say.

"Oh. Nice." The tight expression on Brody's face eases. He's probably relieved that I'm choosing to have a polite conversation instead of ripping into him.

He hunches his shoulders. "Look, I'm sorry for the way things ended between us."

I bite my tongue to keep from saying, "I don't want to hear your shitty excuse for an apology." Even though it's deserved, it wouldn't make things better right now. And despite how he hurt me, I sincerely hope that he and his girlfriend work through whatever issues they have so they can provide a stable environment for their baby. It's sad to think of a child growing up with parents arguing all the time.

His phone buzzes, interrupting us. His eyes go wide as he looks at the screen. "Shit."

"What is it?" I ask.

"Laura's water just broke."

"Oh my god…isn't that kind of soon? I mean, if she just found out she's pregnant and we broke up, like, not even three months ago…"

Brody's face twists. And then it dawns on me. Laura didn't just find out she was pregnant, like he said. He lied about that part—probably to make himself sound less like a dickbag. His current girlfriend must be toward the end of her pregnancy to be going into labor… which means that she was well into her pregnancy when he was still in a relationship with me.

My chest cracks in half at the realization. Not because I'm heartbroken at losing Brody—but because he didn't have the decency to end things with me when he should have. Because he strung me along for months while at the same time seeing a woman who was pregnant with his child. There I was, coasting in our relationship, clueless about the horrible secret my partner was keeping from me.

"Naomi, I'm so sorry—"

I hold up a hand. "Shut the hell up."

Brody's eyes dart around the room, probably because my shrill tone has caught the attention of the people around us.

His phone buzzes again. He frowns at his phone screen. "I really need to go."

"Then go," I say, my voice breaking.

He stumbles back a few steps, then turns to sprint out of the room.

Someone comes up behind me and gently puts their hand on my arm.

"Naomi." Simon's calm, soothing voice sounds behind me. "What's the matter? What happened?"

He spins me around, his golden brown eyes bright with concern. All that dismissiveness that has riddled our every interaction this past week has evaporated. The kindness in his tone, the worry in his eyes, the gentle way he holds my arms shows me that he's there for me—he's my friend again.

I open my mouth, but all that comes out is a cry. All I can do is shake my head.

Simon grabs my camera bag and slings it over his shoulder. Then he wraps his free arm around me, leading me out of the room. "Let's go sit down somewhere, okay?"

I stumble with him, grateful for his support.

Under the dim overhead lighting, my glass of bourbon on the rocks shines. Looking up at Simon, I take in his expression. His forehead is wrinkled to high heaven and he hasn't blinked since I told him about what Brody did.

"That's just…holy fucking shit," he mutters before downing the last of his Scotch. He signals the waiter at the hotel bar and asks for another.

"My thoughts exactly," I mumble before taking a drink from my glass. I wince at the burn.

Simon frowns at me in concern. "You sure you don't want something lighter?"

I narrow my gaze at him. "I just found out my ex

got another woman pregnant while we were together. You're lucky I'm not downing moonshine right now."

He nods his understanding. And then he reaches over and pats my arm with his hand. "I'm so, so sorry, Naomi."

"Me too," I say quietly. "Brody and I weren't going to go the distance. I knew that. I just wish he would have ended things if he was so unhappy. I hate… I hate thinking that the end of our relationship was so incredibly fucked up. And I had no clue. Maybe if I had paid more attention…"

"Hey. Don't for one second feel bad about any of this. None of this has anything to do with you. Brody is apparently the kind of guy who could lie to his partner while having a secret pregnant girlfriend on the side. That's one thousand percent his fault—those are his own issues that led to this. Absolutely none of it has anything to do with you. Do you understand?"

There's a new sort of conviction in Simon's voice when he speaks. It's in his stare too. It's like he cares so much about me and my feelings in this moment and he's trying with everything inside of him to get me to believe him.

And just like that, my head stops swirling. I stop doubting myself. I believe every word he says.

I let a small smile slip. "Thanks." But then another awful thought crashes into my head. "Fuck. I'm going to have to get an STD test. If he was brash enough to do that to me, who knows what else he got up to."

Simon's face falls. He gives my arm another soft squeeze. "It'll all be fine. I promise."

He moves his hand from my arm, then squeezes my hand. It's the perfect calm and comforting move.

"Brody won't be welcome in any of my seminars anymore."

"Simon, you don't have to do that."

"Yes, I do. He needs to see a therapist one-on-one. I'll even give him a referral to a few. He has some serious personal issues that need immediate addressing if he's capable of such a huge, long-term betrayal. And you shouldn't have to see him ever again, least of all in my seminars when you're trying to do your job."

My chest squeezes the tiniest bit. Yeah, it's probably ridiculous, but it feels good to know that Simon's loyalty for me runs deep enough that he would reject a paying client just for my sake.

"I just… I can't believe what a shitshow my personal life has been. I'm such a lost cause when it comes to dating and relationships. Clearly." I try to laugh it off, but it sounds like a strangled cry.

The area right under my eyes burns. Quickly, I blink. That burn is like a subtle warning for me to get my shit together or get ready for an onslaught of embarrassing, unwelcome tears. And I definitely don't want to break down in a hotel lounge full of people.

I clamp my mouth shut, and for a while we say nothing. I peer around the room, my head hazy from the nearly full glass of bourbon I've ingested. I fixate on his hand over mine. Such a tiny gesture, but it means so much right now. I let out a small sigh.

"Naomi."

"What?" I'm barely able to mutter. I'm so done with talking, with thinking, with feeling like utter garbage.

"Look at me."

I take another sip, slam my glass back down on the table, and finally force my eyes to meet his. He gazes at me with an intensity so raw, I can barely keep eye contact with him. But at the same time, I don't want to look away. There's something behind his stare that's magnetic, that makes me want to gaze at him forever.

"Listen." When he pauses, he leans across the table, as if he's trying to underscore his words with his body language. "Brody made the decision to betray your trust, and that's what led to the end of your relationship. It's not because you're cursed or bad at dating."

Slowly, Simon slides his hand down my arm, resting it gently over my fingers. As good as this feels, it's on the edge of too intimate and it shouldn't be, not when Simon is seeing Desiree. I slowly pull my hand from his. He frowns like he's confused.

"We probably shouldn't be touching," I say quietly. "It's disrespectful to Desiree, and I don't want to hurt her feelings again."

He leans back in his chair. "We're not together anymore."

"Shit, I'm sorry. I didn't realize—"

"It's okay." He looks off to the side before looking at me. "We ended things a couple days ago."

"Oh."

We share a few silent seconds of staring at our drink glasses.

"She wanted to move a lot faster than I was ready to," Simon says.

"I'm still sorry."

He flashes a sad smile. "Thanks." Then he purses his lips and his brows wrinkle as he focuses on me. "Look, I know… I know you think I'm just saying this because I'm your friend. But even if you were a total stranger who spilled your story to me, I'd say the exact same thing. Brody is a jerk. You're a million times better off without him."

His words, the conviction in his tone, the way he holds me, it all soothes me. Like I'm being tucked under a warm, fuzzy blanket. I take a moment to clear my throat so I'm certain my voice won't crack when I speak.

"It's just…sometimes it's easier to think that I did something wrong, you know? Because if I believe that, that means there's something I can improve in myself—something I can change and control." My throat tightens as I speak this deep truth I haven't had the courage to say out loud until now.

He frowns at me, clearly confused at my phrasing.

"Because if I did everything right and I still ended up with a failed relationship, then that means there must be something fundamentally wrong with me. It means that no matter what I do or try, I'm still not good enough to have the one thing so many other people are able to have: a loving, lasting relationship."

And there it is, the one thing I've dreaded verbalizing for so long. My biggest insecurity.

Simon's frowning and vigorously shaking his head while giving my hand a squeeze. "That's not it at all, Naomi."

I shrug, letting out a joyless chuckle just as a tear finally breaks free. I quickly swipe it away. "Why do you think I've sworn off relationships, Simon? I've never made a single one work. I'm the common denominator."

"You've sworn off relationships because a lot of guys are unworthy asshats," he says without missing a beat.

This time when I chuckle, it's genuine. But tears still roll down my cheeks.

"Maybe," I mutter.

"Not maybe. It's true. I, of all people, would know. I spend most of my days with those asshats, trying to help them," Simon says.

Another laugh-like sound falls from my lips. I sniffle, then Simon yanks a napkin from the dispenser on the table and leans over to dab at my eyes. Such a small and simple act, but it has me warm all over with how attentive it is. I don't know if I've ever had a guy literally wipe my tears away before.

"I mean it, Naomi. You're incredible. Like, beyond incredible."

"I definitely don't feel incredible right now." When I blow my nose, it's so loud that the guy sitting at the table next to us side-eyes me. But then Simon glares at him, and he immediately looks away.

"You are, Naomi. You're smart, funny, kind, driven, beautiful, adorable, and so sexy."

*Sexy.*

My lips part. "Sexy?"

His eyes do that thing where they widen for a split second, but then he dials it back to a normal expression so quickly that I almost doubt I saw it in the first place. But I did. It happened. And it has my head spinning.

His jaw clenches. "Without a doubt. You're beyond sexy, Naomi."

He knocks back the rest of his drink, sets down the empty glass, then pats his hands on his knees. I assume he's going to stand up to excuse himself to the bathroom or outside for some air.

But he doesn't do either one of those things. He stays sitting and redirects his warm, intensive stare back at me.

"You are the sexiest woman I've ever seen. And

that's not just because of your beautiful face or your amazing body or any other smoking-hot physical trait you have. It's in the way you move, the way you talk, the way you look at me. Everything about you sets me off, Naomi. It always has."

"Oh…"

I trail off, leaning across the table. With each second that passes, I inch closer to him. It's not like this is a major feat. This corner table is practically microscopic. But even if it were a ten-person dining table, it wouldn't matter. There's something magnetic in our interaction tonight. I'm drawn to Simon in a deep, visceral way and my body will do whatever it needs to do to get as close as possible to him as soon as I can.

When our faces are just inches from each other, I stop. Simon leans in even closer. I part my lips, his breath hitting my skin. He's practically panting, and it makes every single nerve inside of me stand to attention.

There's a shift happening between us. It's so clear. I feel it everywhere—in my bones, in the blood rushing through me, in the goose bumps claiming my skin. This isn't just an instance of Simon my friend offering moral support. This is heat. This is passion. This is fire. This is—

My cell phone ringing jolts us. Landon is calling me.

"Sorry," I mutter to Simon.

He purses his lips, his expression taking on a hardened edge.

My head spinning, I answer. "Hey."

"Baaaabe," Landon yells into the phone.

I wince at the volume and hold my phone away from my ear.

"Babe, where are you right now?" he hollers.

In the background I hear shouting and music. He must be at a bar drinking everything in sight, judging by the way he sounds.

The muscles in my shoulders tense. Landon and I have definitely enjoyed our fair share of alcoholic beverages, but he always seemed to be the kind of guy who could responsibly gauge how much to drink and not let himself get too carried away. But maybe he was just displaying his good behavior to impress me.

"What's up, Landon?" I say through a sigh.

"How fast can you make it to my place?" he growls through the phone.

My head spins at how demanding his tone is. "Um, what? I don't know. I don't even know where you live. I've never been to your place. And what the hell, why are you calling me asking me to come over now all of a sudden? I haven't heard from you in a week."

He booms a laugh. When I glance at Simon, I catch him frowning at my conversation for a split second before he looks away and sips his water.

"Well, baby," Landon croons. "How about I text you my address and you come on over? I'd love to see your sexy ass tonight."

I bite my tongue at how he completely ignored my last question.

"I don't have the energy to deal with this right now. Why don't you just stay out and call me some other day? It's been a rough day for me, and I don't feel like doing anything."

"Damn." Landon lets out a low whistle. "Someone's moody."

I grit my teeth.

He burps, then lets out a sigh. "Okay, okay. I'm sorry. Tell me what happened."

"I found out today that my ex got another girl pregnant while he was still with me."

There's silence at first, but then I hear a hiccup, then a giggle.

"Are you fucking serious?" Landon asks before snorting a laugh. "Holy crap, that's some Jerry Springer-level drama right there."

He falls into another string of giggles and my jaw drops. "Fuck you."

"Oh come on, Naomi," Landon groans. "I'm just kidding. I've been a good boy so far, right? I've taken you to dinners and drinks. I've made out with you and not once pushed you. I deserve a little something more, don't you think? You must be aching for it by now," he slurs.

I clamp my mouth shut, gritting my teeth in anger. The pressure builds so much, I start to feel the beginnings of a tension headache in my temples.

"Never, ever call me again."

I hang up on him, shove my phone in my purse, and dart up from the table. Tears blur my vision as I struggle to untangle the strap of my purse from the back of my chair.

"Whoa." Simon holds up a hand, but I ignore him, instead punching my fist inside my purse to dig out cash to pay for my drink. I come up empty-handed and realize I don't have any cash. I'll have to wait and pay with a credit card.

I sniffle, tears dripping down my cheeks. "I can't... I need to get out of here."

Simon stands up and rests his hand on my shoulder. "It's okay. I've got it."

Even though I'm not looking at anything other than the ground, I know all eyes are on me, the weepy tipsy girl who tried to have a quiet phone conversation in the middle of this hotel lounge, but it devolved into pathetic shouting and crying for everyone to witness.

When I look up, Simon's eyes center me. He's not looking at me with pity or annoyance like everyone else is. All I can see in his stare is kindness, and it grounds me in this god-awful moment where I've been humiliated twice in one day.

He fishes two twenties from his wallet and leads me out of the hotel lounge to the lobby. I stumble forward through the revolving glass door, then walk to the right. I have no idea where I'm going. I just know I need to get away from people so I can break down properly without the fear of embarrassing myself in public even more.

Several feet away there's a recessed arch in the brick exterior of the hotel. I trudge there and fall back-first against it. My heart races as I struggle to breathe.

Simon stands in front of me, propping me up with both his hands on my shoulders.

"It's okay. Just breathe."

My mouth twists as I fight and fail to hold back an especially pathetic crying noise. More tears fall, but Simon uses the sleeve of his jacket to wipe them up. A salty breeze cuts against the building, cooling over my wet cheeks.

"I'm… I'm sorry, Simon. For just leaving like that… and that you had to cover my drink. I… I promise I'll pay you back when I get cash."

"You absolutely will not, don't even worry about it. What happened on the phone to make you so upset?" he asks gently.

I stop to catch my breath, my shoulders shuddering as another chilly gust kicks up around us. When my hair flips in the wind, Simon smooths it behind my ear. I let out a low hum at how gentle and caring his touch is—and how much I need it in this moment.

I relay my conversation with Landon to him. When I finish, Simon's jaw is clenched so tight, I'm scared he'll break right through the bone.

"Piece of shit," he mutters.

"You were right about him," I say. "He was a textbook douchebag. And deep down, I think I knew it too. I just wanted something easy, you know? Someone I didn't have to commit to, someone I could just meet and have fun with a couple times a week. But then I forgot that the kind of guys who are up for that sort of thing sometimes treat people like garbage. It's my own fault."

Simon cups his hands around my cheeks, gently turning me to look at him. I go breathless. Because right now, our faces are inches apart, we're both panting, and I can't help but notice the hungry look in his dazzling eyes. I'd bet anything it's identical to the look in my own eyes right now.

"It's absolutely not your fault that Landon is a piece of shit." His tone is soft, but growly. It makes my mouth water. "He chose to act that way. He should have shown you kindness and support when you needed him most, but he chose to be a creep. Don't blame yourself."

I nod, my unblinking stare locked with his.

"He's not even in your league, Naomi. Not even close. He was lucky you gave him the time of day."

I swallow. "Are you going to kick him out too?"

"Yeah."

He says it without blinking, without a tremor in his voice, without a single discernible doubt.

"I'm so sorry."

"Naomi, I already said—"

"You're losing business because of me."

"Fuck business. You mean more than any of it."

He pulls his lips into his mouth. And that's when my stomach flips into itself. Because right now, I know he means every word he says—and it makes me want to kiss him until he can't breathe. And everything he's doing—everything he's saying, the way he's touching me, the way he's looking at my lips like I'm his last meal—tells me he wants to kiss me too.

His hands still cup my face. For a split second, I close my eyes and hum, relishing how even on this cold October evening, I feel so warm under Simon's touch.

I lick my lips, lean forward, and touch my mouth to his. He exhales slowly and I can practically taste him. But that's nowhere near good enough. I need my lips on Simon's lips, my tongue on Simon's tongue. I want to taste him, to tease him, to savor him.

We move our mouths slowly against one another, and I relish the taste of Scotch on his soft, firm tongue. Only a few seconds in and I can feel the electricity of our kiss as it bolts through me. Through my chest, pulsing to my heart and my stomach, getting hotter and hotter the lower the sensation floats, all the way between my legs—

And then my phone rings. Again. Fucking hell.

I fall back and out of his touch at the sudden sound and hit my head against the brick.

"Ouch!"

"Are you okay?"

I nod, then dig my phone out of my purse. "Sorry, just let me turn this damn thing off already."

When I see it's Harper, my heart sinks. She's calling me because of the panicked, all-caps text I sent her an hour ago. And as much as I want to ignore her call so I can keep kissing Simon, I can't. I know Harper. She'll keep ringing me and texting me until I finally answer her because she knows an all-caps text is equivalent to an emergency in our book.

I grimace down at my phone screen, then look back up at Simon. "I have to take this. It's Harper. I'm so sorry."

The way he slow-blinks then purses his lips and nods broadcasts his disappointment.

"It's okay," he says softly. "I'll get us an Uber to Nob Hill. You talk to Harper."

I answer just as Simon backs away from me a few steps and pulls up the rideshare app on his phone.

"Hey, Harper."

I follow Simon a few steps away to the curb and stand while we wait for our ride. We get into the car and the entire ride to Simon's I relay my sob story to Harper. The driver stops at his apartment first and he gives me a small smile and a quick wave before hopping out of the car. I mouth, "Thanks again. Bye," to him as I half-listen to Harper's take on Brody's betrayal. And then I head to her apartment, my body buzzing out of pure shock, the taste of Simon Rutler on my tongue.

# Chapter Sixteen

The longer I stare at my laptop screen, the more the colors from the images on the screen blur together. I blink, then try to focus. But I can't get anything done. I've been trying to edit the latest episode of *Simply Simon*, but it's no use.

That kiss with Simon last night has wrecked me. I can't do anything other than think about it—about him.

I switch my position on Harper's couch yet again, but I still can't get comfortable. Every time my brain replays it in my head, I feel that drop in my stomach. My knees go weak. My throat goes dry and I forget what time it is, what day it is, and what exactly I'm supposed to be doing in that moment.

Because all I can focus on is Simon's hot breath on mine as we inched closer to each other, the hard feel of his body under my hands, the way his mouth felt velvety soft against mine, the Scotch taste of his tongue.

What would have happened had Harper not called me? Would we have just made out in the street and called it a night? Would he have been up for going home together? I would have.

I scoff to myself. All this effort over the past couple of months to keep things professional between us for the sake of work clearly didn't hold much water once I got a taste of Simon. Such a flimsy excuse that ended up being.

I tug a hand through my hair as more questions swirl in my brain. Is he spending as much time obsessing about our kiss as I am? What the hell is working together going to be like after this? I'm supposed to film him and his family at Napa this weekend.

I slump over, letting out a groan against the couch cushion. My phone beeps with an email alert, so I sit up and check it. It's a message from Fiona.

Great work on the latest episode! Last week's video got nearly a million views. I have to say, Naomi, I commend you for the professionalism and maturity you're showcasing with this project. Not everyone could navigate this series with the creativity and vision you have. I'm beyond impressed.

I grin. I'm kicking ass on this project, and my boss who's notoriously stingy with compliments has showered me in praise. But then my smile starts to fade. She's commending me for my professionalism and maturity, but she has no idea just how close I was to setting fire to my professional standards after one kiss with Simon.

I purse my lips, focusing once more on my computer screen and the mountain of unedited footage I've yet to finish. Time to get back on track. Yeah, my professionalism excuse was flimsy before, but it won't be from now on. If I want to continue to excel at my job—if I want to keep impressing my impossible-to-impress boss—things with Simon can't go any further. That promotion Fiona hinted at would likely disappear if she knew that we were messing around. I've spent the last few years establishing myself at Dash. I absolutely will not blow my chance at this career move because I couldn't keep it in my pants.

I immediately text Simon.

Me: Hey. You busy?

He responds right away.

Simon: Nope, I've got a few minutes. What's up?

Me: I just wanted to apologize for last night.

Simon: Why?

Me: Kissing you wasn't the smartest thing in the world to do. I was really upset and feeling kind of vulnerable after everything that happened with Brody. And Landon. I think I got a bit carried away.

Me: Plus, alcohol.

Simon: Ha, right.

Me: I just think we should keep things firmly in the friends/coworkers camp.

I hold my breath as I watch those three gray dots appear on my phone screen.

Simon: Okay :)

I let out a breath. Wow. That was way easier than I thought it would be. I stare at my phone, mystified. There's something about the pure simplicity in Simon's response that reads endearingly confident with the tiniest hint of playfulness. Like he's not one bit worried about what happened between us and what effect it's going to have on our dynamic. Like he's one thousand percent certain it'll all work out just fine.

That realization sends a wave of intrigue that I tuck to the back of my mind so I can focus on the task at hand. We hash out the details for this weekend via text. I'll drive to Napa early Saturday morning, film footage of Simon with his mom, sister, and grandma, do a few quick interviews with them, then take off. It'll be a long day, but manageable.

As I dive back into editing, that intrigue lingers. It registers as a tiny ball of excitement in my stomach. I try not to read too much into it. It's probably just that I'm relieved—and very, very happy—that one kiss with Simon didn't ruin everything.

We're back to being friends and colleagues, like before. Everything will be fine.

I was wrong. This is absolutely, positively not fine.

As I put away the camera equipment after I wrap up filming Simon and his family, I take a slow, deep breath and try not to look at him.

He's just a few feet away on the back deck of Truss winery, sitting at a table with his mom, grandma, and sister. And even though I can only see him from the corner of my eye, I'm an absolute goner.

Thinking that we could stay solidly in the friends and colleagues category after we kissed was a ridiculous and naïve thought, especially after what I've witnessed today. Listening to his family tell stories about what an adorable and sweet little kid he was and then to see him as a doting son, grandson, and big brother has shot that theory to hell.

I've always known Simon is a hottie, but now I see him as a super-sweet, sensitive mega hottie who helps walk his grandma up and down the stairs because she has a bad knee, who refuses to let his mom pay for anything on their day out, who asks his little sister how her car's been running since the last time he rotated her tires.

He is a trifecta of attractiveness: good-looking, gainfully employed, and a total sweetheart. I want to jump his bones.

I shake away the thought as I zip up my camera bag, but then something pink catches my eye. I whip out my phone and text Harper.

You packed a vibrator in my camera bag??? WTF is wrong with you??

She texts back a devil emoji.

Harper: For good luck. The last time I packed a surprise sex toy in your bag, you and Simon almost had sex. You two kissed the other night, so this is me giving you a much-needed nudge. Let's hope for more successful results this time, shall we?

Me: I'm going to kill you. Like, seriously murder you. I'll be featured on Dateline when I get done with you.

A million laughing emojis are her response.

I huff out a breath, willing myself to stay calm. The last thing I want is for Simon or his family to notice I'm freaking out and ask what's wrong.

"Naomi! Come have a drink with us." Amy smiles at me.

I check the time. It's early evening, which means with traffic it'll take close to three hours to get back to San Francisco, maybe more.

"Oh, um… I should really head back…"

She waves a hand, like my excuse is no good. Under the wide brim of her floppy sun hat, her gold-brown eyes turn adorably pleading.

"Come on! One glass! You worked so hard documenting our Simon." She pats his shoulder as he downs the last of his wine. "You deserve a break. We ordered a bunch of food too. You have to help us eat all of it."

My resolve starts to crumble at the mention of food. When I say okay, she lets out a cute squeal. Miriam and Barbara smile.

I walk over and take a seat next to Amy.

Simon smiles at me. "Glad you're staying for a bit. I was worried you'd head back with zero food in your stomach. I didn't see you eat anything today."

The spicy smell of his cologne hits my nose and I have to bite my lip to keep from groaning. I glance at his throat, mesmerized at the slow movement of his Adam's apple as he swallows. I force my gaze down to my blouse, tugging on the hem like I'm trying to smooth out every single wrinkle.

"Ha, yeah. Guess I just got caught up in work."

He's seemingly unaware of just how hard it is for me to keep my shit together around him. He's been relaxed this whole day, which means he's not feeling anything close to what I am. All the more reason to ignore the heat inside me.

"No wonder you two get along so well. Both such workaholics," Amy says, chuckling.

Barbara frowns at her. "They're not workaholics. They're hardworking. There's a difference."

"I know, I know," Amy says from behind her wineglass as she takes a sip. I catch the beginning of an eye roll before she turns to look off to the side.

Barbara reaches over to pat Amy's hand. "You're hardworking too, sweetie. And someday you'll finish your degree and get a great job, just like your brother."

Amy scoffs and Simon grimaces before he gulps more wine.

"Thanks for that low-key dig, Mom."

Barbara's face falls slightly. "Oh, honey. I'm sorry. I didn't mean it like that. I just meant that I'm proud of you no matter what."

Amy lets out a frustrated sigh and turns to me. "Good thing you didn't get this part on camera, huh?"

"Amy's doing great, Mom," Simon says. "She's on her own path, there's no need for her to rush through school. She's happy and supporting herself. I think that's pretty great."

The sour look on Amy's face fades.

"You're right, honey." Barbara reaches over and pats her hand. "I'm so proud of you kids."

I quietly take in the family dynamic, how Simon seems to be the caretaker and peacekeeper during conflicts. It makes sense given he's the oldest and their dad isn't in the picture. That's probably why he's such a good therapist—he's empathetic and tries to resolve conflicts as he sees them arise. Inside I soften even more to him.

Amy hands me a glass of Riesling and I take a sip as two food runners drop off dishes of food. Soon the table is crowded with two bottles of wine, a charcuterie board, stuffed mushrooms, bruschetta, and chips with artichoke dip.

An hour later my stomach is full from all the food and my face is sore from smiling.

I catch Simon eyeing Amy as she finishes her fourth glass.

"Pace yourself. You're still getting over that stomach bug, remember?"

She sticks her tongue out at him. "I'm aware."

"I feel your pain," I say to her. "I have an older brother too."

I tell her my older brother spent our childhood bossing me around.

"Is there some club where they train older siblings to do that?" Amy teases.

Simon says, "Haha," before finishing the last of the artichoke dip.

"They mean well. Still insanely annoying, though." I internally applaud my blood pressure when it doesn't skyrocket as I glance at him. A bit of joking about what we were all like growing up has gone a long way in lessening the hotness factor from before. I can look at Simon without breaking into a hot sweat. Way to go, me.

"Only younger siblings understand what we go through," Amy mock-whines.

"Should we start a club where we drink wine and vent about it? No older siblings allowed."

"That's it. We're officially bonded." She leans her

head on my shoulder. I pause when I feel just how hot her skin is. When she sits up I notice her cheeks are flushed too.

But before I can say anything, Miriam lets an "oh dear" slip as she squints at her phone.

"What's wrong?" Barbara asks.

"Just got an alert. There was some horrible multicar pileup along the freeway on the way from here to San Francisco. The entire roadway is closed for the night."

Miriam's worried gaze flits to me as I sigh, processing what that means. I'm stuck in Napa.

"Well. Shoot." I'd swear in normal circumstances, but I want to keep it clean in front of Miriam and Barbara.

Barbara reaches over and pats my hand. "Oh don't you worry, honey. You can stay with us. The rooms at the Rancho Caymus Inn are so spacious. Mom and I are sharing a room, but you can stay with Amy. She'd be happy to have you, right?"

When I look over at Amy, I'm shocked at just how pale she is now. She runs her palm over the front of her romper, lingering on her belly. She offers a forced smile. "Of course you can stay, Naomi. You don't mind a bit of a mess, do you?"

Simon scoffs. "That's putting it lightly. What she means is, you don't mind sidestepping piles of clothes and not having any counter space in the bathroom, right?"

"I survived sharing a bathroom with you in Tahoe," I tease. "I think I'll manage."

Simon winks at me, and my throat goes dry for the briefest second.

"You sure it's okay, Amy? I don't mean to impose. I can always get my own room."

She shakes her head as Barbara speaks. "Nonsense. You're practically family now. No need to spend all that money on a room at the last minute."

My chest warms at the kindness in her voice, how she and everyone in Simon's family have been so welcoming.

I'm in the middle of thanking her when Amy darts up from the table. "Gotta run to the restroom."

She speedwalks toward the building, reaching for the door as it starts to open. The people coming out hold it open for her and she darts in.

"I told her to take it easy on the wine," Simon mutters.

The couple who held the door for Amy walks toward us, and I realize it's Cole and Tamara.

Cole's cheery face lights up as he sees Simon. "Hey, man! What are you doing here?"

The two shake hands, and Simon introduces Cole and Tamara to his mom and grandma. He explains that I'm filming Simon's family for an episode.

"My younger sister, Amy, was the one who almost ran you over when you walked outside," Simon says.

"What brings you two to Napa?" I ask.

The two glance at each other, both of them biting back smiles.

"A bit of a romantic getaway," Cole says. "I asked Tamara last night at dinner to marry me again. We're renewing our vows."

Tamara holds up her left hand, showcasing the brand-new silver band lined with delicate diamonds that Cole surprised her with. Miriam and Barbara both squeal and offer their congratulations. Simon and I stand up and congratulate them both with hugs.

Cole turns to Simon, his blue eyes glassy. He clears his throat. "We wouldn't be here today if it hadn't been for you. I'm sure everyone you work with would say the same. Thank you. For what you did to help us get to this point."

The look on Simon's face melts me. Pure joy for Cole and Tamara.

"You're the ones who did the hard work," he says. "I'm so happy for you both."

Miriam and Barbara pester Tamara for the details on the proposal, which Tamara happily gives. Then they dive into questions about the vow renewal.

Everything about Tamara glows: the red lipstick she's wearing, her deep brown eyes, the rosy hue of her cheeks.

"We're still hammering out the details, but we're hoping to do it next month sometime."

"And it would mean the world to us if you could come, Simon," Cole says.

I could swear I see Simon's eyes glisten as he beams at Cole and Tamara. He tells them an enthusiastic yes. Then he signals a server and orders a bottle of champagne and fresh glasses. A minute later we're all toasting to Cole and Tamara. People at the nearby tables look over and cheer in celebration.

Just then Amy walks back to the table, hand on her stomach, and plops down in her chair.

"I threw up," she mumbles. "Twice."

Her mom presses her palm to her forehead. "You do feel a bit warm, sweetie."

Simon asks the server for a big glass of water. When it arrives, Amy downs it in a few gulps.

She glances at Simon, dark bags forming under her otherwise dewy eyes. "I take it back. I should have listened to you, big brother. That was way, way too much wine."

Instead of gloating like some big brothers would, Simon pats her shoulder and tells her he'll take her back to the hotel as soon as everyone finishes their champagne. Cole's and Tamara's expressions turn and insist that we don't have to stick around for them.

Amy insists she'll be fine, then she smiles weakly and congratulates them.

"I can drive you back to the hotel in my rental, Amy." I turn to Barbara and Miriam. "That way you all can stay and take your time finishing the champagne."

"I'll come with you," Simon says, standing up.

I start to object but Simon insists and helps hoist Amy out of the chair. "I've helped her enough times when she's been sick to know that it's a two-person job."

Amy wrinkles her nose but mutters a thanks as she leans her weight on him. Miriam and Barbara pop up to give them hugs and kisses good-bye. Cole and Tamara wish us good luck with Amy and thank Simon once more for the champagne.

I walk alongside Simon as he helps Amy walk back into the building, then out to the parking lot to my rental car. Simon buckles her into the backseat and takes the front seat while I get behind the wheel.

"I don't feel so good," Amy mutters.

I look in my rearview mirror as I pull out of the parking lot and head to the hotel.

"Hang in there," Simon says. "Just a five-minute drive and we'll get you to your room."

"Thanks for this," he says quietly as I drive. "I'm sure you didn't think you'd be spending your weekend taking care of my sister."

"It's not a problem. Honestly."

Simon directs me to the hotel, and I pull into the parking lot and into the first free spot I see. I hop out and round the car to help him pull Amy out of the back-seat, but then I hear a lurching noise. I freeze. I know what that means. Amy falls back into the seat and starts to dry heave. When I realize she's about to upchuck in my rental car, I go to grab her, but Simon has the same idea because he pulls her by the arm so that her torso hangs out the open door. She promptly spews onto the pavement.

He winces, then looks over to me. "And sorry for that."

"Yeah. So sorry." Amy wipes her mouth with the back of her hand.

I hold back a sigh. "It's okay. You didn't get it in the car, it's all good."

Simon pulls Amy out, supporting her left side. She's so wobbly that I'm scared she'll fall, so I immediately take her right. I noticed he's slung my camera bag over his shoulder too, and I tell him thanks.

"You think you'll get sick again?" I ask Amy.

"Nope. I mean, I'm pretty sure I won't."

The three of us slowly make our way to the hotel lobby. Even though I'm partly distracted with Amy, I still take in the stunning design and décor. The earthy adobe tile roof shrouding the building and the cream-hued stucco exterior set a rustic tone. We make our way along a stony pathway under a wrought iron arch with the words "Rancho Caymus" greeting us. Heavy wooden doors lead to a cozy reception area. We walk through and make it to the outdoor courtyard, which boasts a pool and a hot tub. Individual rooms line the perimeter.

"Wow," I muse. "This is such a cute—"

Amy breaks out of our hold and darts to the nearest trash can, vomiting once more.

A heavy sigh rockets out of Simon. I walk over to where she's hunched over and gently rub her back.

"That's it. Get it all out."

Simon fishes her room key out of his pocket and walks over to her room just a few doors away.

I help Amy stand up and we start to walk over, but then she halts. A panicked look crosses her face. She starts to turn toward the trash can but it's too late. She lurches before I can move out of the way, and then it happens. She spews all over my chest.

## Chapter Seventeen

Amy's eyes go wide as she looks at me. "Oh no... I'm so sorry, Naomi."

I bite down and try not to gag at how wet and warm and chunky her vomit feels on my skin.

Simon spins around, horrified.

"Just...hold on. Let me get her in bed with a trash can next to her and make sure she'll be okay, and then I'll help you get cleaned up in my room." He stares unblinking at my face, like he can't bear to look at the vomit a second longer.

Gritting my teeth, I force a breath through my nose and nod. "Just. Hurry. Please."

Holding my hands away from my torso, I close my eyes and force deep breaths in and out, trying with everything in me to ignore the hot, wet liquid coating my favorite cream blouse. I hunch over so I don't drip all over my jeans, but it's no use. It soaks through my shirt to my bra.

The door opens to reveal Simon's panicked face. He mumbles that his room is the next one and whips out his room key.

I stand behind him and bounce up and down on my

heels while wringing my hands, like I'm doing some sort of awkward dance.

"Hurry hurry hurry! It's warm and wet and so gross!"

It's a struggle to keep my volume low when I'm squealing out of sheer disgust. I've never had another person's vomit on my body before and it is absolutely vile. Is this how Simon felt when I vomited on him?

He opens the door. I walk into his room and drop my purse and camera bag on the stone floor.

When we're inside, I eye the bathroom door on the other side of the room. "Shower. I have to shower."

Simon nods and quickly moves out of my way as I dart to the bathroom. He hollers for me to take the robe hanging on the outside of the door.

"I haven't used it," he quickly adds.

I say thanks and turn on the shower and as fast as I can, I peel off my vomit-soaked blouse and rinse it in the sink while I wait for the water to warm.

"God. For two people who have known each other three months, we've had to deal with vomit a surprising number of times," I say through the crack in the door.

Simon laughs.

I kick off my ankle boots, take off my jeans and underwear, then jump in the steaming-hot shower. I scrub my skin with soap for a good ten minutes in the pristine, white-tiled shower. When I finish, I turn off the water, dry off, then snag a small bottle of complimentary lotion from the white marble counter and slather it on.

"What if Amy's vomit permanently stains my blouse?" I groan-yell out the slim opening.

A faint chuckle echoes from the other side of the door. "I'll have it dry-cleaned and make sure she covers the bill," Simon hollers.

I snuggle into the plush hotel robe and walk out of the bathroom. Simon stands in front of the couch by the coffee table and flashes a pitying smile at me, like he's looking at a wet kitten. I almost laugh. He's probably never seen anything less sexy than me in this moment… except a few minutes ago when he saw me covered in his sister's puke. All that heat I was battling in his presence less than a half-hour ago is long gone too. I guess vomit is the universal killer of arousal.

"I owe you an apology," I say to him.

"For what?"

"For freaking out when I was covered in vomit a bit ago. You kept your cool so well that night we met when I threw up on you. How? I wanted to burn my skin off just now."

He chuckles. "Like I said before, you barely got my shoes. If you had hurled on my chest like Amy did to you, I wouldn't have been as laid-back about it."

I glance around at the cozy Spanish hacienda-style room with a gigantic king-sized bed decked out in white bedding. The massive wooden headboard boasts nail accents. Wood beam ceilings, textured walls, and wrought iron accents give it a decidedly artisanal feel.

"This is a really cute room."

I plop down on the edge of the bed. Simon stands just a few feet away by the coffee table. There's a wine bottle on it with a note from the hotel staff.

"You haven't opened your complimentary wine yet," I say.

"Wanna have a glass with me? I was saving it for a special occasion. Like tonight when my sister vomits on an unsuspecting poor soul."

I laugh and say sure. He pops open the bottle with a

cork then walks over to me, but as soon as he looks at me, his face turns serious. "Sorry… I um…" His gaze falls to my neck, then my chest. Not quite my boobs, though.

I peer down, and notice that my robe is open wide at the top and a hefty amount of cleavage is showing. Thankfully no nip slip.

Quickly I cover up and let out a chuckle of my own, feeling my face grow the slightest bit hot. "Sorry," I mumble.

Simon clears his throat before pouring wine into the glasses. "It's, um, fine."

I plop onto the bed. He takes a step toward me, glass of red wine in hand. "Drink?"

"Gimme."

He grins as I snatch it out of his hand. When he starts walking toward the armchair in the corner of the room, I stop him.

"You don't have to sit there." I pat the spot of plushy comforter next to me.

He lowers down next to me and we sip in shared silence.

"Napa wine has a different taste than other types of wine," I say after I let the flavor coat my tongue.

"Really? How so?"

"It's more pretentious." I crack a smile at him, and he booms out a laugh in response.

We take dual long sips while looking at each other, the smiles on our mouths lingering even as we swallow. The bitter, earthy taste lingers with each subsequent pull I take.

Simon twists his neck to face me. "More?"

I nod, and he tops me off.

"You know, for someone who claims not to drink much, you really seem to be enjoying that pretentious wine."

I shrug with the glass to my lips. When I finish swallowing, I look at him. "It must be the charm of Napa rubbing off on me."

When I glance back at him, his eyes are kind. And serious. "I'm sorry about tonight."

"It's okay, Simon. It's not your fault Amy vomited on me. And it's not like she could help it. She was sick."

"Yeah, but I should have paid attention to her more."

"I know you're her big brother, but you can't control her. If she wants to drink, she's gonna drink."

"True." He clears his throat. "I don't think it's good if you stay with Amy. You might get sick too."

"Right." I sigh, the nerves in my stomach kicking up at what that means: I'll be rooming with Simon.

"I, um, can run to the front desk and see if they have a spare room," I say quickly.

He shakes his head. There's something shy behind the warmth of his eyes. The longer I stare at him, the more it makes the inside of my chest flutter.

"It's fine that you stay with me. We've stayed together before, at the Airbnb in Lake Tahoe. We can share a hotel room for one night." He looks over at the couch. "You take the bed. I'll take the couch."

I start to protest, but he shakes his head.

"It's only fair. My sister was the one who threw up on you. It's the least I can offer."

I chuckle. "Okay. Thanks."

He stares at his lap while slowly swirling the wine in his glass. "Unless you're...uncomfortable staying with me."

I stop mid-sip, pulling the glass from my lips. "Why would I be uncomfortable?"

He bites his lip, his cheeks rosy. "It's just, the other night when we kissed…" He coughs. "The next day when you texted me and said that you wanted to forget it and keep things between us firmly in the friends and coworkers camp, I just figured you'd want to maintain that space between us. It feels like sharing a hotel room would maybe cross the line for you."

"Simon. It's fine. I'm not uncomfortable. Not even a little bit."

"You're not?" He speaks with the slightest growl in his tone. I shake my head.

The moisture in my mouth evaporates. Maybe it's the way his jaw tenses or the way his eyes pierce into me like they're looking right through me. It makes me want to curl into him and run my hands all over his skin.

"Because I couldn't handle it knowing that I made you uncomfortable." His brows knit in concern.

For a few seconds, I contemplate the right way to word this. If I tell him the truth—how that kiss between us ignited a fire inside of me, how I wanted to drag him home with me and do a million filthy things to him, that I bit my tongue to keep from howling in disappointment when Harper's call interrupted us—it could end in disaster. If he didn't feel the same way, and I admit that to him now, it could make this evening of sharing a hotel room a whole new level of uncomfortable.

But then I fixate on his gaze. This close up, I see that something rests behind those golden eyes of his; something hungry and hopeful. So I take a breath, squeeze his forearm once more, and spill everything.

"Truthfully? I've never been more disappointed than

when I had to break that kiss with you the other night," I say, my voice low and soft. "In that moment, I didn't give a shit about work or our boundaries as friends. And to be honest, a part of me still doesn't care. I'm still so attracted to you, Simon."

For a second, he says nothing. He just stares, that hungry expression on his face remaining. But then the corner of his mouth twitches up along with one of his eyebrows.

"Seriously?" he asks.

I nod, reminding myself to swallow so I don't choke on the breath that's been lodged in my throat ever since the air in the room between us thickened all those seconds ago.

"Well, damn." He knocks back the rest of his wine and sets the empty glass on the side table. "Here's a bit of truth from me too, then: I'm insanely attracted to you, Naomi. I always have been. And that night, I would have given my right arm to keep kissing you."

Something inside of me ignites. It's like all of my organs, my blood, and my bones are on fire with passion. Screw work, screw boundaries, screw everything that isn't us.

And so I set my glass down on the side table and grab Simon's deliciously stubbled face in both of my hands, look at him, and say, "You can kiss me again. If you want."

That whispered request is all it takes. Simon's mouth is on mine in a hot second. But instead of the desperate kiss I expect, he's softer. Sweeter. Almost tentative. It's just his lips slowly moving against mine, not even the hint of tongue yet, and it makes every hair on my body stand on end in delicious, glorious anticipation.

When he slips his tongue against mine a second later, a tiny, imaginary bolt of lightning strikes between us. It's so powerful, so arresting that my shoulders jump. Then I sink back into the kiss, following Simon's slow, steady rhythm. I hum in satisfaction.

He breaks our kiss and grins at me. "Did I make you laugh?"

I shake my head. "No. It's just… I can't believe we're finally making out. After all this time. We both wanted to and I guess we just talked ourselves out of it in our minds."

"I have a bone to pick with my brain for sure. Later, though."

I'm mid-chuckle when Simon wraps his massive hands around my wrists, slowly pulling my hands away from his face and guiding them against his chest instead. I fall into his mouth just as he captures me in another kiss, only this time he's firmer, like he urgently needs me inside of his mouth.

With each tease of his tongue, I'm moaning. Simon kisses like a demon. I always knew he was good with his mouth. There are endless online videos that serve as proof of that. But I always wondered just how good he is at something as simple as a kiss. Yes, he's stellar at administering mind-blowing oral pleasure. But twenty-something me always fixated on the kiss. Because as much as it rocks to have a guy who's dynamite in the sack, I've always thought it was just as important that the same guy could make you swoon with a kiss. Even though sex is indisputably fun, nothing teases like a kiss. You can kiss almost anywhere—at home, in public, in the car. You're not limited by space or public decency laws. You can put your mouths together almost anywhere. A guy who can make you weak in the knees with three seconds of his mouth on yours is worth his weight in gold.

And Simon is a one-hundred-foot solid-gold monument based on the magic he can work with his mouth.

It's only a few minutes until our kisses devolve into something filthy and rabid. I'm straddling his lap, tugging at the buttons of his shirt, when he gently pulls away.

He gazes at me, flushed, his thick hair deliciously disheveled. It's his turn to hold my face in his hands when he speaks. "What do you want me to do to you, Naomi?"

I wonder just how honest I should allow myself to be right now.

"What do *you* want?" I ask, instead of giving him a straight answer.

"Literally anything as long as it's with you."

If college me were to answer this question, it would be real simple. I'd want Simon's mouth between my legs until I come, then I'd want him to rail me until he comes.

But that's a wildly unsophisticated answer.

"You can be honest with me, Naomi," Simon says when I say nothing for the next few seconds. "You telling me what you want would be the hottest thing in the world."

"Really?"

"One thousand percent."

"Okay." I huff out a sigh, sending my nerves retreating back to where they belong. "I want your mouth here." I press the palm of my hand between my legs, which is still shrouded with the robe. "And then I want to use your dick to get off. If that's okay."

I have to clear my throat when I finish speaking, I'm so nervous. But then the smuggest smile crawls across Simon's face. "Gladly."

He maneuvers slightly and I think he's going to switch spots so I can lie down on the bed. I move to stand in front of him and he holds me still with both hands on my hips, gazing up at me. Then he runs his fingers along the thick, fuzzy belt of my robe. My heart pounds at the movement. My breathing is a mess too. I have to press my lips together to keep from panting too hard.

His stare fixes on the belt of my robe. It's such a focused look. Almost like he's studying it or trying to memorize it. When he finally unties it, he slides his hands along my bare waist, parting the robe along with it.

"Goddamn, Naomi," Simon says, his eyes now on my midsection.

This is the first time I've heard him swear in a while and I'm giddy with pride. Simon is not someone to curse frivolously. I must bring something out in him.

I let the thought tumble through my head while I soak in the craziness of this moment—that I'm about to get down and dirty with Simon, my friend, work colleague, and college me's biggest fantasy. Before I can let the thought drive me crazy with anticipation, he distracts me with his mouth once more. This time it's endless light kisses across my stomach.

It's as innocent as a kiss could possibly get—closed-mouth and above the waist—but it's winding me up tighter and tighter with each passing second. I run both my hands through his mass of perfect honey-brown hair while trying to keep steady on my feet and keep my gasps under control. I never knew stomach kisses could be such dynamite foreplay.

Just then my eyes fly open with a very important thought. "Oh! I'm clean!"

Simon leans back, clearly confused.

"My STD test came back clean, I mean." I try to laugh off the absolutely ridiculous way I chose to bring that up. But I can't help it. My brain is mush with arousal. "So, um...we're good to go."

"Yay," he rasps before lowering his lips to my stomach once more. "Can I ask you a question?" he says, his mouth against my belly button, his breath wetting my skin.

"Yes. Anything," I whine.

"That day...when I saw you in the bathtub with your vibrator. What were you thinking of?"

My eyes fly open at the boldness of his question. For a minute I contemplate lying, but what's the use? Being honest up until this point has gotten me quite the reward. I may as well keep it up.

I glance down at the top of his head, glad that I don't have to look him in the eye when I admit this.

"Promise you won't think I'm a loser if I tell you?"

"Promise," he says before giving me another kiss, this time just below my right hip.

"Okay, um. Here's the thing." I take a breath, steadying myself by digging my fingers into the thickness of his shoulder. "I was going through comments on one of the Simply Simon videos, and someone linked to an old camming video. I didn't realize what it was at first when I clicked on it, but then...um, when I did... I just... it turned me on so much. I tried to ignore it and keep working, but then I saw you working out in the backyard, all shirtless and sweaty and grunting. I couldn't help it. I had to do something about it."

My heart races as I admit this to Simon. I trail off just as he glances up at me, eyes shining bright and a smile that's downright devilish on his face.

"I was hoping you'd say that. That you were thinking of me, I mean."

"Really?"

He nods before turning back to my midriff and gently scraping his teeth against my skin. "You were so hot that day, Naomi."

My breath catches as he runs his fingertips gently up my back. It's so light, like feathers touching my skin. It sends goose bumps everywhere.

He leans back so I can see his face fully. Just then he runs his nails gently up and down my back. Every single pulse point inside me throbs. My head falls back at how surprisingly pleasurable this sensation is. Just the smooth movement of his hands has me panting.

"You were so, so sexy. There you were, all wet, your hair was messy, your legs were splayed out. You had that cute pink vibrator pressed against your pussy." His jaw tenses when he stops speaking, like he's reliving the memory in his mind and it's taking everything in him to keep it under control while he recounts it to me. "You have no idea just how badly I wanted you to be thinking about me in that moment. To know I got you that hot is the biggest turn-on."

He pauses once more to direct his gaze to me. And then he runs his hands up my chest and starts massaging my breasts. With his fingers, he teases my nipples. I gasp at the sensitive feel of his rough, thick skin teasing my soft skin.

"I was absolutely turned on by you," I say before my breath catches. "I wanted you so bad then. Just like I do now."

With those words, he pushes the robe from my body and just as it falls to the floor, he lowers his face between my legs.

I don't even have time to think before it happens. In an instant, Simon's tongue is between my thighs, teasing me. My knees buckle.

"Shit," I yelp with a gasp.

He lets out what sounds like a low groan. All I can do is claw at his scalp with my bare hands in an attempt to hold on while ecstasy claims my body. Another long lap, another firm press of his soft, wet, warm tongue.

It's not even one minute before my legs turn to complete jelly. I don't have a snowflake's chance in hell of holding myself up, but when I try to open my mouth and tell Simon this, all that comes out is another gasp. Then another yell. Then another moan.

Soon I'm doubled over, clawing at his shirt. I've yanked it halfway up his back before he pulls away from me.

With his hands cupping my hips, he sits up straight.

"Sorry, I…" With one hand on his shoulder to steady myself on wobbly legs, I use the other to tuck away a chunk of my hair. "I just…it's hard for me to stay standing when you're doing that," I finally say.

"Sit on my face instead?" he asks without missing a beat.

Even though I can't see my own expression, I know without a doubt that I'm sporting the cheesiest grin possible. Because evidently Simon is on the same page as me. I would have asked him to do that had I been brave enough when we started all this minutes ago, if my nerves hadn't completely overrun me.

But I shove away the momentary regret as I watch Simon lie back against the bed.

"Wait," I say before his head hits the sheets. "Can you take that off first?" I wave my index finger along the length of his body.

He grins, then reaches both of his hands for the collar of his shirt. He unbuttons the top buttons, then tugs his shirt off from the back of his neck, a delicious move that all guys seem to know.

"I just don't think I should be the only naked one," I say softly.

When he stands up, presumably to take off his pants, he still wears that clever smile on his lips. "Fair point," he says before running his thumbs along the waistline of his trousers. "Help me?"

I bite my lip, steadying as I reach my hands to his belt. It's a hot second before it's on the floor. It only takes another second for me to unbutton and unzip his pants. Soon they're on the floor too.

His hands find my hips once more after he steps out of his trousers and boxers and bends down to remove his socks.

Before he's back up again, he stops between my legs. I gasp when his tongue steals another long kiss. The pressure and pleasure compound, climbing all the way up to my chest. The sensation is a squeeze to my lungs, preventing me from taking a proper breath. It builds and builds until once again my legs are rubber and my knees are no more.

I tug his head away with both my hands gripping his hair, gasping and moaning.

"Sorry." The way his eyes glimmer when he gazes at me tells me he's not the least bit sorry. "Couldn't resist."

I give him a playful shove and he falls back on the bed, sliding all the way up so that his head rests at the edge. Now it's my turn to indulge in a distraction. Because as I stand before him, I'm given a perfect view of his length.

My jaw drops. Then I'm smiling. It seems that in Simon's case, the camera does not lie. He is just as impressive in person as he is in every video I've ever watched him in.

He's lying parallel to the pillows and he bucks his hips, which snaps me out of my moment of extended and unashamed gawking.

He wags an eyebrow at me. "Do I have to beg to get you over here? Because I'm definitely willing to do that."

"I was just…admiring the view."

Grinning is all I can do after that admission. Then I begin the slow crawl up his body. I start by straddling myself over his waist, relishing the feel of his smooth, warm, thick skin against the backs of my thighs.

When I catch myself softly moaning, I can't help but blush. "Sorry," I mutter, barely able to look at him. "It's just…you feel so good against me."

The smile he gives me is tender and confident. "Don't ever be sorry for putting your body on me, Naomi."

He leans up and grabs my arms to gently lead me up to his face.

"Is this okay?" I ask, my stomach flipping once more. "I—I don't want to hurt you."

The rumble of his laugh tickles my thighs. I almost buckle and collapse on his head at the orgasmic feel.

"You won't. This is my favorite. Don't worry about me. Just let go and enjoy."

With those words of reassurance, he presses his tongue against me once more. Pleasure shoots from between my legs to every inch of my body. I thought it would be hard to keep myself steady and balanced on his face while writhing, but Simon's impressively strong arms have got me securely by the waist once more. And it's a good thing because without the support, I suspect I'd topple over on the bed.

I try to stay steady and together, I really do. To fall apart this fast, to come undone so soon, to shudder uncontrollably while making all these feral noises is just the tiniest bit embarrassing. It's our first time together. Part of me wants Simon to work for it a bit.

But in a way, he has. All those times I've watched him on camera and pleasured myself right along with him were a sort of long-game foreplay. Never in a million years did I think I'd ever get to be with Simon for real. But that's part of what makes this moment all the more unreal and mind-blowingly hot. This moment on this bed with Simon was years in the making—I just didn't realize it at the time.

His mouth and tongue move faster, as if I weigh nothing at all. The ease at which he moves, the lust that's dilating his golden eyes turns me on even more. But I can't look at him for longer than a few seconds. If I do, my head will explode. It's too much lust and desire for one human being to absorb in a single moment.

Inside, everything builds. Everything is hot. The pressure, my panting, my racing heart, the throb between my legs that's now pulsing so hard, I can barely take it. I'm an explosion, aching for that first spark to ignite so I can combust already. Soon I'm grinding against Simon's tongue and the whole of his face, not the least bit worried about how I look or sound. Because it feels too fucking good to care about anything else.

Then finally, the spark hits. It starts from where his mouth touches that spot between my thighs and rumbles like a crack of thunder, leveling me from limb to limb. I'm trembling, panting, and shouting. One hand fists his hair to keep myself steady while the other hand grabs at the wall. Simon's still got me by the waist as the thrashing weakens with each passing second.

And then he lowers me down to lie beside him. I roll to my side, chest heaving, and wait a second before I can finally speak.

"Simon… You… That…"

He flashes another heart-melting grin at me before wiping his mouth with his forearm. Then he sits up, straddles me, and pulls my body flush with his.

"Just wait."

He leans back and twists around to grab his pants from the floor. Out comes his wallet, then he pulls a condom from it. When he rips it open with his teeth and spits the shard of foil onto the floor, my mouth waters. Such a feral, impatient move. And he did it because he wants more of me.

Again my chest squeezes so tight, it feels like I can't breathe. But then he lines himself up with me, slides in, and I'm gasping until there's no air left in the room.

"Oh my fucking god, Simon." I press my head against the mattress, eyes closed while I process the unholy pleasure of him stretching me out. "That's…"

Before I can finish, he treats me to a slow thrust. My eyes pop back open and I turn my gaze back on him.

Even in the dim light of the nearby lamp, I can make out every single feature of the body that's always driven me wild. Those strapping arms, a million times thicker than mine, that hold me up with such ease. His chest and stomach, which glisten with beads of sweat. Those veins that seem to course forever under his skin. The dark hair that pools at the center of his chest and runs all the way down to that hard, impressive length. His rugged build that's always driven me wild. He's muscular, but not cut to hell like a fitness model, and I love it. His strength is functional, developed from hours of building things and hauling things and breaking things down.

I take it all in with hungry eyes. I am starving for him.

But even more than how he looks, it's how he moves, with confidence and care. It's how he gazes down at me, like nothing else in the world matters except for me in this bed and us in this room. Together.

Leaning up, I wrap my arms around his neck and plant a sloppy, desperate kiss on his mouth. He tastes like salt and wine and skin.

"What else is your favorite?" I huff out a breath. "Show me. Please."

He straightens up, sliding out of my grip to a sitting position. I fall back on the bed, holding my breath as I wait for him to demonstrate.

"This is my favorite." He grabs one of my legs and balances it on his shoulder. "And this." He picks up the speed of his thrusting, this new deep angle intensifying the pleasure sensations claiming my body. My calf muscles shake uncontrollably in response.

"And this," he grunts. "Always this." He wets his

thumb against his tongue before pressing it gently to the most sensitive part of my body.

The quick yet soft way he swirls is indicative of his expert technique. Paired with the smooth and steady rhythm of his thrusts, which are hitting my G-spot like the bull's-eye on a dartboard, this is my new favorite too. And no matter how much I thrash or how hard I grab at him, he doesn't stop. He works like a machine programmed for my pleasure.

It's not that I'm surprised at all that this is Simon's favorite move. It's honestly so beyond sweet that a position engineered to maximize my enjoyment is his favorite—and it makes total sense given he spent most of his camming days maximizing the satisfaction of his partners. It's the fact that this move has got me on the edge of release in record time. Again.

Once more my jaw falls open and I'm making sounds that are no longer human. It's no time at all before I'm an explosion of curse words, animal noises, and convulsions. Again.

A few thrusts later, Simon tenses. He leans down over me, buries his face in the side of my neck, and lets out a noise like a mix between a grunt and a growl.

I clutch at him, my arms and legs wrapped around him like I'm intending to remain attached to him forever. Our bodies slick with sweat, I practically slide off him as he leans up and away from me.

"No cuddling?" I babble.

It's a second before I process exactly how desperate I just made myself sound. But it's that post-orgasm giddiness that has me speaking without thinking. I eye a pillow to smother myself. I've already pushed far enough tonight. I've already had toe-curling sex with my off-limits friend…and colleague. We've already thrown our status—and our future—into jeopardy when we finally gave in to our attraction for one another. Asking for anything more, even a cuddle, is too much.

But Simon smiles down at me, halting that train of self-doubt dead in its tracks. He steps off the bed, walks to the trash can in the corner, and throws the condom away. Then he jumps back on the bed and spoons me from behind before pulling the plush down comforter over us.

He nuzzles my neck, the stubble from his jaw tickling me. I let out a soft squeal and close my eyes. Every worry flies out the window.

"Come on, Naomi. What kind of a guy do you think I am?" He runs his mouth along the side of my neck, in a slow, long kiss. "Of course there's cuddling."

## Chapter Eighteen

I wake to the sound of light snoring above me. When I peel my eyes open, the room boasts the telltale dimness of early morning. Slivers of sunlight peek through the partially closed shutters above the bed.

Behind me, Simon stirs. I close my eyes and smile, snuggling my ass and hips into him. This is exactly how we fell asleep last night. I hum quietly to myself in satisfaction. It seems like neither of us moves much when we sleep.

Even in my groggy, half-asleep state my grin grows wider. Because if this isn't the best way to wake up, cuddled into a sexy and sweet man, then I don't know what is. Slowly I inhale, then let out a silent exhale. I could get used to this. I could do this every day and never, ever get sick of it.

And that thought is what sends my eyelids flying open again. That thought shouldn't be crossing my mind at all. One night with Simon shouldn't change what I've spent my entire adult life learning. One night of crazy-good sex doesn't magically fix the truth: that I'm a disaster when it comes to dating and relationships.

Yes, it would be amazing to have this every day—this comfort, this post-sex hard sleep, this waking up with a smile on my face. But I can't. It's not possible. Because I've tried it so many times before with other guys and sometimes it lasted, for a bit…but then eventually something goes wrong. Always. We get on each other's nerves. We realize our long-term goals don't line up. Someone loses interest. Feelings get hurt. Then it ends.

And that's exactly what will happen if this thing with Simon goes any further.

I can imagine it now: we'll end up arguing nonstop about one of us working too much and how we don't see each other enough, like so many other couples. Once the hot-and-heavy phase dies down, our spark will fizzle. Or maybe we'll get jealous of each other and it'll all end in a huge blowout.

My chest tightens when I think about how I—or both of us—will be left heartbroken.

I know better. And that's why I need to leave now before I fall any deeper.

Last night was a fantasy for sure. And now it's back to real life.

Holding my breath, I wait a minute until I hear Simon's snores grow louder, signaling that he's in a deep sleep. Then I quietly, slowly slide out from under his arm and crawl off the bed. I carefully turn around as I step away, taking in the image before me. Simon rests on his side, eyes closed, hair messy, his chest slowly rising and falling. I bite my lip, my heart thudding at how peaceful and enticing he looks. As much as I owe him an explanation for what I'm about to do, I don't want to wake him.

So instead, I dart to the bathroom and pull on my underwear and jeans, thankful that they narrowly missed being spewed on during Amy's vomiting episode last night. I eye my soaked blouse, which is still sitting in the sink. There's no way I can wear that in its current state or even take it with me. I scan the bathroom floor, relieved when I see a T-shirt of Simon's near the door. I throw it on, then tiptoe out and scan the darkened room for my purse. I spot it near the coffee table. I scoop it up along with my camera bag and creep to the front door. My hand is on the doorknob when I hear sheets rustling behind me.

Simon clears his throat. "Going somewhere?"

My heart sinks, but I make myself turn around anyway. "Um. Yeah," I say softly.

Simon sits up in bed, sheets pooled around his waist. He rubs his eyes with the heels of his hands before running his fingers through his hair. I have to silently remind myself to stay put. The sleepyhead version of Simon is a whole new kind of scrumptious. I'd leap back in bed with him right this minute if he weren't looking at me with suspicion in his groggy eyes.

"You were sneaking out," he says.

I'm surprised at how non-accusatory he sounds. I take a breath, wishing my heart would stop pounding. This is my body dreading the impending disaster. It won't stop reacting like this until I'm far, far away from this mess.

"Wanna tell me why?" He frowns.

I shake my head.

He lets out an annoyed sigh. "It would help if you used words, Naomi."

"Okay, look. I'm sorry you caught me trying to leave, but… I'm freaking out a little."

He eyes his shirt shrouding my torso. "A little?"

"Okay. A lot."

There's a flash in his golden eyes. Like pain and frustration mixed together. It makes my chest crack in half.

"What the hell even is this, Naomi?"

"Last night was amazing. You were amazing. But aren't you worried at all?"

"About what?" He looks genuinely confused.

"We're friends. We work together. We just blurred the lines in the most epic way. We did the one thing you're never, ever supposed to do with your friend or your coworker."

The twist in his expression eases a bit, like he's trying to understand exactly how I feel and why I'm freaking out.

"Okay. I understand what you're saying," he says. "We definitely threw a wrench in things last night. But do you honestly think that running away is the way to handle it?"

"I don't know what else to do."

He lifts an eyebrow. "How about talk to me?"

A hot flash makes its way across my skin. "Please don't talk to me like I'm a client you're trying to treat."

"Then don't act like one. I get that you're freaked out. But sneaking out like a coward? Really? I can't believe you would do that."

"I'm sorry if I didn't wake up psyched out of my mind to have some super-awkward conversation about what happened between us. I just need a moment alone to process things."

"All you had to do was wake me up and tell me that you needed some time to think, Naomi," Simon says, his tone still hard and hurt. "I would have understood. But this disappearing act? I don't do well with crap like that."

His jaw bulges right as I clamp my mouth shut so I don't spew off another flippant comment.

"We're friends, Naomi. We've navigated and talked through a lot of awkward things since we've known each other. All that and we're still solid." His chest rises with a breath. "What do you want to do? Do you want to talk or run away?"

Right now every muscle in my body, my heart, my lungs, my skin, my bones, wants to run as far away from this room as possible. But I know what the right answer is. Staying and talking.

I walk over to the coffee table and set my purse and camera bag down. I look at Simon.

"I want to stay and talk."

The corner of his mouth lifts slightly. "Would you be patient enough to let me piss first?"

I smile and nod. He crawls out of bed and walks into the bathroom, and I take a seat on the foot of the bed and wait for him. He walks back out and stands in front of me, stark naked. I focus on his eyes, though.

"I know you hate it when I go all therapist on you, but it's kind of what I do."

The corners of my mouth quirk up at his phrasing.

"Can I tell you what I'm thinking?" he asks.

"Sure."

He settles down next to me. "It seems like you're expecting us to fail before we've even started up because every other relationship you've had has failed."

"Yeah, that's pretty much it."

He pauses, like he's choosing his words carefully. "Remember what you said to me when we were drinking at the hotel bar after you found out about Brody getting Laura pregnant? How you said that it felt like no matter what you did, there must be something wrong with you because you've never been able to have a loving, lasting relationship?"

I nod.

"I think that you're being really hard on yourself. And you shouldn't be."

"I'm just speaking the truth." I shrug as I say it, it comes so easily. Like an automatic defense.

He shakes his head, the look on his face the slightest bit pained. "Look, I know that it's easy for me to sit here as an observer and say that you shouldn't feel that way. It's a lot harder to internalize that, actually believe it, and act on it."

His gently spoken words land in the center of my chest.

"You're right," I say softly. "It *is* hard."

"We can take this a little at a time. No pressure, no expectations."

"I'm just…really, really scared."

"Scared of what?" he asks lacing his fingers in mine.

"Of where we go from here… What we're supposed to do now."

"What do you mean by 'supposed to do'?"

I glance down and with my free hand fumble with the hem of his shirt that I'm wearing before looking at him. "You're an amazing friend. And so great to work with. And as it turns out, we have mind-blowing sex together."

That last bit earns me a small smile. It makes the pressure in my chest dissipate the tiniest bit.

"It's just…there's a lot of amazingness happening between us right now." I power through the urge to flinch at my god-awful phrasing. "I've never had things go so well before with someone. And it's just…as good as it feels, it's also unnerving. It's hard for me to handle that feeling, especially after I've had so many relationships crash and burn." I pause and look him straight in the eye. "When failure is all you know, you get scared of success because it feels so different. It almost feels wrong."

I let out a quiet breath, hoping I don't sound as ridiculous as I think I do.

Simon's expression eases. "I get it. Thank you for being open about how you're feeling. I know it's really scary to talk about. But we don't have to come up with some sort of elaborate game plan. Last night happened because it felt right. It felt natural. Didn't it?"

I nod.

"What feels right to you now?" he asks.

I take a few moments and think about my answer. The longer I stare at Simon, the hungrier I become. I want his mouth on me, his body against mine, the bedsheets tangled around us.

"I don't know if you want to hear what I have to say," I finally say.

"Why's that?" He lifts his eyebrow at me. It's just the right amount of playful.

"Because it could get really, really dirty," I admit.

His mouth tugs up in a sly smile. "Don't fret about it. You of all people know how much I like to get dirty."

"You know, this might sound weird, but 'don't fret about it' is like the sexiest thing you could say to me."

"I know."

"How do you know?"

He tucks a chunk of my messy hair behind my ear. Then he scoots farther onto the bed and gently grabs both of my hands, coaxing me to stand in front of him, in between his legs. The sides of my thighs skim the inside of his. I'm nearly flush with his crotch. Simon's right. All of this—touching him, feeling him, talking to him this close, this intimately—feels just right.

He slides his hands under his shirt, then rests his palms on my waist. Gazing up at me, his eyes turn mischievous. "You blush every time I say it. I first noticed it when you chatted me up at Spud's. And every single time I've said it since then, it's had a similar effect."

I bite my lip, my face hot again as I contemplate just how to word what I want to say. "Do you know why it makes me blush?"

He reins in his smile. "I have a suspicion. But I'd like to hear you say it."

I take his face in my hands. "You used to say it all the time in your videos right after you'd make the person you were with come."

A toothy grin spreads across his face. "That's kind of what I thought."

"It was super hot knowing that you were skilled enough to be that impressive in bed, but then you brushed it off like it was nothing. It was like an endearing humble brag."

That earns me a throaty laugh. A few seconds later, his stare turns focused. "I just don't want you to freak yourself out, Naomi."

My hands fall to his shoulders. "We have to be smart about this, Simon. My last relationship—well, all my relationships have left me a bit broken, so the thought of things going wrong with you scares me. You're really special to me."

When he says nothing, I stiffen in his hold, but then he gives my hips a gentle squeeze with his hands.

"Don't say that. You're not broken."

My hands wrap around his wrists. "Simon, what are we doing?"

"You're standing, I'm sitting, and we're talking."

"You know what I mean."

"I'm enjoying spending time with an amazing woman," he says without missing a beat. "What are *you* doing, Naomi?"

I sigh, unable to keep my annoyance at bay. "You're incredible, Simon. And I won't lie, so was last night. The best I've ever had."

A smug smile tugs at his lips. "Is that so?"

I nod.

"Say more things like that."

"Someone likes their ego stroked."

"I like other things stroked too."

I let out an exasperated chuckle and yank gently at his wrist. "You're okay with taking things slow? No pressure, no expectations? Just whatever feels good and right at the time?"

"Absolutely."

"We can't let Fiona find out."

"I'm not exactly planning on running out and telling your boss or your coworkers about us. Are you?"

"Of course not."

"We'll be discreet. It's no one's business what we do together privately anyway."

The confidence in his tone convinces me instantly. To think I spent all this time worrying what Fiona would say if she found out about me and Simon…but she doesn't have to.

He spreads his legs wider and pulls me closer to his body so that I'm against his crotch, which is getting harder by the second. "We're two consenting adults, right?"

I nod.

"We like each other a lot, right?"

I nod again.

"Can we agree that if we ever hit a snag with something again, we'll talk to each other about it? That way there's no confusion or hurt feelings."

"Yes, absolutely."

"We can do this on our terms, at our pace. Is that okay with you?"

His words sink in, simple and true. He's right. As long as we're having a good time and are considerate of each other's feelings, there's no reason we can't give this a try.

Despite that, the tiniest flash of doubt hangs at the back of my mind. I want this—I want *us*—to work out more than anything…but do I really have what it takes not to screw this all up?

I push away the doubt and focus on the moment. I focus on Simon, the warmth of his skin on my skin, the heat behind his eyes, the fact that he's willing to give us a shot.

I smile down at him. "That sounds perfect to me."

He lets go of my waist, unzips my jeans, and slowly slides them down along with my panties. And then he pulls his shirt over my head. Once again I'm naked and vulnerable to his touch. My skin tingles at just how bad I want him.

But he does more than just touch. He kisses and caresses. My belly, my thighs, my waist. Then he goes in for the kill between my legs.

I'm gasping. My hands are in his hair in an instant. I'm tugging and panting and teetering on wobbly legs, just like I was last night.

"Now for the most important question," Simon says. It comes out muffled with his mouth pressed against me. "Do we throw out your blouse or is it salvageable?"

I gasp when he starts to swirl his tongue.

It goes on like that for a solid minute. Simon driving me mad with his tongue, and me barely capable of speech. And then he pulls away and stands up. My chest heaving, I lock eyes with him. His stare is a million times more intense now but somehow still tender.

"Is that really what you want to talk about right now? My blouse?" I ask him.

"Nope."

He kisses me until I'm aching and throbbing from the inside out. I can't even think straight.

"Bed. Now," I pant.

He pulls away and has me sit on the edge of the bed, guides me to lie down with his massive, callused hands, then kneels in front of me.

I peer down at him, my chest rising and falling in a rapid rhythm. His palms fall on the tops of my thighs. Just the heat of his skin on mine makes my mouth water. It's like my body knows exactly how good he can make me feel and is aching in anticipation.

"Better?" he asks.

"Very much so."

He turns his face to the side and presses a firm yet soft, lips-only kiss on the inside of my thigh. My head falls back and I let out a breathy yelp at the heat of his mouth on that sensitive patch of skin, how heavenly his thick lips are as they tease my flesh. Pulling away for just a second, he lets out a breath. The wet warmth coats my inner thigh like an invisible blanket. It's the most comforting and arousing feeling. He kisses me on that spot once more, this time grazing me with his tongue.

The sensation it sends to that aching spot between my legs is like a lightning bolt. It's such a tiny and soft touch, but it possesses so much power. And pleasure. My chest rises as I fight for more air. Good lord, does Simon know how to tease.

Closing my eyes, I soak in the pleasure sensation once again when he gives my other inner thigh the same treatment.

"That inner thigh twitch," he groans. "I had dreams about that thigh twitch all night."

"You did?" I say, eyes still closed. Between my legs I'm throbbing. If he so much as grazed the inside of my thigh with his finger, I'd come right here, right now.

"Mmm-hmm," he answers with his mouth on my thigh, but pulls away after a half-second. "The muscles in your inner thighs twitch like crazy when you're turned on. Did you know that?"

I shake my head no.

"Too bad you don't have your vibrator on you."

"Actually…"

Simon's eyes widen. Propping myself up on my elbows, I nod over to the camera bag next to my purse.

"Harper packed it as a joke. She has a twisted sense of humor."

"Damn. I like Harper even more now." He half-smiles. "I'd like to use it on you if that's okay."

My face catches fire as I try to fight my own grin. It breaks free anyway. I can't help but feel nervous at Simon's request. I mean, sure, this is my biggest fantasy come true: Simon Rutler is actually going out of his way to please me. I can hardly believe it. My stomach does a million somersaults at just the prospect. I remind myself to breathe so I don't pass out from pure anticipation.

"Of course that's okay."

He grins and stands up, then waltzes over to the coffee table where my bags are and pulls out the hot pink vibrator.

"Tell me how you like to use this," he says when he's back on his knees in front of me. By now his light brown eyes are dilated and there's a cloudy haze to them. He's so very turned on—by me and my vibrator. It makes me want to pounce on him and ride him until we're both screaming. But not yet. I want to see Simon showcase his skills a bit—and I want to see how hot I can make him even in a moment when he's dead set on focusing on me.

"Can I show you instead?" I ask, biting my lip.

His brow shoots up. "Um, hell yes."

I grab his hand that's wrapped around the base of my vibrator and bring it to my face. Then I slowly run my tongue up and down it, all the while keeping eye contact with Simon. His eyes go wide. When he swallows, his neck turns beet red. And then his chest heaves.

"Holy shit," he mutters, eyes wide.

"Put it inside of me," I say. "Slowly."

"Yes, ma'am."

He obeys my order. My head falls back and I groan. My vibrator is smaller than Simon, but it still feels amazing, especially when he's the one at the helm.

I fist both of my hands into the bedsheets. "Turn it to the medium pulsating setting. Then use your mouth on my clit."

"My pleasure." The smile in his voice is clear as day.

The vibrations start low and steady, the sensation pulsing through me in a deliberate rhythm that has me gasping and pleading immediately.

With my eyes pressed shut, I tell myself to focus on one thing: savoring the heavenly combination of sensations. But when Simon adds his mouth, I fail miserably.

As soon as Simon's tongue is on me, I'm shouting. The pleasure amps up to a thousand. It's all because of his tongue. That magical tongue that somehow instinctively knows how to play my lady parts like a fiddle.

My jaw falls open and I howl, then pant, then howl again. Inside, every muscle of mine is tensing, is winding up to endure the mind-blowing orgasm that's inching closer by the second.

I try making it last by counting the seconds. The heat builds anyway. I can feel it from the tips of my toes all the way to the top of my head. I try tugging a hand through his hair. That only makes him groan and flick his tongue faster.

When heat and pleasure collide, my entire body breaks. I've never been more ecstatic to lose a battle of wills. Climax thunders through me, taking my limbs and muscles and breath and brain with it. My entire being disintegrates into just noises and movements. I thrash and convulse and moan and groan. I wrap my legs around his head, then yell his name. He seems to like my positively wild and dirty response a fair bit because he lets out the most delicious, approving groan.

Finally, when my body eases and I stop shouting, I fall back against the bed. I can barely lift my arm to wipe the beads of sweat on my forehead. I roll to the side so I can get a better view of Simon, who's still staring at me, wiping his mouth with the back of his hand.

I quietly admire how messy his hair is after I spent the last several seconds tugging at it.

I gesture at his head. "Sorry about that."

"Don't fret about it." He climbs up onto the bed and moves me so I'm on my back. I zero in on his impressive length. He kneels between my legs before reaching for his wallet, which is sitting on the nightstand. Then he pulls out a condom. Still grinning, I blink up at him as he rips open the wrapper with his teeth.

I let out a growl-like noise. "That's such a caveman move. I like."

He winks at me, slides it on, and positions me flush with his body. Then he leans down, shrouding my body with his. I reach my arms around his neck, suddenly aware of how heavy and tired my body feels.

"I hope it's okay with you if I just lie here. Your stellar sex toy-mouth combo skills really took it out of me."

He grins wide, seemingly unfazed at what I've said.

He slides in, that delicious full feeling claiming me from the inside out. My skin tingles at the slow, deliberate rhythm he employs.

"Do you have the energy to dig your nails in my back and wrap your legs around my waist while I do this over and over?" he asks.

"Mmm yes." I groan, my head pressing into the mattress.

He kisses me, then picks up the pace. My legs tighten like a vise around him; so do my hands. He leans down to suck on the side of my neck. My eyes roll back as my body instinctively moves the way he requested: my nails drag up and down his back while I steady myself with my legs wrapped around him. Stars cloud my vision as the intensity picks up.

He leans up and grins at me. "Then we're all good."

# Chapter Nineteen

Simon slips his arms around my waist from behind, nuzzling the side of my neck as we stand together at the stove in his kitchen. Closing my eyes, I hum and smile. That's my body's go-to response after spending this past month holed up in his apartment with him. We've been out to go to work, of course, but other than that, it's been sexy times galore for us.

Tonight we're taking our requisite break to cook dinner. When he trails kisses along the side of my neck, goose bumps flash across my skin. I start to giggle, but then he pulls away.

I make a pouty face, but Simon gestures to the pot on the stove.

"The pasta water's about to boil over," he says before stirring it with a wooden spoon.

I bite my lip at the scene in front of me: a very handsome and sweet man who also happens to be a sex god is cooking dinner for me. I still can't get over it.

Just then my phone rings. It's my mom.

"Hi, *anak*! We're all so excited to see you tomorrow!"

"Tomorrow?"

"Yes, tomorrow. We're having a welcome party for Auntie Gigi, remember?"

"Oh. Right." The important family event planned months ago fades back into my mental focus. Auntie Gigi is Mom's cousin from the Philippines, and she's visiting for two months with her husband, Uncle Reuben, to catch up with our family in California.

"Of course, yes. I can't wait."

Mom goes on about what she's planning to cook for the gathering while I mute myself and look over at Simon.

"What's wrong?" he asks.

"I can't come over tomorrow. I forgot I have this family thing."

"What family thing?"

"My mom's cousin is visiting from the Philippines so everyone is going to my parents' house in San Jose tomorrow. It totally slipped my mind, sorry." I quickly unmute myself.

"*Anak*, who are you talking to?" Mom chimes in.

"Um, Simon."

"Oh! Have him come tomorrow too."

"Well, I don't know if he's even—"

"Bring him! It'll be fun. He'll get to meet the family. And oh! We can have him taste-test the different *pansit* everyone will bring! Oh, this will be perfect! We'll have an unbiased taster to help us figure out who really makes the most delicious one."

I sigh at the prospect of poor Simon being force-fed endless plates of *pansit* from my relatives and him politely saying that all of them are equally yummy.

"Mom, you're not going to make him do that."

"We'll talk about it tomorrow when he's here, okay? Can't wait to see you both!"

"Mom, I'm not even sure—"

"And don't bring anything, okay?" she says, cutting me off. "We'll have more than enough food."

She says I love you, hangs up, and leaves me staring at the phone. I glance up at Simon, who's sporting an amused face.

"Good phone call, then?"

I let loose an exasperated noise. "My mom just invited you to our family gathering tomorrow. She's insisting that you come, but don't worry, you don't have to. I'll make up an excuse."

"I can come, you know."

"Seriously?"

"Yeah. You went to my family dinner. I'd like to meet your family too."

I swallow as nerves whir inside of me. Simon takes a step toward me, his smile deliciously smug. "You're freaking out."

"I'm not."

The way he tilts his head tells me he doesn't buy my lie one bit. "Come on, Naomi. You don't have to hide your nervousness from me."

I step over to him and hug my arms around his torso. "It's kind of a big step, meeting family."

"Is it? You've met mine. Three times, if you count that FaceTime conversation at Lake Tahoe."

I chuckle into his chest. "Okay, fair point. It's just different this time. Since we're officially together."

I hold my breath, wondering what he'll say.

"I get it."

I lean back to look at him.

"Really, I do," he says with an easy expression on his face. "And if you don't want me to come because you're not comfortable or you're not ready, that's okay. But I'd like to. I think it would be fun to see your family. And we don't have to put any pressure on things. You can introduce me as your friend or work colleague, not as the guy you're seeing. I know the kind of frenzy that would cause at a family gathering."

I kiss him.

"You'd really give up a free night on your own to do whatever you want to hang out with my family?"

"I really would."

I snuggle into him once again. "I can't believe you'd rather see my family than hang out with your friends. Or have the day to yourself."

"It's got nothing on you."

"My mom wants you to judge everyone's *pansit*. It's going to be like an episode of *Chopped* with everyone presenting you with plates of food and waiting to hear you say which one is best."

He grins. "That sounds awesome. And delicious."

"You honestly don't mind?"

"Now you're making me nervous. Is your family full of criminals or something?"

I laugh. "No, not even close. They'll just make you eat until your stomach aches, then offer you even more food. One of my aunts or uncles will probably ask you a million times if you know how to play mahjong. And one of my little cousins will probably make you sing karaoke with them. I love it, but it can be a little over-whelming if you're not used to it."

"Sounds like a blast," Simon says.

"Okay, then. Come with me."

He presses a kiss to my forehead that makes me go gooey on the inside. I think back to that morning in

Napa after our first night together, when we agreed to take things slow.

*Whatever feels good and right to the both of us... We can do this on our terms, at our pace.*

It'll all be fine.

A second later Simon's phone buzzes on the counter. I release him then move over to the stove when I see that the sauce is starting to bubble over.

"Oh. Wow," he says at his screen.

"What?"

He glances up at me. "Cole just texted me. He and Tamara set a date for their vow renewal. This Saturday. At the San Francisco Mint."

"That's really quick. And what a setting."

The San Francisco Mint is a stately venue with a classic revivalist aesthetic. It's a popular place to host swanky weddings and parties.

"I guess when you're madly in love, going all out is the only option," Simon says.

I catch the look in his eye. It's that gleam of intensity again. I can tell he's so moved by Cole and Tamara's re-declaring their love for one another. It's so, so sweet.

"I'm sure you and the other guests will have an amazing time there," I say.

"You're invited too." He holds up his phone to me. "They're hoping you'll feature their vow renewal in *Simply Simon*."

A wave of excitement bursts through me. I almost drop the wooden spoon. "Oh, that's a great idea! What an epic way to close out the series—with a wedding!"

"Vow renewal," Simon corrects.

"Vow renewal, wedding, same thing." I swipe my phone from the counter so I can email Fiona. I quickly type up a pitch to film the vow renewal as the finale. It'll push back the scheduled airing a few days, but it'll be worth it. With how successful *Simply Simon* has been, it's running longer than most Dash series usually do because Fiona wants to ride the viewership wave for as long as possible. I can cut a couple teasers to air in the meantime all the while hyping up the wedding. That's sure to garner loads of views.

I set my phone back down on the counter, then check the doneness of the pasta. Simon cuddles me from behind once more as I bite through a noodle.

"Is this al dente to you?" I ask, feeding him one.

He chews, his cheek pressed against mine. "It's perfect," he says after swallowing.

He trails light kisses along the side of my neck. Goose bumps jump across my skin as my eyes roll to the back of my head.

"So. Will I get to see you wear something sexy at this vow renewal?"

I let out a breathy giggle as he squeezes his arm around my waist in an especially cuddly hug.

"Hmm…there's this tiny black cocktail number that I haven't worn in a while."

"How tiny?" Simon growls softly, his mouth pressed against the back of my neck.

"Microscopic."

"You absolutely have to wear that."

"Oh, is Simon giving me an order? Are we playing a dirty version of Simon Says?"

"I love that idea. Simon says you have to wear that dress. Then take it off the minute we're back at my place."

Against my ass, I feel him harden. It makes me grin

so wide that I can rile him up with just the image of me in a dress.

My phone alert goes off, but before I can check the message, Simon cups my face with his palm, tilting me to the side so he can pull me into an especially sloppy kiss. Twice more my phone dings as we engage in a filthy makeout session.

"Hang on," I say between kisses.

Finally, he drops his hand from my face. I grin and wink at him before checking my phone and see three messages from Harper.

Harper: Hey.

Harper: Are you staying with Simon again?

Harper: Just wanted to check ;)

Me: Yup :P

Harper: Aren't you glad I packed that vibrator? Told you it was a good luck charm.

Me: You're ridiculous.

Me: But okay, yes, I admit, I'm very glad. Being with him is pretty amazing.

Ever since I told Harper that Simon and I finally hooked up in Napa, she's been ecstatic for us.

Simon plates the pasta in two bowls. He rips bits of fresh parsley from the bundle sitting on the counter, leaning over both bowls with a look of pure concentration in his eyes, as if he's dedicated to making the most perfect meal. For me. My heart hammers as I take in the sight.

Me: FYI I'm bringing him to my parents' house tomorrow for Auntie Gigi's welcome party and I don't want to hear a word of teasing about it from you. Understand?

A surprised face emoji is her reply. I leave my phone on the counter and accept the pasta bowl Simon offers me with a quiet "thank you" and a smile. We sit down and dig in. If this is what relationships could be—cuddling while making dinner, endless days of crazy-good sex, fun conversations, flashing looks that give you butterflies forever—I'd happily do it.

He peers over at me. "We make a pretty good team in the kitchen. And at work. And in the bedroom."

"You think so?"

"I know so. We're a triple threat."

I chuckle through a bite.

"Oh you think that's funny, do you?" Simon asks in a mock-offended tone.

He moves his hands to my waist and hoists me up to sit on the counter. My giggles fade. All I can focus on is the raw desire shining in his light brown eyes and that hard set of his jaw. I know that look well by now. It tells me just how hungry he is—for me.

I run my fingers through his short-cropped hair.

"I think I need to be reminded of just how good we can be," I say.

Simon gently takes my chin in his hand, then presses a soft kiss to my lips. When he leans away, he's smiling.

"I might need the assistance of one of those toys you

dropped in my nightstand the other day," he growls. "I caught a glimpse of a couple that looked like they'd be a lot of fun. But first."

He slips his hands under my shirt and cups my bare breasts. Instantly I'm moaning.

Again our mouths fall into a rhythm of filthy kisses. A second later I'm pulling off his shirt and he's tugging off my shorts. In a minute, we're both nearly naked in the kitchen, our mouths and our hands going wild all over each other.

Simon's gaze fixes on mine. Then he drops to his knees and positions his face between my legs.

When he hooks his finger over the crotch of my underwear, I'm shuddering. "Show me," I pant. "How good."

"Can do."

"Thanks for driving," I say to Simon as he pulls into the driveway of my parents' house.

"It's no problem." He twists to the backseat and fetches the two bouquets of flowers he picked up this morning from a florist in his neighborhood.

"You really didn't have to bring anything." I climb out of the car and shut the door. "Especially with all the cookies and muffins I'm bringing."

I grab the three Tupperware containers from the back.

"I thought your mom said not to bring any food," Simon says.

"She did, and I know she'll tell me off for it, but I had to. I can't have three dozen peanut butter cookies and banana chocolate chip muffins sitting around. It's too much."

I spent most of this morning stress baking in anticipation of bringing Simon over to meet my family. Even though we're not making a big deal about our status, my family will make comments about him and us the moment we walk in, and just the thought of that gives me hives.

"Anytime you want to cook giant batches of cookies and muffins, I fully support it. They're delicious and it makes me go all gooey inside to think that you baked me something."

When we walk in, we're hit with a blast of conversation and laughter. I kick off my sandals and move to the side so Simon can stand next to me in the entryway. A dozen people sit in the living room, chatting away, not even noticing that we've walked in the door. Two of my younger cousins are setting up the karaoke machine the family breaks out every time there's a gathering.

Harper walks out from the hallway. With her jean shorts, blue flannel button-up, thick-rimmed glasses, and the messy bun she's sporting, she looks more like a hipster college student than a mega-successful corporate architect.

"Hey, you two!" She greets us both with hugs right as our cousin's toddler son ambles up to her and tugs at her hand. He holds up his sippy cup.

"Auntie Harper, milk? Please?"

I aww at his puppy dog eyes.

Harper's expression softens. "Of course, baby."

She leads him to the kitchen, where another dozen family members are zipping around cooking, setting up plates, and snacking.

I gesture with my hand. "Meet the Ellorza clan."

Just then Mom darts from the kitchen to the living room. She runs a hand through her shoulder-length black hair.

"*Manong* Seb, can you help Gordon light the grill? I

swear he's going to set the whole backyard on fire the way he's trying to do it." She smooths down the front of her floral print blouse with a hand, turns around, and breaks into a wide smile when she spots me.

"You're here!" She squints at the stack of Tupperware containers in my arms. "Ay, what is that?"

"I brought dessert."

She shakes her head and, just like I thought she would, she tells me I shouldn't have brought anything. She scoops the Tupperware from my arms and puts them on top of the nearby console table. Then she pulls me into a hug before turning to Simon. "Simon! It's wonderful to finally meet you in person!"

"It's so nice to see you too, Ms. Ellorza," he says, handing her flowers. "These are for you. Thank you for having me."

"Oh my, these are beautiful. Thank you! And please call me Marla. Come here."

Even though she's half his size, she jerks him into a one-armed hug that is shockingly powerful judging by the look on his face.

When she finally releases him, she turns around. "*Ading* Gigi! Come here and say hi to Naomi!"

Auntie Gigi appears from the nearby hallway and grins at me. "Oh, *anakko*! It's been so long!"

She hugs me tight and I'm smothered into her permed hair. I haven't seen Auntie Gigi since I was in college more than ten years ago. I tell her how wonderful it is to see her and how amazing she looks.

She waves a hand, the gold bangles on her arm clinking together. "Oh, I don't know about that. But you look so lovely! Such a pretty dress."

I tug at the long sleeves of my chambray shirtdress.

"Where's Uncle Reuben?" I ask.

Auntie Gigi's smile wavers for a split second. "He couldn't come. Had family stuff to deal with back home."

"Oh." Inside I deflate the slightest bit. I haven't seen him in just as long and thought he'd be here too. They're the kind of married couple who do everything together—travel, go to the store, cook, watch TV, read the newspaper. It's weird that he's not here.

"Is everything okay with his family?" I ask.

"Oh yes, it's fine," she says with a wave of her hand before turning her attention to Simon. "And who's this?"

"This is Simon. My friend."

From behind Mom I catch a glimpse of Harper in the kitchen, rolling her eyes and shaking her head at how I've chosen to introduce him.

I do my best to ignore her and keep my smile as Simon hands Auntie Gigi the other small bundle of multicolored blooms. Just like Mom, Auntie Gigi fawns over what a lovely and thoughtful surprise it is.

Mom pulls on Auntie Gigi's arm. "Don't you think he looks like that doctor on *Grey's Anatomy*? That handsome one that was in the military who stapled his own leg?"

Auntie Gigi's eyes go wide as she shakes her head. "Oh yes! Except you look younger."

I shake my head and smile as they spend the next minute talking about Simon's physical similarities to the actor. I mouth a quiet "sorry" to him, but he just grins.

Finally, I grab his arm and tug him toward the kitchen. "I'm going to show Simon where all the food is."

"Oh yes, eat up!" Mom says. "We have so much food."

She and auntie run to the garage to find vases for the flowers while we make our way to the kitchen, stopping to say quick hellos to relatives along the way. Dad pops in through the sliding glass door, clad in an apron that says "Kiss Me I'm A Giants Fan," grill tongs in his hand. He runs up to give me a hug.

"Oh, honey bear!" He squeezes me tight. "So good to see you."

I smile at his childhood nickname for me that's stuck well into adulthood.

He pulls back and grips me by the shoulders, beaming down at me. He's Simon's height but has a slimmer frame because of all the distance running he used to do before his hip surgery last year.

"Let me look at you, honey bear. Yup. Still beautiful. And still got that gorgeous hair I gave you."

He pats the top of his head, which is speckled with gray stubble. He started shaving it when he began losing his hair years ago. Simon chuckles behind me.

I turn around and gesture to Simon. "Dad, this is Simon. He's the guy who I'm filming for work. And he helped Mom repair the vase you made for her. Simon, this is my dad, Gordon."

Dad turns to give Simon a handshake and thanks him for helping Mom.

"Good to meet you, sir," Simon says.

"Likewise. You guys should get some food. Then maybe you could help me out back with the grill, Simon?"

"Of course."

Dad gives me a soft squeeze on the shoulder before walking out of the room. I do a scan of the kitchen. Endless dishes of food line the island and counter. A few more relatives come up to us to chat before insisting that we eat. I quickly introduce Simon, then hand him a plate.

"Hope you're hungry," I say.

He winks at me. "Always."

# *Chapter Twenty*

An hour later, we're stuffed and sitting in the living room, listening to my cousin belt a Whitney Houston tune. Simon sits at the end of the plush sectional with me next to him.

"Gotta say, I came today thinking you'd be the best singer in your family, but everyone is so good."

"Maybe it's a family trait. Most of us can carry a tune."

"You're way better than just being able to carry a tune. You should hear how off-key my family can get even when we try to sing 'Happy Birthday.'"

"So you're having fun, then?"

"A blast. Everyone is so warm and welcoming. I can see how you're so amazing because your family is too."

My chest starts to warm, then tingle. The longer he stares at me, that sincerity and warmth in his eyes, the more that sensation grows.

"It means a lot that you brought me here to meet them," he says, his voice low and soft.

He shifts his leg, where his hand rests, so that he's touching my thigh. And then he moves his hand so that his pinky is touching my pinky. It's so minor, but god does it make my heart soar. It's like he can sense I don't want to be touchy-feely in front of my family, and that's what makes this tiny bit of skin-to-skin contact so special. Especially when I look up and soak in the expression on his face. Like he's so, so happy to be here, with my family—with me.

When I glance away, I catch Mom staring at us from across the room. But then she turns around and pulls Dad into a chat.

"Simon! Will you sing Britney Spears with me?" Auntie Gigi's eight-year-old granddaughter, Abigail, gazes at him from where she's sitting on the floor.

"Oh my gosh, Abby. Don't rope poor Simon into that."

He squints at me. "You don't think I can do Britney justice?"

I swallow back a laugh. "Okay. Let's see, then."

He slides off the couch and plops next to Abigail, who hands him a microphone. When she chooses "Gimme More," Simon turns around and flashes me a smug look, as if he's silently saying "watch this." Once the beat drops and the lyrics crawl across the screen, both Abigail and Simon croon along to the song while grooving their torsos. Around them everyone cheers. I shout a few woos while laughing at how Simon is unafraid to get silly.

I could swear my heart gets bigger the longer I watch him. He fits right in with my family. Everyone loves him.

And then an image takes hold in my brain. It's an image I never thought I'd have. It's of Simon and me together at some random family gathering. Relatives surround us. It's loud and crowded like always, but this time, he's holding my hand, in full view of everyone. He leans over and kisses me. My heart ceases beating.

Maybe things with Simon could work out long term. They're working out pretty well right now.

I close my eyes for a second so I can soak in the visual, relishing how every beat of my heart feels like a leap into something mysterious and wonderful. Everyone starts cheering and clapping, and I open my eyes. Simon and Abby stand up and take a bow. He plops back down next to me, tugging at the hem of his T-shirt.

"Well, damn." I laugh, hoping the surge of emotion coursing through me isn't obvious.

"Never doubt my karaoke skills," he says. "What I don't have in pitch, I make up for in enthusiasm."

Holding his eye contact, I pat his leg, keeping my hand on him for a few long seconds. He raises an eyebrow, clearly intrigued that I would risk this much physical contact between us in full view of my family.

"I think that deserves a beer."

I pop up from the couch and head to the kitchen. I fetch a beer from the refrigerator and then turn around to see Mom behind me, a knowing smile on her face.

"Your friend Simon seems very nice, *anak*."

"He is."

She flashes me a dubious look while leaning on the kitchen island. "You sure there's not more going on with you two?"

I hesitate for a second. Had she asked me when we first walked in, I'd be in full-on denial mode. But right now? Right now I'm someplace else. Someplace happy and hopeful, where the idea of Simon and me together in the long term makes me giddy, where I can watch him fit into my family and not feel one ounce of panic or uncertainty.

"It's complicated," I finally say. I wince when I realize just how ominous that sounds.

A knowing smile dances on her lips. It's the same

look she used to give my brother and me as kids, when we thought we knew better about something, but she knew better all along.

"Mom. Come on. Don't give me that look."

She holds up a hand, the expression on her face a sort of feigned innocence. "I'm just saying, you two seem to like each other a lot. And so many of your aunties and uncles and cousins have come up to me today to say how cute you are together."

I hesitate once more.

This time she holds up both hands. "That's it! That's all I'll say." She pats me on the shoulder before grabbing a nearby dishrag and wiping down the counter.

I turn to walk away, but then she starts up again.

"Okay, I'll just say one more thing."

I turn around to her.

"This is the happiest I've seen you with someone, *anak*. I've never seen you smile so much. You say you're just friends, but you could have fooled me. It doesn't look all that complicated from what I can see."

Usually whenever Mom tries to pry into my dating life, I tell her I don't want to talk about it because it's such a disaster. Then she tells me to give love a chance, I roll my eyes or say something dismissive, and we bicker.

But her comment about Simon sends a wave of giddiness through me. It starts at my stomach and rises all the way to my chest. I walk out of the kitchen back into the living room and observe Simon chatting with Harper, who's sitting next to him on the couch now. He's genuinely happy to be here.

I walk over and hand him the beer. When he smiles up at me, the ache in my chest pulses and my face starts to warm. I'm thrown off at this feeling, this excitement and comfort that converges inside of me. Because if somehow, some way I could have it like this—Simon with me, fitting into my life so seamlessly—I'd want it. It would be perfect.

"Be back," I say. "Gotta run to the restroom."

I flit off to the hallway bathroom. I don't really need to pee, I just need a moment to collect myself. This feeling—this realization that I'm willing to throw out the rule book, to take a real chance on Simon, is akin to feeling light-headed times ten. Am I having some sort of epiphany?

I reach for the doorknob but stop short when I hear Auntie Gigi on the other side of the door.

I start to back away, but then her voice breaks. She sniffles and lets out another cry before speaking rapidly in Ilocano. I freeze. I know I shouldn't be eavesdropping, but I want to make sure she's okay.

It takes a second for me to understand what she's saying, she's speaking so quickly. But when I do, my jaw drops.

"What do you think I did, Reuben? I lied for you, like I always do. You need to just figure out things on your end…"

There's a long pause before she starts again.

"Well, what did you want me to tell them? That we can't stand the sight of each other anymore?… Of course not… Look, they'll be upset enough as it is when they find out about us splitting up. Just get your things and be out by the time I get back. That's all I'm asking you to do."

There's another long pause, a few more sniffles, and a muttered curse. The door swings open.

Shit.

I register the look of heartbreak on her tear-soaked face and grab her hand in mine.

"How much did you hear?" she asks, wiping her nose with a tissue. Her tone is so broken, such a painful contrast to how cheery she sounded when I saw her visiting with family just minutes ago.

"Enough. I'm so sorry, auntie."

When her mouth starts to wobble, I pull her into a hug. She mumbles, "Thank you, *anak*," before pulling away a second later. Then her gaze darts to the side, as if she's scared of anyone seeing her like his.

"Here." I gesture for us to go back into the bathroom together. I shut the door behind me as she sits on the edge of the tub.

"Well. Now you know. Uncle Reuben and I are getting divorced." She stares at her lap before fussing with the gold bangles on her wrist.

"What happened?" I ask gently. I know it's none of my business, but at the same time I'm aching with curiosity. I file through every memory I have of them. They always looked so happy together. They would always hold hands, always kiss, always look at each other with adoration in their eyes. I never once saw them argue growing up.

She shrugs, and I hand her the tissue box from the bathroom counter. "It's hard to say. We used to be so happy. Then one day, we weren't."

"But…how?"

"I wish I knew." She shakes her head, studying me with her bloodshot brown eyes. "You know, sometimes you just get used to a person—in a good and bad way. I think when the kids grew up and moved out, we realized we didn't have as many things in common as we thought we did. We were just going through the motions for so many years. In a lot of ways, we felt more like friends. Roommates even. And then when it was just us and no one else there, it felt...different. We started getting on each other's nerves and fighting so much, about the littlest things. We weren't happy anymore. I can't keep living like that, neither of us can."

I open my mouth, speechless, my head in a daze. If one of the most loving and affectionate married couples I know can't make it work, what hope does anyone else have?

Auntie Gigi stands up and walks over to look at the mirror. I watch as she tidies up her eye makeup. Her lipstick has faded to a light pink and most of her mascara has been cried or wiped away.

She turns to look at me and grabs my arms. "I'm sorry to unload all of that on you, *anak*."

The guilty look in her eyes is too much. I start to tear up, so I pull her into a hug. "Don't apologize. I'm so sorry for what you're going through."

When she pulls away, she keeps hold of my arms. "Please don't tell anyone, okay? Not even your mom. I... I still need to tell her. She knows something's wrong, though."

I promise her that I won't. The heavy sigh she lets loose echoes in the small space. She slips out and I'm left standing in the bathroom, unnerved in a whole new way. A barrage of memories crash in my head. I recall every other time I've introduced a boyfriend to my family. It inevitably ends. Always.

The only reason things with Simon feel so fun and easy right now is because we're early days. We'll reach our disastrous end eventually. And someday, I'd end up just like Auntie Gigi, crying in the bathroom when it all comes crumbling down.

I go back to where Simon and Harper are sitting. For a while I just sit and say nothing.

"You two are getting quite the reaction," Harper says as she nudges me.

Simon's stubbled cheeks redden. He starts to grin. "Really?"

Harper nods and chuckles. I grit my teeth.

"Auntie Cindy asked me while I was playing mahjong with her a bit ago how long Naomi has been dating the guy who looks like the handsome army doctor from *Grey's Anatomy*."

Simon laughs, then immediately stops when he looks at me and notices I'm not joining him.

"Oh, come on," Harper says. "You know that's just typical family talk."

"Yeah, well, it gets kind of annoying after a while." I flick my hair of out my face. When I look up, I notice Harper's brow is slightly raised, probably at how hard my tone is.

"I don't need you on top of everyone else teasing me about a relationship," I say. "You more than anyone know how much that annoys me."

Harper's brow is to her hairline by the time I finish talking. She pushes her glasses up the bridge of her nose and frowns. "Fine. Sorry."

I hazard a glance at Simon, who looks equally shocked.

Thankfully no one else noticed my little outburst. Cousins are still singing karaoke in front of us. Behind us relatives are still chatting and eating.

I turn to Simon. "You ready to get out of here?"

His eyebrows crash together, but he nods anyway. We stand up and say quick good-byes to everyone, then drive back to San Francisco in silence.

"Everything okay?"

It's the third time Simon's asked me that since we arrived at his apartment. And every time I give him the same answer. A terse "Yes, it's fine" with zero elaborating.

I know he doesn't buy it. But I'm not ready to say more.

"Naomi."

His soft tone compels me to turn around from where I stand at his kitchen counter, squinting at my laptop.

The concern in his eyes is an arrow to my heart. "What's wrong?"

"Nothing." I force a cheeriness to my tone that isn't normally there.

"You don't have to pretend you're fine when you're not." He says it softly before gently grabbing my hand in his.

I pull my hand away. "Nothing's wrong. I'm fine."

I suspect the tight smile I'm displaying isn't convincing, judging by his heavy sigh.

"I don't know why you're not being honest with me," he says. "We've always been honest with each other. What changed?"

"Maybe we should cool things off a bit."

I bite the inside of my cheek, angry with how meek I sound when I say it. I should at least have confidence when I propose this.

Simon's eyebrows smash together, like he couldn't be more confused at what I've said. "Why?"

It's a fruitless search for the right words. Probably because there are none. So instead I stammer until he speaks.

"Naomi, I thought things were going really well between us. I thought we had a great time with your family."

I tug at my hair and try not to groan. "We are. It's just…well, you said we do this on our own terms, right? At our own pace, and it's just moving a bit fast for me."

"Okay…" Simon's eyes search my face, like he can't quite make sense of what I'm saying.

"Look, I think… I can't have things between us get serious. Ever."

Something changes in his gaze. "What is going on? Did something trigger you or—"

I hold up a hand, exasperated. "Could you just for once not talk to me like you're trying to coach me through a therapy session?"

When he flinches at my irritated tone, I feel like the biggest jerk on the planet.

"I'm sorry. I just…can you just tell me your raw feelings and not be therapist Simon right now?"

He nods.

I take a breath. "Do you sometimes think that we could be something…more? Like, more serious than what we are now?"

His expression falls the slightest bit and it makes my chest feel like it's going to cave in on itself. He knows. He knows exactly what I'm about to say.

"The truth? Yeah. I do think that. I like you, Naomi. I like spending time with you. I like having sex with you. I like waking up next to you. I like coming home to my apartment with you. There's no one I'd rather spend time with than you. And I want so much more than that with you someday. How's that for raw and serious?"

He says it all without flinching, with a confidence I've never heard before. It's like he's calling my bluff, daring me to say more.

"That's just it. I can't… I can't do that. I can't give you all that."

"Why not? What happened?"

And then I tell him everything, how I walked in on Auntie Gigi crying in the bathroom, arguing with my uncle about their impending divorce, how she told me they grew apart over the years, how there's so much animosity and resentment between them, they can't speak without arguing.

"Next to my parents, they were one of the most solid married couples I knew. They were so in love for so long. And now they're done. And I just… I don't want to end up like that. Like them. Resentful and hateful of each other."

A long moment passes before he says anything.

"Naomi. Why do you do this? Why are you hell-bent on sabotaging a good thing?"

He tugs at his hair, shaking his head, like he's mustering the last bit of patience to talk to me.

"We aren't your aunt and uncle. I'm sorry things ended for them, but that doesn't mean they're going to end for us." His chest heaves as he breathes. "And newsflash: I know you think your parents have some perfect marriage, but I can guarantee that they don't. I'm sure they've had problems. I'm sure they've had times when they fought and couldn't stand each other. Every couple does. You just figure out a way to work through it together."

He reaches for me, but I jerk away before he can touch me. "That's just it, Simon. I've tried. So many times I've tried, with every relationship I've had. And I've never, ever gotten through it. No matter who I've been with, no matter how many times we try to talk it out or work it out, it's never happened. No matter what I do, it's always wrong. It always ends up a disaster. And I don't... I don't want that to happen with you and me."

My voice shakes at the end. I swallow hard, willing the tears that are pooling in my eyes not to fall.

"Naomi."

My name is a whisper on his lips. It's so soft, so loving. I have to close my eyes and breathe, it's too overwhelming.

When I feel his hand on my face, I hesitate for a second. But then I lean into the warmth of his palm. I almost moan, it feels so damn good.

"This is different. *We* are different. Don't you feel that?"

I relish the growl of his whisper before opening my eyes. My heart skips at the look in his golden brown gaze. Raw and open, just for me.

"I feel it," I say. "Of course I feel it."

He presses his lips against my forehead and every muscle in my body loosens. He always feels so good against me.

"I'm not saying that we'll never have to work through anything difficult," he whispers against my skin.

He slips his arms around my waist and I fall into him completely.

"I'm not saying it's gonna be easy. But I want to at least try. Don't you?"

Again I press my eyes shut, so hard my eye sockets

begin to ache. I don't know if I can give him the answer he wants, and that kills me.

"I... I don't know."

I feel his body tense against me and I lean back so I can look at him. "I want you, Simon. More than anything. I just... I hate the thought that this could all end and we could end up hating each other."

Just saying those words hurts. Like I've just bitten my tongue.

"Naomi." My name is a soft growl on his breath. "I don't hate you right now. Do you hate me?"

I shake my head.

"How do you feel about me? Right here, right now. Tell me." He holds my gaze, refusing to blink.

I can feel his heart beat against me as it thuds in his chest. That familiar ache hits once again, starting from my core and gliding like heat between my thighs. I'm practically shaking.

I grip him tighter as I struggle to steady my breath. "I want you. Right here, right now."

Our mouths crash together. It's like we haven't seen each other in months. We claw at our clothes like they're on fire. I don't remember moving or walking, but the next thing I know we're in Simon's bedroom, a trail of our clothes behind us.

He breaks our kiss to hold me by the waist and gaze at me. Every inch of my skin feels like it's on fire. We've seen each other naked so many times up to this point, but never like this. Never with our hearts bursting out of our chests, never after laying bare all of our feelings.

"Naomi. I..."

He bites the tip of his tongue between his teeth. But instead of saying anything more, he kisses me. It's so hard and deep I can barely breathe. But I love it. He's never kissed me like this before.

"I want you too," he says through pants, resting his forehead against mine. "I've never wanted anyone the way I want you."

I claw at his hair, kissing him until we're both gasping. "Same. Same, same, same."

We fall onto the bed and just like every other time, he coaxes me to lie back, puts his face between my legs, and kisses me until I'm a shouting, shuddering mass.

Legs twitching, I watch through blurry vision as he wipes his mouth with the back of his wrist, then climbs up to me. But I press my hand on his chest, holding him there. He starts to ask what I'm doing, but when I push him onto his back and get between his legs, he loses all his words. They're not needed right now. All he needs as I take him into my mouth are gasps and grunts. He's a mess of caveman noises until he pulls me by the shoulders up to his face.

Our kisses are so sloppy by now. We're biting and teasing and grabbing and moaning. He slides on a condom, and I hold his gaze as I lower myself onto him. Even as he stretches me out, I don't blink. I keep looking at him as I ride him slow and deep, until the pleasure and pressure becomes too much and I can't take it one second more. I circle my clit with my hand, my head falling back as I moan. He guides me, thrusting, with his powerful hands digging into my hips.

It doesn't take long for me to fall apart. And when I do, he's not far behind. I collapse on his chest and for a few minutes we just lie there, our skin slick with sweat and our hearts thudding out of our chests. He rolls me over to the side and steps away, but soon he's back and pulls me against his chest. I close my eyes, aching to sleep. Every muscle in my body is loose and relaxed and not just because of the two incredible orgasms Simon gave me. Everything about this moment and this place feels like home.

Once again my eyes are burning and I have to press them shut to keep the tears from escaping.

"Please don't go," he whispers as he tucks his chin above my head.

"I won't."

I keep my promise and fall asleep in Simon's arms.

When I wake, it's pitch-black out. The only way I'm able to see a thing is from the glow of the streetlights as they stream in through the cracks in the blinds.

As Simon snores in bed, I slowly, quietly creep out of bed and use the bathroom. When I come back out, I stand at the foot of the bed and gaze at him. That messy mop of light brown hair, the way his broad chest heaves with each breath, the way he always rests his arm over his face when he's in the deepest part of sleep.

I could crawl back in right now and he'd cuddle me back into his chest. It would be so perfect.

My arms and legs twitch at the thought, aching to snuggle with him. I almost do it.

But it won't always be perfect. Something will give. All that excitement and attraction we feel for each other right now will eventually give way to hurt feelings and disaster. Something will go wrong between us. It always does.

Best to end it now.

I turn around and pick my clothes up off the floor. Then I get dressed, grab my things, and quietly leave.

# Chapter Twenty-One

I stretch out on the couch in Harper's living room and blink at the ceiling. No more tears are allowed for the rest of the day. I was calm as I made my way back to Harper's place, but the moment I shut the door behind me, I broke. Ugly sobs overtook me. I had to cover my mouth, they were so loud and I didn't want to wake Harper, who's sleeping in her bedroom. So I sunk to the floor, head in my hands, my shoulders shuddering as I cried quietly.

I still managed to text Simon though, so he wouldn't worry when he woke up and saw me gone.

Me: I can't do this. I'm so sorry.

He read the message minutes after I sent it, but there was no response. And I don't expect one. I left like such a coward—in the exact way he told me hurts him the most.

Four hours after I left his apartment in the wee hours of the morning, Simon and I are done. Even though I know it's what's best, it still shatters me to think about it. I blink furiously at the ceiling, ordering my tear ducts to stop overflowing. Yes, my time with Simon was amazing—*he* was amazing. He was the best man I've ever been with.

The longer I think about him, the more I miss him. The more I want to swing the front door wide open and run back to him.

As much as I adore Simon, it would have ended eventually. Best that I left now instead of putting off the inevitable. My head spins as I think about what it will be like to see him when we film Cole and Tamara's vow renewal for *Simply Simon* and how the hell I'm going to navigate that. I'm sure he despises me and never wants to see me again, but I've got a job to finish…

Harper's bedroom door creaks open, and I look up from the couch. She's rubbing her eyes as she yawns, then stops dead in her tracks when she sees me.

"What the hell are you doing here?"

I sniffle, hoping my face doesn't look too puffy. "I, uh, decided to stay here today."

"Okay…" She frowns, opens her mouth like she's going to ask me something, then clamps it shut and darts to the bathroom. After a minute I hear the toilet flush and the faucet run. Then she's back out, and she walks over to the couch and perches on the arm, facing me.

"Shouldn't you be at Simon's? You've been there almost every night this past month."

I shake my head, annoyed at how hard my lip is wobbling.

Harper's gaze softens. "Shit. What happened?"

I spill everything that happened with Simon. When I finish, a confused frown paints Harper's face.

"So wait…you didn't even want to try?"

Her words sting like a slap to the face.

"Harper, I'm a disaster when it comes to that stuff. You know that. It would have been the same with Simon."

"How?" She plants a hand on her hip. It's her signature I'm-about-to-tell-you-off move and I brace myself because I know I'm in for it. "How in the world do you know that it would have ended the exact same way with Simon when you didn't even try? He's a therapist, remember? Not an insensitive douche. He's aware of how to navigate a relationship in a healthy way."

"Therapist or not, look at my track record. Every relationship I've had has ended in flames."

"Naomi. Do you honestly think *you* were the problem in all of your past relationships? You really don't think those cheating, insensitive, selfish jerkoffs were the reason things ended?"

I tug a hand through my hair. "Okay, fine, I see your point. But I'm the one who chose them. Clearly I'm the problem."

"You chose Simon too," she says without missing a beat. "He's a pretty quality guy."

I open my mouth, but I've got nothing. She's right.

"You've definitely picked some duds in your life, Naomi. I'll be the first to tell you that. But you also picked an amazing guy—Simon. That shows how *you* have changed. You're clearly not going for the same kind of crap-weasel you used to go for. Look how far you've come."

I let out a teary chuckle.

She glances at the window overlooking the San Francisco skyline, shaking her head slightly. "I know this is gonna sound weird to bring up right now, but I swear I've got a point."

"Okay…"

"I quit my job."

"What?"

She tugs at the hem of the ratty Pepperdine T-shirt she wears to bed almost every night. Then she hops off the couch and heads to the kitchen to make a pot of coffee.

I follow her. "Harper, are you serious?"

She spins around, hand on her hip. "Dead serious. I gave my two weeks' notice on Friday."

My jaw hits the floor. When I can regain the ability to speak seconds later, I'm sputtering. "Wh-why didn't you tell me?"

"Because I needed some time to process the news alone first."

"Wow. That's… Harper, that's awesome." I let myself smile. This is the first and only spontaneous thing I can ever remember her doing.

"What are you gonna do now?"

"I'm moving to Half Moon Bay." She gives a shaky smile. Even though I can detect nerves behind it, I haven't seen her look so excited in forever. Even the puffiness from sleep does little to hide the joy in her expression.

She explains that once she finishes up work, she's going to rent out her place and head to Half Moon Bay.

"I don't even know where to start. I've just… Okay, so it's no secret I've been unhappy at my job for a while. I felt like I was going through the motions. I used to be so passionate about architecture. I loved going into work and staying late most days to see my vision come to life. But I just got sick of it after a while. The passion faded away. I don't know when or why it happened, but I guess it doesn't matter."

She pauses once the coffee is done brewing. Then she pours us each a mug and motions for us to go sit on the couch again.

"I stayed for so long, longer than I should have. For the money obviously," she says. "I was able to save, pay off my student loans, and buy this apartment. You know how much that means, right?"

I nod, understanding her completely. Thankfully mine and Harper's families have never been poor or desolate, but we've never been close to rich. We still aren't, especially not by the insane cost of living standards in San Francisco. Harper is the most financially successful member of our family and even she's careful with her money. Our grandparents were immigrants from the Philippines who moved to California and worked hard to provide for their families. We never went without, but we never had expensive things. Even though I make well above average with my job, Harper made almost four times my salary. I can completely understand why she stayed at her job for so long. It gave her the kind of financial security we've always dreamed about. That would be almost impossible for most people to walk away from.

"But then the other week, I was sitting at my desk, looking at these plans for another multimillion-dollar sports complex the city is building…and I couldn't get myself to care about it," she says. "I tried all day to make headway on the project, but it was like pulling teeth. And that's when it occurred to me. I don't like my job anymore. And I didn't want to do it for one more second."

Harper's eyes light up as she relays how she walked into her boss's office and gave her notice.

She takes another breath. "I'm going to fix up *Apong* Vivian and *Apong* Bernie's house."

My jaw drops once more before I pull her into a hug. "Are you serious? Harper, that's amazing. I'm... I don't even have the words. I'm so, so happy."

Our grandma and grandpa bought a small house in Half Moon Bay, the quaint and cute sleepy coastal town half an hour south of San Francisco. It was their first and only home purchase in the US. That's where Harper and I would spend the holidays with the rest of our cousins growing up, crammed in that tiny two-bedroom house, sharing yummy family meals, opening presents, singing karaoke, chatting, and laughing.

When they passed away years ago, they left the house to Harper's parents, but it's needed so much remodeling and structural work, and no one has had the time or money to undertake it.

"Wait, you're not going to do the remodeling by yourself, are you?"

"Oh god, no way. I'll hire contractors. I just...when I was sitting at my desk, I asked myself what would make me happy. Like, truly blissfully happy. And the only thing that came to my mind was that house. I always loved staying there as a kid. I thought about how if only I had the time, I could go up there and start fixing it up. And it just clicked in my head. I thought, why not?"

I pull her into another hug. "I'm so happy for you. Truly. This would make them so, so happy."

"Thank you," she says softly. When she pulls away, she holds me by the shoulders, her hickory-brown eyes boring into me. "You say people can't change. Did you ever think I'd just quit my job on a whim?"

"This is different. It's not work. It's so much more personal."

"It's really not," she scoffs.

I shake my head as I let out a sigh. My knees ache from sitting cross-legged on the couch for so long. I start to turn so I can reposition, but Harper grabs me by the arm again.

"Listen, when you told me three months ago after things ended with you and Brody that you were banning relationships forever, I thought it was the worst idea I had ever heard of."

"I remember," I mutter.

"I don't mean that as an insult to you. I get why you did it. You were hurt—and you were tired of getting hurt. But when did Simon ever hurt you? Like, truly hurt you in the way that your past boyfriends did?"

I open my mouth, but nothing comes out. Because she's right. Simon has never once betrayed my trust or hurt my feelings on purpose. Yeah, he got protective and jealous with Landon, but then he apologized for it and changed his behavior. He handled it more maturely than any other guy I've been with.

"No. He never hurt me," I finally say.

She raises an eyebrow. "Exactly."

"Harper, things between Simon and I have only gotten romantic recently. We've been together a month. There's no guarantee it'll work out."

"There's no guarantee anything will work out, ever," she fires back. "Friendships, jobs, where you live, long-term plans. You're not skittish about any of those."

Okay, she definitely has a point there. "Naomi, I've seen the way your past relationships have wrecked you and made you doubt yourself—you don't trust yourself to have a healthy, loving, lasting relationship because of your history with those jerks you dated. And it killed me. Because you absolutely are capable of it. You're loving, honest, loyal, and attentive. And you were that way to every single one of your exes. The reason those relationships ended was because they ghosted or cheated or lost interest or had their own personal issues to work through independent of you. Not because you're some flawed, unlovable person. You're amazing. You just needed the right guy. And I really do think Simon is that guy for you."

She pauses, presumably to let me soak in what she's said. I'm thankful for the pause because everything she's said lands like some heavy-hitting revelation. She's spot-on.

"You're punishing Simon because of what your douchebag exes did to you."

I try to speak, but she cuts me off.

"I get it. Really, I do. It sucks to be hurt by someone you love. But don't treat Simon like he's broken your heart when he hasn't. You know you're in love with him."

I balk at the word "love."

Harper rolls her eyes yet again. "You're joking me, right? You're not going to try and tell me that you're not in love with him. I've seen the way you look at each other. I've never, not once, seen you as happy with any guy ever than with Simon," she says softly. "Didn't you realize that? Didn't it ever occur to you how things felt different with him than with everyone else?"

My head spins at all the truth bombs she's dropping left and right. When I don't say anything in response, she continues. "Did you ever pay attention to how Simon looked at you like there was no one else in the room? You did the same with him."

My stomach drops when I remember it, the way intensity and kindness somehow perfectly merged in his golden brown stare. Every single time.

"He looked at you like he was in love with you, Naomi. You guys were friends *and* you fucked," Harper says. "That's the jackpot. And you're willing to throw it away because of your past and your insecurity. That's so sad."

I struggle to process what Harper seems to have figured out so easily.

She reaches over and gives my shoulder a squeeze. "You cried after you ended things with him, didn't you?" she asks softly.

Eyes watering, I nod. "For hours. Basically from the moment I left his place until you woke up," I admit.

"You've never cried like that for anyone. Sure, you cried when you found out that Brody got another woman pregnant, but that was more anger that he would be so hurtful and deceptive than feeling sad that you lost him."

I mutter that she's right.

"Simon is different. You care about him in a way I've never seen you care about a guy. You were the happiest I've ever seen you when you were spending time with him. And I can tell how much you miss him. Because you love him. You know in your heart you love him. Your head just needs to catch up."

She pats me on the shoulder once more, flashing a sympathetic smile. Then she hops off the couch and gazes down at me. "Just think about it, okay?"

"I will."

She pads back to the bathroom to take a shower, while I sit on the couch and toy with the idea that maybe—just maybe—I'm in love with Simon.

I eye my phone sitting on the coffee table. There's only one person I can talk to right now who can help me make sense of everything. I swipe it up and dial.

"Mom?" I say when she answers.

"Hi, *anak*! How are you? Gordon!" She shouts my dad's name before I can even answer. "Come say hi to Naomi!"

I smile to myself. We saw each other yesterday and she's still thrilled to hear from me. A second later I'm on speakerphone listening to them bicker good-naturedly about who gets to hold the phone.

"I told you. I've got it," Mom says.

"Whatever you say, beautiful," Dad says. "How's things since we saw you yesterday, honey bear?"

"Um, okay." I clear my throat, hoping I don't sound too pathetic.

"You sure everything's okay, *anak*?" Mom asks. "Your voice sounds funny."

Closing my eyes, I let out a slow, quiet breath. Of course she can see right through it. She always can.

"Actually, um, I was hoping I could talk to Mom, Dad."

"Say no more, I understand completely."

There's a muffled puckering noise on the other end. Then Mom makes a "muah" sound.

"You girls have a fun chat. Love you!"

"Love you too, Dad."

There are a few more seconds of muffled sounds before my mom speaks. "So! Tell me what's on your mind."

"I have a question." I clear my throat. "How…how did you know you were in love with Dad?"

I'm sure I could have asked my dad the same question, but he claims to have fallen in love with Mom on their first date. As adorable as that is, I'm not a hopeless romantic like him. I need to approach this from a different angle.

"That's an odd question, *anak*. Why are you asking? Do you think you might be in love with someone?"

"Maybe… Yes… I don't know."

"This is about Simon, isn't it?"

"Um, yeah."

"Ah, I see." I can almost hear the smile in her voice. "Well, here's the thing. No one can tell you you're in love with someone. It's a feeling."

"I know that." I sigh. "It's just… What if your feelings are a mess? And your brain is a mess too? So you have no idea how to feel or what to do…" I drift off, fully aware that I'm making zero sense.

The sound of Mom's chuckling throws me. "*Anak*, there wasn't a moment where a light bulb went off in my head and I suddenly knew I was in love with your dad. It was just this sense of comfort and joy that kept growing the longer I was with him. No one before him ever made me feel that way—so taken care of, so comfortable, so happy."

Her explanation sends a jolt to my chest. That's exactly how Simon makes me feel.

"That sounds amazing. Easy, almost."

Her laugh echoes against my ear. "Oh, *anak*. It wasn't easy."

"Well, you and Dad make it look easy. You're the perfect couple. You're a hard act to follow."

"There's no such thing as perfect, Naomi."

"Maybe not, but you two come close."

"*Anak*, what makes you think we're perfect? We fight just like any other couple. We get on each other's nerves. Sometimes we can't stand each other."

"Mom, I don't remember any of this growing up. I mean, I remember a few arguments, but they were never serious."

She sighs. "That's because we purposely didn't fight in front of you kids."

"Oh."

She pauses for a moment. "You said something a bit ago. 'You're a hard act to follow.'"

"Well, yeah. My whole life you two made marriage look easy. I've always struggled with my relationships. They've all ended in flames. I figured I was doing something wrong, picking the wrong guy. I kind of assumed I was bad at them."

"Oh, *anak*."

I flinch at the dejection in her voice.

"Maybe I should have told you this, but I suppose now's the right time."

There's a quiet moment where it sounds like she's taking a breath.

"Your dad and I were separated for a while. Before you were born, when your brother was a baby."

"What?"

If a light breeze happened to blow through the living room at that moment, I'd topple over. Never in a million years did I ever expect to hear my mom say that.

"You and Dad were separated?"

"For a short time, yes."

"What happened?"

She sighs. "I had postpartum depression after having your brother. Your dad was so busy with work and wasn't giving me the support I needed. I ended up almost having a breakdown. So I took your brother and left. And I only came back when your dad promised to change his work hours so that I could get the help I needed."

Her voice shakes, and my eyes start to burn.

"Mom, I'm sorry."

"It was hard to get through. So hard." She stops for a few seconds. "When I left, it really shook your dad. I told him I wasn't coming back unless we got marriage counseling to figure out how to move on together. So we did. We saw a therapist every week for almost two years after that. And we still see a counselor from time to time, on and off over the years. Whenever it feels like we're arguing too much or hitting a rough patch or one of us is going through something difficult and emotional."

"Wow. I…" My head spins as I search for the right words. There's so much I didn't know about my parents' marriage. "I don't know what to say. I guess I'm in shock."

A sad chuckle echoes on her end of the line. "I think that's why I didn't want to tell you. You've always looked up to our relationship. It's the most special feeling in the world, when your kids truly admire you."

"I still admire you, Mom. I admire the heck out of you and Dad for getting through that and having the marriage you have today. You're so loving and affectionate and kind to each other."

When she sighs this time, it sounds lighter. "You know, all the counseling and therapy we did over the years, it's why we're still together. And I'm sorry I never told you about it. I just didn't want you kids worrying about our struggles. I wanted you to always see us as stable figures in your life. I guess that backfired a little."

"I get it. I wonder if Auntie Gigi and Uncle Reuben tried counseling before they split."

It's a few seconds before I realize what I've said.

"Crap," I mutter.

"It's okay, *anak*. I know already."

"She told you?"

"Not yet. But it was easy enough to figure out what happened. She showed up without her husband, who she's been attached at the hip to for almost forty years. And every time I ask about him, she changes the subject. I knew trouble was brewing."

"Oh."

I explain that I accidentally overheard auntie talking about her divorce and she asked me not to tell anyone. Mom promises she won't.

"I hope you give things with Simon a chance," she says after a moment. "It won't be perfect, but you shouldn't be concerned with perfection. You should strive to be with someone who you care about, who you love, and who you want to face the tough times with. Someone worth fighting for—and fighting with."

I blink and a tear falls. I've never met anyone who I even cared to fight for—until Simon…and I threw it away because I doubted myself and I conditioned myself to be cynical.

"You should tell Simon you love him," she finally says.

"Mom, I'm still not sure—"

"Is there anyone that compares to him?" she asks,

cutting me off. "Is there another person on this planet who you'd rather spend a day with?"

I don't even have to think. "No. I only want him."

"Does his well-being and happiness mean anything to you?"

"Yes. More than my own." I'm shocked at how quickly I answer her. But it's the truth.

"Then I think you love him, *anak*."

"I… I think I do love him." It feels so weird to say it out loud. But also so incredible.

"I just… I'm not sure if he loves me."

"Oh, he does," she says. "I saw the way he looked at you. No man looks at a woman like that unless he's in love with her."

My heart races at how even though she only saw us together once, she could tell. And then it sinks at just how oblivious I was to my own feelings for so long.

"Tell him, *anak*."

I sniffle. "Okay. I will."

We hang up. I contemplate running back over to Simon's place, but I check the time. He's leaving the city early this morning to spend the day with his mom and grandma. Holding my breath, I dial him. My chest tightens with each ring. I get his voicemail. And it's full.

I let out a groan. You've got to be kidding me. But then I remember that text messages exist. I pull up our thread of messages on my phone and type out four simple words:

I love you, Simon.

I stare at the words, my heart thudding as if I've had

a shot of adrenaline. My thumb hovers over that arrow button. One click and he'll know exactly how I feel.

I jump when my phone rings. It's Cole.

I answer it, trying to steady my voice.

He practically screams my name instead of saying hello.

"Tell me you're free tomorrow night!" he says. My head aches at how unapologetically chipper his tone is.

"Um, I think so. Why? What's going on?"

"Tamara and I are hosting a cocktail hour for everyone who's coming to the vow renewal on Saturday and we'd love for you to come."

"Oh. Um, sure. Thanks for the invite."

"Of course! You're filming our big day."

"Will Simon be there?" I ask, my brain catching up.

"Absolutely! I just called him earlier today and he said he's coming."

My heart flutters. Screw texting. I'll tell Simon exactly how I feel tomorrow, in person.

"I'll be there."

## Chapter Twenty-Two

When I walk through the massive glass doors of Meyer Lemon near Saint Francis Square, my heart is pounding so hard, I'm certain I'll puke. Once I'm inside, I take a deep breath, then catch my reflection in a nearby accent mirror. Christ. My skin appears sallow in the dim lighting of the bar.

I dig through my purse for my lipstick and reapply the bold red hue to my quivering lips. Then I run my fingers through my waves and smooth a shaky hand over the front of my dress. It took me almost an hour to figure out what to wear. This is the first time I'm telling a guy I'm in love with him. I want to make sure I looked memorable, but not over the top.

With Harper's help, I settled on a navy blue maxi dress with a leather jacket. Cute, put-together, and perfect for the chill on this early October evening.

The hostess leads me through the crowded main bar area down a hall to a room in the back. There stand Cole and Tamara, glasses of champagne in their hands. They both sport giddy smiles on their faces as they chat with a group of people gathered around them.

I do a scan of the room, but I don't see Simon. I count more than thirty people, all with drinks in their hands, eager to toast to Cole and Tamara's rekindled romance. I smile to myself, genuinely happy for them.

I walk up to them. "Hey, you two. Congrats."

They pull me into a joint hug.

"We're so glad you made it!" Cole says. He gestures to a bottle of champagne on a nearby standing table. "Be sure to drink up. No work tonight, okay? Save all that for tomorrow, the big day!"

I accept the champagne flute Tamara hands me, then take a step back to make room for another person who walks up to congratulate them.

"Simon's running late," Tamara says.

I twist my head to the side to look at her. "Oh. Okay."

I can't think of anything else to say, so I just awkwardly stand in place, taking another sip while looking around the room.

"I thought you two would come together," Tamara says.

"Yeah, well…um, we didn't."

She nods and her eyes take on a sympathetic stare. She opens her mouth, but before she can say anything, someone bumps me in the back and I spill champagne all over the front of my dress.

I spin around to an early twenties server who's wide-eyed and cupping his mouth with one hand. In his other hand is an empty tray.

"Oh god, I'm sorry!" he says, his face twisted in worry. "It's my first night at this job, I've never been a server before. I'm so, so sorry, I—"

I let out an understanding sigh and force a small smile. "It's okay. Really, don't worry about it."

Tamara puts a gentle hand on my arm. "Bathroom's

just down there," she says, nodding to the end of the nearby hallway.

Once inside the women's restroom, I clean up with paper towels and walk back out.

And then I hear Simon's voice behind me.

My heartbeat stutters as I turn around and see him standing six feet away, right in front of the men's restroom, his blazer-clad back to me. I'm about to walk over to him when he pivots to the side and I see he's on the phone.

I purse my lips, and stand off to the side behind a giant decorative vase that separates the entryways between the men's and women's restrooms. I don't want it to look like I'm creepily listening to his phone conversation.

Closing my eyes, I take another deep breath. This is it. As soon as he's off the phone, I'm going to tell him I love him. My body is vibrating with how close I am to him.

"Uh… I don't know how Naomi's doing, Grandma."

My eyes fly open at Simon's words. He's talking to his grandma. About me.

He lets out a heavy sigh. "I do. More than anyone I've ever been with."

I gasp, then immediately cup a hand over my mouth. My mind runs the gamut of possible questions Simon's grandma asked him about me.

*Do you care about her?*

*Do you want to be with her?*

*Do you love her?*

Even though I can only hear one side of the conversation, I fixate on that last hypothetical question.

Because that's what I hope. That Simon loves me, just like I love him.

I spin around and peek at him around the giant vase. His back is still to me.

"It doesn't matter," he says. "She didn't want to... It'll be fine... I'll figure out a way to get over this."

My eyes well up at the defeat in his voice. My throat aches to speak, to tell him that he doesn't need to get over it—get over me—that I don't want him to. Because I love him.

But I can't tell him that, not while he's talking to his grandma.

Yet the more seconds that pass, the more that sinking feeling at hearing his broken voice cuts me. He's already given up on me—and I need to do something to change that ASAP.

I take a breath, step out from behind the vase, open my mouth, and am promptly interrupted by a wave of shouts.

"What the..." I mutter while cupping my hands over my ears. I spin around to where the sound is coming from.

Behind me a group of people chanting and clapping marches in the direction of the party room that Cole and Tamara have reserved. The six-member group of people dressed in all black formal wear start belting out an a cappella version of Tony Bennett's "The Way You Look Tonight" in deafening multipart harmony, just a few feet away from where I'm standing.

Cole and Tamara beam. Tamara's eyes glisten while Cole sways along, grabbing her hand in his. The melodic sound thunders around me as I stand there and observe for the next minute. How the hell can six people make such a thunderous, collective noise?

My head spins. I need to think of a plan B. I spin around, determined to grab Simon by the arm and drag him outside so I can tell him without any interruptions that I love him and want to be with him.

But he's not standing there anymore. Where the hell could he have gone? I'm contemplating busting into the men's bathroom when I realize that he probably went outside because he was on the phone and it was too loud in here with the music.

I sprint down the other hallway, in the direction of the entrance. Rounding the corner, I spot him outside, just a few feet in front of the glass doors. His back is to me and both hands are at his sides now, which means he's done talking on the phone.

Yes! No more loud noises, no more interruptions. I can finally tell him how I feel.

I'm reaching for the door handle when Simon turns around. The second his eyes lock on mine, I start to smile. But when I focus on his expression, my smile drops. Instead of opening the door and running to him, I pull my hand back to my side and stay standing in place.

The mix of pain and anger on his face as he gazes at me is wrenching. It's like a glare, but with an edge of heartbreak.

My eyes burn, my chest aches, and my throat squeezes as I look at him. I'm hit with the urge to speak even though I know he can't hear me. I ache to tell him how sorry I am for leaving when he was asleep, how much I wish I could take back that god-awful "I can't do this. I'm sorry" text.

I start to open my mouth, but he shakes his head at me, his stony expression unmoving.

The silent rejection hits like a brick to my face. In

this moment, it's crystal clear: Simon wants nothing to do with me.

*I did this. I made him feel this way. I broke him.*

He turns away and walks to a car parked along the curb. He climbs in the backseat and shuts the door, and the car speeds away.

*I deserve this... I broke his heart.*

When I blink, the dam inside me bursts. It's not until that hostess from earlier gently touches my arm and asks if I'm okay that I realize I've been standing there, silently crying. I blubber an apology, wipe my face with my hands, then stumble outside. I pull up the rideshare app on my phone and fall inside the car when it pulls up. The driver says nothing as I cry all the way back to Harper's place.

"Are you sure you want to do this?" Harper asks over the phone as I set up my camera in the corner of the courtyard at the San Francisco Mint.

"I'm sure," I say.

With the phone pinned between my cheek and shoulder, I adjust the camera height. Then I straighten up and gaze around the space. The classic revival architecture of the building along with the endless strings of tea lights hanging above set the perfect romantic scene. At one end is a wooden platform with a white sheet hanging over it, which serves as the makeshift stage where Cole and Tamara will renew their vows. Standing cocktail tables and small round dining tables, all covered in white sheets, dot the rest of the space.

"You don't have to keep checking in, you know," I say as I finish setting up. "You've sent me three texts since I left your place two hours ago asking me this same question."

Harper sighs. "Yeah, well… I felt a little guilty the way I left things earlier. And I didn't want you to feel forced into anything."

"You mean the way you forced me into this dress?" I smooth my palm along the side of the form-fitting hot pink knee-length cocktail dress Harper insisted that I wear. When I squirm, the cap sleeves feel snug against my shoulders. The gold zipper in the back, which runs the length of the dress, is cold against my skin.

"You look amazing in that dress, Naomi. You wanted to wear that sad gray thing you wear to funerals, but no. Not when you have to see Simon."

Closing my eyes, I sigh and momentarily regret spilling everything the moment I got back to Harper's place last night. But I was sobbing. She knew something bad happened. There was no way I could get away with telling her nothing.

"I really don't think Simon is going to care what I look like," I mumble. "He made it pretty clear last night that he's done with me."

"That doesn't mean you have to start dressing like a sad sack. Especially if you're planning on going through with what you've planned."

I swallow in an attempt to quell the nerves whirring in the pit of my stomach. I'm fully aware of just how badly I screwed things up with Simon. I owe him an apology for how I hurt him, and I plan on doing that when I see him today.

I don't expect that to change anything between us—I don't have that right. I blew my chance with him the moment I decided to take the coward's way out, when I walked out on him the other morning as he slept instead of staying and talking things out. Maybe if I had done that, I'd have realized my true feelings and we could have stayed together.

It's too late now, though.

Harper huffs a sigh. "It's okay if you want to say screw it and come home."

"Can't. I've gotta film this for work."

"Fine. The moment they say 'I do' again, come home. Then we'll drown our sorrows with sheet masks, prosecco, and whatever takeout you feel like."

I smile softly for the first time all day. "Thanks, Harper."

I hang up just as Cole and Tamara walk into the space, holding hands with their two elementary school-age kids dressed in adorable pink tulle dresses. Cole props their toddler on his hip. The two of them are clad in matching tuxes while Tamara wears a stunning sleeveless lace white gown with a deep V-neck. Gazing at the decorations, they all squeal in delight. I can't help but grin. Even in my heartbroken state, I'm ecstatic for them. They're declaring their love for each other again in front of their family and closest friends. Not everyone is able to do that. I swallow back a lump in my throat.

Cole spots me, hands the toddler to Tamara, and scurries over while tugging at the bow tie of his tux.

"Congratulations. This place looks amazing. And thanks again for letting Dash film your ceremony," I say.

"Of course. Anything to promote Simon and what he's helped do for us. We wouldn't be here if it weren't for him."

My heart pulses at just the mention of his name.

Cole looks off to the side. "Speaking of the devil."

I look up and my mouth falls open. There's Simon, decked out in a charcoal gray suit with a white shirt underneath, collar unbuttoned, no tie, looking like he stepped straight out of a *GQ* ad. His light brown hair is cropped close to his scalp on the sides. The top is thick and long like usual, but slicked back. He must have gotten it cut. It takes a few seconds, but I eventually clamp my mouth shut. My eyes bulge the tiniest bit, even though I mentally order myself to keep it together. He looks mind-blowingly handsome and I can barely handle it.

When he walks up to us, I see that he's left some stubble on his cheeks. My mouth waters. I always, always loved his stubble.

Before I have to muster the strength to greet him politely and pretend that my heart isn't totally shattered, Cole yanks him into a hug. Simon lets out an "oof" noise.

They pull apart, but Cole keeps hold of Simon with his hands on his shoulders. "None of this would have been possible without you." His voice shakes and his eyes water. "Thank you."

Simon starts to speak, but Cole pulls him into another death hug that turns his face red. Just then one of Cole's kids calls for him and he runs off. Simon and I are left alone together.

I hold my breath, wondering if now is the right time to tell him what I need to say—what he deserves to hear from me.

That I'm sorry I walked out on him the other morning while he was asleep instead of talking things out. That was so beyond hurtful.

That I'm sorry I doubted my feelings for him.

That I'm sorry I let my disastrous dating past dictate my future with him.

That he's the most incredible guy, I'm the biggest

fool for letting him go, and whoever he ends up with is the luckiest.

And maybe, just maybe, if I'm bold enough, I'll tell him I love him too.

Just thinking about that last one makes me want to vomit. Because how humiliating would that be, confessing my love to the guy I can't have?

*You did it to yourself.*

My gaze falls to my heels. And there goes my nerve.

"You look incredible, Naomi," he says softly.

His compliment throws me off. My head whips up. He's gazing at me with that same intensity I saw the last night we were together.

"Sorry, what?"

"You're beautiful. Absolutely stunning," he says without missing a beat.

"Oh. Thanks. You, um, you look like a freaking male model."

His eyes turn shy. "I don't know about that, but thank you."

Once the momentary lightness of exchanging compliments fades, we're back to awkward standing and staring.

"So how do you wanna do this?" I finally say.

He frowns at me. "What do you mean?"

"I was planning to get commentary from Cole and Tamara before the ceremony, film it, then interview you afterwards. Viewers submitted a bunch of questions for you and I thought it would be nice if you could answer some."

"Oh." A bewildered look clouds his face, like he's just now remembering that I'm here to film this for his series. "Right. Sure."

"Great." I let out a sigh while fidgeting.

"About last night," he says after a moment.

"What about it?" I ask softly.

"When I was outside of Meyer Lemon and saw you at the entrance…"

"Yeah?"

He hesitates.

"You looked so upset. So hurt," I blurt when he doesn't say anything more.

His face twists for a moment before he swallows. "Yeah, well. I was."

"I'm so sorry for hurting you, Simon. You didn't deserve the way I treated you."

For a few seconds, all he does is look at me, his unblinking stare tinged with pain and something else. Something I can't quite nail down.

I push on, fully anticipating that once I get this all out, I'll be wrecked from the heartbreak. But it's what I deserve.

"I was going to tell you that last night, but then I saw the hurt and anger on your face, and I didn't want to upset you more than I already had." I force myself to pause and breathe. I sound like a babbling maniac. "I was going to say that I wished more than anything that I could redo our last time together. I should have stayed with you. I should have told you how I truly felt about you. I should have said screw it to all my doubts and insecurities and finally just said that I…that I…"

*I love you, Simon.*

As I gaze into his eyes, my heart pumps a beat so frenzied, I feel like I'm going to pass out.

He doesn't even blink as he looks at me. His gaze turns pleading and intense as he steps closer to me.

"You what, Naomi?" he whisper-growls.

*Say it now!*

"Simon, I—"

Cole and Tamara walk back over to us. Damn it.

"If you want to film our commentary before the ceremony, we'd better do it now," Tamara says, looking over her shoulder as people start to file into the space.

I turn away from Simon and hesitate for a second before telling them okay. The smile Simon flashes them is so tight, it looks like he's in pain. He walks away to one of the standing tables.

My head spins as I struggle to pay attention to Cole and Tamara all the while processing what happened between Simon and me just now.

Simon was clearly upset with me last night, but judging by how he approached me today, how he was willing to hear me out, that pleading look on his face, maybe all hope isn't lost.

Maybe we still have a chance to work things out. I just need to talk to him.

As Cole and Tamara answer an interview question, I scan the now-crowded space in search of Simon. There must be at least fifty people in the courtyard milling around. I don't see him anywhere. Then the event coordinator of the venue pops over and ushers them to the front to kick off the ceremony.

"Everyone!" she calls out. "The ceremony is starting! Please have a seat so we can start."

I force myself back behind the camera. I have a job to do. I just need to be patient, film this vow renewal, then Simon and I can talk and maybe work this whole thing out.

## Chapter Twenty-Three

After the ceremony, all I can hear is everyone chatting about how beautiful it was. And it was. It was heartening listening to Tamara and Cole exchange vows in front of their kids and loved ones. I already know viewers are going to adore it once this episode goes up on the Dash site next week.

But I'm a barrel of nerves because I still haven't gotten a chance to talk to Simon. As I wander through the crowd to find him, Cole's voice booms over the speaker system.

"Everyone, thank you so much for coming! We love you all and it means the world that you're sharing this day with us."

Everyone claps while I'm still searching the crowd, taking small, careful steps so I don't crash into anyone. Cole says they're going to start dinner service soon, but not before he thanks the one person who's the sole reason we're all here today.

I stop walking instantly and turn to the stage where he stands, beckoning Simon from the crowd. He walks up, flustered grin on his face.

Cole pats him on the back. "Because of Simon Rutler's counseling, I became a halfway decent husband."

Laughter and applause follow.

Cole turns to Tamara. "Thank you, Tamara, for these first fifteen years. And here's to many more decades together."

There's a collective "aww" sound from the guests as they kiss.

"And now," Cole continues. "I think it would be great if the man I owe everything to could say a few words to help inspire and encourage everyone here."

Simon starts to shake his head no, but the crowd cheers him on. People chant "speech!" until he gives in. Cole hands him the microphone and pats him on the back before standing off to the side, leaving Simon front and center.

He clears his throat, briefly glancing at the ground before focusing back on the crowd.

"Well, don't expect this to be anything good. That's what you get for goading a guy into giving a last-minute speech with no preparation."

Everyone laughs. Simon gazes across the audience and catches eyes with me.

"But I've always wanted to do this, make a big, impromptu speech. So here goes nothing."

I hold my breath, realizing he's referencing his fuck-it list.

He pivots to Cole and Tamara. "First, let me just say congratulations to you both. That was such a beautiful ceremony. You made me tear up, well done."

Tamara holds Cole's hand in both of hers while their kids smile on at a nearby table.

"As far as advice goes, that's a bit tough. This is pretty last-minute." He rubs the back of his neck before running a hand through his hair.

As he looks up at the crowd, he locks eyes with me

once again. My mouth goes dry as he holds my gaze in those silent seconds, where everyone waits for his next words. And then something in his stare changes, almost like looking at me has set off something in his brain.

"Actually, I can say this." He turns to address Cole and Tamara. "Cole, you said in your vows that you always knew Tamara was the one for you because you could do the most boring things with her and you'd still prefer that over anything else in the world. Because simply being with her is what makes you the happiest."

Simon pauses as Tamara and Cole embrace once more.

"And that's the advice I'll give to you all today. If there's someone in your life who makes you happier than anyone else when they do the simplest, silliest things with you, that's the person you should be with." He swallows. "Life is short. Too short to be wasting your time with people who don't drive you wild in the best way. That person who makes your stomach flip when you get a text from them? That person whose voice sends heat all over your body? That person whose terrible cooking you'd rather eat over your favorite take-out just because they made it for you? They're the one."

A few soft chuckles and "awws" follow. He pauses to take a breath and looks at me again. I pull my lips into my mouth, my heart in my throat.

"That person who could vomit on your shoes, and you'd still rather see them over any other human being on the planet. That person who you'd happily argue and make up with over and over again. Because everything and everyone else pales in comparison. You're *that* in love with them. You date other people, but all you think about is them. You'd run to the bakery at the crack of dawn because egg tarts are their favorite snack. You'd spend your Saturday night on the couch wearing a sheet mask on your face and drinking prosecco even though you're a Scotch drinker who never washes his face."

Another wave of soft laughter follows. But I can't make a sound. I'm too stunned.

"Because being with them makes you the happiest. You could be offered anything else in the world, and you can look that person in the eye and say, 'It's got nothing on you.' And mean it."

With those words, my heart ceases beating. I'm that person for Simon; he's that person for me. And he's in love with me. Just like I'm head over heels in love with him.

"If there's someone in your life who makes you feel that way, do yourself a favor. As soon as you can, tell them exactly how you feel about them. Even if you find out they don't feel the same way, yeah, it'll hurt, but at least you'll never wonder what if. And for those of you who do this and end up with that special person, congratulations. You're in for one hell of a happy life."

The entire crowd applauds and cheers. Half of the people raise their glasses to toast Simon's words.

But me? I don't have time for cheering or toasting. I'm running straight up to Simon. I grab his hand and pull him with me to the back corner.

"Hey," he says. "I hope I didn't—"

"Just, shush," I say, breathless. "Everything you said, that's exactly how I feel about you. I just…so many of my relationships before you were a disaster. And I thought it was because of me. I thought I was doing something wrong. But I wasn't. For the longest time I was with the wrong guys and everything was a train wreck, but then I met you and everything was different. Everything was fun and sexy and blissful and felt right and I… I just thought it was too good to be true. But that's bullshit. That's such self-sabotaging bullshit. I don't know what the future holds for us, but I want to find out. I want to fight for us. I want to be with you and I just…"

I'm panting at my frenzied pace of speaking. I realize I haven't said the most important thing of all, the one thing that matters more than anything—the one thing I've been dying to say to him.

"I love you, Simon. I'm the happiest when I'm with you…and I hope… I hope…" My throat squeezes as I struggle to keep from crying. "I hope you can forgive me for walking out on you the other morning. I'm so, so sorry I did that. That was horrible and if I could take it back, I would. I hope you can forgive me for ever doubting us and our feelings. And I hope that I'm not too late in saying all this to you."

I know I've already said this to him, but I need him to know just how much I regret messing up.

"I love you too, Naomi."

With both hands on his cheeks, I pull him to me and kiss him. He grabs me by the waist as we engage in a smooch far too filthy for such an elegant venue. But then applause and cheers and whistles thunder around us. We jolt apart at the sudden noise and laugh at everyone cheering around us.

"I thought this corner would be more private," I say, my face hot at all the attention. "I guess I was wrong."

Simon pulls me back against him. "I don't care. As long as I have you, I don't care about anything else."

"If you want to glare at me forever, that's okay. I'll happily take it because one, I deserve it. And two, you look insanely sexy when you scowl."

He lets out a soft laugh that makes my heart literally flutter.

"The only reason I glared at you was because I was hurt. But then I realized that even though I was hurt, I still wanted you. I still wanted to try and work things out," he says.

I pull him closer to me. I slide my arms around his shoulders and we kiss once more.

Out of the corner of my eye, I notice a few people pointing their phones at us.

"One of those pictures is going to probably end up online, you know," I say.

Simon shrugs.

"So you're okay with everyone knowing that you— former camming stud, beloved therapist, and one of the most wanted single men in the Bay Area—are taken?" I ask.

He grins wide. "God, yes. It'll give me a whole new level of legitimacy in my job now that I'm in a committed relationship."

"Oh, is that the only reason?"

"Well, that and the fact that Naomi Ellorza-Hays is officially my girlfriend. That's definitely something to be excited about too."

I grab the lapels of his jacket, pull him to me, and lay on yet another kiss. We break apart after several seconds.

"I'll probably have to put a disclaimer on the series finale letting everyone know that we're a couple now. And have a chat with Fiona," I say. "Journalistic integrity, you know."

"Of course." He winks.

We walk to a nearby standing table. The feel of Simon's hand in mine makes me buzz from head to toe. We're holding hands. In public. For everyone to see.

I release his hand when a server walks by, and swipe two champagne flutes off the tray. I hand him one and take a sip while he gulps.

"Careful. We've still got your interview to do. Don't want you wasted on camera," I tease.

He flashes a sly smile, downs the rest of his champagne, then wipes his mouth with the back of his hand. "Let's do this."

"Okay, first viewer question: What was your favorite part of filming this series?"

"Meeting you." Simon smiles at me from where he's sitting in a room off to the side of the venue, just a few feet away from where I'm standing with the camera.

I try my best to keep composed, to keep my professional hat on. But I can't help but break out into the biggest smile.

"Nice," I admit. "Next question: What was the most unexpected thing that happened while filming?"

"Falling in love with you."

My breath actually catches. And I thought that was something people exaggerated. But no. The person you're in love with really can take your breath away.

"You're killing me over here," I say. I don't even bother to hide my grin. I'm too blissfully happy. Even if I tried to frown my smile away, it wouldn't work. As long as Simon's next to me, I won't ever stop smiling.

"Are you embarrassed about anything that aired in the series?"

"Nope. You're too good at your job. Thanks for making me look way better than I actually am."

"You're smooth. How will I get through the rest of this interview without swooning to death?"

"Don't fret about it." He winks.

"You know what it does to me when you say that."

"Oh, I know."

Clenching my thighs and clearing my throat, I attempt to focus once more. "If you could go back and do one thing differently while filming the series, what would it be?"

His eyes take on a totally different sheen as he looks at me. I can see the rawness in his stare. His smile softens and his voice drops. "Nothing. Except maybe telling you I loved you sooner."

I'm breathless once more. "When did you realize you loved me?"

"When I saw you naked in the tub with your vibrator."

I roll my eyes.

"It wasn't an exact moment," he says. "But when we were cooking together in my apartment before I met your family, I had this realization. I'd never been happier than in that moment with you. And that's when I knew."

I have to look down at the ground to keep it together. Then I walk over and kiss him. "You can't say *me* as the answer to every question, you know."

"I can. And I will."

I turn back around and turn off the camera. "You're going to get so, so lucky tonight. And tomorrow. And pretty much every day after that. I don't know if we'll be able to leave your apartment for the foreseeable future."

There's a naughty gleam in his eyes.

"You've got a fully stocked fridge, right?" I tease. "Because we won't even have time to go to the store."

"We'll get groceries delivered."

I move to sit on his lap. He snakes his arms around me, pulling me against his chest. Despite the layers of clothing between us, I can still feel the warmth of his body on mine. I hum softly. I love being this close to him. We share another sloppy, wholly inappropriate kiss.

"The camera's off, right?" he says between kisses.

I hum "mmm-hmm" while keeping my mouth on his.

"I love you."

"I love you, too."

"Sorry, but I can't bring myself to be very professional right now with you on my lap," he says against my neck.

I let out a moan, then giggle when it starts to tickle too much. With my hands cupping both sides of his face, I gaze down at him. Those beautiful golden brown eyes shine up at me like he can't get enough of me. It makes my entire body go warm and gooey.

Around us there's music playing and people chatting and laughing. No one seems to have noticed our little display of affection.

We finally break the stream of kisses, but our eyes remain locked together.

"I guess we'll have to remember to maintain a more professional etiquette if we ever work together again," I joke.

"Our one weakness." He tucks a loose wave of my hair behind my ear.

I snuggle into him. My heart swells as I beam down at him. I love Simon. I love him so, so much.

He presses another kiss to my lips. "I take it back. We're doing pretty damn well if you ask me."

"I'd have to agree."

# Epilogue

*One year later*

"Don't fret about it. You're gonna do great. Like always," Simon says.

The nerves swirling inside of me turn to heat. He knows his cam guy catchphrase is the right thing to say to distract me. "Thanks."

Standing next to me at the front of the hotel conference room, he reaches over and gives my hand a squeeze.

This is how Simon has always kicked things off the handful of times he's featured me as a guest speaker during one of his seminars. As attendees walk in and find their seats, that's when my nerves hit their peak. But just a few encouraging words from him, and I feel a million times more centered.

If you had asked me a year ago if I would have ever considered speaking at a relationship seminar, I would have cackled in your face. But after we became an item, Simon's seminar attendees mentioned wanting him to bring on guest speakers now and then. After the tenth time he pitched the idea to me, I caved. Part of me was curious to see if I could try something out of my comfort zone. It turns out that I can. Today marks my third time doing this.

It's a natural progression, I suppose. *Simply Simon* was a hit—it earned the highest ratings and viewership of any online series ever produced on the Dash website. It also earned me a promotion to executive producer. I have full control over any and all series I want to film along with a small staff. And now I can add guest speaker at my boyfriend's relationship seminars to my list of professional accomplishments.

Fiona wasn't even mad when I told her about my and Simon's relationship. Probably because of how I timed it. I waited until she returned from her anniversary trip to the Seychelles, when she was all loved up and in a bliss bubble, to disclose our relationship. She was totally fine with it. I worried for nothing.

Simon's work has experienced a similar boost. His seminars are always full and his therapy practice is busier than ever. He has to refer inquiries to his colleagues.

"Thank you so much for coming today," Simon says to the packed room.

He introduces me as his guest host and asks if anyone has any questions they'd like to ask. I call on a guy who's raised his hand. He's late twenties with a nervous smile on his face. Under the overhead lights, I spot small beads of sweat lining the top of his forehead.

"Yeah, hi, um, Naomi," he stammers. "I'm just… I have a question and I'm not sure what to do or how to go about it or…"

I flash what I hope is a comforting smile. "It's okay…"

"Tanner." He takes a deep breath. "I want to propose to my girlfriend."

I smile. Out of the corner of my eye, I see that Simon grins too.

"Aww! That's wonderful. Congratulations!"

Soft claps and whistles echo through the room.

Tanner flashes a flustered smile before mumbling a thank-you, then looks between Simon and me. "The thing is… I'm nervous she won't say yes."

"Why do you think she won't say yes?" I ask. "Haven't you talked about getting married?"

He shrugs. "Yeah. Never in depth, though. I try to bring it up, but I get so nervous sometimes. We've talked about getting married someday. I just don't want it to be unromantic, you know? I want it to be spontaneous and a surprise. I don't want it to come off like a business negotiation." He clears his throat. "And I guess… Well, I just want to know what you think. Would you want to talk a lot about marriage more before a proposal? Or would that take the romance out of it for you?"

"Honestly? If a guy were to sit me down and say that he wanted to talk marriage, long-term plans, family, all that, with me, I would swoon. That's romantic as hell. Because it means he sees a future with me and that's the most romantic thing he could ever do."

Tanner flashes a relieved smile. "Really?"

"Really." I sneak a quick side-glance at Simon, who's nodding along. "I don't care if a guy proposed to me on the Eiffel Tower with a rock the size of my head. If I can't actually envision a future with him—if we've never had a serious conversation to make sure we're on the same page about building a life together—I would say no to the proposal. I'm not saying that every woman is like me. There are plenty who would say yes, I'm sure. But the more you talk about marriage, the more comfortable you'll feel, and the sweeter her yes will be when you finally propose. Because that way, there's no doubt. Those butterflies you'll feel when you're down on one knee waiting for her answer won't be from uncertainty. They'll be from pure joy. And those are the best kind of butterflies."

I look over at Simon, who mouths "Nailed it" to me. I smile a thanks, grateful that he has no idea what I'm planning.

Tanner thanks me and I ask if there are more questions. When I finish, everyone applauds, and I walk to an empty chair at the back of the room and check my phone while Simon leads the rest of seminar.

I see an email that throws me off completely. I squint at the message, my mind racing. Keywords pop out from the text.

*Deposit... Overseas emergency... Closing...*

I can't wait any longer. This has to happen. And soon.

I focus on Simon. His easy posture and relaxed smile send a tingle through me. We've talked about this a million times. We'd do it today if we could. Suddenly all that uncertainty evaporates, leaving behind the best kind of butterflies.

I glance up at the door every few seconds. Simon is due home any minute. My phone buzzes and I check it.

Harper: Holy shit you're actually doing it? Like, tonight?

Me: Yup. Wish me luck!

Harper texts a million crying and heart emojis.

Harper: Call me later with all the details! I want to hear everything!

Me: Will do. And I want to hear how the remodel is going too. How are you liking Half Moon Bay?

Harper: It's amazing here. But the remodel is... JFC I honestly don't even know where to start.

Me: Issues with the contractor or something?

Harper: Sort of. Actually, not really.

Harper: I'll tell you about it later, but for now, sending all the good vibes your way!

Simon's keys jingle in the door.

"Whoa," he says as he walks into our apartment. His eyes land on the kitchen counter, where there are a dozen plates of cookies and muffins.

He turns to look at me standing in the tiny kitchen. I'm shrouded in an apron, dusted in flour.

"Thought you might want a snack before your flight tomorrow," I say.

He swipes a cookie and devours it in two bites. He grins at me while chewing, then swallows. "How did you know I was craving these?"

He drops his bag on the floor, then walks over to kiss my cheek. When he finishes swallowing, he pulls me into him, then plants a long kiss on me.

"Mmm," I hum, sliding my arms around his neck. "You taste like peanut butter."

"Blame the cookies."

I giggle, then swallow back my nerves. "Are you all packed up?"

"Not even close."

I give him a playful smack on the shoulder.

One thing I've learned about Simon after a year of living with and dating him is that he's a last-minute packer, no matter the destination. Whether we're planning a road trip or an international flight, he always waits until a few hours before leaving to get everything together.

"Come on." He squeezes my waist and I squeal. "You know I'm incredible at packing."

I kiss his smiling mouth. "I just don't want you to forget anything or be in a rush."

Simon's taking his mom, sister, and grandma to Alaska. It's a trip they've been looking forward to for months, ever since he surprised them on Mother's Day.

"Thanks for keeping me accountable. I'm just sad you're not coming with us. They are too."

"I wish I could go," I say softly. "I just can't right now with how crazy stuff is at work. I've got one series wrapping up this week and another one kicking off right after. But I promise we'll do a trip together once work calms down."

I turn toward the carefully arranged stack of muffins I plated while waiting for Simon to come home from work. "You should have a muffin. They're banana chocolate chip. Your favorite."

I try to keep my voice as casual and calm as possible. I pull away from him and he walks the two steps to the muffins. I move to wipe down the already clean kitchen sink, but I need a distraction. If I'm not doing something, I'll just stand and stare at him, and he'll know something's up. I want this to be the surprise of his life.

He starts to ask a question, but then goes quiet. I let out the breath I've been holding and turn around.

My grin grows wide when I take in his expression. Utter shock as he stares at the piece of paper I tucked between the muffins, right on top of the tiny black velvet box I hid in the middle of the plate.

Holding the paper in his hand, he glances up at me, his eyes wide. "Naomi, what is this?" His mouth curves up in a surprised smile.

I scan the words I wrote earlier today.

*Fuck-it list item #2: Ask Simon Rutler to marry me.*

My eyes water, but a few blinks and I get myself under control. "I finally thought of another thing I wanted to cross off my fuck-it list."

Still smiling, he tries to speak, but he stutters.

"Open it," I say quietly.

He picks up the velvet box from the plate, opens it, and stares at what's inside. "Naomi..."

I whip off my apron, revealing the T-shirt I bought weeks ago. Then I get down on one knee.

When he finally looks back at me, his golden brown eyes are practically bulging out of his head. They glisten and the lump in my throat grows.

When he scans the words "Marry me?" on my shirt, he beams.

"Hear me out," I say, a tear streaming down my face. "This isn't how I wanted it to go. I was planning something amazing. Like, a fancy dinner, that tiny black dress you love so much, a stroll through Palace of the Fine Arts, the works. But then the jeweler messaged me yesterday because he had a family emergency and had to leave town for the next two months, so he said that I needed to pick up the ring way earlier than planned, like, yesterday. And so I did, and I guess I could have just waited and hid the ring somewhere in the apartment, but all of our stuff is mixed together, so you'd probably find it, and if I had to carry it with me all the time, I'm terrified I'd lose it and..."

I finally stop babbling because I'm out of breath. I inhale, then I wince at the pain in my knee from kneeling down on the tile floor.

I sniffle as more tears stream down my face. "But then I realized, I didn't want to wait, I just... I just love you so much. And I want you to be mine. Forever."

Tears shine in his eyes as he smiles down at me.

"I know we've talked about marriage and I know we're on the same page... I know I never asked you about how you would feel about me proposing to you, but I just—"

"Naomi," he says through a breathy laugh. "Just ask me."

Wiping both my cheeks with my hands, I beam up at him. "Simon, will you marry me?"

He booms out a yes before hunching down, grabbing me by the shoulders, and pulling me back up. When he kisses me, I melt. We go at it for so long, I lose count of the seconds. When we finally break, he cups my cheeks. Our foreheads pressed together. It's a struggle to catch our breath.

"So I did okay, then?" I whisper.

He leans back, still holding me by the cheeks. "You were perfect."

I plant another kiss on him.

"My family is gonna be psyched when I tell them we're engaged," he says, pulling me into a tight hug.

"Hopefully they won't be too upset that I broke tradition and asked you."

"They're fully aware of how nontraditional our dating story has been," he says. "They'll be fine with it. As long as I get you a ring too."

"Only if I can come with you to the jewelry store and pick it out myself."

"Absolutely."

I glance at the silver band gleaming at us from the open jewelry box, which sits on the edge of the counter. "Now when you look at your hand while you're on vacation, you'll think of me. And it will kind of be like I'm there with you."

Simon hugs me tight. "I'm so lucky to be marrying you."

"Come on." I lead him to the bedroom. "We have an engagement to celebrate."

Simon's smile turns mischievous as I pull off my top and slide off my jeans. He starts unbuttoning his dress shirt.

"Maybe we can play a sexy game of Simon Says?" I ask.

He lifts an eyebrow. "Simon says lose the bra and panties and climb on the bed."

I bite my lip, get all the way undressed, then jump on the bed. He eyes his laptop, which is sitting on the nightstand.

"Should we?" he asks.

I nod excitedly and make a come-hither motion with my hand. He flips on his computer and the webcam.

"Ready for a close-up?"

I wink. "Always."

Simon rakes his gaze across my body. His eyes practically catch fire. "How am I going to make it two weeks without you?"

I yank him by the belt to the edge of the bed, then start to free him from his pants. "That's what the video is for, silly. Just be sure to wear earbuds when you're watching it. Wouldn't want anyone overhearing—or seeing. Like that one time when you were at your cousin's bachelor party in Vegas."

His face turns red. "Can we please not make me relive the embarrassment of that? I was drunk and hadn't seen you in like, four days."

"I'm just flattered that you'd prefer to hole up in your hotel room and watch a video of me rather than get a lap dance."

His hands skim along the sides of my torso before they rest on my ass. He gives both cheeks a firm squeeze. "Any time you want to give me a lap dance, I'm open for business."

Giggling, I lean up to nibble his bottom lip.

He grins just before capturing me in another long, hot kiss. When he pulls away to look at me, his eyes hit that perfect balance of intense and tender. When he gazes at me like that, I swear I can feel just how much he loves me. Simon. My best friend, my boyfriend— my fiancé—my heart, my fantasy-turned-reality, the person I love most.

"I can't believe I get to marry you, Naomi."

"That goes double for me."

\* \* \* \* \*

# Acknowledgements

This book was SUCH a long time coming. Getting to this point was a wild and arduous journey, and for a while I thought *The Close-Up* would never see the light of day. But it did. It's finally out in the world, and I have so many wonderful people to thank who helped make this happen.

Thank you to my agent, Sarah Younger, for never giving up on this book and believing that we'd be able to find a home for it. I was ready to give up more times than I care to admit, but you never lost faith. You're the best.

Stephanie Doig, thank you for loving Naomi and Simon as much as I do, and for bringing such brilliant insight to this book. This book is a million times better than it was because of you. I'm so lucky to be able to work with you.

To Stefanie Simpson, Sonia Palermo, JL Peridot, and Skye McDonald, thank you for beta reading *The Close-Up* in its various early versions. Your insight and enthusiasm gave me so much joy. I love you all to bits.

Steph Mills, thank you for all the encouraging emails. Your positive words helped keep me going when

I was ready to throw in the towel with this book. You're a ray of sunshine.

Thank you to Gemma Burgess for responding to my fangirl email all those years ago and for critiquing my early outline for this book. Your novel *A Girl Like You* was a huge inspiration for *The Close-Up*. You inspired me to start writing romcoms, and for that I'll be forever grateful to you.

Thank you to Psychology In Seattle podcast and YouTube channel for educating me about relationships and therapy.

Thank you to all the authors who unapologetically and happily write sex-positive romances and romcoms. You give me life.

To my husband, thank you for being the most supportive and wonderful person. I'm so fortunate to call you mine.

To my friends and family, thank you for loving me, supporting me, and cheering me on.

Huge thanks to all you lovelies on Twitter and Instagram for cheering on this book from day one.

And to everyone who reads this book, thank you a million times over. It's the most special feeling to know that you'd take time out of your day to read something I wrote. This book means everything to me, thank you for giving it a chance.

## *About the Author*

Sarah Smith is a copywriter-turned-author who wants to make the world a lovelier place, one kissing story at a time. Her love of romance began when she was eight and she discovered her auntie's stash of romance novels. She's been hooked ever since. When she's not writing, you can find her hiking, eating chocolate, and perfecting her lumpia recipe. She lives in Bend, Oregon, with her husband and adorable cat, Salem. Follow her on Twitter and Instagram (@AuthorSarahS) and on her author website, www.sarahsmithbooks.com.

*A meet-cute gone wrong is the start of a surprising courtship in this fresh, modern take on the workplace romance.*

*Keep reading for an excerpt from* Hot Copy *by debut author Ruby Barrett.*

# Chapter One: Wesley

This elevator is sweltering. Or maybe it's just the combination of my nerves and this suit that's making me feel like the air is thick enough to choke on. I tug at my tie. After two years of wearing nothing but jeans and T-shirts, the silk feels like a noose. The only piece of clothing I am comfortable in are my socks.

I stand shoulder to shoulder with a guy almost my height, in a similar suit and tie. Though his looks much more expensive and he seems more at home in it. His blond hair and Rolex glare under the fluorescents. The volume on his phone is turned up so loud I can hear his horrible taste in music clearly through the earbuds.

"Hold the elevator!" a woman calls as the doors start to roll closed.

I step forward, pressing my hand to one side of the sliding doors as she darts in. Her head is down, her thumb scrolling quickly across her phone's screen.

"What floor?" I ask, but she doesn't respond, instead tapping the toe of her high-heeled shoe in a metallic rhythm. She sighs audibly, shaking her head at the screen. I shrug and step back again.

"You part of the Hill City internship?" Bad Music Guy pulls an earbud out. The tinny sound of his music fills the small space. What I wouldn't give for the dulcet tones of the Beastie Boys' mid-'90s discography so I could avoid conversation with him. I was such a nervous wreck this morning I forgot my earphones on my bedside table.

I nod and hold out my hand. "Wesley Chambers."

"Mark." He smiles wide, showing all his teeth. Like a chimpanzee. "Who's your mentor?"

My father's friend Richard Skyler is the CEO of Hill City Marketing & PR, one of Boston's premier agencies. Dad considered his paternal duties fulfilled when he got me a spot in this program two years ago. After that, it was back to sporadic emails and missed birthdays. I'm not mad at him, though. My father is just a dick. He can't be fixed.

Luckily, his buddy Richard isn't an incurable phallus.

"Uhhh." I scratch the back of my neck, stalling for time. "I actually interviewed for this internship two years ago and I was going to be working with Richard? The CEO? But…" I clear my throat. Sneak a peek at Mark. The sharp edge of his smile assures me that I will not explain the past two years of my life to *this* guy.

"But I had to defer it," I say. "So, now I have to work with Corrine Blunt." I can't keep the dismay from my voice.

I'd met Richard Skyler when I was a kid and he'd remained friends with my parents until their divorce. When I interviewed for the program, Richard and I got along like old buds. And when I had to decline his offer of mentorship to take care of my mom, Richard promised me a spot when I was ready. And he kept in touch: emails, even the occasional phone call.

"Honestly, I'd assumed Richard would be my mentor again. But…it didn't work out."

I rock back on my heels, surprised by how disappointed I feel in this moment. The woman is a powerhouse, after all: graduated with an MBA from Boston College at twenty-four. At thirty years old, she's one of the youngest executives at Hill City Marketing & PR and the only woman in the executive suites. She's won countless awards for her marketing campaigns and was Richard's protégé in the first Hill City mentorship program years ago.

Plus, I know I'm not supposed to think about my boss this way, but it's not the worst thing that she's pretty. In her picture on the website she sported a bouncy, dark bob and a bright smile. She seemed happy and welcoming and young, like whatever they mean when they say "bright-eyed and bushy-tailed." I'd felt an affinity with her immediately. I shouldn't complain about having to spend a whole year working with her. In truth, I'm excited, if not mildly intimidated.

I open my mouth to admit that but bite my tongue when Mark says, too loud in this small space, "*Dude*, your mentor is Corrine Blunt?"

I rub my hand over my closed mouth and wince through a nod.

"The lady boss?" Mark laughs, and the cruel sound sends a shiver up the back of my neck. I've been the subject of a laugh like that before.

"You know what they call her, right?"

I stifle a cough and avoid his gaze, staring at my fuzzy reflection in the chrome elevator doors, at the digital numbers counting our ascent. I look anywhere but at this asshole. My eyes finally come to rest on the back of the woman standing in front of me. She stares up at the numbers as well. Her neck is long and elegant. The red temples of her glasses hooked around her ears are the only pop of color on her otherwise crisp black outfit. The scent of coconut wafts from her long, dark hair, pulled up into an intricate, tight bun, not a single strand out of place. It looks painful, to be honest.

She's wearing a black blazer and the type of skirt that makes a woman's ass look spectacular. And the blazer has that ruffle thing around the waist. *"Peplum, Wes,"* Amy's voice echoes in my head, tinged with frustration at the number of times she's had to repeat an irrelevant fashion-related fact to me.

"Wes, my man, you're in for quite a year," Mark says, as if I haven't ignored him for the past thirty seconds. The elevator dings our arrival on the Hill City floor and the woman walks down the hall, her head lowered over her phone again.

"My frat brother Sean got an internship here and worked with her. He coined her nickname: Blunt the Cu–"

I make a spluttering sound. A combination of *no* and *what* and *stop* that comes out sounding like, *"Nuhwst."* I don't need him to finish his sentence to know what he was about to say.

"Look, buddy," I say, and a shocked, stilted laugh tumbles out of my mouth before I can close it. Relief that she didn't hear him washes over me. "Can you *not* say that word?" I hiss into the empty hallway.

Mark throws his head back and laughs, the sound booming down the halls, solidifying exactly how much I don't like him. He grabs my shoulder, shaking me roughly. "Oh my god, Chambers. You're precious."

* * *

All the interns gather for a breakfast meet and greet in one of the conference rooms. I lean against a wall with a plate of fruit and a mini chocolate chip muffin, chasing a piece of melon around with my plastic fork. Everyone here seems to know everyone else. They're fresh from the same graduating class and it shows in their excitement, the overlapping convocation stories. After two years, my own graduation is a distant, hazy memory. I've launched a few smiles at some fellow interns, but mostly I eat my complimentary breakfast alone, watching people avoid eye contact with me.

While I've grown into my legs, feet, and hands and gotten better at shooting the shit with the guys, I still feel like the sore thumb in any crowd. Amy calls it Ugly Duckling Syndrome. I call it being lucky a twin is a built-in best friend.

The piece of melon slips off my plate and bounces off my shoe. I hike up my pants to stoop down to get it and when I rise, Mark stands in front of me.

"Come on, bro. Let's mingle."

By mingle, Mark means hit heavily on the only women of color in the room, two interns from Finance. Marisol, a Northeastern grad from Pennsylvania, ignores us for her phone. But the one Mark lays it on thick for is clearly uncomfortable with the attention. With every one of his jokes, Abila's smiles morph into cringes. Her shoulders inch toward her ears when his hand brushes her arm. He stares at her chest and she pulls her cardigan together. I open my mouth. Close it again. If Amy were here, she'd let fly with some asshole-puckering swear words. If my best friend, Jeremy Chen, were here, he'd find a calm way to explain to Mark why his behavior was inappropriate.

I'm just afraid that if I open my mouth to do either, another nervous laugh will end up escaping, especially if Abila has it in hand. I catch her eye, lifting a brow. She rolls her eyes, shaking her head.

"I'm…going to get another coffee," she announces, earning a glare from Mark for interrupting his story of "epic drunken debauchery." "Please don't follow me," she says, her voice laced with quiet disdain.

"Christ, uptight much?" he mutters.

*Or maybe she didn't feel like being sexually harassed on her first day, Mark.*

Mark's elbow digs into my ribs, spilling my, luckily, lukewarm coffee. I pat at my hand with a napkin, putting the cup on the conference table behind me.

"Wesley! I see you've met my intern, Mark."

Richard pats my back hard enough that I buckle a little under the pressure and I'm so glad I'm not still holding my coffee because I would have spilled over more than my hand. Mark and I greet Richard, Mark smiling that chimpanzee smile again.

"If you'll excuse us, Mark. I need to borrow Wes for a moment."

Something shifts in Mark's smile as we walk away, his eyes snagging on Richard's hand on my shoulder. He suddenly seems a little less primate-like and a little more sharklike.

"I'm so sorry I couldn't be there for Laura's funeral," Richard says, once we've found a private space in the corner of the conference room away from Mark's dead shark eyes.

At the mention of Mom, my stomach drops.

I really don't want to talk about this today.

"Did you get the flowers I sent?" he asks.

I nod, swallow past my dry throat and dread, and try to get the words to come out. I'm at that point where I think it's okay. I think I'm okay with my mom being gone. But then someone asks about her or how we're doing and my stomach clenches, my tongue ties. I realize I'm not okay. I'm small again, a skinny, scared kid who really, really misses his mom.

"Yes, we got the flowers. Thank you," I manage.

Richard smiles and not for the first time, I wonder how this kind man could ever be a friend to my father. Richard speaks fondly of Mom, repeating stories he's already told me about the three of them—my mom, my dad, and Richard—in college. The longer he talks about her the less my lungs feel like they're being crushed in someone's fist.

"I'm sorry." He smiles ruefully. "I'm sure I've told you all of these before."

He has, and each story hurts like a knife to the gut, but I'm starving for them nonetheless. Memories of Mom where she was the happy, healthy version of herself. Our last few months together, when she was sick and so tired of being sick, are imprinted on my brain. It's a relief to be reminded that she wasn't always that way.

Richard walks me through a maze of hallways, pointing out departments. We pass a large, open concept area he calls the Pit where teams already work together, walking until we reach a sandblasted glass door, the words Marketing Director etched across it. He claps his hand on my shoulder and squeezes, smiling warmly.

"This is Corrine's office. I know the two of you will

get along well." He points to me and winks as he walks away. "Pay close attention. You'll learn a lot from her."

I take a moment alone on this side of the door. I check my tie, catch a glimpse of any stains on my suit in the reflection of the glass. But all I see is a blob of brown on top of my head and dark shapes where my glasses sit. Fuzzy and undefined. That feels depressingly on brand.

I adjust the pant leg I'm in an ongoing battle with, but it creeps up my leg again, displaying my lucky socks. Taking a deep breath, I knock.

"Come in," a voice calls from the other side of the door.

I step into an all-white office. It's so bright I squint. So clean, so sterile I want to take off my shoes to not to leave footprints. A small white couch, an armchair with no arms, and a glass coffee table sit in the open space in front of a white desk. Two pocket doors bracket the crisp white wall behind the desk.

And standing across the room, one dark eyebrow arched, her red lips tightly pursed, casting a stark black silhouette in this crisp white space, is the woman from the elevator.

My brain stutters, stalling on the image of her there and now here. Her hair shining under the elevator lights still lingers on the backs of my eyelids. The smell of coconuts doesn't belong here. That scent belongs back in that elevator. But after two good sniffs, here it is still.

I close my eyes tight, like if I turn my brain off and on again it will work better. But when I open them, it's still her, with that severe bun and the peplum top and red glasses. The Corrine Blunt I found on the company's website looked nothing like this woman, who glares at me like she eats bright-eyed and bushy-tailed things for breakfast. Whatever similarities I thought we had have been surgically removed. Every possible reason for why this woman is in Corrine Blunt's office runs through my head. But it keeps returning to the only horrifying explanation:

Corrine Blunt *is* the woman from the elevator.

*Don't miss* Hot Copy *by Ruby Barrett,*
*out from Carina Press.*
*www.CarinaPress.com*